Dancing
ON
ARROWHEADS

Dancing
ON
ARROWHEADS

REHAB ABU ZAID

PARTRIDGE
A Penguin Random House Company

To order additional copies of this book, contact
Toll Free 800 101 2657 (Singapore)
Toll Free 1 800 81 7340 (Malaysia)
orders.singapore@partridgepublishing.com

www.partridgepublishing.com/singapore

DEDICATION

For every person who planted seeds of goodness inside me and let them grow to bear fruits; for every eye that saw the dimmed light inside me and followed it; for those feeling lonely and those who are alone; I hope that my experience and agony resonate with you.

PREFACE

When Ms Abu Zaid first made contact with me regarding the translation of her novel, I did a quick research on author and book, and knew that this would be a fascinating project to take on.

The beautiful language used throughout the novel, rich with figurative expressions, poetic flow, entwined with some deliberate ambiguities, make this an exciting read. On the surface, this is the journey of a young Saudi girl into womanhood, rediscovering herself and learning to define her identity; a story of trials, bitter relationships, disappointments and love. However, behind the protagonist's journey lie many messages calling for social equality, fairness and respect.

These universal themes know no religious or social boundaries. I am confident that non-Arab readers will appreciate this work not only for these themes, but also because it provides a wonderful insight into life in a part of the world with which they may not be familiar.

Finally, I would like to thank the team of translator, editor and proof-reader who worked on this novel. Without their dedication and professionalism, it would not have been possible to have the English version of this gem of a novel. I would also like to thank Ms Abu Zaid for her trust in us, and wish her many more successes in the future.

Nayiri Mississian
Director of Nairi Translation Services
www.nairitranslationservices.co.uk

CHAPTER 1

He used to take pleasure in blowing his cigarette smoke in her miserable young face, watching it wrinkle as she bore his abuse, while her dreams and aspirations, which defied the rules of his house, crashed into pieces. He was an egotistic, backward-thinking, master-of-the-house type of father who failed to see that his actions were oppressive towards the family members living under his roof. She was in the prime her life; optimistic and buoyant as a tulip. Despite living by his rules, she let her dreams flourish – which was vital to breaking the shackles that crippled her hopes. She was a young woman who had to endure more than she could handle, yet never allowed her circumstances to diminish her yearning for a joyful life.

Whenever she talked to her closed-minded father, it always ended with the triumph of his ailing ideology. He had to have the last word – and his last word never held true wisdom. Just like the preparatory meetings of the Arab League's annual conventions, their conversations were not constructive. They were filled with ruptures that humiliated her, but she believed that for as long as she would live, she would not let anyone destroy her dignity. She was just like Palestine. Palestinian people, who have the right to possess their own lands, are exposed to violations by fake deeds of ownership. In the same way, her thoughts were invaded by her father's suspicious, controlling and vindictive attacks:

Is it right for parents to destroy their children with their harsh, vengeful attitudes? And what purpose does that serve? Parents only harm their children, break their hearts, and kill their dreams, by unleashing on them their latent anger and deep-rooted grudges that had been caused by other people. How can they punish their children for sins they have not committed? They see their children as channels to vent their mephitic desire to feed their selfish and egotistic needs – subconsciously or otherwise.

Each of her siblings was treated aggressively by their father – a man whose heart was heavily laden with live bombs that could explode any moment, terrorising everyone living under his roof by taking a sharp turn in the path in the blink of an eye!

Al-Batool's[1] mother, who was also subjected to her husband's oppression, reminded her to say a prayer before talking to her father. She wanted to give her daughter strength, but she never took a clear stance in these battles. On the one hand, she wanted to support the breadwinner of the house; on the other, her heart would cry for her squawking children. In the end, she would impulsively back the side that won the battle – a mistake she repeatedly committed.

It was a normal family gathering and they were in their living room with its Bedouin-style seating. Along each of the three walls, there were high, cushioned seats with drawers underneath that contained anything that they needed to have at hand. There was a television against the fourth wall. He was in the room, seated opposite the television and, as usual, he was switching from channel to channel all day long without getting bored. Perhaps he would find his lost cause... He tried to kill time and avoid the mundane daily conversations.

The father's personality was peculiar and contradictory. At times, he could burst into a rage when provoked by the news, at other

---

1   Al-Batool is used as a proper noun to refer to the female character. In Arabic, it means *the virgin, the pure one.*

times he would exhibit utmost sympathy for the needy, the oppressed and the war casualties around the world. He had an unpredictable character. He could shift, when needed, from his oppressive self to one who was compassionate towards the oppressed. He both loved and gave conditionally.

As usual, he was reclining on his favourite seat, leaning on his right hand, when she wavered towards him; she was trembling as she was about to invade his private moments with his lovely mistress, the television screen. With a quavering voice inhibited by her dry mouth, she tried to grab his attention, all the while gripped by the fear of being repelled by a man she loved.

She did love him. She recollected her childhood memories, which she held dear in her heart. She could remember him teasing her, and driving after her as she went to school to make sure she did not lose her way. Despite all the pain, she always loved him.

"Baba…"[2]

He did not respond. He pretended to be preoccupied with the song of Egyptian pop singer, Roby, playing on the screen.

She tried again. This time, he half-turned in her direction, twisted his lips with disinterest – a clear sign that her request would be denied even before it was heard – and gestured to her to start talking.

"I was offered a grant for administrative and secretarial training at work… on the condition that…"

He interrupted her without looking at her face, "No!"

"It will only take two hours every day after work…"

"I said NO and that's that!"

Trying to remain unperturbed by her humiliation, she held her breath and in the same shaky voice, exclaimed, "But it would lead to a big promotion next year!"

---

2   *Baba* is the Arabic word for father.

3

Barely a few seconds had passed when she was shaken by a slap to the right side of her face, which left her swirling in a whirlpool. Her head floated in the air, and her eyes saw nothing but dots all around her. She had always endeavoured to protect herself from emotional pain by hiding behind a locked gate, refusing to allow any feelings of humiliation to creep in. Staying strong meant that she had to put up with the repercussions of dealing with inadequate people. Her head filled with dilemmas every time she thought of how she was living under the roof of her father and enjoying the luxuries provided by him, but not the luxury of a stable relationship with him.

While he was losing his temper, enraged with his untamed slurring that brought out the worst in him, she stood there frozen with fear, astonished, and submissive, waiting for the effusive volcanic eruption to end. Her mother had the very same fears but, unlike her, she was a person who would stand back and let her man spit in the fresh pot of milk she had prepared...

"Don't you know about the notoriety of secretaries – their bad reputation? Now, tell me the real reason you want to change your job! You must have something else in your mind and I will find it out!"

Instead of bursting into tears to relieve her pain, she was struck by an electric shock of anxiety and confusion. This became an exclamation mark that would haunt her for as long as she would live! Examining the facial expressions of those around her, raising her head towards the heavens, searching the tunnels in the ground, looking underneath the grass and above the waves of the sea, she desperately tried to find a rational explanation for such rage. Perhaps she could solve this riddle, and rid her mother from swinging between confusion and subservience.

The sadness of her mother and siblings filled the room after they came to ask about what happened but, as usual, he took the lead and mockingly concocted a different story; one that suited his own desires and whims.

Her eyes were filling with tears, her only private consolation, as she swiftly ran up the stairs to the second floor to bury herself in the darkness of her white-walled room, where her pain had dwelled for years, and her books and papers piled up at every cosy corner. Inside her room, where two windows opened to the garden and dark brown curtains blocked the air from interrupting her solitude, she found herself isolated from the outside world and wrote like she never wanted to stop. For her, writing was a means of reconciling with herself and a peaceful way to reassess life.

I think often of where this path will lead me. I question myself too many times but the answer is always: I do not have many options. My poor, pitiful soul, you are torn between desperation and hope. I must overcome all challenges in order to attain peace of mind and reach my desired destination. I must be patient and hopeful of finding a way out. You do not need to answer me; I know you sympathise with me because you see what people do to me and you know how my own mind tortures me.

She had another idea now – a more intelligent one, a more pressing issue.

Do you believe that I will be able to find my hero soon? Is he somewhere out there looking for me while I keep wandering here and there? I float with my thoughts in the world of my dreams, and it tires me. Do you think I will ever meet him?

Perhaps... I fear that the beats of my heart will stop before I can touch his flesh, and that my joyful feelings will stop when he arrives. I am scared that they will introduce me to a face that does not belong to the man of my dreams, and force me to marry one who is not my true love, my other half.

Should I agree to marry a man just because I must be married? Should I stop chasing true love? Should I accept a relationship without love just for the sake of marriage, and join the many married women on their loveless and dreamless journey?

I do not want to be the new fabric that they will shape to fit his car seats, yet he would be a wrecked car that will need a lot more than good seats to provide a comfortable ride! No, I won't settle for less. My mirror shall only reflect the face I am waiting for.

During her daily internal monologues, her inner self always intervened: Stop it! Haven't you had enough of waiting? Do you still have hopes and dreams?

She responded assertively: My birds of love are calling for passion, and my trees of hope are digging deeper roots inside me and their leaves are growing bigger every day. The whole world must listen to what I have to say; they must support me by holding the sword of beauty in the face of corruption, oppression, and misconceptions of norms and traditions!

Repeatedly, the investigator cross-examined her throughout the dark folds of the night. She posed the question and she replied.

Are you insane or have you been hit by an electric shock of foolishness? Are you not living in the same age as we are, or is this only your ghost? Have you buried yourself in a graveyard a thousand miles away from our times? What world are you talking about? Who do you think would want to know about you? I did tell you to stop it!

Despite being challenged, all her responses remained positive and confident. She short-sightedly but confidently remarked: They are just like me. A lot of them out there are just like me. I can feel them going through pain and torture, and I also know they can feel mine. Their voices move me, and the echo of my voice touches their hearts. When I am pained, I can see them hurting with me, and when I am happy, I can feel them jumping with joy. Believe me, I do not know their names, nor do I know their whereabouts, but I have faith in them and I am waiting for the day we can meet.

These controversial monologues often ended in the victory of one side. Then the defeated side would hurriedly move to another act in the drama of life to make her laugh again and avoid facing up to the loss.

She was young, but her life was nothing but a lost battle. She focused her mind on contemplating people and all living things, analysing her thoughts, and achieving her goals – albeit only through her pen. Through the exploration of her pen, she found brilliant new ideas, and she was reborn more than a thousand times in just one year. She was a woman who seemed to have come from a different time in the past when prisons were the only abode of women like her. Her eyes spoke to all people. As fast as an eagle, her voice transformed people's fears into tranquillity, flying them to islands of peace – their everlasting abode.

Beautiful eyes are not those, which are big with a marked contrast between white and black. Real beauty is a reflection of the eye of the beholder – a look that defines all meanings of world beauty. Beautiful eyes impress others, hold meaning, and have deep insight. You can see the light flashing out from them, but you will wonder if they are looking at you or just reflecting that light within.

Her eyes revealed what she tried to hide. Her eyes yearned to discover the depth of everything in life, sending out rays of aspirations that miraculously blended ambiguity with clarity. Inadvertently and timidly, her eyes exposed the darkest secrets of the realities beyond fundamental traditions and facts. Her eyes saw what others could not, and drew with the brush of her eyelashes an imaginary picture, a deep insight, with which she hoped to initiate a change in society.

Her voice was similar to *daraseen*, a cinnamon drink. It was delicious, with an unrivalled aroma that lingered long after she had gone. The tone of her voice was like a wave rising up and going down swiftly from the purity of her spirit. With the slightest sigh, she captured people's ears and hearts.

Her femininity and purity of heart, unrestrained by pretention and deceit, often triggered suspicion in others. She had to face not only the doubts of females who supported sexist, male-dominated ideologies, but also of men – especially men of intellect.

CHAPTER 2

S he kept twirling her hair with her fingers as the voice of the professor, talking about the secretarial and administration course, went deeper into her soul. After battling a long day at work, she tried to focus on what he was saying and listen to every word attentively, while he tried to test how many of the attendees sitting behind that brown glass barrier were listening to him. He wondered whether they were actually listening, or he was talking to a blank wall.

The place was gloomy, quiet, and insanely spacious, to the extent that any girl coming into the educational centre would feel as if she was the only one standing there like a fool. Similar to many old public buildings in Riyadh, the centre used to be a traditional Saudi residence, tailored to meet the growing prerequisites of the family. There were divisions between the zones of both genders, even inside the house. The women's zone now served as the manager's office most of the time, while the men's zone, which was located a few steps away from the main building, had been turned into a waiting area for female students. All the other rooms in the building had been converted to classrooms.

No one could ever be attracted to the so-called charm of these buildings. They were cold, with pillars that barely stood erect under the banners fixed onto them, rotting wooden chairs, and dust and damp covering every surface. Every part of the building attested that it had been abandoned, deprived of intimacy. Even though the temperature both inside and outside was high, the place looked forlorn, cold, and bleak. You could only hear the ringtone of mobile phones coming from the square-shaped rooms with their strikingly white walls and blinding fluorescent lights. This is where some female students were seated on grey iron desks, lashing out against their husbands, maids, or drivers, over their phones. Despite the private nature of these phone conversations, none of them paused when another student walked in. Nothing could stop them.

Drawing comparisons between meeting rooms and tables, the instructor stated that they were different and served different purposes. Then, to test how much attention the female students had been paying his lesson, he posed some questions.

"What is the purpose of the round table? When do we use it?"

Samar, another young female and her co-worker, said that she thought all tables were the same and it never occurred to her that there was any difference... was there any difference?

He smiled and asked again, "Why is it that meeting rooms and convention halls have different tables: rectangular, round, oval?"

Al-Batool responded, as everyone in the room looked at her scornfully: "Regarding the rectangular table, it might entail the presence of leaders and those they lead. As for the round table, it could mean that the different attendees are of the same footing."

It appeared that he liked her intelligent answer. He engaged her in discussing it further, before moving on to explain the different ways of categorising office files, and the important relationship of this task with the type and place of work. Her mind began to wander, and she started wondering about the relationship between girls. Her thoughts were triggered by the reactions the girls had given to her input, even though they had not had the chance to meet her yet. They were under the impression that she was the kind of girl who used such cunning ploys as asking questions or giving answers in order to draw the instructor's attention onto herself. Jealousy and resentment dominated the relationships between these girls. Most of them were antagonistic towards girls who were different from them, and with their backbiting and condemnatory attitudes, they devised rules on who could join their club, when, or where, and drew up the terms based on their whims and moods.

This was the kind of relationship she had with Samar, who always kept close to her, boastful of the fact that they were the only girls in their class who were working for a major corporation. Samar had squinting eyes, and her lips were like those of a fox. She let her true colours surface again the following morning at work.

"You like the instructor, right? I don't find him funny!"

Startled and shocked by the question, al-Batool tried hard to suppress her urge to provoke Samar in return.

"Oh, Miss Know-it-all! What makes you think that?"

Biting her lower lip as a sign of infuriation, "You responded, showed interest in him, you were proactive!" uttered Samar, with an attitude that was accusing al-Batool for participating in class in order to present herself as an intelligent student and gain the male instructor's admiration.

"So, you think that whenever I converse with a man, any man, I am aiming for his heart? You have always been too shallow, Samar."

"Who said anything about love, you crazy girl! I meant that you're just looking for a fling! You want to have an affair."

Hearing this, al-Batool reacted in an exasperated tone: "May God give me some respite from your absurdity! So that's why more than twenty pairs of eyes looked at me with disdain when I opened my mouth during the lesson. I am now coming to realise a very important thing…"

"And what is that?" asked Samar, with a smug smile on her lips.

Al-Batool tried to maintain a steady tone to end the conversation, although her whole body was struck by storms of rage, spiralling and blowing like a tornado.

"I discovered that you know nothing about chastity! If there were something going on between us, I wouldn't have answered his questions. I would've acted innocent and remained quiet to hide our secret, wouldn't I?! You have twisted ideas in your head. So every time I talk with a man, does it mean I'm having an illicit relationship with him? Even if that were true, why would that be any of your business anyway!"

Leaving Samar behind, she walked out of the room, put on her black robe and hijab, and headed to the car. As the chauffeur drove her, she sat there with vacant eyes, reflecting on the prejudices that prevailed in her community. The depth of her thoughts consumed not only her mind, but also her body, which was overcome by a sudden sexual urge. Just like the car key that had turned on the engine, her mental state revitalised her senses.

She knew that in the eyes of Saudis, she was not as beautiful as Samar, yet Samar was so uncontrollably jealous of her that it governed all aspects of their relationship. Jealousy is like fire that needs wood to burn; and when it burns, it destroys everything in its way.

Samar was the product of a clash of civilisations between the freedom coming from foreign countries and the backward community at home. The community could not deal with the sudden flow of foreign ideologies, which were regarded as an infection, and no one was prepared to deal with such thunder. Thus, the community was divided into two extreme groups, both of which denounced moderation. The first was an extreme, closed-minded group that chose willingly to block all its receptors and prevent any foreign ideas from permeating the deep-rooted convictions of the community. The second group was like an unleashed gipsy, careless of any standards. Samar held the beliefs of the second group. She was a gossip-loving, egotistic and self-centred person, striving to feed her offensive, shallow and uncontrollable desires.

"How I hate being a woman!" she murmured while the driver was rambling about an earthquake in Pakistan and expressing relief that his family had not been harmed. Suddenly, Samar's attention turned to the clock, and she urged the driver to go faster because it was almost 8:30 pm and she had promised her father not to be late. This was the second of the two conditions her father had imposed on her before giving her his approval to join the course. The other was that she would never consider working as a secretary, no matter how lucrative the offers were.

CHAPTER 3

It was a wonderful morning, sunny and humid. The air was filled with soft rays of sunlight, a breeze that captured the minds of wise men, redolence of jasmines, and symphonies played by the beautiful cestrum bidding the dawn farewell. Wintertime in Riyadh is delicious! It fills people's hearts with happiness and washes away all bitterness. It elates everyone – even the Religious Police[3] who do nothing all year round but dutifully roam the city with spiritless and emotionless expressions.

Would you believe that it has been a very long time since I last looked at our back garden, especially the palm tree, which is two years younger than I am? I pass by it every single day in the morning and afternoon on my way to work and back, but I never see it.

I wonder why I work. Is it because of the money? Well, everyone needs money, but I lament the fact that people work only for the sake of money. I want to see people appreciated for their honourable efforts of spreading knowledge and serving others. I do not know why I work. I have a lot of time in my hands, but am I only trying to fill my time? If so, then why is it that my work occupies most of my time? Perhaps I work because I am creative and eager to use my skills at work. Yes, most likely this is what motivates me. A professional work environment is a fertile soil for the enrichment of my talents. I have studied too hard to gain my

---

[3]   The Islamic Religious Police is a term often used to refer to Saudi Arabia's Committee for the Promotion of Virtue and the Prevention of Vice (Haia), and stands for a government agency employing members to enforce the Islamic teachings within the kingdom.

degree… Oh, this has never crossed my mind before! I have not been married nor had any children; I am free from family responsibilities, social obligations, marriage conflicts and divorce proceedings! Could this be why I work hard from dawn to dusk, wasting my energy, and drifting my mind away from my world of dreams?

As she left the house the next morning and got into the car on her way to work, all that was floating inside her head were her internal monologues. She found herself succumbing to self-interrogation during her routine daily activities, or recollecting memories from her past and creating imaginary stories about her life. Like many girls her own age, she could not fulfil all her dreams because of the ignorant views of society.

She thought of her friend Wejdan, who wanted to continue her education and get better job prospects, but lived in an environment that prohibited modernity and discouraged knowledge. Her face carried an enlightened aura of satisfaction[4] that was the result of her intelligent mind and gracious heart. Whenever she met with al-Batool on the weekends, she talked of how much it troubled her that the religious icons she looked up to rebuked her aspirations.

Astonishingly, those icons regarded themselves as the best people who could implement the tradition of the Prophet (peace and blessings be upon him). They believed that their historical background and lineage, which traced back to the noble Prophet, qualified them to act as superiors. They had a deep-seated conviction

---

4   According to Sufism, a branch of Islam, Muslims should appreciate every little thing in life and pursue a more humble life to emulate the life the Prophet Mohammed lived. Being a follower of these teachings, Wejdan accepted God's preordainment, and respected the wish of her father, but never stopped wishing she could attain higher education. Wejdan embodies the resilience of Sufi women who never fail to show gratitude for what they have in their life.

that they belonged to the highest levels of humankind. In order to spread their reputation and successfully establish their religious edicts and rulings, these clerics appointed members of their own group as supreme spiritual leaders, and they all embraced and lauded each other at every opportunity. Alas, Saudi girls had to carry painfully heavy loads as big as Mount Uhud. Their situation was deadlocked, just like Egypt's High Dam, with no holes even for a small ray of light to pass through.

Her inner voice cried out at her: Be grateful that you are working, using your skills to help people. Didn't you always believe that the true meaning of life rests in helping others and sharing their pains; that such interaction is the source of your life? If your motive is to serve with that spirit, then you are a true human being with principles. A decent man, a precious breed, is out there looking for you. You are a pearl, hidden inside the shell, charming the eyes of all who dive to the bottom of the ocean, but only one diver will lay his hands on you, and when he holds you, what will you want from him?

These people are but opportunists taking advantage of me and giving nothing back. People have always treated me with selfishness. Once their needs are fulfilled, they bid me farewell and vanish in the sporadic walks of life. They rush back to me in desperation when they need me again. Absolutely not! I will never again fall in the trap of giving and getting nothing in return. And my feelings will never be used in the name of love!

People are often unreliable and opportunistic. Some are emotionally mature, but many others live their lives with a constant need for attention. To satisfy their egos, they feed on the dignity of noble people and take pleasure in trapping their prey. They particularly enjoy taking advantage of gentle, pure women, who have maintained their dignity and respectability despite the troubles life has thrown at them. Those who manipulate others are, in fact, the prey of their own insecurities and weaknesses.

Wejdan had a generous nature, and her devotion had no limits. She gave up on her aspirations for the sake of keeping the peace with her parents and her husband. It was extraordinary that despite the sacrifice she was forced to make, she never lost her belief in the beauty of her dreams. Instead of receiving love from her parents and husband as a fundamental right, she had become accustomed to bidding for it. Her obedience had given them more fuel to control her life as they wished, in the mistaken belief that they were giving her the best she would ever get. Her love of her family was not reciprocated, but they did not hate her in the way that many movies feature such relationships. She was the weaker side in this equation, and her beloved ones, the stronger side, treated her as if they owned her. She had no right to expect, or demand, love. Her life was in the hands of the egotistic desires of her family, who never felt compelled to give her anything in return for her sacrifices. Wejdan was cognisant of the unjust circumstances of her life. Her parents had married her at a young age and deprived her of an education. They had blocked her from following the light that always hovered in her horizon, yet they continued to believe that they were doing her a service worthy of gratitude.

Inside al-Batool, a trumpet made a loud noise in protest: Why did you start your day with sad thoughts? What made you think of Wejdan now? Think of the man who will guard you forever as a treasure; the one who will cherish you because of your personality, not because he can possess you; the one who will fall in love with the conviction in your eyes, not their confusion.

Suddenly, she gasped as she noticed the clock strike midnight.

What? Is it midnight? Did I go to work? When did I come back? What did I have for lunch? Am I sleepwalking? Is my imagination playing tricks on me?

Twenty-four hours of her day were filled with endless conversations and fluctuating feelings of trouble, safety, confidence, and panic.

She had to prepare her body and mind for another day of self-interrogation. She tried to go to sleep, although she was reluctant to stop her spontaneous, soothing conversations with herself, as they allowed her to enjoy a sense of freedom. She could talk with herself for hours with no restrictions.

Is my imagination playing tricks on me?

The question aroused in her the kind of pain that she always battled to ignore. She did not want to address it now. She did not want to alleviate the pain. Ignoring it was the best way to deal with it, she decided, but the pain did not let her sleep peacefully. She became angry with herself.

Sakan el-Leil [5] was playing; the voice of Fayruz reminded her of the roar of waves in the translucent waters of the sea. She turned off both the radio and the light, but her mind remained switched on.

Who will close the door and turn off the light troubling me inside my head? Dear God, isn't it time for my mind to be calm as the night in Riyadh? I only want to sleep for a few hours. My pillow endures the noisy heartbeats pulsing in my head, and it aches as my head throbs every night.

She woke every hour and pushed aside her pillow, hoping to silence the sound of the horn in her head. But the pillow cried out in pain; and so did she.

---

[5] *Sakan el-Leil*, meaning "The Night Became Calm", is an Arabic song performed by the famous Lebanese singer Fayruz. The lyrics are based on one of Gibran Khalil Gibran's poems, wherein a man is calling upon his lady to explore the beauty of the night and dispel her fears.

This was how she slept. She envied those who enjoyed the pleasure of peaceful sleep. She could make use of a training manual on how to sleep. Why wouldn't her mind call upon sleep with the same passion as it entertained other thoughts?

Who are the happiest: deep sleepers, shallow sleepers, or those who struggle to sleep? I think it ought to be those who continue sleeping after their alarm has been put on snooze multiple times ... If only this was something we all could do!

O, this dark night is eerie. Darkness always takes me to places I do not know before bringing me back home and leaving me in peace.

She was a woman who never slept peacefully. She was trapped inside a dreary jungle, yet tirelessly content to analyse the raging thoughts in her head, navigating mountains, cliffs, and crossroads, and running away from the lava erupting from the volcano only to find her path obstructed by a river. She laughed and cried, became angered and troubled, argued and screamed, until she would collapse from the pain. Remarkably, she pulled herself up with strength and pride after every fall. Contemplating her darkest secrets gave her immense pleasure because it helped her see the truth, and transported her to faraway places where there were no dams, drought, or earthquakes. It kept her inexhaustible candles lit; whenever they melted, her tears made new ones. No matter how hard she cried, agonies found their way back to her heart.

As she looked in the mirror the next morning, it cunningly murmured to her:

"Good morning! The start of a new day must be full of hope. I wish I could protect myself from the arrows coming from your sad eyes. I wish you would smile!"

She serenely gazed at her image. That morning she looked better, despite the groaning of her pillow the night before. She opened the window and looked up to the sky.

"This reminds me of the sky at university. But how?"

O, what a silly question! It is making me laugh. Of course the sky is the same everywhere. Don't muddle with my memories, leave me alone! Why do you always take me back to the pain of the past? Please, leave! A new day has come.

When I was at university, everything seemed bigger to me and even the smallest of problems appeared prodigious. The scars in the sky carried a deeper resonance with my soul. The university building, the broken lifts, the damaged stairs, the old trees on campus, and the autumn leaves fallen under the shadows of the trees, all bore a different meaning. They held my hopes and aspirations as I walked towards the gate and said my farewells each day. In the morning, they welcomed me again with a new breeze of dreams. Now, the sky and the land do not look the same as before. I look at the world differently; I have even re-evaluated my relationships with people.

'*We will see life as beautiful if our soul is beautiful.*' Elia Abu Madi[6] was right. Beauty stems from the soul first and foremost. Nowadays, people are more impressed by violence, ugliness, and all that is bizarre. Even when they know that the fake glow of appearances will soon fade, they are lured in by it. When their possessions lose that glow, they move on to grab a new brand or fashion before anyone else. This is the era of mobiles and pagers, where everything is artificial and cloned. People are not thrilled by what is genuine or real, and do not appreciate beauty or value. They only chase what benefits their personal, materialistic interests.

Death. The cars that we see on our roads are deadly because they take us to unknown destinations when, in fact, they were created to transport us safely from one place to another, and make long-distance

---

[6] Elia Abu Madi was a Lebanese-American poet whose poetry was commonplace and memorised in the Arab world.

travel easier. Over the years, new designs have been introduced primarily to bring innovation and improvement to our lives. Now, cars create envy, competition, and distance between different social groups. Showing off and speeding result in death – not only of the drivers involved, but of innocent people too. When we sit in our cars, we never know where we will end up.

Dear God! What has possessed these drivers today? Why are they racing each other? Why are they in such a rush, putting their precious lives at risk?

Those few minutes on the way to work filled her heart with fear, as she doubted if she would reach her destination safely. "Thank God we made it!" she murmured when they arrived at her work place. "Now off to start today's battle against these lunatics!" she quietly added.

We have to deal with different kinds of people in our life. Every time we step out of the familiar boundaries of our home, we have to be ready for psychological warfare, which comes and goes; it ebbs and flows and does not always end decisively in victory or defeat. Today, as always, I must stay alert at work to be able to confront warring people. Although fortitude and vigour are some of my strongest characteristics, my sensitivities are often as fragile as twigs. What a contradiction, don't you think?

I am enduring what only iron could resist. By nature, I am inquisitive and eager to dive into the ocean to explore its depths; but I spiral like a leaf every time the heavy winds blow. This is not a sign of weakness. I always choose to follow the road filled with challenges; hence, I must face all opposition that crosses my path. No matter how harshly they attack me, fill me with insecurities, or spread rumours about me, I will keep my course and meet them with a brave smile. I will confront them with grace and dignity. I will remain tough until they become hopeless. They will lose and I will win. They will fall and I will rise. Similar to a centuries-old tree, which has stood strong against the storms, I will persevere! Their attacks will only leave a scar on my deepest roots.

Samar was a person who resented al-Batool's elegance and eloquence. For her, al-Batool was an object of wonderment. She wondered if her silence and calmness were signs of inner peace or a cunning character. Of course, Samar would always prefer to think of the latter.

"You know, people were giving me compliments today about the way I was walking, as if they'd never seen a female in heels before! I am the best dressed girl around here today."

It took al-Batool a few seconds to notice the antennas above Samar's head sticking out to scrutinise the other females in the room.

God, what shall I do now? Shall I respond in the affirmative to reassure her or just tell her to get the hell out of here and leave me alone? In fact, I think I too should start wearing heels to work!

"Yes. Heels suit you," she said with a smile.

With an ego that had just been pumped by that compliment, and with a ludicrous gait, Samar moved her antennas to the desk next to al-Batool, who was glad to see her go, though the smell of her perfume lingered behind.

It was only then that she was able to immerse herself in her notebook to record that most worthy incident of her day.

God, I can't catch up with time, it is going too fast! A life of lies... But I am not a victim; it is the creators of lies who fall into their own traps. Have you ever looked for a seat only for no one to offer you help? Have you ever looked for a shoulder to cry on, without knowing which of your friends to confide in? Why do women like Samar occupy themselves with the futile affairs of women and their relationships?

She recalled the day she first came here to apply for a job. They were getting her paperwork finalised before hiring her. An American female senior manager walked into the office, and turning her head towards al-Batool, gave her a friendly smile and a nod of approval.

Moments later, a Saudi female employee came in and their eyes met. Being good at observing people, al-Batool could not miss the look of condemnation on her face, as if yelling at her *who do you think you are?* Then she deliberately attempted to ignore the newcomer, and to make her feel inferior, she started using facial expressions and hand gestures directed at her when communicating with the other employees. She had felt threatened by the American manager's glance at the new girl, as she had always thought that she would never meet her match. Women like her emotionally attack any female whose appearance makes a statement. They fight for a plot of abandoned land before the army of a real, beautiful queen makes an entrance.

As these deep thoughts gradually receded in her mind, she tried to focus on her work, which was the only thing that mattered right then. However, anything could happen in the course of the day to spark interest or bewilderment in her, provoking the bee in her head to start buzzing again without permission.

CHAPTER 4

S he touched the faces of people in the photos to feel her bygone childhood. She wondered how different those faces would look now.

Does distance change our feelings? Can our feelings be alive in a particular place and time, but die in another? When I was younger, I strongly believed in the so-called notions of love and loyalty, dreams and aspirations. I had a set belief system and rejected everything else that did not fit with my definitions. Regardless of how hard life became, I clutched tightly to my beliefs. It always infuriated me when people remarked "out of sight, out of mind" with a mocking smile. I labelled them as ungrateful and reckless because I refused to believe that distance made people grow less fond of one another.

I was too innocent. I believe there is a lot of truth in that saying. I must not feel guilty for believing in it now, but I feel sad for losing my innocence – something no willpower will be able to bring back. These friends from the past live miles away now and we only see each other on special occasions, but our lives are probably much alike.

Ah, this is his photo! Where did this come from? Why now? Touching the photo, I can feel him here with me; his voice is filling the room. Shall I call him? But I never did so in my worst times!

She did not want him to think that she was falling into the crime of being needy, nor did she wish to hear him say that he was desperately missing her. She decided to write to him; putting her feelings on paper was better than talking to his stern face in person!

Her thoughts poured out onto the paper and she recorded those valuable moments of her life.

Was it my heart, my soul, or my mind, which intrigued you? They shared their love for you. You captured my whole being. You imprisoned me with your silence when you listened to me so well; but you also overwhelmed me with your voice when you spoke. Even though your words were measured and reserved, they penetrated my vacant heart.

There were intricately tangled forests of riddles in the depth of my heart, where only the gentle echoes of soft words could be heard. You spoke with honest words and an honest tone of voice, which inspired me with the certainty that you were speaking from your heart. In fact, that was the only thing about you of which I was certain. The scrupulous language you used charmed me and carried me to many beautiful, imaginary places.

Your words were not your only charm. Your soft whispers were the wings that flew me to far-away places. When I recall your voice, I become terrified because I lose track of where I am and where I am going; which road to take; and whether the path I choose will take me to the abyss or to the river of true love.

Did you know that the stone you threw in my waters created waves that took me on many high and low journeys? Whether you intended to clutch me that way, I do not know, but I know that all my senses loosened, and my love for you grew every day until all the creatures of the world became aware of it. They could hear your footsteps on my vast grounds. The penguins and gulls felicitated me, the dolphins clapped for me, and I rejoiced in listening to your voice ring the hidden bells of my heart. Alas, only I could hear them, and no one but you knew how to ring them.

Did you know that I only loved my name after I heard you pronounce it? I only believed in my writing when it was about your eyes and soul. You knew me better than I knew myself.

I scream in pain. Can you hear me? Can you hear the voice of the girl who did not call for you? I hear a voice, but I cannot tell if it is the echo of my own voice, or a recollection of your whispers. The voice is telling me that there are fingerprints on the pages of your heart and that you are going to find the person who left them. It is telling me to follow the light that will guide me to your heart.

Why were we afraid of love? Why did we always talk about its pains and agonies? Why did I expect you to take action while I cocooned myself and waited? Why did I remain chained while you ran around, oblivious of the fact that you owned the key to set me free? You might respond that I was the one who put my heart in chains – that it was not your fault. If this is what you think, then I must stop loving you. I can see a new light, which I will follow to change direction and steer away from this land of dreams.

Why did I write to you? Was I trying to prove that you existed in my life? You occupied a big part of my mind, which strived to find a solution to my pain, but in vain, so it sought the help of my heart. The two engaged in heated discussions and reproachful remarks.

I ask again, what was the reason that my pen could address no one but you? Why did it express all my heart's treasures, yearnings, and secrets to you alone? It was only in your chest where I could surrender all my coyness. Why, I ask.

I wish you could hear my whispers in the wind, see my smiles, and discover their deep-rooted source in the privacy of my soul's depth.

I wish you could unleash your suppressed emotions, allow your mind to think freely, and find home in the vast space of my land and my sky.

I wish you could come back to sit with me and listen to my talks. You had an insight into my soul. You would see the depth of the river of sadness and compassion flowing within it. You would smell the fragrance of my oasis of roses, orchids, tulips, dianthus, and carnations, and pick infinite bunches of my flowers. You would see the scars in my heart, and know that I have been hurt. My pain almost killed me.

I wish you would return. Please do!

I wish I could hear your silent thoughts and relearn how to contain you. Return, so I can hear you say to me, "I am all ears". I wish my ears would hear you say why you sounded harsh and what hurt you the most.

I want to draw your face, visualise you, and see you closely. My feelings were always expressed in writing, but will we ever meet so I can tell you more? Would you hear these words one day?

She did not know that he would never read her words. She had to write, as she had no other option. Her deep love for him controlled all of her senses, and forced her to write. Despite her confidence in putting her words on paper, she was a coy person. She was never under the delusion that they would be together in the future, that she was the one he was looking for, or that he was the missing half of her moon.

The interrogator posed some questions again, but this time she had no lawyer to defend her. Why won't you meet him if you both expressed love to each other in the past? Both of you know that you were meant for each other. What are you waiting for?

She hurriedly and anxiously grabbed her mobile phone. His name was Turki, but his number was added under the name of a female friend, Arwa. The things that detectives will try hard to uncover must be masked.

We were similar. We both fought hard to stop our feelings for each other, but how could we escape from the decisions taken for us by destiny? We pretended that they were our own impulsive decisions but they were, in truth, predestined for us.

They agreed to meet in the nearest luxurious hotel. What a risky adventure!

Turki had always loved the good and the bad in her. Her outgoing nature and sense of humour raised him up so high that he could touch the sky and reach the heavens. He understood her deep need for affection, so he showered her with his love, knowing that she was a faithful lover. He had a special way of containing her, and he did it skilfully. He loved her with a kind of love that could evolve over time.

She rushed to hide between his arms and kissed him passionately. She kissed and never thought whether it was right or wrong to do it. Her instincts controlled her. The heat of their encounter mixed with the fumes of hope. He did not give her a chance to think because missing her had ignited a fire in his body. She had conquered his imagination as he waited for days and months for that phone call. He took off her white shirt and kissed her breasts fervently. She looked like a delicious red apple. He devoured the curves of her body. He did not talk. His lips passionately invaded every part of her, and she allowed herself to indulge.

In his hug, she felt the warmth of the desert sand and the protection of the sunshade. She was captivated by his tanned complexion, the sharp edges of his face, and his dark hair, every time she looked at him. When he kissed her, his lips made her feel reborn.

It is strange how we become absorbed in a particular moment in time and lose control of our senses.

In a split second, she felt a sour taste in her lips as he stroked her left breast. Instead of pleasure, this time she felt offended by his invasion. She felt a kind of emotional pain unlike any she had experienced before. Amidst the sounds of sexual pleasure, she pushed him away, which he mistook for a flirtatious gesture.

They did not talk, but stood there exchanging looks of reproach and confusion. He was visibly engulfed by sexual desire, but she quickly put on her black robe and rushed out. She felt light-headed with the pain of invasion, and agitated with the realisation that he had touched a very dear part of her body, her breasts. She thought of her breasts as the miracle of life and motherhood. They were the essence of her dignity. What a stupid girl, she murmured to herself. For the very first time in their relationship, she could not divert her conscience from the feeling of guilt.

In the lift going down to the waiting car, she was shocked to see her reflection in the mirror. The trembling of her lips sent a clear signal that she did not want to hear anything but her own inner voice.

Turki was shocked too – by her reaction. He phoned her many times as she sat crying in the car. She decided that she ought to ignore his missed calls forever.

In that rainy winter's night, she remained awake and her tears poured down heavily like the rains. Her inner world was as fragile as the world outside. She thought about life and sought answers to her many questions. Despite the consolation she found in lamenting her status quo, she wondered if tears were the answer.

What is the purpose of tears? Do people deserve the tears we shed for them? Do tears bring us any reward when we cry with all our heart or shed them in a specific place and time? What are tears: drops of salty water, or expressions of true emotions? How can our tears be expressive of what our mouths cannot say? Are tears stronger than words? Are they more powerful because they can perform when all of our senses fail?

Which is the more constructive: tears that burst out vehemently to save us from fainting, or the compassionate tears that relieve the sadness in our eyes, heal the wounds of trauma, and alleviate our pain?

Do our cold tears explode to soothe the volcanic anger that has engulfed our land, to wash away the ashes, and to purify our nature?

Is it better to shed tears in the embrace of a loved one who will wipe them away and relieve our pain, or should we cry alone in a dark room because we do not want to be judged by others?

Should we cry over the painful moments that we spent with those who walked away and forgot us, or should we only cry over the loss of people who were close to us, and not waste our emotions on those who are not worth it?

I cannot find answers to my questions. I only know that a woman cries when she feels helpless and hopeless. She has no shelter where she can take refuge from the harsh criticism of society. She cannot hide from the scrutinising eyes of people who are trying desperately to uncover the reasons behind her crime – pardon me, her tears. Her only panacea is to detach herself from this world and surrender to deep sleep. She turns into a prisoner, not knowing whether she should cry and get accustomed to living with her pain, or freeze all her emotions lest they erupt.

Dear God, help me! I am overcome by a fever of questions! I have no remedy. This fever adores me and does not want to leave my body. I cannot make it go away. I am not strong enough. It is happy that I am suffering. I cannot live without questioning!

O longest night! I so await your morn, though my thorny cares won't by morn be shorn.[7]

She reached the epitome of her pain and succumbed to outbursts of anger. She tried everything she could to overcome the destructive feeling, but to no avail. The outbursts varied in time, but no matter

---

[7] A poetic line from *Mualaqat* by the prolific Arab writer Imriu al-Qays.

how short or long, they were painful and made her heart bleed in agony. In these moments, the colour of everything around her changed into shades of grey. Eventually, the torrent of fury receded and decided to wage war another time.

She was excellent at putting on a brave face and keeping the truth to herself. If you looked inside her, you would find a fierce battle, deadly protests, and a struggle to attain freedom. She could not share her protests publicly. She had to shed her heavy tears in solitude.

I wonder how my death will come. Will I die during these protests? Someone might trample over me and kill me. Will I be rescued? What will be my end? Shall I declare war against my emotions and die peacefully with dignity, or shall I choose the route of wisdom, which will help me cross the rivers of sadness without engaging in this evil war?

She felt a sudden, uncontrolled urge to write – an impulse as deep as the ocean and as fierce as its waves. But for whom? Writing was not always the solution because her words were meant to be read by him. She was torn now between writing for him and thinking of him. "I cannot find my pen, I cannot find the words," she murmured while crawling into bed. She wanted to sleep to escape her reality.

She tossed and turned, but could not sleep, so she decided to continue writing – to him. She grabbed her pen and paper. Love had won her, but wanting to be sure of it, she allowed that moment to last longer. Her dreams had grown bigger, but despite the years that had passed, she had gone nowhere. Writing was her only achievement.

I do not know what it is, but something about you is pulling me towards you, reminding me of your words and drawing your image in my mind. I cannot suppress this vision. I cannot sleep. I cannot even write to you now.

I always admitted that writing about you was easier than writing to you. Whether I feel compelled to do it, I do not know, but I like writing about you. I sit here now, reminiscing about the beautiful moments that we once shared, but all I see is your pessimistic, stubborn self, which destroyed the harmony we once had. Please do not ruin the beauty of my memories.

We are standing in a closed auction room, you against me. Take anything you want, but leave me the green lands of love, which I have watered with my rains. Do not take a single flower from my lands. Please do not touch the love I have for you inside my heart. Do not destroy any good memory I have of you – not only because I want to keep it alive, but because you also want it to live.

I am satisfied with what's left from you: a memory. I am happy with my role of an ex-lover. I will take care of these lands. I will be their cultivator. I will irrigate the fields, which have witnessed the best celebrations of honest, spontaneous love. Let me be the keeper of these lands. I will not ask you to pay me for taking care of them. I will not reveal the secrets you have buried there. I will protect your treasures, but you will never have them back.

I waited as time went by, but nothing changed. I will continue to wait, although I know nothing will change. Time is defeating me. I am losing this battle. O, how I want to destroy all those feelings that force me to wait for you! I hate that you control my whole being. I am angry with you! Do not control me!

Just as my heart was filled with hatred against you, the phone rang, and I found myself running towards it with all the rush and longing in the world. I was shocked that I could not recognise your voice. It was unfamiliar, and tougher than I remembered it.

I remembered the day we had agreed to part. We had thought it would be the end and I had shed my last tear over my loss.

When you called, time stopped, and my heart beat so fast that my breath was caught inside my lungs. I could not breathe. I could not hear, or talk. I could not tell what was real and what was imaginary.

My fantasies and nightmares became one and the same. I did not know what I wanted, but I had to wake up to the reality. I have no idea how I summoned up the courage to do so, but I listened to your voice again, and it conjured up a true image of your heart.

As my subconscious mind watched your naked soul, my waves carried you to the shore of my compassion, and docked you at the port, where I could examine the yellow rust on your ship – the extent of your vanity. I wanted to help you despite being angry with you. I found myself drying up the sweat on your forehead and combing your curly hair. I tapped on your shoulders. I wanted to blame you.

My mind and heart could sense how much you needed me and how much control I had of your uninhabited heart. I knew your secret, though you did your best to conceal that you still loved me.

You have no idea how much I detest you now.

Did our love end because of my naivety; or did it end because I was too good for you (although you never acknowledged it)? I have never liked playing games and I know that I never plotted to direct our love to its end. I communicated my sincere feelings for you through my spontaneity and spirituality.

You never exploited my beauty. On the contrary, you were gentle and honest, and keen on protecting me from the shocks that life would cast my way. When you said the 'L' word, I froze as if my life had ceased. I could not absorb the moment. I could not assess my sentiments. Why did you feel the need to apologise for my silence?

You had a deep faith in our love, which I know woke you at night, distracted you at work, and triggered your tongue to tell me the most beautiful confessions of love, again and again. When we parted, you said that you would be strong. I know that you are. Unfortunately, your strength weakened our love.

The 'L' word is dying. You are falling into the darkness of my thoughts. I am dying as my hope of having you back fades.

Yes, I loved you the way you were. I loved your imperfections; your conflicts, fears, and stubbornness. I even loved you when you were not courageous enough to conquer my world. I loved all of your rudeness and abruptness, as you would describe yourself. I saw you through a very narrow lens, and I saw nothing but you. I was blinded by your love. I saw my soul in your eyes. Like a mirror, they reflected the essence of my soul. I wish I could rid myself from your cuffs and untamed impulsiveness.

Through my lens, I saw the rivers of compassion in your heart. Alas, I will never swim in your waters again. I smelled the delicious fragrance of your basil and lavender fields. I saw how your sweet herbs stood the heat of your desert. Every time you picked bunches of them, they grew again. I loved the cheerful symphony of your canaries and bulbuls. They sang, even when frightened by the eagles hiding in the gloomy forests of your kingdom.

In every beat of your heart, I heard songs of love and betrayal.

The north and south poles met inside your heart – a universal miracle first of its kind. And you lived just there, at an imaginary equator, where it was not too cold or too hot; where there was no drought, but few trees could grow; where living creatures could visit, but not live; where the hot sun shone every day, but the ice on the mountain peaks never melted; where people went for a drink to quench their thirst, but the snow never turned to water.

I loved your paradoxical nature. I found pleasure in coexisting and interacting with your mystifying perplexities. I thought I could move the mountains inside you, make the rivers of feelings flow, and inspire you to talk and release all the pain you held inside you.

I vividly remember the day when I first saw your eyes. I fixated my eyes on yours, and did not notice the distance between your paradise and your fire; your goodness and badness, your stubbornness and mildness, your pureness and ugliness, your hesitation and impulsiveness, and your generosity and avarice. I delved into the deep waters of your blue eyes, and did not see the sediment beneath the serenity of your blue waters.

Do you know what I am thinking of right now? If only I could remove my voice from your ears, and erase my face from your memory, I would. It could be the harshest thing I could ever do to you; or perhaps it would mean nothing to you.

Do you remember that time in the winter when we met? I restrained myself from meeting your eyes and touching your hands. Your body did not keep me warm that night, but our hearts met and we connected spiritually. That feeling made me crazy for you. The tribulations of love, which controlled me for years, are long gone now.

You were my dearest illusion. I always thought of you as the most absent and present person in my life. I had deep faith in the power and magic of feelings. My imagination took me to your home, where I left my imprint in all the rooms; to your office, where I teased you in secrecy. You became friends with my soul and played with it.

We took your car and went for a ride. I did not know where we were going. I just wanted to be with you. I could not fight that need. You drove to empty streets to convince me that we were alone. Your eyes were searching for a woman to fill the empty space next to you – a woman to escort you to a place where no police officer would stop you.

You divulged your sinful desire to me, and in that moment of confession, you stabbed my heart and tore up the virtuous image of you that I had carefully placed there. You destroyed our spiritual connection in one honest moment. I wish we'd never met.

I want to stop the pain you caused me by offending me with your many attempts to tempt me, but my heart is bleeding heavily. There was a beautiful side to your greed, and your acknowledgement of it, and nothing is dearer to my heart than the pain you caused me. I want you badly now. I want you to be with me forever.

I touched the highest clouds every time I heard your voice pronounce words of love to me and shatter my peaceful existence. The resonance of your voice raised me up to the heavens. With your whole being, you tried to hide from me your shortcomings and uncertainties, but I locked myself in your castle of arrogance and destroyed all your gates of darkness from inside. I demolished the bridges of protection you built around your castle, so you would not see too closely the truth of my deep, noble love. You gave the impression that you were happy with my achievement, but your happiness was not genuine and it could not last. You resented the new reality.

I destabilised you when I pulled out your pillars of wild thoughts with which you flirted as you chased your desires. I maintained my calmness and reconstructed the beautiful you while you maintained a sense of resignation. In that awkward moment, we united. The lava of our passion merged us, against your will. You looked confused. Your desire for immoral love overcame you, but you did not lose your pure love. It lived in another world where your purer self merged with the shining stars, and people stretched out their necks looking for your light. I whispered that you looked beautiful before raising my flags of victory over you. Deep in my heart, I loved your imperfections.

I used to find excuses to save you from feeling guilty, yet you make me feel guilty for ending our love. Please, do not blame me. I have never regretted the moment our hearts came together and I never will, but I am in deep pain.

It is remarkably rewarding to express my feelings to you: painful, precious, foolish and effortless... how I miss saying your name! I want to see you and hear your voice.

I am trying not to say it aloud to stop my ears from hearing it, but it begs me to say it. It haunts me wherever I go, and takes me to unfamiliar places so I lose myself and say it. I distract myself with people's affairs to avoid thinking of it, but it keeps begging me to say it, and hurting me until I cannot bear the pain. I have to let it out. All of my senses proclaim *I love you!*

With the first sign of dawn, the pen fell down from her tired hands. She listened to the words of wisdom in the song of Umm Kalthoom, which relieved her agony. The lyrics filled the early morning air with a soothing sensation:

> *Is not it the time for this heart to feel love? That heart is longing to fall in love. My day is useless if I never experienced love.*[8]

Although her emotions soared into the clouds, she could not write any longer. With the last word that she had written to him that night, she had felt her painful feelings of guilt and grief dissipate into non-existence. Finally, she could retire when others were starting their new day. She knew that she had to stop wasting her time in places where there was no love. She had to be brave and take a decision. Her future lay ahead of her and she had to prepare herself to face the unknown. She had to fall in love with herself in order to find love.

She woke the next morning, feeling excited about the new day. As she walked to work, she breathed in the sweet smell of roses. "What a beautiful life!" she thought.

---

[8]   This is a line from a song by a well-known Egyptian singer, Umm Kalthoom. It is entitled *Robaiaat al-Khayyam*, which is a trilogy written by poet Ahmed Ramy, who translated it from the Persian poet *Omar al-Khayyam*.

CHAPTER 5

"You know, dear friend, something inside me was buried alive. I could not write, smell fragrances, or enjoy the make-up I wore. The inventor of make-up was a genius! His invention hid the sadness from my face. I excelled in pretending that life was cheerful and beautiful, but I could not bury my pain. Dust piled on my heart, as it did on my desk. I gave neither of them much attention. Are these my eyelashes feeling like the spines of a cactus?"

"Wait a second, my dear; I thought you let it all go after your divorce. I was expecting to see a new person, a happy and hopeful al-Batool. Your life with your ex-husband had reached a deadlock. Aren't you glad to be out of that deep, dark well? Didn't you tell me you were having your first book published in a couple of days?"

"I am certain everything will go back to normal when the right time comes and once I am ready for a new beginning. It is hard to stop thinking about love and marriage, and replace those thoughts with others. It takes time to heal. I am like raindrops on rose petals, feathers of birds, and leaves that fall from the trees when the wind blows. Change is a natural process," al-Batool tried to explain, unable to focus her thoughts.

It was too early to order food, so they spent the time chatting. Al-Batool had come back to Riyadh, after leaving Jeddah where she was married for five years. She had returned to her old job, which she had started after her graduation, and where she had first met her friend Eman. Al-Batool's painful marriage had kept them apart for a while, but Eman had always urged her to stay positive.

They used to meet up twice a week after work, and often go to a ball. Al-Batool loved dancing as it relieved her pain, and provided her with a route to escape the fumes and dirty smells hovering over the city of Riyadh. For Saudi girls, dancing was a temporary distraction from the puzzling extremes of conservatism and the moral degradation in their communities. It was a relief from the double standards of life, from which they all wanted to escape. They could not publicly declare their wish to lead a free life because the country rejected all such notions. They would be shunned and punished for doing so. Dancing was the only way for them to express their hope.

Those days had passed like the white clouds.

In the coffee shop overlooking the coast of Jeddah, al-Batool was sitting in her favourite spot, mindless of the noise around her. The place was filled with the fumes of cigarettes and the fruity smell of the hookah. She was at a table facing the sea, where she could feel the cold breeze of the most beautiful time of year touching her face and blowing away all her dreams and pain. She watched the waves hit the shore and thought of them as lions that rebel without any fear of dying.

Many questions filled her mind, and with a fragile look in her eyes, she looked up to the sky trying to find answers. She looked stunned.

How is it that I used to be so strong, but then became the weakest person alive? I should have been stronger and refused to marry him. Now I am left with a life of painful memories.

Is it true that people change not only physically, but also in character, as they grow older? If so, why am I still the same? I can feel the world around me moving at a fast pace while I stand still in the middle of the ocean.

"My dear Eman, to write poetry you need to have a clear position and I have not picked mine. How can I be honest in my writing when

I am the mother of all lies? Poetry is the ability to make decisions and read the feelings of others. Poetry is the gift of the eccentric. I cannot be a poet because I am, like most people, weak. I would bring shame to it."

Filled with sympathy, Eman hugged her friend and they both wished each other a wonderful time together. Neither of them wanted to interfere with the other's life, although Eman was keen to learn about life from al-Batool's stories.

"Could time ever make us grow apart?" asked Eman.

Al-Batool smiled as she saw her younger self in Eman's face. "I missed your eyes. They saw me grow. They know me more than I know myself."

Eman touched a place in al-Batool's heart, despite knowing that she had to be cautious with her words.

"Then why did we not keep in touch all this time? I've missed your insights. Your words always touched the deepest feelings in my heart. You gave me guidance and were always there for me whenever my emotions burnt me with fever. You helped me know my worth. Where are you now?"

Al-Batool took a deep sigh and opened up to her friend.

"Do you recall that statue my mother kept on the living room table in our old house? It looked like a metal ball that stood on a pillar to make the guests feel welcome when they spent time at our house." She continued with a smile: "Do you remember it? That ball is my mind and the pillar is the duty I cannot ever relinquish. That statue represents both the love and hate inside me: the important and the trivial, the indifferent, the caring, the wise and the insane. Isn't it just a farce to live and watch a part of you die? That is where I am now – just swinging."

Her friend cleverly asked, "What about the horizontal bar?"

"It is that line in the horizon which separates the earth from the sky. Both go in parallel," al-Batool quick-wittedly explained.

Eman sailed in the sadness of her dearest friend's eyes, in the waves of her defeated passion.

"You refused to live in hell. You ran away from it when your life turned into hell. Alas! How could you not express all that in writing?" exclaimed Eman.

"There were men, like Maram and Pascal, with whom no love blossomed. I used my writing as a shield to protect myself against their shallowness and small-mindedness," al-Batool added with a fearless smile.

The conversation of these two friends reflected the belief of a whole generation of women who believed that marriage was the essence of all living things, and without it, there would be no existence for them.

"Turki was my biggest motivation to write again, but it was painful to write. Every stroke of my pen stabbed my heart. It bled and I drowned in my pain, unable to regain my strength to fight back the memories. Yet he did not help. On the contrary, he did everything to make my wounds deeper.

My dear friend, did you know the reason I stopped writing was not that I'd run out of thoughts, but I was conquered by fear and despair. I was also somehow lazy, slow as a turtle. I'm growing older! And whether I like it or not, time will not go back.

Do you remember how fond I was of photography? I thought the photos I took would keep the beautiful moments forever. Now they only cause me pain. I hate those moments that I once thought were a blessing.

I shut thousands of doors to block that painful past. I wanted to fill my memory with new photos, new images, but the reality still haunts me; my imagination is even worse than the reality. That scene will not leave my sight. When Waleed took me to Dubai to spend our honeymoon, we went to a luxurious hotel. The weather was phenomenal, mild, and made us fall in love even more. I suggested we take a photo in front of a gift shop.

'Let us record this moment so we can tell our children of our love story.'

'I am not in the mood for that! You are so silly, just like all the other girls. Don't you think this is childish?' he blurted out.

'My love, let us be children tonight…'

'OK. Go and ask how much it will cost,' he yielded.

The price was much less than the joy it would give me. Nothing was as precious to me as the moment we were trying to capture.

As I was preparing myself for the photo, beaming with happiness, he suddenly yelled at me in front of the photographer, 'Hold on! We do not want a photo. Let's go!'

'What happened?' I asked sheepishly.

'Nothing! I just changed my mind. I am the man. I do not like taking photos,' he answered rudely and walked away, leaving me behind. I felt like a fool as I walked briskly to catch up with him. People stopped and looked at us, wondering why I was following a man who had just left me in that way. He did not care how humiliated I felt. He did not know that it would hurt me forever. It was the beginning of the end of our marriage.

Believe me, Eman, sleeping with a disrespectful, worthless man is like an illegal sexual relationship. It only makes you more humiliated. I have no idea how some husbands can make love to their wives and be happy with it when there is no spiritual connection between them. How can they make love without sensing their heartbeats in their toes?"

"Maybe Waleed thought that his good physique was enough to compensate for his emotional and mental shortcomings. He thought he could control you."

"That's true. He was too arrogant to give himself a chance to understand me. He was locked in his own ego."

Unable to look into Eman's eyes, she turned her gaze away into the horizon and continued to share her pain.

"I have pain in every part of my body where his hands have been. The same pain lives in every part of my wedding dress! Do you remember it? The pearls on it look like tears shed over a failed marriage. When I put it up for sale, no one wanted it! Even though, like other women, I had chosen to wear white on my wedding day, I was not blessed with happiness. I've always thought that women who wear white have no character, no style. That's why a bride wears it on the most awkward night of her life when she cannot tell what her true feelings are, or whether she is yearning for a new future or a memory from the past. She is anxious about sharing her life with a man who is no more than a stranger to her. A woman will only feel comfortable when embarking on a journey with the man of her dreams. I think white is the only colour that embodies that state of loss."

She looked at Eman, full of beautiful dreams and unspoilt innocence, and longed for her past when she used to be like that. Her soul burnt with the sensation of longing, but she knew she could never bring back what she had, who she was, and what she aspired to be.

"What about the 'orange' man? Do you still think of him?"

Al-Batool giggled at Eman's reference to the 'orange' man. "You mean Turki! I have erased from my mind all the regretful memories of the nights he used to visit me. We have not met at all and I never think of him now."

"That bastard! After all the sacrifices you made for him, all he could do was ask for your hand in a secret marriage!"

With a hearty laugh, al-Batool divulged the details that troubled her in the past, but only served to make her laugh now. "Yes! He said that it would only take a pack of oranges for him to visit me every time! And that my family should be happy that a man of respectable tribal lineage had agreed to marry their divorced daughter!" She chortled until tears came down her cheeks.

"It's good to see you laughing after years of crying over him!"

"My pain runs like a river between my loss of love and the destruction of divorce. Should I cry over my present, my future, or my past? Does our past have an impact on the positive and negative outcomes of our future? My past has gone and taken with it all the good times and all the sorrows I have had. I stand here today, with nothing in my bag. I no longer try to manipulate my life by taking decisive actions about my future. It's clear to me now that the thrill of the future lies in the secret bag of surprises it holds for us."

Eman took out the hookah tip from her mouth and exhaled a smoke of pain. She could not withhold her tears as she moved her hands to her face to fix her black hijab.

Moved by her friend's sadness, al-Batool tried to console her.

"Don't be sad, my dear. Life does not deserve your tears. I wish I hadn't said a word to stir such unhappy feelings in you. I know how you feel towards your so-called husband. It is tough to live together in the same home when you are separated. My love, the most important thing is not to feel like you are trapped in prison. Although you are sharing the house, don't give up on protecting your femininity from neglect and abuse. I know very well how emotionally draining it is, but no matter what, be yourself. Always be true to your soul."

Fighting back her tears, and with a renewed confidence, Eman said, "Today, I will not let sadness control me. Ask me how?"

"How?"

"I will treat myself to dessert with a cup of coffee and forget my boring diet!"

They ate their food just like children, paying no heed to the table etiquette that their parents had taught them, and not worrying about what anyone else would be thinking of them. There had been nothing more exciting to them in the past than sitting together at a table of delicious food, chatting and laughing.

Raising her head in a sudden movement, "But what is wrong with having a secret marriage?" al-Batool asked in a gleeful tone.

They both giggled, as each came to the quiet realisation that the beliefs they had held for ten years had changed direction.

Looking at the sea, al-Batool wished she could drown all her secrets under the waves. She wondered if she could do it all over again – not with Turki, but with someone new.

Each of them took their cars to go back home. That night, they both reflected on their conversation and knew that only death would part them. She never felt ashamed while opening up to Eman, and she never regretted it. There were no boundaries between them. Even during their sleep, they communicated telepathically.

CHAPTER 6

A s al-Batool moved the radio button left and right to switch between channels, her fingers stopped where she could hear a man reciting in a soft voice the following verse from the Quran: "A divorce is only permissible twice; after that, the parties should either hold together on equitable terms, or separate with kindness."[9]

Why do people recklessly violate God's commandments, which were revealed to guide us all? Aren't they only chasing a mirage? But God permits divorce. I heard the words. Was he sending me a sign to support my choice for divorce? Will I be punished for liberating myself from the worst pain ever that life has inflicted upon me?

Her head started spinning. She rested it on the wall to keep her balance, but the wall moved at her touch. She recalled that time when she was leaning against a worn-out wall in a musty room with fetid, frayed carpets, where many women had walked back and forth in agony over their legal cases. She visualised the water dripping from the drain of the tattered air conditioning unit, which made a valve train noise like an old, high-strung race engine. It was in that pathetic room where the divorce settlements of these pitiable women were being finalised. There was no light gleaming on the walls of the room; nor was there any spark of light in the women's lives.

Al-Batool watched the women closely. Wrapped in their niqabs, with only their eyes showing, they walked in, one after another,

---

[9]   Quran: The Cow Chapter: Verse 229

looking for a sofa to sit on, to steady their tired bodies before their verdicts were read out. The upholstery was torn, just as the women were. Some sofas had no backs or arms, and others looked ugly with dirty foam fillers hanging out from their punctured leather cushions. Al-Batool observed each of the women balance herself on a sofa, trying to avoid falling any further than she already had.

She could not read their stories on their covered faces, but their body language expressed it all. She could hear their heavy breathing and see the scars on their faces even from behind their niqabs. These scars were left by all the hostile accusations launched at them simply because they were women. The community labelled them as sinful, disobedient to God.

Al-Batool was always puzzled by how Saudi women insisted on covering their faces in front of their own gender. She wondered if they were afraid that others would take a bite from their faces. They were kept in dark cages, and they never had the urge to ask their masters to release them. She always found this shocking. Perhaps Saudi women preferred to be introverts – not because it was in their nature to be reticent, but because they were afraid to make close connections with each other. Nevertheless, they loved gossiping and uncovering the hidden secrets of other women.

A new woman came into sight, looking reserved and quiet, but it was not long after that an irksome older woman asked her, "What is your case?"

The younger woman did not respond.

She asked again, "Are you the plaintiff or defendant? It must be a case of custody." (It is ironic how Saudi women ask a question and answer it at the same time.)

The younger woman looked weary. She nodded in affirmation and started to recount a string of distressing stories.

"I have nine children. He refuses to spend a riyal on them. How can I feed them? Shall I beg for a living or become a prostitute? God is my only avenger!"

It was disquieting for al-Batool to see how easily women opened up to strangers and shared their personal troubles. As both women struck up a conversation, they brought their chairs closer in the same cautious way as they had walked in and looked for a place to sit.

"Why did you leave him dear? You should have remained in marriage for the future of your girls. May God save you!"

The divorcee went quiet for a moment, and looked at the older woman first, then at the others in the room who were listening carefully with a look of rage and cynicism. From their eyes, al-Batool knew that they were passing harsh judgements on the poor woman, blaming her for making a decision that contravened the image of women as weak and subordinate to men. Driven by fear and insecurity, Saudi women condemn someone of their own gender for becoming stronger and breaking the norm. They prefer to remain apathetic, conformist, and substandard in their achievements, and in doing so, they trample on anyone who dares to be different.

"How could I live with a drunken loser? He treated me like a mistress. He humiliated me, without a care for my feelings or opinions. I was not worried about myself, but when my beautiful girls hit adolescence, I had to take action to protect their soft hands. I wanted to kill him. God saved us."

Upon hearing this, the women in the room roared louder than the winds. Some said prayers to God to save the girls and their mother from all evil while trying to calm her down as she had started sobbing. Others asked her for more details.

The divorcee spoke in an angry but troubled voice: "My girls mean the world to me. I would kill anyone to protect them. He is a lunatic psychopath. He sexually harassed one of them. It was the day

49

I turned into the fiercest creature on earth. He fantasised about his own daughters in sexual positions. The looks he gave them offended their modesty. He is a pervert."

Al-Batool could not say a single word. She just wanted to escape from the ugliness of that room. Feeling utterly sick, she rushed out looking for the ladies' toilets. Her mind burst with questions that she could not answer, although she knew she could find the answers if she thought harder.

Why did my father and I decide I should get a divorce? I feel I will regret this decision for the rest of my life because the prospects of getting married again will be dark after my divorce... Why am I thinking about this now?

Why did I act as if I did not care about the divorcee's misery; as if I had the upper hand on her? Why was I passive, acting as if I was better than she was? My misery is endless, just like the questions in my head.

Life sends us all kinds of problems we never imagined we would go through. When we meet people whose problems are far worse, we sometimes mock them for a laugh or show total empathy. Then life shocks us by forcing us to go through situations which are the worst of all.

Al-Batool finalised her divorce papers on that day. She left the court building, uplifted to have solved the biggest problem of her life, but her heart was filled with the pain of the women whose predicament was still unresolved. She thought of their troubles as she earnestly welcomed her freedom from the prison of her own mind, which had been trapped in the corners of the community's expectations throughout her marriage. She could not help but feel a little gloomy, but an exhausted smile appeared on her face as she pondered that divorce was the beginning for a new, exciting journey. Similar to those who are rescued from a fatal accident, but despite their broken joints and burnt body parts, feel that they have conquered death, she contemplated the vast future ahead of her and thanked God she was still breathing. She had a second chance in life.

It had been two years since she regained her freedom. Her memory of the divorce could never die. It was hard to recover from the pain of the past. Inside her heart, the memory of the past quarreled with the present moment. She knew that we, humans, never forget painful or joyful memories, which visit us every morning as we sip our coffee, and control every part of us. We sink in the vast oceans of our memories and like small pieces of sponge, we try to absorb as much of the water around us as we can. We only remember bits and pieces of the bigger incidents and can no longer tell the details. Yet the feeling never goes away. Life goes on and we try to overcome the sadness of the past by believing in a happy future.

Al-Batool made a resolution to continue life's journey with happiness in her heart, to take pride in her daily achievements, to be grateful, appreciative, and not to forget to smile. She was confident that she had picked the right path. She saw happiness as the green plant that sprouts through the hard ground of a pavement. To her, happiness was not a destination, but a journey.

It was a peaceful night. She tried to find comfort in her bed. She wanted to dispel the trauma of the past from her heart and replace it with tranquillity. How she wished she could be like a virgin, untouched by scars, innocent and pure like a child, with a heart soft as silk and precious as pearls.

She wanted to have the strength to forgive those who did her wrong and to forgive herself for making a wrong choice in marriage; to disengage her mind from negative thoughts and have a heart willing to love again, and again. She wanted to reach inner peace through forgiveness, not resentment about life's failures.

She recalled Fouad's face as she opened the drawer to get out her journal to write. She did not know why she was writing. It was a daily routine. Her notebook sustained her and she had kept writing in it since her divorce. Besides, it was too early to sleep.

When you visited our office that day, you brought the warmth of sunshine with you. I cherished that moment. I felt like a bird that had been flying between robust trees and finally perched on one of them to sing. You looked tired, Fouad. Actually, you seemed sad as a thousand sighs. I could see sadness in your grey hair, in the thin wrinkles under your eyes, and the tired skin on your face, but that glow was still there at your older age. Your valiant spirit had not been defeated by the steep hills and narrow straits you had crossed. When you spoke, you sounded like a runner panting at the finishing line. Your voice quavered, just like the beeping or buzzing sound of a digital heart rate monitor.

That day I drank in the sunlight, and tasted the sweetness of my writing. I wonder if that was because it was you who had instilled in me the motivation to write – motivation that I try hard to keep. I do not know if it will lead to big achievements in my life, but I try hard not to lose it. No, I have not lost it.

How could we fall in love without having any control over our emotions? Had you always been inside my heart, but waited for a long time before making your appearance? Were you the iron ball that destroyed my wooden gates of self-defence?

The first time I saw you – four years ago or maybe more – you looked happier and more energetic, but when we met again, after my divorce, I saw a shadow of sadness following you. I wonder if you were always sad but hid it from me. We were similar. We did our best to hide our true feelings.

That day, your light filled the office and soaked my heart with happiness, despite the fact that you looked so weary. You sat down next to our male colleague, and when you talked, your voice was like a nightingale calling me to live in your cosmos of dreams and forget the sorrows of this world. It had a unique vibe to it, reassuring me that you cared for me. I listened to it intently, and it penetrated me deeper and deeper until it took control of my whole being.

After my divorce, I returned to my old job. I breathed the familiar smell of my old office: its yellow post-it notes, its packs of paper files of that year, the previous year and the year before, its oil paints, and its small plant. I used to open the windows to get some fresh air. Everything was as it had always been.

Why is it that we do not appreciate the value of what is dear to us until we lose it? It was our fate to meet that day, and from the moment you walked in, I saw the light and realised that you had a deep place in my heart.

You were older. I had always dreamed to be with an older man for he would be more mature and have a deeper understanding of life. He would share his insight with me, help me rise and contemplate my naiveties only to smile back at me with kindness. He would value my sincerity in exposing my weaknesses to him – to the man who loved me. Even though I am a strong person, I would see him as my backbone, my source of wisdom and guidance. Besides the appeal of your age, it was your refined nature and strong vision for tomorrow, which impressed me most.

Fate flew me to the office on that day, and when I saw you, I landed on your tree. Your shoulders attracted me with all the gravity in this world. I was weak and vulnerable, and that drew me even closer to you. I had surrendered to you a long time ago. You had had a lot on your plate too, yet you were always there for me, surrounding me with warmth so I could maintain my strength. Your feelings were stronger than anything else in the world.

On that day, I saw my future in your eyes and hoped to be with you forever. For a moment, I fell in love with my mind, not my heart. I felt shy as we greeted each other. You were reserved, as always, and quietly studied my eyes, perhaps wondering if, or how, you knew me. I wanted to keep you wondering.

"Have you two met before?" our colleague asked.

You gazed at me with great respect, and uncertainty.

"Mr Fouad, I am al-Batool!" I exclaimed. I had always called you *Mr Fouad*. I had never had the courage to address you directly by your first name.

"Al-Batool! Welcome back. Where have you been hiding all this time?" you said with excitement.

You were spontaneous, unlike me; I could not show you how much I had missed you.

I did not know how to respond. Luckily, you did not wait for an answer, but asked me another question instead.

"Are you still passionate about reading, or has writing charmed you?"

"I still prefer reading. Writing is an act of the moment. You seize a moment of satisfaction just to express the feelings that you cannot always unleash."

Wanting to change the subject and show you that my memory had not failed me, I asked, "How is your son, Omar?"

A look of dismay and regret appeared on your face. "He is doing fine, growing up to be strong and tall as Lebanon's trees," you said with a quavering voice and a shine in your eyes that only parents can have.

I allowed you a few moments to contemplate my face while I told our colleague about how we had met through several journalistic projects that you were leading. You both asked me if I would ever write articles or investigative reports again. I grabbed that moment and cleverly tried to send you, and only you, a message because I knew you would understand the hidden meaning behind my words: "Just recently my life started settling back into normal. I will get back into journalism soon."

You understood me; I could tell from your nodding. You knew that the previous episode of my life must have been hard, as if you had shed every tear with me. Your eyes wondered about my situation, but you changed the course of conversation and challenged me with a question.

"What do you think about poets nowadays?"

I sighed before commenting.

"I've started to believe that poetry is the biggest trick in the history of art. A poet dwells in the soul of his beloved. He numbs his own feelings and passes all his agonies, frustrations and dreams to her, vanishes into her soul, and waits for a poem to be born. Then he just continues living as if nothing has happened. That's why I believe poetry is a crime which law does not sanction."

"Do you mean that poets are schizophrenics?"

"Perhaps!"

"Thank God I am not a poet!" he added with a smile.

Our colleague was amazed at the instant spark of chemistry lighting our lane. He was visibly enjoying our conversation, but I tried to avoid looking directly into his eyes. You and I spoke the same language with almost the same depth of thought. A woman can live with her husband or family for years without speaking the same language, yet it can take her one conversation with another man to have full understanding of his character.

I posed a question swiftly as if struck by a sudden thought.

"Have you read Patrick Suskind's novel *Perfume*?"

Our colleague joined the conversation. "I've heard a lot about this novel," he said.

Not commenting on his input, I continued: "In short, the novel focuses on the theme of self-absorbedness of human beings. The protagonist is an ordinary, poor man, who turned into a murderer because he was allured by the scent of beautiful virgins. He did not want to sleep with them. He only wanted to extract their sensual scent and preserve its essence. He wanted to look into their soul because it was the most delicious thing he would ever taste, but his mission was truly hard to accomplish, nearly impossible, except through removing their skins."

You looked at me deliciously as my colleague asked, "What did he do?"

"The story talks about body remains and creative natural perfumes made from soul extracts. He could fall in love using only his nose. He loved the victims' scent from the moment he took control of their bodies, and he loved the scent that he extracted into a bottle after murdering them. He only loved their scent. My point is that writing poetry is so much like this kind of torture. Both of them involve killing and gruesome processes to achieve great results."

"I will buy it right away. Bottles of perfume, is it?" you interjected with a hearty laugh, and added, "I don't have to buy the novel. The scent in this place is enough to make me happy. I enjoyed being here. I was touched by a lot of great scents."

I had to leave, but I hoped that I would communicate with you again. We had always exchanged cards, letters, and the shortest of notes that soothed the pain in our heart. We preferred the old-fashioned way of communicating; it was the best, truly better than short text messages and emails. We had written a lot to each other without knowing where our relationship was heading. We had analysed many issues and opened up to each other about everything, but we had never talked about love. I never missed a word of what you wrote. I read with compassion about the troubles you had been through with your wife. You were sad that you had a child with a woman who could not be a good mother, and that the marriage had to end in divorce. I had stopped writing to you when another man raided my life; like me, he was daring and immature, but he left me – and it was well-deserved for me.

O Fouad, the stories of love inside us are like volcanoes; some are active and others dormant. I hold many stories of pain inside me, but I have many responsibilities too. A part of me is burning deep inside, pushing me to the front of a road to light up the way for others. I will blame neither myself for this divorce, nor my family for their lack of moral support.

I surrendered to sleep, my memory wrapped in sadness and hope. I heard the Star of the East, the Egyptian singer Umm Kalthoom, singing the following lines from *Al-Attlal* (The Ruins):

> "My darling everything is fated
> It is not by our hands that we make our misfortune
> Perhaps one day our fates will cross when our desire to meet
> is strong enough
> For if one friend denies the other and we meet as strangers
> And if each of us follows his or her own way
> Don't say it was by our own will
> But rather, the will of fate."[10]

How beautiful it is to consider possibilities!

She recollected Fouad's features; his white complexion and how the goodness of his soul made him look burly, handsome and wise. He had wide shoulders, which were a sign of his strength, honesty and nobleness. He had thick eyebrows and dark, curly hair. He was dignified. His physique reflected his determination and peaceful nature. Just like the mountains of Lebanon, he was robust and resolute. He was like an object of reverence, prestigious as the late Lebanese prime minister, Rafiq al-Hariri.

---

[10] Translated by Blog of Arabic Song Lyrics and Translations
http://www.arabicmusictranslation.com/.

The profound melancholy which had taken over her mind, vanished instantly as Fouad preoccupied her thoughts. He had the power to turn her frozen desires into a blazing fire. The whisper of his voice had never left her mind. She continued writing until she could not rub the sleep from her eyes.

As she recounted the entire story about the murderer in *Perfume* to Fouad and their colleague, she was also writing the first chapter of her life with Emad – an amateur poet with whom she had fallen in love. She did not know she was heading into a dark future. She loved writing since it relieved her, but she disliked trying to predict her future through her writing.

CHAPTER 7

It was a Thursday morning when she woke up to a phone call from her friend, Wafaa, who wanted to come over at noon to watch the televised events of the National Meeting for Intellectual Dialogue. They conversed on the phone as al-Batool prepared her morning cup of Arabian coffee. Her mind was roaming between two different worlds. While communicating with Wafaa, a part of her was thinking of how revolting the conference was. Al-Batool's mind had the incredible ability to analyse serious matters that touched her wild spirit while she was busy with everyday tasks. For an hour, they both discussed whether this conference would ever bring about real change to push forward the so-called creative plans to bring reform, change, and progress by the government.

Wafaa confidently quoted a verse from the Quran before stating her position: "*God does not change what is in a nation unless they change what is in themselves.*[11] I am not optimistic that these conferences will bring about actual change. What do you think? Is it possible that a community's deep-rooted norms will drastically change because they are sharing the workings of a conference with the public? Change can't be achieved through meetings at luxurious, air-conditioned halls with secret locations!"

As her friend was listening quietly, she continued: "Take my word for it al-Batool. This is the reality of our community. I'm not being gloomy, but my instincts tell me I am right about this. In our country,

---

[11] Quran, Chapter 13, Verse 11.

politicians claim they are doing all they can to bring about reform, but the real reason they invite high-profile figures to conferences is that they want to give themselves importance, a good reputation. I don't believe in their efforts!"

"Oh, you are here already! Hold on a minute; I'll open the door for you."

At the door, al-Batool and Wafaa kissed as the former jokingly said, "Couldn't you wait until you got here to discuss it? Do you have relatives at the telephone company that you want to make rich?"

They laughed and continued to discuss the so-called plans for reform. Wafaa had always shared every detail of her life with al-Batool. They had laughed and cried together. Wafaa valued their friendship, which dated back to their childhood. Al-Batool also played a very important role in Wafaa's life, being the muse behind her success in journalism, and an enriching source of information. She was always there when Wafaa needed her. Al-Batool admitted that close relationships between women were rare to find in Saudi Arabia, where women only met to slander others and gossip about the latest news in the world of dating – something that controlled the mind of many girls who deeply believed that they should have a boyfriend once they reached puberty and their bodies started to change.

Many of al-Batool's close friends at school and work saw her as daring, strange, controversial, and vague. While some women described her as 'a nice person', an expression that could hold many meanings, others believed that she was only putting up an act of being respectful while deep down, she was a cunning, deceptive woman. Jealousy between Saudi women meant they held grudges against each other. They remained forever suspicious of every woman in their lives.

Al-Batool and Wafaa talked about their friendship and what it meant to them.

"We've truly had a close and long friendship, Wafaa, and that is rare to find."

"My dear al-Batool, I've known you for years I cannot count (because I don't want to remember how old I am!); I hope we will always be friends."

"My dear, you've been a loyal friend. Don't you agree that the length of a relationship reflects its depth? I think a successful friendship is one which depends solely on honesty, tolerance and trust in each other. Those who lie to their friends for personal gains can never maintain true and honest ties."

"We've always had good intentions towards each other, and no interest in exploiting one another. I liked your wittiness and your interests when we first met. We've been good friends since then."

"We were destined to meet, Wafaa. God made our paths cross."

"So... Do you have faith in Saudis now? Are you going to have more than two good friends?" Wafaa asked with a playful smile.

"Who is the other friend you are referring to?"

Pinching al-Batool in the leg, Wafaa jokingly said: "What a clever quip! You think I don't see your nose growing longer? Tell me, how are things with your family? How are you coping with their fundamentalist beliefs?"

"Oh stop it! Leave my family to one side. As for the 'friend', we've only known each other for less than two seconds, and you expect us to get married right away!"

"I know you love Fouad! I see it in your eyes; your face is lighting up."

Al-Batool tried to avoid looking directly at Wafaa's eyes in order not to give away her feelings, which she knew shone on her face. She knew she was falling in love with him, but did not want it to be too fast. "The light showing on my face was evoked by your visit my dear. Your coffee is getting cold; drink it, and let's watch a new session

61

from the National Dialogue events in its second day. I wonder what will happen now. They already exchanged slurs and hurls in the first session, now what?" she said in an attempt to change the topic.

"Why do you like the National Dialogue conference? Why do you want to find out what the future will bring when all the signs are negative and bleak?"

"My dear, I am only a simple person living in this world. I try to understand what's happening because everything – even the smallest of events – affects our life. I also influence others through my writing. It is only natural to hold a viewpoint and develop a better understanding of the world. This is simply my opinion."

"I do not see any point in debating whether Saudis should have their own opinion about a given debate or if women can be good achievers or not. It requires, I believe, an honest and daring stance of putting our words into action to bring about an effective change. Then everything will fall into place and positive results will follow. What's happening in our country is the complete opposite; they are only holding events, and using the tools of the media, to bring the spotlight on themselves in a country that is not run by thought but petrol revenues! We always believe that others see us as victims, but we actually have a bad reputation for not being able to make successes in the fields of acting, singing or supporting other talents. These people are living under an illusion, preaching their ideology and taking pride in their lineage instead of feeding their brains with knowledge about other communities. We are simply self-absorbed. If someone who holds no power in our community, like me, chose to criticise these habits, thousands of centres would retaliate to prove that they do care for talent, youth and the progress of our nation. How poor our youth is!"

Al-Batool was mumbling the word *'Reform'* as if she was hallucinating. After recollecting herself, she shared her thoughts with Wafaa.

"True reform is always achieved through actions and constructive advice, through open-mindedness, equality, tolerance, and the availability of good opportunities for children. It comes through loving your homeland, Wafaa, not by pedantry or feigned knowledge. Saudi women cannot attend symposiums; they are banned from praying at the Holy Mosque[12], attacked for using the internet, ridiculed, even in front of children, for voicing their opinions on important matters. They are not allowed to shop at grocery stores due to the lack of "privacy", as they claim! Adding insult to injury, divorcees and widows, who are trying to make an honest living, suffer from many injustices too. There are two types of people: there are those with sick, suspicious minds, who decide the fate of others when they should have no right to do so; and there are those who are like rigid doors that close the way to the success of others, not sparing any effort to stop women's lives from moving forward. These types of people live to destroy the dreams of women because they are envious of them. These evil people cannot fight powerful women, so they make the community turn against them. My dear, women are being fought not because they are doing something wrong, but because of their success and extraordinary ability to strike a balance between work and home. Do you believe it is rational that successful women's colleagues, husbands, so-called friends, the unemployed and the failures among her relatives should be jealous of her when she is working so hard to dedicate herself to her family and work?"

---

[12] It is believed that women should not pray at the Holy Mosque in Medina because it constitutes a form of worshipping the grave, according to some conservative clerics in the KSA.

"I know, my dear friend, I know many women who work really hard till they drop from the pain, and many others who are so spoiled that they only care about their outfits for the next festive occasion or the wedding of their neighbour's son taking place the year after!"

Wafaa's words further triggered al-Batool's disapproval of the current situation.

"Wafaa, I am fed up of feeling like an alien in this community. I cannot tolerate living in this cage where backward-thinking Saudis are keeping us – under the pretext of protecting our privacy. They want us to think that our women are like queens whose privacy should not be violated (as if we are the best in this world). They never truly care about women. They are scared of our success, courage, and rebellious nature, and that is why they want to stifle our dreams! I believe that women have the power to achieve their full independence and mute all those evil voices, but women are under the hammer; banned from playing sports at school, driving, or learning languages; pressured to maintain their family reputation and social status when considering a job, like a position in the media. I cannot see any meaning in forcing women to abstain from doing these things. Men hijack our personal freedom because they do not want to see us becoming self-sufficient. We can't even play a role in helping other women who are suffering from hunger and oppression around the Muslim world. We live in our so-called shrines of privacy and that's why we never interact with the world or experience the different trends of globalisation. Our reserved lives prevent us from benefiting others and building constructive dialogue with other nations."

Wafaa interrupted her: "You must write all this down now; I have good connections with the *Al-Amal* newspaper's editor-in-chief, you know, and he will be thrilled to read your different insight on life."

"None of the Saudi newspapers would ever publish my viewpoint; they will regard it as silly."

She poured some hot coffee for both of them, and offered Wafaa *Al-Maknooz* dates. It is the norm in Al-Qaseem province to eat these dates with Arabian coffee given that the sweet taste evens the sourness of the coffee. With the hot cup of coffee in her hands, al-Batool walked to the sofa and sat down. "Yes! In KSA, speaking the truth and voicing your opinion are seen as absurd. What age are we living in! I cannot accept this! Where do you think the lack of women's freedom of speech will lead us, but to hell?"

Al-Batool's feelings of humiliation and alienation made her recollect memories of writing an article about unfaithfulness in marriage and the way Islam justly rewards and punishes men and women equally for it. She stated that Islam does not wrong women; society does. The newspaper refused to publish the piece. Men are revered in the Kingdom of Saudi Arabia. No one should dare challenge them. At the time, the newspaper had assigned al-Batool a weekly column, but without paying her a riyal. She was shocked when the newspaper told her they would not publish her article and that they reserved the right not to publish any articles that violated their editorial policy. When she called the editorial team for some explanation, they connected her with the editor-in-chief, who reminded her that she was writing for a Saudi publication with a readership from the wider Arab world. "How dare you offend Saudi men publicly?" he scolded her.

"Why would I ever voice my opinions if I am banned from making them public? Newspapers in our country only let names of well-known, doctorate-holding Saudi women sparkle on their pages to show off to the world that Saudis read articles by cultured, highly educated writers. Readers are stupid, just as I am for contributing to a newspaper that does not allow me to express myself with honesty. I will be too foolish to ever consider writing again – unless I complete a doctorate first! I could acquire a PhD for 20 thousand riyals by attending any university, anywhere in the Arab world, or through distance education; but what would be the point of it? After all, female professors do not have much to say! They are not good writers; they copy prolific poets and plagiarise information from books that we have read before, and sadly enough, many of us are tricked into believing that we have freedom of expression in this country, and poetry worthy of praise! What idiot made the rules of creative writing in the KSA? Who claimed that Saudi newspapers offer a special and unique style of journalism, which could be referred to as a work of art? If there are certain rules that female writers should not breach, then why have we not been told about them? Freedom of expression is the driving force behind innovation."

She jumped off her seat and went to open the windows. Everything around her was suffocating her.

"How can I escape this? Where shall I go? The palm tree in our backyard knows my story. It knows how much we are bleeding deep inside while appearing perfectly normal on the outside. This feeling burns like fire inside our hearts and the more we are subjugated to men, the hotter it blazes. Our lives have no hope."

Wafaa did not respond to al-Batool's raging thoughts. She respectfully remained silent, and stood up from the sofa to walk towards the library in her living room. It was as big as half the size of the room and had many old, valuable novels. Al-Batool had lovingly placed dry roses between the pages; she cherished her books.

She pulled out three books and wondered if al-Batool would allow her to borrow them for a few nights. Al-Batool allowed Wafaa to take two of the books, advising her that reading more than two books at a time was not constructive.

All Wafaa wanted to do then was to free herself from the depressing atmosphere that had reigned over them. She believed in her own ability to write and influence the public through freedom of expression. She knew that people read her articles. She repeated "*Hadha Hwa Qadroona*"[13] to al-Batool to calm her disquietude, but as she walked out of the house, she struggled to let go of the gloominess her friend had left on her. She hoped that it would not ruin her night.

It was almost ten at night when Wafaa left al-Batool's house. Neither of them could find answers to the questions that troubled them, but unlike al-Batool, Wafaa did not want to reflect on them too hard, lest her night would turn into hell.

---

[13] A phrase that is often used by Arabs to mean "that's life" or "c'est la vie". It is used when referring to situations that people cannot control or change.

CHAPTER 8

After Wafaa departed, al-Batool performed her night prayer. She prayed that her father, and everyone, would one day see her ambitious side, her passion for life. Throughout her childhood, al-Batool's father would tell her to "grow up!", and expected her to act older than her age. She wanted him to see that she had grown into a strong woman and her dreams were big too.

I won't accept my father's unfair views on my life choices, and I won't be weak or dependent on him. My father's selfishness controlled everyone in my family. He had a twisted, paradoxical attitude to child rearing, which turned our home into a cell at Guantanamo Bay Prison. Our dignity was brutally offended. If we do not insist on being treated with respect, we will become worthless. Human dignity, mind, heart and soul are all blessings granted by God. It is our duty to protect these gifts. If we do not, God will punish us. I firmly believe that I would be punished if I remained passive towards my father's offences. The Muslim Caliph, Omar bin al-Khattab, said: 'Human beings are born free and no one has the right to enslave them.' However, Arabs and Muslims are only good at memorising these words, not putting them into action."

Al-Batool's father forced everyone at home to obey his commands. Like military recruits, they felt trapped and disgusted with the attitude of their ironhanded commander. They felt angry too. Al-Batool had always hoped that one day her mother would find that perfect moment to fight against the oppression, but her hopes were in vain.

Writing was her only way out of that misery; it relieved her. Concluding her night-time prayer, she rushed to write down her thoughts on an old newspaper at her dark brown desk.

The world outside my home is moving in a different direction, while my family are holding on to their backward beliefs. I wonder if I should wait for relief – it seems far-fetched, yet possible.

Al-Batool had to find a way to soothe her anger, and to alleviate the misery of her family who put up with the oppressiveness of their father. She knew she did not have much chance to change anything; nevertheless, she felt compelled to fight for her rights. She resorted to patience – her only painkiller. Oftentimes she would try reading to forget about the deadly storm inside her. She never explicitly expressed her anger; it was safer to keep it under the covers of repression.

The fluorescent lights in her room were too bright and she found that they distracted her easily. She preferred the dim yellow light of her antique crystal lamp, situated at the foot end of her bed. The tiny rays of light refracted on the walls of her large room, and as she glanced at the walls, each ray of light reflected into her memory a story of pain from the years gone by. She grabbed the Arabic translation of Paulo Coelho's *Eleven Minutes* and sat on the black chair at her desk to read it. It was not as comfortable reading on the chair as reading in bed, which was what she usually did. However, her eyes suddenly caught the following lines: "How is it possible for beauty that was there only minutes before to vanish so quickly?" and she wondered about a line from Ibrahim Nagy's *The Ruins*: "But where is that light in your eyes?" Those lines prompted her to think about the reasons behind all the unjust treatment she endured at her father's home, at Waleed's home, and even after getting divorced and meeting Turki.

Turki was able to deceive me because I failed to see the destructive desires in the light of his eyes. What is the relationship between desire and the light in a person's eyes? Should I have left my father's cruel prison to find shelter in the shades of a rich, charming man, whose lineage attracted many Saudi women? Should I have agreed to marry Turki in secret because he was ashamed I did not belong to a reputable family like him? Women end up succumbing to prostitution or other illegal acts after divorce as their only way to make a living. Dear God! If only the community knew how hard I tried to make a decent living for myself. I was like a war survivor with torn clothes and nothing left but my dignity, and I chose to protect it at all costs. Men target our dignities and we pay a heavy price trying to defend ourselves from humiliation by the people who matter the most to us.

Suddenly, al-Batool's mobile phone started vibrating. It was Samar, who was more of an enemy than a friend. Her sick mind and hypocritical personality sabotaged all of her relationships with everyone she met. She was devious and had a desire to backstab and scandalise people for her own gains. Al-Batool did not want to answer Samar's call because it was too late in the night and because she wanted to keep a boundary between them. She did not want to develop close relationships with her colleagues, but she was too eager to know what had prompted that late-night call. She answered.

"My family did not agree to our marriage," Samar's voice came.

She knew the details of Samar's love story with Khaled who was 12 years her senior.

"I know you won't accept their rejection without putting up a fight for your love. Why are you worried?" asked al-Batool.

"I hate their interference in my personal life choices, but I am actually afraid to lose my whole family. Their rejection was based on other issues that would offend the entire family."

Al-Batool replied in shock: "Is there another reason other than the fact that you are still a virgin and he is a married man with kids?"

Samar was usually cynical and tough, but this time her voice was shaking: "I think I know what you mean. I should have been married a long time ago, but that is not the reason."

Samar was silent for a moment. Al-Batool knew she was confused and scared. The former said, "He does not belong to our tribe." Al-Batool did not respond.

"Why are you silent, al-Batool? You know I am going through hell now!"

It was a promising confession made by Samar. She was the kind who would never admit she was defeated. Everyone at work saw her as a strong woman. Perhaps she trusted al-Batool with these embarrassing details because the latter did not gossip with others and could keep a secret. Al-Batool did not compete with anyone in drawing a perfect image of her life. She knew her skills and competencies set her apart from her peers. She was different; she knew it and everyone could see it. It was a curious coincidence that al-Batool was thinking about that exact same thing before hearing Samar's confession. Khaled and Turki were very similar; they had the same motives for marriage and believed that they could reach their goals through their wealth.

"I find the community's double-standards disgusting; men set many rules for us, turning our lives into complicated challenges. Women are in a constant battle with themselves, fighting their urges and dreams in order to live up to the expectations of the community. Not allowed to have a say in the matter, Saudi women are pushed to marry men on the basis of their tribal lineage, and we eventually fall in the trap of emotional pain – the torture of erasing the memory of the men we loved but could not marry."

"This is not the right time for one of your ridiculous lectures! Please just tell me what I should do."

Al-Batool understood the complexity of Samar's case, yet she did not know how to advise her. "I was just thinking about running away from my husband's home," she retorted.

"I should too – run away, from this country. That would be the first step to achieving my dreams. Perhaps I will find another man who is richer and more handsome," Samar replied.

Al-Batool encouraged her to flee the country if given the chance.

CHAPTER 9

There is a peak in everything in life: age, youth, beauty, desire, ambition, and the joy of mundane pleasures. In our lives, we have three main turning points; the climax of maturity, wisdom, and gaining confidence to overcome heartaches. Al-Batool was going through a painful time and learning how to be stronger when she met Emad. To her, he was like a long-awaited love.

Al-Batool and Samar had been transferred to the company's branch in Jeddah. This was where she met Emad. Her father had agreed to set her free for a six-month period after she promised him that the company was giving her a promotion and she would bring him more money when she returned. Al-Batool repeated to her father that she would not violate any of his rules and would only go to her work place, nowhere else. At home, she was never allowed to go out, except when accompanied by her father or younger brother. No happiness was equal to being released from Guantanamo prison, even if it was for a few hours, al-Batool thought. She did not care how many rules she had to obey. All that preoccupied her mind was being released from that prison for some time.

Emad was the public relations manager at the Jeddah branch. He was overly caring towards the women and enjoyed playing with his charm to attract their attention. In the beginning, he thought al-Batool would be like every other woman he met at work: easily impressed by his charm. However, he soon realised that al-Batool was guarded, resolute, and difficult to deal with, especially when she did not want to follow some of his orders. Unlike the rest of the women, she was wise and did not allow herself to be misled by a man's good looks. She had an aura of tranquillity about her, a well-rounded personality, a calm voice, and a dignified composure. It was hard for him to get close to her unless he showed her respect.

While Emad assumed al-Batool was playing hard to get, she was actually flying with happiness about her release from the siege that Samar and other devious female colleagues had staged around her at their previous office. She was marching into new horizons of self-confidence and self-appreciation. Emad and al-Batool met almost every day due to their work demands. He was too crafty when it came to words. She sensed that he was trying to impress her with his words. He was exceptionally good at using sweet words, but his words were always ambiguous and could have had many different interpretations. He could play the innocent and the villain; he would tell her that she had got him wrong if she confronted him. He was audacious and bold.

His work was exciting and he had an efficient work discipline. This brought many women his way. He worked in an ideal setting where he could put his manipulative plans to use.

I do not understand how deceit can so masterfully defeat truths, and how hypocrites succeed in deceiving people who are usually astute. Even more puzzling is how these deceivers achieve their simple victories and earn the reverence of others.

Emad studied the keys to al-Batool's shielded heart and intelligent mind, and eventually succeeded in opening all the doors. He controlled her feelings and occupied her mind. She was not strong enough to resist. She was emotionally in need male attention. She had recently lost Fouad – they were destined to be apart – and she compensated her need for love through Emad. He helped her feel complete and desirable; she fell into the trap of love.

The freedom al-Batool was looking for was finally achieved; or so she thought. In six months, al-Batool and Emad got married and she lived in Jeddah, the land of prosperity and progress, leaving in Riyadh the prison that had been curbing her freedom for years. At last, God had changed her fate.

One early morning, she pondered the surroundings of her new home, which was only fifty yards from the sea. She looked into the horizon from her window and prayed to God: "We have reached the morning and at this very time all sovereignty belongs to God, Lord of the worlds. O God, I beseech you to grant me goodness on this day: triumph, light, blessings and guidance." After a short pause, she continued supplicating to God: "O God, please do not deprive us from the blessing of abundance in time, age, and money."

The early morning holds with it a big virtue in our religious culture. It affects all of our affairs throughout the day.

Al-Batool woke up early every day to pray to God (although that morning it was already eleven o'clock). She looked at those morning prayers as treasured moments that held the secret to all of her dreams. She would cry in regret if they were missed. She believed that people's wealth would not be blessed if they did not say their morning prayers.

It was a Friday morning when she got up and walked towards another window that overlooked the highway. She looked outside, but there was nothing to watch; the streets were vacant because everyone was relaxing at home on their day off. She felt tired, weak, and wanted to go back to sleep, but just before she reached her bed, Emad grabbed her from behind. He wrapped his arms around her waist, expressing his joy that she was part of his life (his life of mystery, which she was oblivious to). He was choosing his words carefully and skilfully. He wanted to make her do something that night, which he knew she would not be keen on. He intended to hide behind his soft voice and sweet words.

Emad liked al-Batool's self-respect the most. It was rare to find a woman as hard to get as her. While she was an adventure and a challenge for him, for her, he was the epitome of compassion. His magical voice embraced her heart and soul and transported her into another world. His voice renewed in her a hope for a better future.

Turning her face towards him, he asked her, "When will you be ready?"

"Do we have something planned for today too? I am still suffering from last night's headache!"

"Dear, I told you earlier we will be meeting with my friend Abdul Aziz. He owns big companies and promised to offer us a part-time job."

"You mean, offer you a job!" said al-Batool in an annoyed tone.

"We are but one body and soul! Please take some pain killers and get ready for our dinner party tonight... O, and please don't wear the black robe you had on last night. It was really unstylish."

Al-Batool was shocked, but listened silently as he continued: "Yes! I did not want to talk about it yesterday. You do not have good taste in clothes. Women in Jeddah dress elegantly. This is something you need to learn."

"I have a really bad headache! My whole body is aching! I cannot come tonight. I have to work."

"I really wanted to discuss this with you earlier. I think this is the perfect time."

They both walked to the bedroom. She opened her wardrobe and fumbled through her clothes. "Go on; now what?" she implored.

"My darling, do you know how much I care about you?"

She pulled out a white scarf and wrapped it around her head to soothe her headache.

"Emad, please stop it. What do you want? I feel sick."

Emad shocked al-Batool with his reply: "I think you should leave your job. If you agree, I will start the resignation process tomorrow."

Al-Batool found that too much to swallow.

"Please, leave me alone now. This topic is not open to discussion. Now not only my head, but my heart is aching too with the pain you have caused me – yet again!"

Emad blasted his last order before leaving al-Batool: "We should not be late this evening. Abdul Aziz wants us to arrive as early as possible."

She smiled, resigned to the fact that she had to go with him. With her smile, she embraced her own pain and tried to conceal her true feelings, albeit unsuccessfully. Emad would tease al-Batool whenever he was bored, but on that occasion, he was angry with her and chose to say nothing more. As he left the room, she had a certain feeling that his true colours would show soon. She knew how badly he loved money. She had also noticed that he was starting to fall in love with another woman. Emad believed it was his right to be loved by many women. Her instincts told her that her husband wanted to see Abdul Aziz's wife. He never agreed to meet men without the presence of their wives, even if they were to discuss business matters. Emad, like many men of his generation and status, sought pleasure in impressing women with his charming voice, wide knowledge and kind demeanour.

The barrage of questions invading her mind kept her distracted. Al-Batool was wrong in thinking that Emad's love was engraved in her soul, and that he sheltered inside her heart and would never leave. She was wrong. Emad was the cause of her sadness, but she wondered if leaving him would make her happier.

Saudi Arabian author Raja Alem once said that divorce was a scar on the forehead of the divorcee. Emad was al-Batool's cover to hide the shame left by her previous divorce.

CHAPTER 10

Al-Batool became restless because of an idea that had been occupying her mind each night and keeping her awake. She had been getting up and standing at her window thinking about it…

I feel that my life is like a video game system. A video game player gets only four chances in a particular game. Every time my heart loses a game, it takes its chances again in the next round. My heart keeps on taking its chances with different men. O, will I find true love before the end of the game?

Suddenly, the phone rang and wrenched al-Batool from her deep thoughts. It was Emad, telling her to go down quickly as he was waiting for her in the car. They were going to a dinner party to meet Abdul Aziz. She hurriedly dressed up and put on her lipstick.

As she was adding the final touches of her make-up, many thoughts of her life with Emad crossed her mind. Gliding her fingers on her lips, she was struck by the thought that her lips were responsible for starting and ending conversations with her husband; through her lips she had faked most of her feelings about their life together. She polished her eyelids with silver and black eye shadow to cover the look of humiliation and sadness in her eyes. It was the last drop in her favourite bottle of perfume, Quelques Fleurs Houbigant, which she sprayed on herself; and with that last drop of perfume, she knew that her patience was evaporating too.

He never checked my perfume bottles so he would buy me new ones to try. He was always telling me how I have my own special perfume that I should not change. I was not the woman he was trying to impress. He thought that the reason behind my tolerance of his behaviour was that I had no other option but to remain in our marriage. He could satisfy me emotionally, he assumed. People can be very conceited once they are certain that their lovers will remain loyal to them. They take their lovers for granted and make them feel as if they are indebted to them.

Did I treat Fouad with such conceitedness, not valuing his deep love for me; or was it the difference of our nationalities that prevented us from getting married?

I kicked Turki out of my heart soon after realising his inclination to abide by absurd norms, like keeping our marriage a secret and building a typical reclusive Saudi family. He was under a lot of pressure from his family and he could have made many mistakes, but he chose to be honest with me and told me from the beginning that we could not marry.

She got into the car where Emad had been waiting. She felt as if their car seats were miles apart. She resigned not to give in to his manipulative ways to make her go to any of those parties ever again. She was unhappy that she had not tried harder to win him over with her playfulness, yet she knew he could have turned into a monster if she had not obeyed him.

As the party started, al-Batool felt like a baby learning how to walk. She thought that she was compromising her honesty when exchanging pleasantries with people she did not know. Emad was a liberal man with an open-minded outlook on the relationship between men and women. Their friends were enjoying the music when suddenly Emad suggested that al-Batool should dance and remarked that she was a good dancer. She did not reject his call, but only because the song was getting her in the mood to dance. Everyone cheered "al-Batool must dance"; and so she did.

When people dance, they make a public display of their life's agonies. Dancing reveals a person's dark secrets that are hidden behind closed doors and under blankets. Troubled moves, for example, suggest that the dancer might be suffering from an emotional disorder or anxiety. Dancing releases a lot of frustration caused by many suppressed desires. Just like a spy, dancing hacks into our heart and takes control of it. We move with the beats and we lose ourselves.

With every dance move, al-Batool could sense the stab of Turki in one part of her heart and the tears of Fouad in another. She noticed that her moves were titillating Abdul Aziz and another friend, Essam. The words of praise and the cheering of the party encouraged her to continue indulging in that romantic moment.

Piled up problems are like the rotten remains of human corpses; if they stay unsolved for long, they become putrid.

At the end of her dance, one of the female attendees, Sahar, whispered in her ear: "Emad is over the moon because of your sensual performance!" Sahar had a hunch that al-Batool was unhappy about something.

Al-Batool looked at Sahar with a smile and asked mockingly, "What makes you think so?"

"You were not just dancing, but your body was speaking. Your performance was tantalising. Your curves swayed left and right with every beat of that song. You were like the stem of a flower swaying in the blowing winds."

Al-Batool bit her lip because she could sense that Sahar was trying to uncover what was wrong with her. She wanted to end that conversation, and turning to Emad, she said in a soft but firm voice, "I am exhausted. I have this headache again. Can we go now?"

Emad grabbed his car keys and pulling himself up from the settee, he said, "Let's go my dear. I feel a little tired myself."

She was drinking water to quench her thirst, but as Emad stood up, she put down her glass and ran after him outside. She was visibly outraged by his behaviour that night. She got into the car and slammed the door.

"What is wrong with you? You were great today – very cute too!"

"It's odd that you're not jealous at all and put your wife on public display!" retorted al-Batool.

"What's odd to me is that you do not know what a catch you are. You were really hot. I want to have sex tonight."

Al-Batool blurted in exasperation, "I want a divorce!"

CHAPTER 11

K issing is a great way to feel the burning desire between you and your lover. Equally, kissing can tell you if your partner is lying to you. Those who open their eyes first whilst kissing are probably insecure about the feelings of their beloved. Emad's eyes were like those of a wolf, cunningly checking everything around him; even while he slept, they were half-open. He was always the first to open his eyes while they kissed, doubting his wife's loyalty to him.

With the passing days, al-Batool started thinking that she should continue with her marriage. She cried a river over her decision to divorce him. Her tears were not a sign of weakness. She knew that he was not the right man for her. Her frailty stemmed from having to negotiate her investigator's personality. Al-Batool did not believe in forgiving others; the very thought of it made her feel nauseous. Emad controlled her feelings as if they were a toy to him. Every time he chose to play with her feelings, she sank into misery and torture. His whimsical, conceited, and impudent self would only be satisfied once she did what he wanted her to do. He found pleasure in forcing her to obey all his rules. Like al-Batool, forgiveness was not a trait Emad possessed. His wife had to concede every time he humiliated her, but she never forgave him. She knew his round in the game would end sooner or later. She embraced herself and sank deep into an internal monologue.

One must act like a fool in life in order to live peacefully. Men abuse women because we cannot defend our own rights, but we must suppress their devious means of control. Some women waste their time blaming men incessantly and living like victims. Others try to survive their unfulfilling relationships by tolerating all their troubles for the sake of peace. When I signed our marriage contract, I committed myself to him for life. I must do something to sustain this weak home. I must get pregnant; a child will make our home much stronger. Emad already knows I will never go back to my father's home; it is worse than this home. I will continue living here until the moment presents itself.

Her mind wandered off as she sat in her office, gazing at the walls. In the corners of her mind, she looked for a new mask to cover her injured heart. She only saw emptiness, but did not want to halt her search. Soon, she found a glimpse of hope on the horizon and chose to hold onto it.

Given that there were not many operations at the Jeddah office, al-Batool had a lighter workload than she did in Riyadh. This gave her a lot of thinking time; time to think about Fouad. She had not written to him since their meeting at the Riyadh office. She felt excited by the thought of writing to him now. She wanted him to see that her escape from her father's home, which she thought was a triumph, was in fact an act of utter foolishness. The memories she held of him were not dead; they were buried inside her weak soul.

She wrote to Fouad:

If life threw us to the coasts of death, let our loved ones be witness to our story. I spend my days and nights thinking about you only to realise I lost you a long time ago. I do not engage in trivial talks with other women, as many women do here at the Jeddah office. Chitchatting makes women dispirited, uncultured, and distracted from their goals. It turns them into simple-minded creatures, unable to discuss bigger issues. Fouad, I have missed you a lot. I miss your amazing letters and I miss Riyadh, my home. I miss everything now: my palm tree, the small trees, and the clouds in the sky. The clouds used to follow me as I walked back home from work. I wanted to tell you about my marriage when I saw you last time, but I knew your voice would only make me hesitate. I wanted to do it with a strong heart. I could have emailed you this letter, but instead, I am writing it by hand and sending it by post. You know my passion for exchanging letters with you. I wish that a scent of my fragrance or a lock of my hair would get stuck in the pages. They would comfort your heart and keep you warm. Distance makes us feel lonely.

I think about my fate after deciding to leave you. Perhaps I was a bit selfish when I decided to travel to Jeddah. You were waiting for me. I would like to apologise to you, and please, accept it. I did you wrong. Life is an avenger; it had to come back and get me for what I did to you. And it's here in my life, in the shape of a monster of a husband. Fouad, you are purer and more beautiful than anyone I know. We did not break up because you did something wrong. Our different nationalities were the barriers blocking our path. However, these barriers are breakable, and one day we will be able to run to the other side to establish different ideologies in our communities, and then, Fouad, your eyes will sparkle like never before, and your destination will change. I will be older, wiser, and I will spend the rest of my life breathing inspiration into others.

I now live in this so-called city of "progress and austerity". I run most of my errands on foot, while humming Talal Madaah's song The Age of Silence:

"And when you leave, my screams go quiet in a valley where not an echo can be heard and there are no tears. The Age of Silence, O, the years of sadness and grievance. O, my legs can no longer move because of the suffering I endured over the years."

I have engraved the lyrics and the notes of this song on the billboards, squares, pavements, crossroads, and the streets of Jeddah. When I walk towards the beach, I wish for the high waves at sea to engulf me and wash away my pain. Alas, they bring back memories of you. I embrace them gracefully. I cannot forget you. I still love you. "My Love, I have engraved your name on the chords of my voice, on the gates of time, on the blue skies, on the valleys, on the day I was born and on the day I will die. Yet, you are gone."

May God have mercy on Talal's soul!

Fouad, by the way, Jeddah is a place that no visitor could hate. It welcomes everyone: guests and lonely travellers alike. Visitors are impressed by this exquisite city, which gives them the freedom to roam its mystic streets. It might delude them into thinking that this is a place where residents exercise freedom and their rights are respected. That is far from the reality. When visitors live in this coastal city for long enough, they will find themselves puzzled with its many paradoxes. When I walk through its ambivalent streets, I see magical smiles and scowling faces, liberals and fanatics, and all forms of beauty and ugliness. After two years of living here, I can tell you that I am tired of living here; it is noisy and very expensive to live in. I am not used to it. I have to go with the flow, and I have developed a sense of solidarity with people's craving for appearances! Their first impressions of you are based on the brand of your shoes!

I have been trying to avoid talking about Emad, but I must tell you, my marriage turned out to be a disappointment – a carriage filled with regrets. On horseback, my rider tries to control his untamed horse pulling the carriage. Every horse falls sometimes, but nothing will abate my will and pride. The rider shall not control my ride. Jeddah is the land of the dead. As I live here, I fight against deprivation. Emad has given me lots of opportunity to train myself to become an expert in manipulating the feelings of others.

Don't worry Fouad; I will not waste more paper on describing the ugly image of a person whose facial features are distorted by his burning flames of vileness. I know you are keen to know what I write about these days. Well, I decided to put my trust in God and stop writing. I do not understand how writers can navigate through all the confusion that blurs their minds in order to reach a resolution. It is impossible to write about something controversial without stirring debates or provoking rows. Writers are so different from researchers. Writers can take risks, whereas researchers studying weapons of

*mass destruction in a land filled with bombs cannot.
However, the findings of journalists hit us like bombs,
while the words of writers gently unleash many hidden
truths.*

*Some people write of things that will happen in the
future; and when their words come true, they are looked
upon as fortune-tellers. You know my pen; I have always
thrust myself through the arrowheads of my pen. All I
want from my community is mercy and forgiveness.
I wish they would stop criticising and judging me. I
want them to leave me alone. Don't worry Fouad; I
will always read what you write with your treasured
pen in Arabian newspapers. I will die for it. Do not stop
writing, or I will stop living.*

*"O you sea of Jeddah, the strong beats of my heart
are dancing to a special symphony," I said to the sea,
and the sea smiled at me. I could hear it asking me: "Is
love light as a feather or heavy as a horse?" I have always
laughed at this question. It could be a great theme for
your upcoming piece about passion. You have confessed
before that I was your muse. Grab the chance to dance
on arrowheads. I will send you my email to exchange
messages sporadically.*

Until we meet, stay blessed.
Al-Batool

CHAPTER 12

There is no doubt that we see ourselves in our old friends and those who saw us growing up. Our most precious and bitter memories are written on the wrinkles under their eyes and on their foreheads. In her dreams that night, al-Batool heard the voice of her old friend, Eman, which evoked in her images from her past life, and her ambitions as a young woman. Al-Batool reminisced about her beautiful past as she listened to Eman's voice, hoping she would find in it peace and happiness, which were missing from her life. But Eman's voice was melancholic, which shocked her.

While she was in her car being driven to work, al-Batool decided to give Eman a call. A trumpet of honking cars interrupted their voices.

"Good morning sunshine! I had a dream about you. I wanted to check if you were all right. Is something wrong, Eman? Your voice sounds like you are worried, fearful."

"A sweet morning to you dear, and your voice sounds wonderful. God bless you. It is smooth and soothing like a waterfall and a beautiful melody."

Both of them took deep breaths and smiled, with a look of fatigue in their eyes.

"I work more than ten hours at the hospital. It drains me. I have no time for my four children. I am a wreck of a woman. Mithaffar has been unemployed for two years now. He lives like a ghost; always engaged in stupid online chats, which occupy all his time and kill the last spark of love between us. Sadness has the power to make our voices harsh. It is like the rust on a ship, a cancer that destroys all hope for life. Adding insult to injury, I had no say in my marriage. My father accepted my husband's proposal behind my back. They plotted a scheme against me, to strip me of all my rights. They played their dirty game so skilfully. My father turned from what he should have been, my closest friend, to my worst enemy. He agreed to give my hand in marriage in exchange of a fair amount of money. No amount of money should have forced me into a marriage that I did not want! Whenever I am encountered with the darkness of our backward community, I always recall your words, shining at me like the sun. While Saudi females are always condemned for their slightest mistakes, men in our community boast about their horrible offences and virility, and no one ever blames them. My father scorns me always and claims that my mistake is the cause. This works to the favour of Mithaffar, an unemployed man and a burden on other humans, just like the ravagers of the weaker gender in our societies. If I object to his offences, everyone will join my father in belittling me and labelling me as an unfaithful woman."

"They will do that because we live in a male-dominated community, my dear Eman. In our country, men have an unspoken covenant to bring themselves victory by trampling on women. They are bloody, selfish creatures. They show no care for the needs of women. They must attain victory at all costs — even vengeance that results in death!"

"Do you think everything happening to us is coincidental? I bumped into three mad people the other day, and today three more idiots crossed my path! I'm starting to believe I am the only sane person in this city. Don't you think I am living in the wrong city?"

"Darling Eman, please calm down. We would have escaped this world if we could. Unfortunately, there is only one way out... Women are battling the absurdity of life as they go through a long journey of endurance. The wombs of our mothers were our point of inception, and our graves will be our final destination... Women must remain united and strong to support each other. I swear to God, men in the KSA will never be able to quell your willpower even if they could tie a collar around your neck. Their real challenge lies in breaking your sublime spirit and determination. These two things have no legs to be cut, nor hands to be crucified."

"I hope everything will be fine in the end. I've been babbling about my misery and forgot to ask you, what's been keeping you busy all this time?"

"Time goes by quickly, Eman. I am heading towards the unknown. I have been busy keeping a close eye on the continuous cheating adventures of my husband. I keep fighting day and night to prevent the pain from coming through the doors of my life. I think that men have a real problem with self-confidence. A confident man will only fall in love with one woman. The less confident a man is, the more women he will need in his life. Emad is like a poisonous spider. He built a tight silky web, secured with a hinged trapdoor, and trapped me inside while he enjoys the luxury of living freely. He comes from a world filled with twisted paths and murky waters. However, oppression and slavery will eventually lead to the destruction of the web. While I get squashed every time Emad goes through a fling, he egotistically takes pleasure in watching the devastation his poetic lines cause me. Emad is one of those husbands who flirt with other women, but not their wives."

"Are you certain he has actually betrayed you? Have you seen it yourself?" asked Eman.

"Every day, Emad fantasises about sleeping with scores of women. He is emotionally troubled; a group of mistresses line up in the corners of his mind. Any space left in between is filled with illusions

93

and reveries about women. I will push for my divorce from him, no matter how much I end up losing. You will hear about it soon."

"What about Turki? I have a deep feeling you are begging for his return. He's still got a big place in your heart, hasn't he?" asked Eman.

Beautiful memories of our lovers always put a golden smile on our faces and render a tender tone to our voices. In that special tone of voice, Al-Batool said:

"He sends me messages every now and then to check what's new in my life and to make sure I am still alive. Turki's presence is like the anchor balancing my ship. He holds me still in the centre of a circle with half a diameter. He will always remain my axis, even if he is just a memory. It is a good memory that will continue to light a very big place in my heart. I will write to him soon to keep the fire inside my heart burning. Turki and I will always dance on arrowheads, which neither penetrated our bodies to kill us, nor were they removed so we could heal. Can you believe that what terrifies me the most is living eternally in heaven, more than the idea of death itself? We were created to know that everything in life always comes to an end."

Reacting to her friend's wandering thoughts, Eman said, "Take good care of yourself, al-Batool."

In a compassionate tone and with all the love in her heart, al-Batool told her dearest friend, "You too, my dear. Good bye."

Al-Batool entered her office and gestured to the Filipino maid to make her morning coffee. The maid attentively listened to the daily instructions al-Batool gave her on how to make the perfect Arabian coffee. The coffee arrived. It was spiritless. Since she had hung up the phone, al-Batool's head was going in unending circles. She did not know how to solve the problems in her life.

Sometimes our outbursts of ideas collaborate with laziness and hinder productivity. Vexed with herself, she grabbed the paper to read the headlines and skim through the columns and longer articles.

She sniffled loudly – a sign of the pain she had been carrying in her ribcage for years. Suddenly, her eyes spotted an article written by Wafaa. Without hesitating, she called her friend.

It took Wafaa a while to answer. Finally, in a half-awake morning voice, she asked, "Who is it?"

"Hello!" said al-Batool.

"Yes?"

"Have you lost my phone number, Wafaa?" al-Batool asked in bewilderment.

"I am sorry. Who is this?"

"Congratulations on your article."

Recognising al-Batool's voice, Wafaa said: "Oh, yes, thank you darling. Which one are you referring to?"

"The Privacy of Women Amidst Violations of the Saudi Community," al-Batool read.

"Oh, I haven't told you about it. I wrote that a long time ago but I had to go through a lot to have it published," replied Wafaa.

"You are right, dear. Success takes a lot of struggle and persistence. But don't you think there should be more than one winner here?"

"What do you mean?"

"I am the one who should ask you, how did they agree to publish your article?"

In a cheerful but exhausted voice, Wafaa replied, "We must give up some things in life in exchange for others. There is a price for everything."

"It must have been terribly expensive!" al-Batool exclaimed.

Wafaa commented: "Well, you know, people's views on the value of things may differ."

Al-Batool nodded her head in silent agreement and said a few words of prayer to God to bring her friend many more successes. Feeling shocked with Wafaa's comment and her words of prayer in return, she just wanted to hang up but instead, found herself saying something she did not want to finish: "Will I ever see you s..."

Al-Batool despised the sound of her own voice complimenting Wafaa when her best wishes were not coming from her heart. She did not want to discuss the article because it was now unimportant to her, just like Wafaa.

Al-Batool was shocked that Wafaa had stolen every idea she divulged when she had visited her last. Wafaa might have had a tape recorder hidden under her clothes that night to save every single word.

Al-Batool deleted Wafaa's number from her phone, and her heart ripped over the many beautiful memories of their college years. She had shared her dreams with her friend, who brought them to fruition for her own good. Now Wafaa was honoured for being the daring journalist, and her name, polished with gold, attracted attention. Al-Batool resented the fact that Wafaa had plagiarised her words, her ideas, which she had given birth to while burning in hell.

Human behaviour is strictly regimented by emotional and rational reactions, which are inseparable. People sometimes act in hypocritical ways because they are trying to make peace with their past and pave the way for a happier future. Every now and then, they hear that voice inside their head reminding them not to allow the dirty relationships of the past to pollute their futures.

Wafaa was never a sincere friend. When al-Batool remembered their past, she was only trying to find some meaning for their present. She had thought she was sharing her thoughts with an old friend, not an opportunist using all her ideas and thoughts to achieve a higher status.

While she was engrossed in contemplating her discovery – that the person she had thought was a friend was in fact an enemy in disguise – her phone rang. It was Samar. Signs of bewilderment appeared on al-Batool's face. Her lips pulled a faint smile and she answered the call in a mocking voice: "What wind is bringing all my good friends to my shore today? Welcome my dear!"

"You are such a foul friend! Have you forgotten our good days together?"

"No, not forgotten, Samar. I actually checked up on you and found out you resigned."

"Why didn't you call me? Oh, I bet you are busy getting married and then divorced!"

Al-Batool laughed in a loud burst, and jokingly said, "Of course, change is the best thing ever." She had come to believe there was truth in this.

Irritated by Samar's giggling, she continued, "Your mobile was turned off all the time. Where have you been hiding?"

"Finally, I got rid of the shackles that kept me a prisoner for so long. I travelled to Britain to continue my education, where I met an Italian businessman. Giuseppe and I got married."

Samar was silent for a second, to give al-Batool a moment to process the news.

"It took me a long time to do this. I have not finished my first year there yet. I only came to Riyadh for a short visit. I will be leaving in a week for Britain. We will live there forever."

Al-Batool said, "I am very happy for you; you sound happy. So... is he really Italian?"

"Yes, and he is very rich too. Just as you predicted, I ended up marrying a rich man. I insisted on having it my way and forced every member in my family to accept it. I also threatened to kill myself or run away."

"What about Khaled?" al-Batool asked.

"That chapter of my life ended. Haven't you learnt that lesson yet? You should know to stop the fight when you love someone deeply, but there is no future for you. When your interests are no longer the same, you must be brave and move on," Samar explained.

"You mean that love is not worth our sacrifices and sufferings?"

"That is exactly what I mean. Khaled had always been a lost case; all the way from the beginning, I knew I would not fight my family for him. I knew he wouldn't make me as happy as I wanted to be. Besides, he would have never compensated me for the effort I would have put up for him."

"The only compensation one gets in love is giving without any expectations."

"No my dear, I don't see things that way," Samar said.

They were both silent for a moment before concluding the call.

"I am glad you called, Samar."

"I am glad I heard your wicked voice! Remember me."

"How can I forget you? I will always remember…"

I wonder about the reason Samar called me today, when I was just going to write my last letter to Turki. Is fate trying to stop me from doing it? No. She was sent to assure me that I am on the right track.

Al-Batool suddenly grabbed her mobile phone and wrote a message to Turki. Her lines summed up the amount of pain she had endured over the years:

> *"Be My Friend. Love ruins relationships. If we both lived in a different world and in different circumstances, we would have made a great couple. Our souls were destined to meet. We knew each other in another world. However, we have completely different beliefs and lifestyles. Turki, you are the only one who knows my real motive for getting married: to avenge myself. I wanted you to know that I am happy."*

Al-Batool finished packing her make-up, the files that were thrown in every corner of the house, her precious jewellery, antiques, and clothes. She did not know it would take her a few hours to finish packing. Everything in life can be destroyed faster than a blink of an eye.

She left her home knowing where she was heading. She had planned for that moment very well. Emad was coming home from his trip to Cairo. She left the message in an obvious place beside his bed, knowing that he would panic upon reading it.

Living with you forced me to fold the doors of my heart like people turn the pages of a book. But today, my heart had a rebirth of love. I will just quote from the prominent Syrian writer, Ghada Al-Semman's poem 'Dancing with the Owl' – I do not want to ruin the great evening you had with your new wife in Cairo.

"When you treat me like a ghost, I live like one. Your sorrows penetrate me as a car passing through the shadows. They leave no harm and no traces that would live in my memory. That was how the stories of my love life had always come to an end. My heart is not the hanger on which you would just hang up the banners of love and remove them whenever you want. My darling, the ever-lasting memory of love shall remain for those who keep it; oblivion is for those who don't protect their treasures."

Emad... don't worry about me, I will be fine. And don't ever try to bring me back to live in your prison. I pride myself in becoming a divorcee one more time. It is an honour.

Have you ever felt that you wanted to spit out the evil voices inside your head? There was a voice living inside my body, which had been drumming in my ears for many years. I feel that I want to vomit that voice away. I will bite my lips, my tongue, and my nails, because they touched your body in a woeful marriage. Until we meet again, may you burn behind the gates of hell."

Heading to the airport to fly back to Riyadh, al-Batool's mind wandered in many directions: Palestinians are not the only people suffering from assaults and living in fear and oppression. Iraqis are not the only people suffering from lost identity and torn by corruption. We too, honest individuals, pass through similar experiences of suffering throughout our lifetime.

These memoirs were written and compiled between 1997 and 2007.

Email: rmzaid@hotmail.com
Twitter: @Rehabzaid
Instagram: Rehab Zaid
Facebook: Rehab Abuzaid

YAKUZA
MY BROTHER

YAKUZA
MY BROTHER

A Novel

JACOB RAZ

Translated from Hebrew
by Jeffrey Green

PARTRIDGE
A Penguin Random House Company

To order additional copies of this book, contact
Toll Free 800 101 2657 (Singapore)
Toll Free 1 800 81 7340 (Malaysia)
orders.singapore@partridgepublishing.com

www.partridgepublishing.com/singapore

Contents

Preface ix

Chapter 1 An Oyabun Is Born 1

Chapter 2 1983—Yuki 13

Chapter 3 Meeting the Yakuza—
           Scenes from the Underworld 32

Chapter 4 On Yuki's Trail 105

Afterword: The End of the Day—Siloam Church 209

About the Author 213

In the prison library
I pick a flower
From the dictionary
—From the Prison Poems of Fukuoka Ken'ichi, a Yakuza

.

Preface

After the great earthquake in the city of Kobe in 1995, the Japanese government's response in initiating rescue operations was sluggish. Among the first to arrive in the earthquake zone to pull trapped people out from under the ruins were men whose backs and arms were tattooed in dazzling patterns and whose left pinkies had been cut off. Most belonged to the Yamaguchi-Gumi, the largest Yakuza group in Japan, with more than twenty-three thousand members. Kobe is the seat of their headquarters. The Yakuza rapidly and efficiently opened their emergency storerooms and provided food and thousands of blankets to the victims of the earthquake. They helped many and saved many people's lives. This was repeated during the tsunami disaster in 2011.

*

I first arrived in Japan through the front door, or so I thought. The country echoed in my heart—the culture, the aesthetics, philosophy, theater, poetry, the world of Zen Buddhism. It was a seductive, enchanted world—flawed and whole, perfectly imperfect, human in its sophisticated distortion, captivating in its learned simplicity. In addition, the practice of Zen, an unabating alarm clock for the sleepy consciousness, has been my constant companion.

I did know about shadowy sides of Japan, but I had not yet faced them. *When I get there, I'll probably meet them,* I thought. However, that dark side rushed forward to meet me unexpectedly at home. A short time before I first left Israel for Japan, three Japanese youths, members of the Japanese Red Army, attacked and killed twenty-six people, most of them Puerto Rican pilgrims who had come to the Holy Land to walk in the footsteps of Jesus, at Tel Aviv airport. Two of the terrorists committed suicide, one of them the husband the woman who sent them, Shigenobu Fusako, the JRA leader. The third, Okamoto Kozo, was captured.

I stayed in Japan for many years. I lived, traveled, studied, sat in libraries, sojourned in monasteries, took part in religious festivals, and investigated town streets. I learned what I could about the culture and the people. The more I wandered, the more I encountered the back alleys—as happens to the saunterer. There I found people quite different from the Zen monks, or artists who drew beautiful calligraphies in ink, or teachers of tea ceremony. These were communities poles apart from the diligent corporate workers bent over computer screens late at night, later to frequent nightclubs, sake fumes wafting from their mouths as they whispered banal secrets to hostesses. These different people attracted me.

Many of the decent folk wandered in these back alleys. They crossed the lines almost daily for a few hours of satisfying hidden passions. But the true dwellers of the other side were different: nomads; wandering bards; blind women storytellers; witches and shamanesses; peddlers traveling among the innumerable religious festivals; refugees from society; characters in sunglasses, men whose bodies were tattooed with splendid pictures; recluses; homeless people who took off their shoes when they stepped onto the piece of cardboard that served as their home; Koreans who never outgrew their longing for the Emerald Land; descendants of untouchable people who had yet to be purified; Okinawans who had not forgiven the emperor; young people with cocaine in their veins; wizards and philosophers in isolated huts; crazy potters kneading clay and throwing it into the fiery kiln; cooks who had been singers, and singers who had been cooks; members of parliament who became entertainers and the other way around; writers who became criminals; and all kinds of hybrids who gauged society's normalcy. You can't have one without the other.

There was a need in me to meet them, to see, touch, and sniff these people. Whether it was because of my need for a rounded encounter with every aspect of Japan, or because of my attraction to the darkness within me, I began following them. First the nomads, then the blind women storytellers, and then the peddlers, the cheats, and the outcasts.

Then it was impossible to avoid the Yakuza, the Government of the other side.

It wasn't easy to make contact. Japanese journalists bow obsequiously to Yakuza in return for a personal interview of half an hour with a big *oyabun* (boss) and for a bit of gossip about the most recent battles with the rival family. Newspaper photographers butter up the Yakuza in return for rare photographs of their religious ceremonies. Japanese sociologists and criminologists barely manage to interview them, at best, in detention rooms and prisons. Anthropologists never get their cooperation. Two or three Western anthropologists received single interviews from one boss or another, and heard eloquent lectures about the values and history of Yakuza. However, except for one American study (by David Stark), I could not find a single account of a long fieldwork with them in either scholarly or popular literature. I was told it was impossible, that I should give up. But I wanted no less.

When I finally did manage to meet them, I thought I was carrying out academic research. And indeed, I published a few years ago an academic book in Japanese titled *The Anthropology of Yakuza*. But the academic study bears witness no less to the voice of anthropology than to the world of Yakuza. The more I lived with them, the more the scholar in me faded away. In this book, I wish to give priority to the voices of the people I met.

One of those voices, a powerful oyabun, said to me on his deathbed: "Think it through, *Sensei* (professor). We're all social outcasts. That's what they say about us, right? And we say that ourselves, that we're outcasts from family, community, from the law; we're the ones who can't adjust to society's customs and laws; we're the ones who can't adapt; we're criminals.

"But take a good look, please. We've immigrated from the law-abiding society into the Yakuza world. But in this world of Yakuza, the laws of are more stringent, tighter, better organized, and clearer than those of that law-abiding society. Here the hierarchy is more precise, and it's observed more strictly than over there. In our world, punishments are harsher, more frightening, and more effective than those of the society we were cast out of or fled from. 'Misfits'? Not a single one of the *katagi* (law-abiding citizens) would last a day in our rigid world. Think about what could have been done for those kids before they joined us. Think it over."

Everything in this book is true, as true as truth can be. All stories of fiction here are the fruit of the actual encounters I had during the years I spent with these strange, different, and solitary men, who, as they proclaim, "go all the way." There were good and bad persons, frauds and honest, friends and enemies, squares and madmen, boring and intriguing, threatening and cordial, merciful and ruthless people. There were people whose presence I couldn't stand and others with whom I made rare, heartfelt connections, which continue to this day. All of them echoed in my heart.

The full variety of humanity. How normal.

*

Who are the Yakuza? The word denotes the Japanese underworld, organized in hundreds of small groups and a few big national groups and alliances. As for 2015, there are approximately 60,000 members, along with many more supporters, marginal members, hidden members, hangers-on, and other shadowy circles. The number has been decreasing fast in the last few years; a decade ago there were over 90,000 members. Many are going underground, which makes numbers highly unreliable.

The yakuza took their present form around the mid-eighteenth century. The word Yakuza consists of three words: *ya* means eight; *ku* means nine; and *za* means three—which adds up to twenty, the losing number in a gambling card game. By extension the word means a worthless person, a loser.

But the Yakuza use the word with pride. For them the word means romance, a world of chivalry, crime, liberty, money, isolation, love, and sacrifice. Yakuza is to live a legend to its extremes.

Yakuza often call themselves *Gokudo*, "the Path of Extremes." That is to say the world of those who live life to the fullest, without compromise. They will do everything all the way: friendship, devotion, crime, war, love, sacrifice, loyalty, dedication, determination. Treachery too.

Another name used by the Yakuza is *Ninkyodo*—"the Path of Chivalry." Our ancestors, they say, were wandering noblemen, descendants of masterless Samurai who roamed through old Japan and fought the strong to take from them in order to help the weak.

But the name one is likely to hear most often in the media is *Boryokudan*—"violent gangs," or "gangsters." This name has been used by the police and the media for the last three decades to attenuate the romantic aura of the name Yakuza.

The Yakuza hate that term. "We're not the American Mafia," they say.

A note to the reader:

Japanese names are written in their Japanese order: family name first, given name last.

Chapter One

An Oyabun Is Born

It all began in 1983, ten years before I saw the following story in the *Manila Times*:

May 1993

Activity of Japanese Yakuza on Rise in Manila

Last night the Manila police raided a luxury villa on Roxas Boulevard after neighbors complained of gunshots and screams coming from inside. According to police sources, the villa belongs to Furukawa Saburo, a wealthy Japanese businessman, and has recently been the focus of suspicious activity. According to these sources, the Manila police have reason to believe Furukawa is an ex-Yakuza (Japanese criminal organizations), who has been acting as a lone wolf. Lately the activity of the Yakuza has been on the rise in Manila, so much so that it has become a main target of the Manila police. Yakuza activity concentrates on prostitution, drugs, and arms smuggling. Unofficial rumors say that Furukawa is connected with various crime groups: Chinese groups in Burma, Corsican gangs in Laos, Triad groups in Hong-Kong, and criminal elements here in the Philippines. In Manila he is thought to be in close contact with Mercedes Salonga, who heads the city's largest prostitution syndicate. It is also known that Furukawa has been in contact with a number of the Chinese "Dragonhead" bosses, a connection that is a matter of deep concern to the Japanese Yakuza in Manila.

The police found the villa empty. The screams, it turned out, were of a pet monkey who was frightened by shots that apparently had come from inside the villa earlier. The interior of the villa was in a complete chaos. Furniture had been slashed and the contents of drawers strewn on the floor. It seems a search had been hastily made, and intruders fled when they heard the police approach.

Two photographs from inside the villa accompanied the story: one showed a large, splendid room opening onto a garden and pool. It was a mess. The second was a photograph of the terrified monkey, sitting on a dresser, with an expression of dread on its face. Behind the monkey I noticed a picture frame leaning against the wall, and in it, in large letters, a print of a poem in English. Most of the words were clearly legible. I brought it close to my eyes:

"I will break God's seamless skull,
And I will break His kiss-less mouth,
O I'll break out of His faultless shell
And fall me upon Eve's gold mouth."
—Jose Garcia Villa

I was stunned: Yuki! That man, Furukawa, is Yuki! After years of searching, maybe I found him! This man is not Furukawa; he is Yuki!

2

I grabbed the telephone and, with pounding heart, called up the *Manila Times.*

November 1993
The *sakazuki* Ceremony: An Oybaun is Crowned

A severe-looking man wearing a white silk kimono pronounces these words in ancient, ritual Japanese, to my amazed ears and eyes. "When you drink from this bowl, you, Fujita Tetsuya, senior *Kobun* (ritual son) of the late Okawa Oyabun thereby accept the position of the oyabun of the Okawa-Kai family! Please, drink! Coolheaded knight, polish your manliness! Go out again on the path of wandering; know the inside and the outside of a man's world's tribulations, the path of extremes. Chivalry! Chivalry! This world makes the blood boil in our hearts! Even if your wife and son go hungry, cast your life aside for the sake of the family, and be the great oyabun! The Okawa-Kai family awaits you, coolheaded knight! I, Sakurai Hideo, in the name of Ishida Taro, the elder of the family, hereby do the bidding of Okawa Oyabun and appoint you oyabun of the Okawa-Kai family!"

The man, who announced himself as Sakurai Hideo, talks and looks like a priest. Sakurai is the master of ceremonies, and a senior member of the Okawa-Kai, one of the most powerful Yakuza families in Tokyo. He is the Master of Ceremonies of this event, in which Fujita Tetsuya - for me my old friend Tetsuya - is the appointed heir to the legenday Okawa Oyabun, who died of cancer some time ago. Okawa Oyabun made his wish clear: Fujita Tatsuya is to be the next Oyabun.

Now Sakurai kneels on a red cushion, and at his side are various vessels: two white porcelain bottles, a tray decorated with a cone of salt, and another tray adorned with a big fish. Before him is a white cushion, and on it lies a gilded *sake* bowl. The man's movements are precise, as if the whole world depended on them.

*

The ceremony began a few minutes earlier. Sakurai took the gilded sake bowl, and, with a large, round gesture, stretched out his right arm. An assistant handed him a white piece of paper. Sakurai took the paper and wiped the bowl with broad movements. Then he took one of the white sake bottles and removed the white paper stopper that had sealed its mouth. He recited a short prayer in ancient Japanese and waved his hand over the mouth of the bottle with a wide motion, while uttering a short, loud grunt: "wwwwoooooowooooooooo!," thus purifying the bottles. He then poured a little sake into the gilded bowl. He put the bottle back, replaced the paper stopper, and repeated the ceremony with the other bottle.

After a long chanting in ancient Japanese, Sakurai turned to modern language. He faced Fujita Tetsuya, the nominated oyabun, and asked him to step up to his place in the front of the hall. Fujita, wearing a black kimono, rose from his seat and stepped slowly to the front of the room, next to an altar upon which some fruit and fish offerings had been placed. Ishida Oyabun, the family elder, already seated near the altar, welcomed Tetsuya with a tiny bow, eyes veiled with sunglasses, body tense, emotions untold. Will he accept Okawa's will in a few month time, or will he fight?

Tetsuya bowed to the altar, ascended to the platform, faced the room, and was seated. Body tense. Emotions untold.

The assistant rose, took the bowl, and, gliding smoothly on the white carpet, carried it to the small altar. He laid the bowl at Ishida Oyabun's feet. Ishida Oyabun took three and a half sips from the bowl. The assistant took the bowl and passed it to the new oyabun, Fujita Tetsuya. Tetusya's hands, adept at beating, shooting, and slashing, shook now. He raised the bowl and waited.

And then Sakurai addressed him the words, "I, Sakurai Hideo, in the name of Ishida Taro, the family elder, hereby do the bidding of Okawa Oyabun and appoint you oyabun of the Okawa-Kai family!"

And thereby I lost my friend Tetsuya. My Yakuza brother.

*

I had entered the hall an hour earlier, before the others. I found a corner so I wouldn't stand out, a tall Western man, dressed casually in this crowd of elegantly dressed Japanese gangsters.

For a few hours they had gathered, adept at the world of darkness. Most of them wore black kimonos, glimmering in the light. Some wore black suits and white ties. Many wore sunglasses. First to enter the hall were the members of the family council followed by Ishida Oyabun, the family elder, with his second in command and his chief advisors. Everyone turned to them and bowed deeply. They sat along the path of white cloth, to his right.

The last to come were the guests. They bowed to each other in exaggerated submission. These were representatives of the other Yakuza families from Tokyo, Kyoto, Osaka, and Kobe. They gathered here to honor the Okawa-Kai family and the late Okawa Oyabun. Looking around, I observed some representatives of Yamada-Gumi, the largest family in Japan, a declared enemy of the Okawa-Kai family. Why have they come here?

No one smiles now.

In the back row I see a short man dressed in a black jacket over a red Chinese-style shirt, his eyes narrow slits. He is the Hong Kong boss of the Chinese Dragonhead gang, so they tell me. After a long period of violent rivalry, an alliance had recently been formed between the Dragonhead and the Okawa-Kai families, so say my sources. I also know who formed that alliance, and he is not here. It is Yuki, my long-lost friend.

The last to arrive into the hall was Fujita Tetsuya, the guest of honor. Soon he would become the new oyabun of the Okawa-Kai family, the second most powerful family in Tokyo, and one of the most powerful families in eastern and northern Japan. My family.

Now all bow down to the floor. Sakurai ends his speech with, "Please drink!"

Tetsuya raises the bowl, holds it before his eyes, and says, "It is an honor for me to speak before the honored people here. This bowl, from which I am drinking before the nobles of the family, is a sacred bowl. It is an honor for me to drink from this bowl, and to follow in the footsteps of those greater than I. I, Fujita Tetsuya, a humble son of this family, accept the authority with modesty and submission, to become a worthy oyabun of the Okawa-Kai family. I vow to be a man worthy of this family name and of the memory of Okawa Oyabun. I am honored to drink from this bowl."

He sips three times and takes another half sip. He removes a paper napkin from the sash of his kimono, wipes the bowl very slowly, and places it inside his kimono, next to his heart. He bows deeply to Ishida, the old man. Then he turns toward the great hall and bows deeply again, touching the floor with his forehead. He rises again.

Ishida Oyabun smiles thinly beneath his sunglasses. He bows slightly to Tetsuya, as do all those present, including myself.

Fujita Tetsuya, the new oyabun, raises his hand. The hall falls silent, and he says, "With acceptance of this weighty role, which I take upon myself with humility and with great honor, I wish to thank everyone sitting here for waiting patiently while I was in prison. I wish to thank those who managed the family business with responsibility and prudence, and especially Ishida Oyabun, my most respected brother, who preserved our power and honor in Japan and throughout the entire region.

"I am pleased by the presence here of Charlie Long Oyabun, a senior leader of the Dragonhead Association of Hong Kong, and I am pleased to announce the renewal of the longstanding alliance between the Okawa-Kai family and the honorable Chinese Dragonhead family ..."

He bows to the Chinese man. Not a deep bow, I notice. The Chinese man lowers his head. A little.

"From now on we will work together in all our business in East Asia, in the spirit of these times. The man who was the living spirit behind the renewal of this alliance is not here with us. Murata Yukihira, or Yuki to his friends, lately known as Furukawa Saburo"— he smiles—"did the impossible, and it is thanks to his efforts that the alliance with the Dragonhead was formed. I am deeply sorry that Murata Yukihira is unable to be here with us today. I wish to announce on this occasion his appointment to membership of the Senior Council of our family. As such he receives the full honor of the family, and also its full protection! Let it be known hereby that Murata Yukihira receives our personal protection, after every earlier decision in his regard has been rescinded and is null and void!"

The exclamation mark hangs in the air. No one moves.

*

For a moment I go back in time to October 1983, ten years ago, to a small food stall in Sugamo Square, Tokyo, where a young man is cooking nighttime delicacies with the nervous precision of someone being tested. I have known him as Yuki, the man with whom I bonded in the Yakuza bond, what he called the Brotherhood of Vagabonds. Only after he disappeared did I realize the depth of our bond.

Yuki disappeared one day and never reappeared, except in the stories of people from Tokyo to São Paolo to Manila. I didn't know whether these were invented tales, or whether he is a real person, alive or dead. Or maybe he was a creature of my searching soul, longing for his lost innocence. For ten years I have been seeking the man. I know bits and pieces of his story, but I don't know the shape of his soul. And now he received the personal protection of one of the strongest oyabun of Tokyo. He may be real, after all. Is he?

I remember the long letter he wrote me, narrating the story of his life. I recall the torment gushing from his words. I read the poetry he loved—Baudelaire, Jose Garcia Villa, Octavio Paz. Who is he? Where is he? In Hong Kong? Bangkok? São Paulo? Tokyo? Why isn't he here today?

*

"I wish to conclude my speech. Thank you," Fujita Tetsuya says. Sakurai announces that the ceremony is finished and that the banquet will take place in half an hour in the central hall of the hotel. His voice changes, free of its earlier ceremonial gravity. "Before we disperse," he says, "photographs!"

Fujita Tetsuya, the new oyabun, stands before the scrolls of the patron gods, and at his side stand the important leaders. A camera flash. A photograph. Another photograph, and another. Tetsuya stands at attention, and at his side, as on the pages of an album, quartets of the crime lords of Japan switch off, faces expressionless.

Suddenly he shouts, "Sensei, come for a picture!"

Embarrassed, I also have my picture taken. After the photographs, everyone goes his own way. In a little while the banquet will start.

*

I arrived here yesterday. Two days earlier I received a phone call. "Sensei! The ceremony will take place tomorrow in Koriyama. Someone will be waiting for you at the Koriyama station. Three pm. See you later!"

The next day I boarded a train at the Ueno station in Tokyo. We were approaching the Koriyama station, a region of hot springs in the northern black mountains. As I switched to the local train, I observed more Yakuza boarding, some of them garbed in over-tailored suits donned with white ties. Others wore long-sleeved T-shirts with brightly colored emblems and baggy, colorful trousers. White shoes. I identified them by the metal badges with the symbol of the Okawa-Kai family, pinned to their shirts or suits. Some silver, fewer gold badges. Platinum badges would come in big black luxury cars with opaque windows.

I also recognized them by their swaggering gait, their arrogant-yet-frightened gaze at the *katagi*—the law-abiding citizens. I picked them out by the evasive glances of the katagi. I knew them by their menacing shyness; by their short haircuts or the Afro style they called *pa-ma*; by their ubiquitous sunglasses. Like overgrown boys popping out of manga comic books, they would purposely expose the *irezumi* (tattoos) patterns under their shirtsleeves. Here and there I could see a palm with a missing finger. People noticed and bypassed.

"Koriyama station!" The Yakuza got off the train, not concealing their excitement.

I too got off. Someone I had never met hurried up to me. "Yakobu Sensei?"

"Yes, that's me."

"Come with me, please," he said with submissive courtesy. He pointed toward a polished black, royal, threatening-looking Mercedes-Benz, my reflection shining in the hood. It was the oyabun's car. Many Yakuza were obviously astonished by the honor I was given. They must have wondered who I was. *I* wondered who I was. A Western scholar? A nosey *gaijin* (foreigner)? A peeping Tom under the conveniently titled "expert in Japanese culture"?

We drove in the town for about ten minutes passing rows of hotels, mostly traditional style with little rock gardens at the entrance. Efficient women in kimonos politely ushered guests in and out. Bowing. People walked around in *yukata* (casual summer kimono) robes, their faces calm. I saw a cliff face next to a deep ravine and black basalt mountains across from us.

On the edge of the ravine stood our splendid hotel, a beautiful garden at its entrance. A large calligraphic sign proclaimed the name of the hotel, and it was busier than the others. The Yakuza invited me in, insisting on carrying my suitcase. At the entrance stood a few reception tables with signs carrying names. Men with grave countenances sat at the tables and greeted the Yakuza members. There was a certain hidden order here.

I was taken to my room. On the way, there was plenty of excitement. Old Yakuza strolled about wearing splendid suits with platinum badges on the lapels, and everyone accorded them great respect and deep bows. Their attendants offered them services like lighting a cigarette or placing a chair for them to sit. The young men raced about here and there, looking anxiously at the elders, rushing to satisfy a wish or obey an order that may not even have been voiced. They gathered in small groups, whispering. A new oyabun would be appointed for the Okawa-Kai. A historic event.

No police were in sight.

The staff of the large hotel were doing everything to satisfy their guests. Were they welcome guests? Unwelcome? The service people were submissive, obsequious, deeply bowing. They seemed to be well versed in the rules of the event. Eight hundred men, members of the family, were to gather here by tomorrow, as well as more guests from other families. Eight hundred men. Tough. Fragile. Child-men.

My room is simple and beautiful. I unpacked, drank green tea, admired the black basalt cliffs outside, and waited for what was to come,.

*

A historical event is about to take place here, an informer lectures me. Ishida Oyabun, the family elder, is retiring from his temporary post as the family head and will confer it upon Fujita Tetsuya, the senior kobun of the late Okawa Oyabun. From now on he will be known as Fujita Oyabun. Since the death of the legendary Okawa Oyabun, the family hasn't had a leader. Fujita Tetsuya, whom Okawa appointed during his lifetime, spent two years in prison, now to be nominated to this extremly heavy post. Perhaps now the turbulent spirits of the family will calm down. The informer sighs.

*

The next day I go to the hot springs with some Yakuza friends. The hotel is built on a slope, and we go down deep under the entrance floor. Through the large window I see the water and the boulders, and the law-abiding katagi bathing in the water. Their faces are red, and their eyes are closed. Some have small white towels on their heads. The place is surrounded by bamboo fences. The smell of sulfur is thick in the air. Steam rises from the water. It feels a little like hell.

I strip in the dressing room and put my clothes in a locker. I go out to the rock-surrounded pools a little before my Yakuza friends. I'm still embarrassed. Now they come, like drawings out of a Buddhist hell. They laugh. They speak loudly. To intimidate the katagi citizens. Their bodies are masterpieces of drunken colors of Irezumi tattoos. They are decorated in red and blue, yellow and black, and emerald green. Figures of kabuki actors in red and green adorn their chest. Kannon, the goddess of mercy, is painted on a buttock. A dragon slopes across a back. Two green snakes are coiled around the nipples. A firebird descends from the belly to the thighs. A spotted tiger climbs a shoulder. The fire god in the lotus position rages toward the head. Orange ninja mice dance on the feet. Yellow fish decorate the back of the arms. Here is the god Fudo Mio-o, red and orange, brandishing his sword along the back, spitting fire from his mouth. A bamboo forest trails along the legs.

One only has his shoulders decorated. Another only his legs and hands, like pairs of socks and gloves. Another's whole back and chest is covered with pictures, and another member's feet and buttocks, even his male organ, is covered by a coiled blue snake with orange eyes. Along his stomach, on an angle, is the phrase *Namu Myo ho Renge Kyo* (Praise the Lotus Sutra).

One member, Matsumura, is garbed completely from his bald head to his feet with tattoos that dazzle the eyes. Even beneath his left eye is a swirling drawing in black.

"Come look, Sensei. You are from Israel, they say? You see, news spread fast here. They say that over there in Israel you have a lot of wars. Here too. Were you ever wounded? Do you have scars? Come and look. There used to be a scar here, beneath the Buddha. And here, beneath the dragon. And here too. But Horimae, the irezumi master, managed to hide them all in creations like this that surprise the eyes. I'm a living art gallery. I'm scar upon scar that was turned into a canvas. I'll dedicate my skin to a museum. Let them exhibit it. What do you say? Should we suggest it over there in the Middle East? A way of rehabilitating war wounds?"

The good citizens leave the pools one by one. Surreptitiously. Heads down.

It's getting darker, and we're still bathing. Rain starts to fall. My friends are sitting in the water, white towels on their heads. They drink hot sake and pour me cup after cup.

Beyond the fence the black cliffs breathe white vapors. Sulfur. The pool is red. And my friends are painted with demons.

Chapter Two

1983—Yuki

Meeting Yuki

Sugamo District, Tokyo. Summer. Midnight.

Opposite the southern exit of the Sugamo train station on the Yamanote line in Tokyo is a small square, on one side of which is a small police station. Around the square are about fifteen night food stalls and a few telephone booths. On the glass walls of the booths pictures of naked girls are pasted, promising two hours of the very best treatment for 20,000 yen. All included.

That summer I lived near the station. I was deep inside a research project on marginal groups in Japan. My study took me to remote places, but I had also found some around the corner in the big city. The people operating the night stalls around train stations particularly fascinated me. The lights were turned on at nine and turned off in the morning. They were food stalls, each with its peculiar dishes—ramen, udon, soba, and others.

Next to each stall were two benches. An electric bulb in a red or white paper lampshade hung above. On either side of the stand, five or six men and women ate, drank, and chatted about the day's events: The summer heat, the humidity, the unappetizing food in the company refectory, the puffed-up boss, the summer vacation that never was. The achievements and failures. After work, on their way home they sit here. They feast on delicious, cheap food. It ia crowded here—intimate, pleasant, liberating. People would take off jackets, ties, and their corporate souls for an hour of intimacy.

On the other side of the stalls are the people that serve them. Tough, good people. Cooking, amusing, gossiping, confessing, interpreting, caring, telling stories. Each one with his own loyal customers.

I used to frequent a certain young man's stall, where he served *oden,* a sort of Japanese stew. His name was Yuki, short for Yukihira, after the name of a famous poet who lived a thousand years ago. Gaunt. Sunken cheeks. Long hair tied behind, hanging down to the middle of his back. His eyes bulged like a frog's. One eye looked straight at you, the other looked sideways. About ten years younger than me. He was precise, attentive, busy peeling-cutting-cooking-serving.

Hesitantly, short conversations began. I found myself curious about him. He was obviously curious about me. Gradually I began joining him every evening while he prepared the stand, before the customers came. I helped. I learned how to cut vegetables. I would help him in fetching water, rinsing a cup, and hanging up the paper lampshade. In the center was a square pot with various dishes that he'd concoct every evening. Fragrances wafted from it, the street smell of Japan. You heard murmurs of simmering, bubbling, whispering water.

I came every evening. Scholarship and friendship intertwined. We talked about commonplace things. Sometimes we talked politics. Sometimes he mentioned a book he'd read. He clearly had a broad education but said nothing about the circumstances that had brought him to the food stand.

For a long time I knew nothing about him. Just that when I looked at him, I saw great suffering breaking out of that gaunt face. Sometimes, when he got excited, his left eye twitched, as if to say, nothing serious. For a long time he knew nothing about me. One evening I drew my name and some other calligraphy and a few small ink drawings on the little paper lantern above the stand. I wonder if they are still there.

Bit by bit we exposed ourselves to each other. What I liked to eat. What film I'd seen. The moon behind the cloud. The ways of preparing tofu and the differences according to the quality of water. What district the choicest sake comes from. Very little about our past.

One day, a magazine lying on the bench caught my eye. It was the *Bungeishunju* literary journal.

"Yes," he said, apologetically. "I have an MA degree in literature and one in economics. Yes, both. I wanted to do a doctorate in literature, about the poetry of Southeast Asia. Maybe a comparative study with Japanese poetry. But it didn't work out."

A bashful smile, as though I'd caught him out. He continued his cooking without looking at me. "After completing my degree, I worked in a big financial firm. I was successful, and they anticipated a big future for me in business. But I quit. 'No thanks, I don't want to be part of Japanese business lunacy.' Then a bookstore. I was happy there. A year, a year and a half. Then it didn't work out. I quit. Can't stay in one place. I started to work here. Because my brother knows Hayashi Oyabun."

"Oyabun? You mean a Yakuza boss!?" I ask.

"Yes. A Yakuza boss. Yakuza is the Japanese Mafia. You know that, right? Hayashi gave me this stall. He's the oyabun of this area. It's a good place here. Across from the station. Yes, I'm happy here. I start to work in the evening, finish in the morning, at five. I meet people. I have time to read. I get up at noon. I pay something to Hayashi every month, and I'm content. He gave me a good place because of my big brother. My brother once did him a favor. My brother works in the north, in Hokkaido.

"I like working here. On my own. My own master. The Yakuza protect me. Once a week, on Sunday, I go to the Golden Gai district in Shinjuku, to the Murasaki, Hirano's *nomiya* srkinking bar. Literature aficionados gather there. We read, talk. Play guitar. What's Golden Gai? you ask? You mean you don't know? Golden Gai is the navel of the universe. Come with me next Sunday."

Golden Gai

On Sunday evening we go to Golden Gai.

We leave Shinjuku station, heading east, to the huge, tumultuous plaza, crowded with young people wearing stylish rags. A gigantic video screen overlooks the plaza, on the wall of the STUDIO ARTA Building, showing the concluding scene of *Casablanca* and the beginning of a beautiful friendship. We go down alleys and reach Yasukuni Dori Avenue. Big and broad, a river of cars, lights, colored signs, and people coming and going, going and coming in restaurants of every kind, of every taste and tongue.

Across from us is a sign saying Kabuki-Cho. We go in.

Sign after bright sign decorate the alleys. Red, blue, yellow, violet, green, flickering and sparkling, blinking off and on, off and on. Calligraphic signs with enticing characters. Neon pictures of the Old Man from Kentucky, of giant crabs, or clowns, or Dutch windmills. Across the street, narrow alleys, colorful tunnels of neon lights, in which people sell toys and pictures. If you walk there, you pass bars, *izakaya* drinking establishments, night clubs ("The first drink on the house, the girl is free, come in, come in!"), hostess clubs for men, host clubs for women; music clubs, small theaters, small movie houses, a sex shop ("Peepshow cubicles, amazing toys, come in, *onii-san*, my brother, come in!"), a striptease club ("Amazing girls from Thailand, the Philippines, Cambodia, America, India, Africa. Come in, come in, come in, live show, live show! An African man and a Japanese girl!"). Hundreds of little entrances that promise things for every age and sex ("Onii-san, it's cheap! Come in!). "Lingerie Club," "Touching Club," "Kissing Club." And the king of clubs—the massage parlor titled "Soap Club." Carefully classified pictures displayed, so the customer knows what he's entering and who's serving him: a high school girl, a student, a housewife, or a Western woman. Here is also Hayakawa's club, a former Yakuza, now a musician, who travels all over the country to old-age homes and hospitals and plays his songs to atone for his past sins.

Drooling men tarry, sniff, and look at the pictures like gemologists. Sometimes they are swallowed into a little entrance. Others come out seeming dissatisfied. A Filipino pimp counts money, his fingers heavy with golden rings. Here and there are guys with black looks, short hair, swaggering gait, often with sunglasses. Even at night. They're the kings. The Yakuza.

We walk east until we reach a little alley that crosses to the southeast, on an angle, and along it a row of ginkgo trees. We walk until we reach a small, bizarre neighborhood. Four or five very narrow alleys. Little signs and closed doors. Every house is two stories high. People come and go through the narrow doors. When a door opens, you can see a small counter, and next to it five or six people, and maybe another table or two. The light is dim, and the people, on both sides of the counter, are very friendly. Maybe they'll invite you in. Maybe they'll cross their hands, a sign that means no, no entry for you. Especially if you are a gaijin, a foreigner. Next to the ground floor door is another door, and behind it a flight of very steep stairs that lead you to the second floor, where you will find another establishment. People stagger through the doors, and their breath smells of sake, whiskey, or beer. Or all three.

Here is a small door, and above it a small sign says Murasaki. Outside stands a big man with sunglasses. He wears silk shirt in summer colors over white trousers. He's hugging himself with huge arms. He looks at us, wags his head at me. Yuki nods back. The giant shakes his head.

We go into a dark room, illuminated with reddish lights. The man who greets us is Hirano, the owner. His eyes are deep and his hair is long, down to the waist, tied behind, almost twin to Yuki. About sixty. He's busy behind the counter. Cutting, frying, cooking, pouring, wiping his hands, smiling, laughing, consoling, humming, spicing, flipping, shouting, wiping the counter, removing corks, concocting sauces.

On the walls are posters of film classics. Soft graphics, reddish-orange colors, the soft-tough gazes of Clark Gable, Maureen O'Hara,

Fred Astaire, Vivien Leigh, Marlon Brando, a lot of Chaplin, Humphrey Bogart, Maurice Chevalier, Gene Kelly.

Near the counter a few people are talking loudly. Laughing. Little portions of food are rushed from the little kitchenette where Hirano's hands do miracles.

In the dark corner is a girl wearing a bright orange dress. She's wearing sunglasses with orange frames. She's smoking a cigarette, and in the violet ashtray on her tiny table are a few orange lipstick-stained cigarette butts. A look flashes between the girl and Yuki as if it shouldn't have. What's going on?

Yuki introduces me to Hirano. Hirano smiles, and his eyes become thin crescents. With a deep bow, small dishes are spread out on the counter. Squares, circles, rectangles, diamonds, triangles— and on them are kinds of food I've never seen. Drinks.

"You new around here? Well, welcome to a different Tokyo," says Hirano, while concocting a special drink for me. "Go and take a walk around in Golden Gai and enter the various dens. Do it mindfully. You'll find movie people there, writers, ordinary people, journalists, and Yakuza." He talks with the passion of a priest, who gives a sermon to an ignoramus.

"In this labyrinth of alleys, each just three steps wide, you'll find about a hundred little nomiya. In each one about six, maybe ten people, eating and drinking. Each nomiya is run by a bizarro. We're all special here. Even Yuki doesn't know them all.

"The Yakuza frequent here, but they don't control this place – yet. They own the big business over there - Shinjuku-Nichome and Kabuki-Cho."

He lowers his voice. Almost whispers. Did I see a swift glance at the girl in orange? Who is she? And he goes on.

"They come here to drink, rest, to cool their heads. So far, this is a demilitarized zone. Mind you, it's rather hard to control the crazy people who run the nomiya of Golden Gai. So even the Yakuza use a gentle hand here. But no one can tell.

"After the war, the black market was flourishing here. Then, a lot of Yakuza. And American soldiers. And a lot of cooperation between them. Here in this alley I saw American officers handing guns to the Yakuza oyabuns. So they'd fight against the Korean and Chinese gangs searching for revenge. It was tough. People ate roots and ran their cars on wood for fuel. The Yakuza grew then and turned into a strong army. So this place grew from a pissing alley to a flourishing area. Pimps gathered here, whores, and crazy small entrepreneurs who flourished after the Great War, and they built here the *mizu shobai* water business, that is, restaurants, pubs, clubs.

"Then the whores left, and the mamasans came, the wives and mistresses of the Yakuza, and all sorts of businessmen and businesswomen of the shadow world. Me too. We built a world here. Two hundred nomiya, every one a universe. Sadly, today we're down to a hundred and are gradually disappearing. Ho, hello Kuroda-san. Sit down, sit down. Here is Yakobu-sensei from Israel. Kuroda-san is a famous thriller writer. Best sellers only, I tell you. Only best sellers. Science fiction thrillers. Yakobu-san is a university professor. Fluent Japanese, don't worry."

A business card is magically produced from Kuroda's pocket and presented with a bow. A beautifully designed card with elaborated calligraphy. To my embarrasement I don't have a business card. I blush. Kuroda sends a 'don't bother' smile and without further ado turns to the entrance and waves at a tall man who struggles his way to the stall through the narrow space. Kuroda nods to Hirano, who renews his juggling with herbs, raw eggs, shrimps, and eggplants. In no time four small dishes materialize on the counter, and the two go on their business, ignoring me altogether, what seems to me totally un-Japanese. Hirano promptly returns to lecturing on Golden Gai. He nods at the direction of the new customer and whispers,

"Inoue, a film director. You see, intellectuals come here, artists, writers; movie directors; museum curators; aging Communists; sixties' revolutionaries; serious journalists, as well as tabloid writers on sex, sports, and the Yakuza. Cultural celebrities are all around.

Everywhere you go in Golden Gai you see their faded photographs hanging on the peeling walls of of the little dens around here. Signatures, drawings, pieces of paper sodden with the juices of the world.

"People come here to talk about the world, about politics, apocalypse, solitude, the Vision, the dream, the falling off, art, gossip, the economy, Marilyn Monroe, Pavarotti, the Yakuza wars, who's coming up, who's going down, Kabuki actors, the stock exchange—but mainly who's flying upward and who's in a tailspin and isn't around anymore.

"And they're thrilled when they meet the erotic darkness of the Yakuza-world. Yuki, your friend, too, is an intellectual, although he wouldn't admit it. And he knows them, the Yakuza. You believe me, Yakobu-san, he knows them closely. But he doesn't dribble when he sees them. He's got nerves, I tell you."

I stare at Yuki, who's obviously embarrassed by Hirano's last observation. He asks for another botltle of sake, and lowers his head. I know. I'd better leave it at that. Hirano sees everything.

"Believe me," he says, "I see those intellectuals drooling when they glimpse a tattooed arm. When they rub up against a mid-level *aniki* (big brother) of the Yakuza. You could think they're watching a live show.

"Especially the jounralists. Gossip-hungry, they treat the Yakuza to drinks, hoping they'll be lucky to fish up some news about the high politics of the Yakuza. Who's fighting whom, for what turf. Who's been arrested, who's in prison, who's been ostracized, who's been killed. What's going on with the Taiwanese and Chinese gangs. Whose daughter's getting married to whom."

Yuki, sitting next to me, shrinks. And I wonder, am I missing something?

"There's good jazz here, and opera, and food that can't be defined."

The night goes on, with drinks and delicacies, and an array of types that come and go. A gallery of suits, jackets, T-shirts, jeans, black shoes, white shoes, slippers. The two celebrities next to me rise to leave, but the film producer stops for a second to bow slightly to the girl in orange. Again, I perceive a quick look between the girl and Yuki.

One evening someone comes in, and everyone stops talking. I look back and see the giant goon from downstairs. What's he doing here? The man is tall, wearing a long-sleeved silk shirt decorated with manga figures. On his nose are sunglasses. He walks in with haughty meekness that freezes the atmosphere. He looks around and produces an incomprehensible grunt. Everybody nods a faint greeting with a bow, a bit tense. Hirano goes on with his work. Yuki, I see, shows the man a lot of respect.

Before the man sits down, Yuki whispers, "It's one of them, the Shimada-Kai family."

Who is he? Is Yuki related to the goon?

The man sits next to us. He bows to me. I bow back. He looks embarrassed. Yuki introduces me. The man relaxes when he finds out I can speak Japanese. When he hears "Israel," he goes, "Tatatatatatatatatatarrrrrrrr" and pantomimes shooting a machine gun. He laughs. "Israel is like Yakuza," he says. "Exactly! Tatatatarrr." He laughs at his own joke, stops, and bows again. "No offense. I am. They call me Big Shibata. Nice to meet you. And you?"

"I am Yakobu. Nice to meet you." I introduce myself in the Japanese version of my name, Ya'akov.

"Yakobu? A strange name."

"It's a Jewish name."

"Oh, Jewish! You Jews are like us Yakuza, aren't you? Outcasts!" Bursts of laughter. Then he turns serious in a flash and says, "Keep an eye on Yuki, and he'll keep an eye on you. I'm his aniki, his big brother, you understand? Aniki. And he's my kid brother. And I myself am the younger brother of his big brother, Murata Yoshinori, who's an oyabun in Hokkaido, in the north. Yakuza VIP. You don't understand? Yuki is the real brother of Yoshinori Oyabun. I'm his younger brother, but in the Yakuza sense, and that's more than a flesh-and-blood brother. One more sake! Murata Oyabun, he'll be big-shot in the Yakuza world, believe me."

I look at Yuki. He never told me his brother was a Yakuza. Yuki nods apologetically.

Shibata goes on. "Yuki isn't exactly a Yakuza. But one day he'll be. His brother is an oyabun. He's doing great things. Yuki is half-katagi and half Yakuza. One day he'll understand, and he'll drink the cup of *sakazuki* with us. I myself will drink with him. I promise you." He bursts into hearty laughter, heavy with pungent smell of sake vapors, and then bares his arms. Colorful images astonish the eye with red, blue, and green irezumi tattoos.

He pours sake into my cup and raises his own. "*Kampai!*" he shouts. Everyone around responds with a meek "kampai," except for the girl in orange. I notice that the pinky of Shibata's left hand is missing.

I'm curious to hear more about the Yakuza, but I don't dare ask. That night Yuki doesn't exchange looks with the girl in orange. Later in the evening she leaves with Big Shibata, not looking at Yuki even once.

We don't leave the place until dawn. Yuki is drunk and chatters about everything from poetry to politics and manga. Then he suddenly stops and announces, "I'm going to join the great Sekida family. Or the Murata family, my brother's. Whatever. And you should know now that you too, Sensei, are coming with me, gaijin or no gaijin. You're my brother, and you'll be a Yakuza! An Israeli Yakuza. Tomorrow we're going to get amazing irezumi on our whole body."

After that night, Yuki doesn't talk about his Yakuza family, or why he's there, or who his famous brother is. Nor does he talk about his plans to join this or that Yakuza family. Every once in a while the girl in orange appears, takes her cocktail, and sends a swift glance at Yuki. The girl makes me uneasy.

The People of Golden Gai

Each of the owners of the little places in Golden Gai has a mad story. There is an avant-garde actor, who, along with the food, offers you little plays that he writes, designs, directs, and performs. In another place, the mistress of a midlevel Yakuza demonstrates her supposed independence by showering all men with poems, insults, and curses. There is a retired backpacker who's returned from journeys in Africa, Morocco, and the deserts of Australia. He serves "ethnic foods" that he invents every night. You'll find a former prostitute there who became disgusted with her work and is content to serve food and drinks that she concocts.

They all have stories, and they all have their own customers, their own foods and drinks (which are theirs alone), and their walls are covered with posters, drawings, cartoons, books, and magazines that testify to the places from which the owners have fallen—the famous university, the hi-tech company, the symphony orchestra. Each one of them could fill a novel, and the pages wouldn't contain the power, the pain, and the lunacy that the person carries with him every evening to Golden Gai. The customers here rub together their pains and sorrows, never to be alleviated, while the man or woman on the other side of the counter improvises conversations and real stories of adventure, courage, and suffering, while ceaselessly serving all sorts of tiny dishes, with a lot of drink.

But what you really see is the madness of these shamans of liquor and loneliness, those soul travelers in the narrow alleys of the metropolis. And me, peeping into their innards, taking my own expeditions into the gloom souls of the lower east side of Shinjuku.

For example, Okama Shoji is a transvestite and cook who likes to imitate men more than anything, and as precise as you may be with your observation, you can never tell that he's a man and not a pretty woman.

Or Aida, an ex-opera singer who's become a cook. The walls of his place are covered with theater and opera posters from the twenties, and given the slightest encouragement, he'll break out with

23

an "O Sole Mio" so powerful that it shakes the poster of *Carmina Burana*, exposing the nakedness of the faded wall beneath it. And he does wonders with his knife.

Nearby is Machiko's place, whose walls are bare, but whose hoarse voice attracts customers, and only the old-timers really know how little her boyish body reflects her many years. Only if you listen to her words can you know that she attracts her regulars because her astonishing history reverberates with them in hidden intimacy, at the edge of their bellies. They drink at her place and hear the mirror-image of their lives and the lives of their loves, and, miraculously, they aren't saddened, nor are they happy, but they're here at Machiko's, the temple of great woe and joy, two of a kind.

Nearby is Mayumi's place. She's only twenty-five, and there are various rumors about the circumstances that enabled her to buy her place here. She too washes and cuts, fries and grills, cooks and concocts and sautés while shouting, conversing, asking, arguing, scolding, expelling, and gossiping. Sometimes she sings and shakes her limbs in a tiny dance as far as the narrow space allows, and she consoles and drops her hands and curses and smiles and seduces and rejects—and there's no knowing what the next moment will bring with her.

The owner of Shadow, Shino Tatsuhiro, has been here since he was seventeen. He opened the place so he wouldn't have to do ordinary daytime work. He used to be a member of the Communist party, but now he detests the Communists. He speaks Japanese, English, German, French, and Russian. He doesn't smoke, and he doesn't drink. He comes to work on his bicycle; he's modest and meek, one of the sanest and squarest people in the area. He and his ten clients talk in Tokyoese, the language of the city's intellectuals, the Golden Gai dialect that can't be heard anywhere else in Tokyo or the rest of world. People come night after night for the gossip, the literary journals, the concert posters, and also for the "intelli-Yakuza"—a new breed of the underworld, who are lawyers, accountants, university graduates in history, architecture, business administration, law, political science—a variety of disciplines proving to be extremely useful in the sophisticated Yakuza businesses of the late-twentieth century.

Shadow's menu is French. Actually, it serves omelets, couscous, *fromage du jour*, and wines. Only French. The little nomiya is crammed with objects fished from the trash, a variety of discarded possessions, well suited to these alleys of ex-singers, ex-politicians, ex-men, ex-women, ex-criminals, ex-honest citizens. And Shino, innocently sane and square, masterfully conducts this choir.

The Dadaist bar of Golden Gai is called Jetée. Kawai, the owner, is taller than most of her clients. Jetée attracts film directors, cameramen, and jazz musicians. And Yakuza. Personal bottles of whiskey are kept in a rack on the wall decorated with select drawings by Kawai. You can find servings of salmon and special sake from the distant north. Edith Piaf's voice is in the air. Movie posters are on the wall, including pictures of Francis Ford Coppola, Wim Wenders, and other celebrities who visited the place. "Wim Wenders filmed this place in his movie *Tokyo-Ga*," I am reminded every time I come.

For Kawai, this is Tokyo's Montmartre, a temple to French cinema. Every year she travels to the Cannes film festival and brings back the fragrances of France. As the empress of this little nomiya, Kawai manages, cooks, serves, chats (in French and Japanese), reconciles, scolds, and mainly tells of the wonders of Provence and its mythical foods.

Golden Gai is like nothing else. And I, the frequent visitor, like a chameleon, I'm sometimes a singer, sometimes an impersonator, or a transvestite, sometimes a storyteller of and sometimes a listener to stories of suffering, swallowed up in the nothingness of Golden Gai's alleys.

People here like to lament Golden Gai. "Look, in a little while the end will come," they say. Then the Yakuza persuaders will appear. "Take money, we'll come tomorrow. Leave the place and get yourself an izakaya somewhere else. Take ten million. Take twenty million. We'll be back tomorrow. Think. We don't break anything. We're not the American Mafia. Get another place. Tokyo is so big, is it not? We don't break anything. We'll come every day. Arms bare. Tattoos and all the rest. We behave ourselves, don't we?"

*

Yuki looks at the girl in orange. Always in orange. She always lowers her gaze and puts out her cigarette in the personal purple ashtray. Always in a dark corner. And Big Shibata always waits for her downstairs. Sunglasses on his nose. Yuki doesn't tell. I don't ask.

At the Sugamo Stall

Back in Sugamo, Yuki and I prepare the stall for the night's activity. I bring water, learn how to prepare the sauce, and arrange the sake bottles.

I ask Yuki about the Yakuza. Yuki sighs. "I'm not a Yakuza. Not yet. Maybe I don't want to be a Yakuza. But maybe I'll be one. With family members I feel best. Even if they don't read literature. I'm a failure at home and worthless in my studies. I didn't even manage to work in a store. I don't have a single yen to my name. My work here is thanks to them. They protect me, and they're good to me. They're better to me than the people who think of themselves as guardians of the law. I'm not a Yakuza. But maybe I'll become one. We'll see. In another year, or two. I'm afraid of them. I also love them. They're tough men. They go all the way. And me, I like the middle way, no noise. They're my best friends. I don't have any others. They make things possible for me. Maybe one day, in a different life; who knows? I'm afraid of myself. I'm afraid of my madness. If I become a Yakuza, I'm afraid I'll go all the way, like them. I'm afraid and fascinated."

He sighs again. Looks at me. "I'm a nomad," he says to me.

"Me too," I say,

"I wander among worlds."

"Me too."

26

"The poet whom I'm named after, Ariwara no Yukihira, once wrote, more than a thousand years ago, 'We who pass our days next to the shores, where the white waves break, sons of fishermen are we, and there's no house we can call our own.'

"I once made dolls. I studied literature and poetry, I studied business management, I worked in a finance company, in a bookstore, I played guitar. I ran away from evil, and men of evil protect me. I haven't found a home."

"Yuki-san, I can also list the number of different jobs I've had and the many regions I've wandered in. So what? I came to your country to look for something I'll never find. Have I found a home yet? I don't know."

"But you're a university professor, aren't you. Don't laugh at me."

"How can being a professor alleviate that despair I see in your eyes? What's the use of my studies and my publications here in this tiny space of ours? When the smothering fear comes, nothing I teach can help. I'm helping you with the cooking here. That has nothing to do with my university. The university is just a perfect supplier of good excuses for doing what I do. Yuki-san, we're brothers. You see, don't you?"

He says nothing. On the bench I see three books. Two of them are collections of poems by Octavio Paz. One in Japanese, the other in Spanish. The third, in English, is a poem collection by Filipino poet Jose Garcia Villa.

"Did you know that Paz wrote haiku? That he translated Basho's journal, *Oku no Hosomichi*? I read him in Spanish. Slowly. Jose Garcia Villa? I'll understand him someday. He tells me what was and what will be. He points to my core of being, as if he were writing my own madness. He's my great teacher. Sometime I'll go to his Philippines, to understand, maybe. Read his *The Anchored Angel*. Read his *Have Come, Am Here*. It could have been mine. Read it."

I read. "*I will break God's seamless skull and I will break His kissless mouth/ O I'll break out of His faultless shell and fall me upon Eve's gold mouth/ This is the death I will stand on.*"

"Yuki?"

27

"Yes?"

"Did you like the poem?"

"A blow to the skull. Why did you say it's your poem?"

"Because he's left me, God. On the cross. And when I called, He didn't answer. Read this, too"

I read. *"I can no more hear love's voice/ No more moves the mouth of her/ Birds no more sing/ O my God! I am dead."*

"Yuki. Please tell me."

"Sensei, God has left me. I can no more hear love's voice. The poems are clear, aren't they? Is it so hard to understand? And my palms, they're bleeding, you see—don't you?"

"Tell me!"

"Tomorrow. How can I not tell you? I'll tell you tomorrow."

First Meeting with Yakuza

One night, at three in the morning, on my way back to my apartment, I see a man standing in the center of Sugamo Square, holding an umbrella upside down hitting an imaginary golf ball. His hair is short and wavy. Sunglasses. He hits the imaginary ball.

"Nice shot!" I say, and he halts his movement, looks at me.

"Hi!" he calls to me. "You're the gaijin who hangs around with Yuki. He told me about you. You should know that Yuki is my dearest kobun. You hear? My most precious. He hasn't had the sakazuki ceremony yet, but it's like he did. You live here, yes? I'm the boss here, and I know everything. The bars. The Turkish bath. They're all mine. Here, take my card."

He hands me a business card, and on it, in swirling characters, is written:

Okawa-Kai Family
Shimada-Kay Branch
Hayashi House
Head of the House Hayashi Yasue

Splendid calligraphy. Curling in gold.

"I'm Hayashi, and I'm the boss. And if you want, everything here is available to you. Turkish bath? Ladies' club? Men's? A little palace where they rub your body with honey and then lick it off? My treat. Because Yuki likes you. Think about it. Call me. Anytime. That's my office number. Say that you're Yuki's friend. Say you're Hayashi Oyabun's friend. Come and visit.

"Do you know what Yakuza is? Yakuza is a hard life. Also a good life. Not child's play. One day you're a great lord, and one day, poof, you're nothing. A path of extremes. Gokudo. You see? Call me up. Because Yuki likes you, like a brother. Then it's also like you are my son too, you see?"

He swings the umbrella and hits the imaginary ball into the night.

Brotherhood

And so it goes on. I ask Yuki questions. He delicately escapes away into his exacting cookery.

One evening he arrives at the stand with a fresh, deep scar on his cheek, but he's still tight-lipped. He talks about politics, literature, cooking, philosophy—just not what happened. His left eye twitches more than ever.

"Yuki, the girl in orange. Who is she?"

Silence. Then, "I don't know."

"Yuki, I saw!"

He looks at me in astonishment, as if I'd seen something beneath his skin.

A sigh. "I mustn't look at her."

"Who is she? And that scar, is it connected? What do you mean, you mustn't? It's a free country."

A sigh. "Don't push me. I'm not allowed, and that's it."

One evening he doesn't arrive at the stand. I suddenly realize I have no address or telephone number. Nothing.

29

The next day he comes as usual. Impatient, and before I ask, he says, "Another time, Yakobu-san. I'll tell you, but not today. Yakobu-san, you're like my brother, and I can't not tell you. But not now. It wouldn't be good for you if I told you now. Leave it alone."

Then, suddenly, he takes a little sake cup. He takes the sake bottle from me, quickly pours it into the cup, and says to me, breathing quickly, "Repeat after me, Yakobu-san."

I look at him confused.

"Repeat after me! With the drinking of this cup …"

I clear my throat. "With the drinking of this cup …"

"I, Murata Yukihira from Hokkaido, and you, Yakobu Razu, from Israel …"

"I, Ya'akov Raz, from Israel, and you, Murata Yukihira, from Hokkaido …"

"Have become five-five brothers. Equal borthers."

"Have become five-five brothers. Tell me, Yuki, what—"

"Drink! Three and a half sips!"

I drink three sips and half a sip.

He drinks three sips and half a sip. He exhales a long breath. "That's how they do it; did you know?"

"No. Who?"

"When they become brothers."

"What does that mean, become brothers? Who becomes brothers? Yuki, could you explain—"

"We're equal brothers. You said so, remember? 'Like brothers.' You were the one who said so, right? You chose me as a brother. I chose you as a brother. Every evening. I'm deeply grateful. No one, not even my real brother, was willing to be witness to my wounds. You're willing, and so you're my brother. Now we're responsible for each other. We have *giri,* total obligation. Do you know anything about giri in our world?"

"I know from books … but not really."

"Now let's get the stand ready. The customers will come soon."

Yuki Disappears

I traveled to the distant north for a month on the trail of the nomadic men and women I studied. I return, as usual, to Yuki's stall in Sugamo Square. But Yuki's not there. Another man is standing in his place. A thin man with sunken eyes is preparing the food.

"Where's Yuki?" I ask.

"Who's Yuki?" he asks. "Never heard of any Yuki."

"But Yuki was here. For months and months Yuki was here! He's my friend."

"Don't know any Yuki. Never heard of Yuki. Something to drink?"

"No thanks."

From that day Yuki wasn't to be seen at Sugamo. No one knows any Yuki. I make inquiries at the restaurants and stall owners and friends around the square. They don't know. Some say, "Don't ask."

I wander around the neighborhood and try to find Hayashi Oyabun. After all, he's the boss. He'll tell me what happened to Yuki. But it's also impossible to find Hayashi. I try asking about Hayashi, and there's no answer. Some people hint, quite crudely, that I'd better stop asking about Hayashi. That I'd better not ask anything at all. I go to the Murasaki and check with Hirano. No. He hasn't seen him.

The girl in orange isn't there either.

What happened?

What happened to him? Where is he?

Chapter Three

Meeting the Yakuza—
Scenes from the Underworld

First Steps, 1986

Three years after Yuki's disappearance, and all my efforts to learn anything have been fruitless. I give up and turn to my regular activities: research, teaching, and other things. But the image of Yuki—somewhere in the world—keeps returning, won't leave me alone. As if it were seeking redemption. Then one day I say, I'll try to make contact with the Yakuza. After all, he was almost one of them. And indeed, I did try again and again to contact the Yakuza but failed.

One such attempt began in Takayama town, at the foot of the Hida Mountains, on the day of the autumn *matsuri* (festival). At the time of the festival an open-air market is set up around the Hachiman Shrine. If you walk there at evening time you face a line of red lanterns, behind which you will see stalls offering noodles and shirts and green bottles and toys and lottery tickets, and you can see craftsmen make glass animals—tigers, foxes, and delicate deer.

That evening I stand there with my friend Shiroshita when a big black car approaches, and the whole fair is reflected in its fenders, and everyone behind the stalls jumps to attention. A large man gets out. His hair is black, his suit is black, his glasses are black, his shoes are black. In front of him are two young men who are very sure of their path. There is fear around and a lot of respect. A glass deer falls from someone's hands and breaks.

"Yakuza," Shiroshita whispers. "Until today they never came to our town. What do they want from us?"

I breathe deeply and say to Shiroshita, "I want to get to know these people."

Shiroshita looks at me. "You're out of your mind!"

"I'm a gaijin. Nothing will happen to me. Do you know where I can find a lead?"

"Yakobu-san, you're crazy! They're dangerous!"

Two days later he gives in and says, "In Tokyo, near Fuchu Station, across from the railroad station, there's a pub, Moonlight. The mamasan is Mikako, an old friend. a I'll call her up and introduce you. She knows them. They come there to drink. Try. But you're nuts. Be very careful!"

*

Tokyo. The Moonlight Bar. Noon. Mikako, who was once beautiful and now wears heavy makeup still displays the smile that brought her to sinful Tokyo from her little village in the mountains twenty years ago. She smiles at me and wonders who I am and what and why, and after hearing me out and enquiring thoroughly, she says, "Fine. Tomorrow I'll come with a low-level Yakuza, and you'll talk to him, and then we'll see if we go on to the boss."

The next day she introduces me to Shinoda, a stout, weary man who is sitting sideways, facing the door. Without any preliminaries he asks me what I want.

"I want to get to know you," I answer directly. "I would like to study your society." I'm a visiting professor at this and this university, and I want to study your society so I can understand why you are what you are, why the sunglasses in the middle of the night, and why the glass deer broke at the fair in Takayama when the huge black car

33

appeared, and your connection to Japanese culture, etc. He listens. Says nothing. He then says he'll ask. Then he leaves.

The next day I call up the pub. But there, in the Moonlight, they don't know where Mikako is today. No, they don't know when she'll be back. They don't know. No. They never heard of the Yakuza. They don't know Shinoda. Yakuza don't come here. Mikako has gone away. She's not there. They don't know when she'll come back. She's out of town. Sorry.

I say a careful "sorry," and there is silence on the line. I put the receiver down softly.

1987, First Contact

I fail over and over in my efforts to contact the Yakuza. I try intermediaries. I try with someone who knows someone who knows someone who might show me the beginning of the trail. People promise to come and don't show up. They say they'll introduce someone but then disappear. One person discourages, another warns. Some give me angry looks. Some laugh at me. Some say I'm looking for trouble.

This goes on until November 1987, at the Hanazono Shrine in the Shinjuku Quarter of Tokyo, there is a breakthrough.

It is the Otori Matsuri Festival and amulet market. They sell masks and flowers, deities of good fortune made of plastic or painted wood. A fair for good luck and good business. Alleys of stalls are carefully set around the Hanazono Shrine. At the entrance to every alley is a cloth banner that says "Kinoshita Group," "Shimonoseki Association," or "Love of Homeland Society."

One of the signs says "Okawa-Kai Group," and I remember: the Okawa-Kai is one of the most powerful Yakuza families in Tokyo. I recall that it is headed by Okawa Oyabun, the oyabun of Hayashi from Sugamo whom I met four years ago.

The alley is decorated with colorful lanterns. And next to one of the stalls, there he is, my future friend: Fukuoka Ken'ichi, outlaw and poet. He's short. A cloth cap covers a bald head. He wears a T-shirt and striped jacket and maintains a wide stance.

Fukuoka Ken'ichi is the lord of this place, and everybody bows very deeply to him. He smiles beneficently and is hugged by a pair of bodyguards, one of whom holds a little black bag under his arm, and the other hands Fukuoka a little flame for his cigarette and other small and big services, everything by a hint. A blink of an eyelid, a tiny movement of the head, raising a finger.

Without doubt the man inspires great respect—or fear?—in the people about him. But he looks around as if he wants to be somewhere else. His narrow eyes are worn out from years of merciless survival, and they still seek a good fight.

He stands next to a mask booth and talks to the seller. I approach the stand and ask the seller in Japanese what these decorations are.

Fukuoka observes me, savoring my presence. Then he begins a lecture on the religious significance of masks. "Do you understand?" he asks.

"Yes, thank you," I say.

"Your Japanese is very good!"

"No. Not at all," I say.

Then he suddenly says, "Sake!" Two little cups materialize as if from nowhere. Someone pours sake into both cups. He opens his mouth to say something, but I stop him.

I hand him my cup and take his, and I say, "With the drinking of this cup, we have become brothers, from now on, forever. Go out on the path of wandering, knight of the Gokudo, the path of extremes!"

Silence all around. It was a bad joke.

More silence.

The two bodyguards mutter something guttural.

Fukuoka recovers his wits first and says, "How do you know? Where did you learn it? Where did you get to know that vow? And how do you know we're Yakuza? D'you know this is the most sacred vow in our world?"

35

Is he applauding my daring act, or is he threatening me? I now regret my cheek. I meekly reply, "From the movies I know, from Yakuza movies." Which is true.

Fukuoka ponders for a moment and bursts into loud laughter. He orders his bodyguards to refill our cups.

I call on my courage and take out my business card, in Japanese. He looks carefully at the card and reads it out loud,: "Yakobu Razu, visiting professor. The Institute for the Study of the Cultures of Asia and Africa.

Grumbling from the bodyguards.

He tries to pronounce my name, "Yakobu Razu. University professor?

I breathe deeply and say, "I want to study your world."

Silence. Then he says, "We're gangsters. Criminals. You know that, don't you? What's so interesting about gangsters? Who'll let you in, anyway?"

"I don't know. Maybe you will?"

"Me?"

"Yes. I'd also like to get to know Okawa Oyabun."

Silence.

"Our oyabun is a great man. The greatest. I don't know if he'll give it even a thought."

Silence.

"But I'll talk to him anyway," he finally says.

Fukuoka takes out a business card decorated with fancy calligraphy, swirling with golden characters:

Okawa-Kai Family
Okawa Kai Branch
Fukuoka House
House Head Fukuoka Ken'ichi

He writes his home phone number on the card. The two bodyguards exchange glances. I bow deeply in sincere and dumbstruck gratitude.

Two weeks later he calls, and he speaks in a staccato rhythm: "Yakobu Sensei! Fukuoka here! I spoke with Okawa Oyabun! He agrees! He'll talk with you! Come next week to the Washington Hotel in Shinjuku! The Momoyama Hall! We're having a banquet. Come at six thirty. Before the banquet! Ask for me! He'll come and talk to you. We'll see! I am relieved! See you later!! You don't know how lucky you are!"

*

The Washington Hotel is all white. The waiters are in white. The reception desk is white. On the second floor, in front of the white entrance to the violet Momoyama Hall, a few dozen men are standing. Legs apart. They wear white, pink, violet striped suits. Wide, colorful ties. Platinum, gold, and brass pins adorn their lapels. Lots of sunglasses. Very short hair. Or curly. Aftershaved faces. Scarred faces. Smooth faces. White shoes, pink shoes, sometimes black and white. Hotel guests bypass cautiously. Waiters and waitresses bow very deeply when they serve the drinks. One of the Yakuza catches my eyes. He is blond. Natural blond. His eyes are Japanese, but his nose is European. He is short, sturdy. His eyes are penetrating. Someone calls him Jimmy. He looks an insider yet an outsider to this company of Yakuza. I am curious.

I'm standing at the head of the stairs with a big bottle of sake in my hand, a gesture of gratitude for Fukuoka for introducing me to Okawa Oybaun. *I am here,* I say to myself, *there's no going back.*

At the banquet reception table they know about me. Everyone is polite. Fukuoka is already waiting in a black kimono, irezumi peeping out from under his sleeve. He greets me with a deep bow, replete with fluent Japanese courtesy, and leads me to an empty auditorium.

"You have ten minutes," he whispers and disappears. I wait. A few minutes pass.

Outside a shout is suddenly heard: "*Ooossssssss!*"

He enters.

Okawa Oyabun. Two men at his side. One of them is Fukuoka Ken'ichi. His bald head gleams. He is obviously excited. The other one is in a blue silk suit and a violet tie, with a smallish beard and a face carved of stone, his head covered with short spikes. I see a little bulge under his armpit.

"Meet Fujita Tetsuya," Fukuoka says.

We bow.

"And meet Okawa Oyabun." He bows slightly. I bow deeply.

Okawa looks different from the people gathering outside. Nothing special. I wouldn't have noticed him in a crowd of Japanese businessmen, I note. Glasses in a thin, gold frame. Thinning hair neatly combed. A beige suit. A conservatively colored tie. Nothing special. The tough guys on both sides look like they should—Yakuza inside out. He and they don't belong to the same world. But he's their oyabun, the boss of the gathering gang outside the auditorium. He's their legendary much-feared leader. One of the most respected oyabuns in the Yakuza world. And he looks so normal.

Then he looks at me. Not arrogant or apologetic. Certainly not menacing. It is a relaxed, penetrating, waiting gaze.

He sits next to me. I notice the stump of a pinky on his left hand. He looks at me for a long time, smiling simply, and asks, "What do you want?"

I hand him my card. I explain everything. "I want to do research. You interest me as human beings. I don't want to learn about you from books, from policemen, from the newspapers, or from criminologists who once spent two hours with you in detention. I want to know you from the inside. Not through one or two interviews. I would like to get close to the way you live, think, feel pain, grow your children, get hurt, overcome your loneliness. To know your life history: where you came from, what you escaped from, why you joined this world, how you see your own and your children's future, your hopes and fears, your hobbies, your food. In short, I'm asking your permission to get acquainted with you as human beings, not as knights or demons.

And I would like to know you in order to know Japan better. I don't think one could do it without meeting you." I talk fast, as if I will never have another opportunity. As if I have nothing to lose.

He looks again. He says nothing and stares for several silent minutes. Finally he smiles and says, "Okay. I'll cooperate. Today you'll stay with us for the banquet, and next Sunday you'll come to my house. We'll talk there."

At that moment Tetsuya, who had accompanied him here, pops up at our side. He says to me, "Sensei, I'll come and take you to the oyabun. Your address, please!"

"No, no! There's no need. I'll come by myself."

"No, Sensei. I'm coming to get you. Your address!"

I give him my address.

I stay for the banquet, sitting in a place of honor next to Okawa Oyabun. The first part is amazingly boring, businesslike, with tiresome speeches about political alliances, and other stuff you could see at any business or political gathering at any end-of-the-year party. Greatly disappointed, I wonder whether it is a performance put on for me.

Then comes the entertainment part. A pretty girl mounts the stage. The lights dim, and the restrained decency on the faces of the men in the audience is replaced by leers at the pretty girl. Her breasts are perfectly round. She dances a seductive dance, slowly stripping just to expose her muscular, manly arms and legs. She is a man. The audience cheers and shouts and whoops and demands an encore. He returns to perform another dance.

At the Oyabun's House

It's Sunday. A gigantic black Mercedes Benz with opaque windows appears next to my apartment house in the small neighborhood in western Tokyo. Tetsuya gets out. He's wearing a black suit. He bows deeply. Some neighbors peek. Black cars like that, men with that haircut—well, everybody knows who *they* are. What's the professor doing in this man's company?

I get in the car, into a luxurious salon, a bar stocked with a variety of drinks. A television screen. A *go* board, ready for a game. Black velvet curtains on the windows.

I sit in the back and Tetsuya is at the wheel. First he is tense and formal. After a few minutes he starts smiling. My questions. His questions. Who? From where? Why? He tells little about himself and lavishly praises Okawa Oyabun.

"We Yakuza and the katagi Japanese aren't on good terms," he says. "The katagi hate the Yakuza. All of them. Out of ten Japanese, ten hate us." He fears the katagi Japanese, I note.

He has never traveled by train, just taxis and planes. We chat. I forget that I'm an excited scholar. He forgets that he has to represent the Yakuza. The drive in Tokyo is long, an hour or so. At the end of the drive, we become friends. He invites me to his home next week.

After a long drive through winding streets, we are at Okawa Oyabun's home in a decent upper middle class residential area. Private homes. Gardens. Private parking lots.

We enter the parking area and get out at the entrance to the house. We remove our shoes. At the entrance stands Okawa's wife, pleasant and courteous. The entrance hall is surprisingly middle class. No bodyguards seen. If they're here, they're well hidden. We are invited to the living room, half-Western in style. Armchairs. A high table. A sofa. A big piano. Who plays it? On one of the side walls is a large glass picture of a large peacock, shifting colors by means of some electric device, which is hardly a Japanese common middle-class style.

I'm in the home of one of the most powerful, respected, venerated, and feared bosses in the Yakuza world, Okawa Oyabun.

A pretty young girl passes by. Her mother introduces her as their nineteen-year-old daughter Machiko. She's studying Christian studies and Western art at the university. The girl is acutely polite, but her eyes are inquisitive. Then another girl comes in, Kimiko, the younger sister. Both girls call Tetsuya Uncle Tetsuya, and there's evidently mutual affection among the three. For the girls, Tetsuya is certainly not one of the three "terrors" of Northeastern Japan, as his reputation goes. Here he serves tea, his head bowed submissively. Okawa's wife brings refreshments and drinks. Tetsuya helps her and then disappears somewhere with her. Okawa and I are alone in the room now.

I take out a tape recorder and ask if I may. Okawa Oyabun says, "Please."

I turn it on. For the following six hours we talk. From time to time Okawa raises his voice and requests something. His wife or Tetsuya swiftly respond at the drop of a word. Sometimes it's a question about a date, someone's name, a document, a request for food or drink. Everything materializes in a flash. For six hours I ask and he speaks. A flow of words. Pleasant, intelligent, witty. He doesn't try to prettify. No stories about Yakuza being the Japanese Robin Hoods. He is totally different from the oyabun figure appearing in books, in comics, or in the newspapers.

He rarely asks me to turn off the tape recorder. For six hours he tells me of his life and his Yakuza worldview: That he was born in Korea, that he was imprisoned for robbery during the Second World War. That he found a home with the Yakuza. That he loves Korea and his daughters, and his wife, and his many kobun sons in the Yakuza. That he's looking for honor and dignity in this world. That he knows he won't succeed. That he sees the gangsterization of the Yakuza. That he's worried. That he's not healthy. That he's terribly worried.

Evening comes, and we are tired. Then he calls Tetsuya and says, "We'll start with the *shoba-wari*. Bring him to the shoba-wari. It's the ceremony for allotting places before the matsuri"the Japanese festival. It is the working of the delicate balance of Yakuza powers behind the scenes. That way you'll understand a lot. The day after tomorrow there's the shoba-wari ceremony at the Hachiman Shrine near Waseda University. Tetsuya, take him there.

"Gradually I'll introduce you to the kobun, my sons, and to the various oyabuns. Slowly. Never hurry. We'll see how things develop.

Gradually you can see things and meet people. Go to Tetsuya's home, and you can see what things are like in our homes. He has a sweet kid. Start, and we'll see.

"You're from Israel. You Jews ought to understand us because we're of the same cloth. Rejected wanderers. We developed our own ways of getting respect and making a living. And our own language. Same race, Sensei."

"Thank you," I say at the end of a long day.

"Before I leave," I say, "I have a request. I want to find a friend who disappeared a long time ago. He's precious to me, and I'm worried about him."

I tell him Yuki's story. He listens and says, "You understand that I have a lot of power here, in this Yakuza world. Still, I can't promise anything. Yakuza is a world of vanishing people. Sometimes it's their wish. Sometimes because of other things. Usually they don't want us to find them. But I'll check. I'll do my best. Good night."

Okawa Oyabun Speaks, Part One

"I'm Korean, not Japanese. My real name is Chong. I came here as a child from Korea with my father, to find work in Japan. Those were times of poverty and distress in Japan. My family lived from hand to mouth. At that time, during the Second World War, the Koreans were Japanese citizens, but there was discrimination, like today. It was hard. I started to make friends with a rough crowd.

"One day I got sick and tired of poverty and abuse. One day we're hungry. One day somebody says come with us. Somebody organizes, brings together, gives a pistol, brings a car, leads, threatens, tempts. One day we assemble. We drive, hearts pounding. Outside the city, we learn to shoot. Bang-bang into a tree. The tree's heart shatters. One day we drive. At the end of the city—a house. A bamboo fence. It's dark. Here's money. Here are art objects. Here are nice clothes. A moment of joy. A moment of fear. Of boiling blood. Here's the bag. Here's the loot and the end of shame. Then, the police! The sound of a muffled blow. Somebody falls. His face twists. He's not here anymore … seven years in jail. The end of the war. They say the Americans are giving out guns. I change my name from Chong to Okawa, a Japanese name …"

Behind the Scenes of the Festival

"Come and see shoba-wari, where we allocate pkaces for the different families before the festival. Matsuri, the Japanese religious festival, is the soul of Japan. Matsuri last from a day or two up to about ten days. There too we make a good living. Hundred of people come to a little matsuri. Thousands come to middle-sized ones. Tens of thousands come to a great matsuri. And there are some matsuri that attract millions, the matsuri for Kobo Daishi in Kawasaki, for example. Gigantic. That's a lot of revenue. Millions of yen. Mostly without income tax. What do you say? Maybe you'd like to be a fortune-teller, or sell sweet ices, or fried octopus? Come and see."

I go with Tetsuya. Two days before the matsuri at the Hachiman Shrine near Waseda University. Tough-looking Yakuza gather in the temple courtyard. All smoking. Clusters of Yakuza. Someone must to be organizing this gathering.

In a corner far away from the temple, beneath a tree, is a table. Two men are sitting there, and at the side, an awning, and the man sitting under, in sunglasses and black kimono, appears to be receiving great respect. Young men rush to serve tea, to light a cigarette, to hand him a fan.

The men whisper to each other. Tense. Sideward glances.

"What's going on?" I ask Tetsuya.

He whispers, "Not here; not now." He leads me to a deserted corner and tells me, "Recently, men from the Yamada-Gumi family have been trying to squeeze into Tokyo any way they can. Until now the Yamada-Gumi, following an agreement among the big families, could be active only in western Japan: Kobe, Osaka, Kyoto. They didn't go past Nagoya to the east. Now they're trying harder to move in the direction of Tokyo and the region. Not long ago a little clash started in Sapporo, on Hokkaido Island, where we're strong. If we don't stop them in time, there will be a war here."

"And what's happening today?"

"They're trying to get into this matsuri. This is a medium-size matsuri. The profits aren't bad. They'll try to feel out how solid we are here."

From far away you can feel the growing tension. Three men arrive. Yamada-Gumi, I'm told. Suits, ties, sunglasses. The swaggering gait. Their heads slightly down. That blend of arrogance and meekness. They stand at the side. One of the standing men approaches them. They huddle together. The man points in the direction of the awning. The three men straighten their suits. They pull themselves up tall and walk toward the awning. The man sitting under the awning seems to be ignoring them. He's smoking, eyes hidden behind black sunglasses.

The three men approach. They stop about fifteen feet away. One advances a little closer and stops. Suddenly he bows forward, spreads his legs, places his left hand on his back and his right hand on his right knee, with the palm up—announcing that he's unarmed—and says in a meek voice, "I, Matsumura Hideo, a man of meager deeds, my birthplaces is the Nagano prefecture. I come here from the Matsudaira area of the Nagano prefecture. I am a member of the Kokusui family, headed by the great Inaba Oyabun the Seventh. My father is the great and honored Matsumura Oyabun the Third, who lives in the city of Matsudaira; him and his fathers and his fathers' fathers, since the Edo times. I am a worthless son of the great Matsumura, a doormat for you to tread upon. I have no weapons, and I place myself in your hands, Maeda Oyabun, that you might offer refuge and livelihood to the lowliest of sons and teach me the ways of Gokudo, the Path of Extremes.

"Behold, I am in your hands. Protect me. I am a stranger in this city, and the *satsu* (police, in Yakuza slang) are on my trail. Whatever you give me, I will accept. I have made my way here to support my wife and children and to bring honor and a livelihood to the great Kokusui family in the Nagano prefecture. Please accept me under your protection during the matsuri and give me a modest place on the edge of the fair so I can bring rice to my family."

The man under the awning, Maeda Oyabun, doesn't move. He keeps smoking. He looks in the direction of Matsumura, and his face is expressionless. Then he turns his gaze upon the two men at his side, and then toward the two sitting at the table. All of them move their heads very slightly. He turns his gaze back to Matsumura, who is still bowing. They stare at each other. Matsumura inclines his head even more. Then Maeda Oyabun also bows, just with his head, a slight bow.

"Very well," he says. "The Path of Extremes will not abandon the persecuted. We will give you some of the little that is in our hands. This matsuri is modest, and there isn't enough to earn for our sons. But we'll share it with you. Go to the table with my blessing, and you'll receive a place, a stall, and may you make a good living."

Matsumura straightens up. Then he makes a very deep bow. He is about to go, and then Maeda Oyabun adds, "And return to me after you've put up your stall."

Matsumura stops and looks at Maeda. He bows and walks to the table. On the way he notices me. Stops again. Goes on. Near the table he bows again. Bows are exchanged.

A map is spread out on the table, and everyone gathers around. He approaches and looks at the map on which are marked row after row of stalls. Each stall is numbered, from the shrine outward. The main row is the one leading from the temple to the main street. A place near the shrine is a good one. The further you go from the shrine, the worse the location. Worshippers on the way back from the shrine, after receiving the sacred blessing, stroll back along the stalls, ready to eat, drink, buy toys, clothes, goldfish, sweets, amulets. There's where the good money is.

"During the week of the matsuri," Tetsuya says, "you can make a lot of money, Sensei, a lot of money! Straight money. No income tax. And there is also protection money. Anyone who's not a member of the Yakuza pays protection money, and I keep hassles away from him. How much protection money? Depends on the place. Depends on the income. Depends on the man's face. We used to take just a little from Israelis. Now we take a lot. Why? Because they earn pretty well. Because they're bold. Because they have their own oyabuns, and that raises the price. Whomever belongs to an organization has to pay more, no? Whomever's a lone wolf or has no protection, so I protect him, right?"

The man in charge of allotting places starts by announcing: "Kurokawa, number seventy-five!"

Kurokawa bows, places an envelope on the table, and goes to erect his stall.

"Sumiyoshi! Seventy-four!" and so on.

The waiting men are anxious to know their placement numbers. Where will they put the men from Yamada-Gumi? At whose expense? Who will be angry? Who will make a little note for himself? Who, maybe, will pull something out of his pocket? The tension rises.

Then: "Matsumura! Forty-seven!" Matsumura from the Yamada-Gumi puts down an envelope, makes a deep bow, and goes to put up his stall. A pause. Men huddle. Whispers. Grumbles here and there. They return to the table.

Only Tetsuya is quiet, almost amused. "Most of the people know in advance where they'll get a stall. The map has been ready since yesterday. Most of the places are known for years. This and that place to this and that family. Yesterday I got a telephone call from an oyabun in the city of Sendai, asking me for a good place for his new kobun. He promised a good place for my kobun when he goes to Sendai for the big matsuri there. That's how it is. It's a sensitive business. Can be lethal. Whoever tries to go against it is in very big danger. This map is the map of power relations in the area. Behind it is a very delicate network of relations among the families, among the oyabuns. Give and take. You only change it if you're willing to pay for the change. Or with a pistol. But it's a very delicate balance.

And you'd better have a very good reason to dare to use a gun to get a good place at the matsuri. A very, very good reason.

"Those three men from Yamada-Gumi came today, and the delicate balance is thrown off. It's impossible to refuse. If a Yakuza declares that he's running away from the police, you can't refuse him. So they're using the Yakuza code to penetrate us. That's dirty, and they'll pay for it. So what do you say to my offer? Do you want to be a fortune-teller or to sell fried octopus? What do you say? Your stall will be very popular. A gaijin fortune-teller. Oooff! That'll be a hit."

He breaks out in laughter.

Everyone is busy now putting up the stalls, carrying the goods. Some of the peddlers are rehearsing their musical patter to lure customers at the real show, which is tomorrow: "Hey! You! You nice kid! Come! Come! Goldfish! Transformer, Autobots! Cute animals! Tell Dad!"

*

The matsuri opens the next day, and the place is bursting with colors, sounds, music, the cries of peddlers, the voices of children in colorful kimonos: girls in red, boys in blue. In the evening, there are rows of red paper lanterns, and their faces glow with sake and beer. Children cheer. Even the tough characters on the other side of the stalls soften, sometimes, at the sight of the children. Others, I notice, stare with animosity. Still others are far behind the stall, enclosed in a capsule of loneliness and hostility.

The stalls are flooded with colors. Along the alleys you can find cookies in the shapes of deer, frogs, giraffes, and pandas. Mats are spread heavy with art objects, antiques, statues, and traditional tools. You can eat fried octopus, or omelets sprinkled with vegetables and a lot of ginger, bland sushi, colored ice, and a huge variety of spices ("Seven kinds of spices that you don't know yet, madam! A special mixture for you! Look, I'm making it especially for you! Taste it, taste, madam! A secret formula from Mount Osore! A formula from the priests of Yamabushi! Good for your health! Good in bed! Good for cooking! For slimming! For the memory! For forgetfulness!").

You can find T-shirts here, cheap yukata robes, and secondhand kimonos piled high. There are shooting galleries and games of chance, toys, tropical fish, bonsai trees, religious articles, masks, medicines, charms. Craftsmen make jewelry, glass animals, paper dolls, and the Buddha images. An assortment of spiritualists come to the matsuri to offer you salvation: yin-yang priests, palmists, astrologers, physiognomists, witches, and fortune-tellers looking carefully at the your ear, fingernail, eye, hair, and whatnot. There are jugglers, acrobats, storytellers, clowns, benediction givers, sutra chanters, and masters of happiness.

Young people, singles or couples, sit, faces worried, in front of a fortune-teller in black caps and cloaks, or a veiled women lit by small paper lanterns. They anxiously wait for the pronouncement of their verdict: what's going to happen with the university exam, the job interview, the unfaithful spouse, the next incarnation, the stomach ache, the mother's illness, the neighbor's envy, the loneliness in bed, the enormities of pain and sorrow.

For three days I sell shaved ice with colored syrup. I earn my rice quite nicely, maybe because of the ice flakes soaked with syrups or maybe because I am a foreign clown from a distant land selling slush to Japanese kids.

A Tour of the Backside City
On New Year's Day Tetsuya takes me to Kawasaki, to the huge matsuri in honor of the Kobo Daishi, the prominent Buddhist teacher of the ninth century. During the first three days of the year, the matsuri attracts three million visitors from the whole Tokyo area and from distant districts. Tetsuya takes me to the Yakuza city behind the stalls to introduce me to its shady citizens.

"This is my elder son," "This is my eldest daughter," "This is my 'equal' son—five-five, as we say," "This is my kobun," and so on.

"How is your boy these days?" "Show me a picture of your baby," "Send greetings to Masako Chan," "How's your leg?" "How did the shirts sell?" "Take off these girlie shoes! What are you, a homo?"

He leads me down the alleys of the temporary city that has been erected here, to closely meet its laws and customs and ways of living. Gradually I discover the shoddy goods, the half- or fully fake. I see the tiny chicks sprayed with a glowing yellow dye to attract children's eyes. I hear the corn on the cob sold on the stall is a product of the wonderful farms from Hokkaido Island, although it was bought just now in the local supermarket. I see the bonsai pots that will break apart before the customers get home.

I hear peddlers loudly announce the supernatural powers of miraculous drugs and potions and charms. I listen how they extol the scientists, the researchers, and the magicians who concocted them after years of meticulous experiments. And I say to myself, there might be a powerful root or herb here after all, some secret charm in the horn of an African rhinoceros; the liver of a Siberian bear; the paw of a Bengal tiger; the powdered shell of an Indonesian tortoise; the grounded lizard from Szechuan; the skull of a monkey from Hokkaido; the giant flower from Sumatra; the dried seahorse from Tahiti; the green mushrooms from the Amazon; the bird's nest from a cave in the Halong Bay; the saliva of a frog from Kyushu— maybe there is something in them that will cure pain of heart or back, failed digestion, faded hopes or incurable loss, curvature of the spine or stiffness of the knee. Who knows? And by now I'm an experienced peddler.

The New Generation

Yes, you admire the veteran peddlers who are skilled at selling, displaying, dancing, winking, and seducing. You enjoy the strong voices, the mad words, and the dance they perform for the crowd.

But I observe the young ones too. Different, withdrawn, hostile. The new Yakuza generation. I talk with them. The work here is only a beginning, they say, basic training, to go over to "heavier" places in the world of the Yakuza, where the big money's to be found, they say. The honor, the risk, the excitement, the show, the status, human dignity. The big game is in gambling, prostitution, amphetamines, drugs, real estate, the world of business, the political connections. That's where they'll show the whole society and their families at home who they really are. There they'll throw back to society the fruits of rejection, contempt, the looks, the nicknames, the low grades, the oppression. They'll strangle. They'll throttle shamelessly. They're a new generation. They'll be like Okawa, Watanabe, Taoka—legendary giants of the Yakuza. They'll be bigger. Much bigger. In fact, they won't be like them. They'll be a new generation, different, bold, violent, ruthless, without the namby-pamby codes of the old generation. They'll make a new Yakuza. Like a sword. Cutting, sharp, shining, with delicious blood spread on the metal. They'll fight hand to hand with the disgusting so-called honest people. They'll have silk suits, beautiful women, gleaming cars, lots of bodyguards, irezumi tattoos on their whole bodies. Journalists will beg them for a three-minute interview. Bows of submission, lots of bows. And lots of honor. A great deal of honor. And if death comes, let it come. They'll die ornamented with their tattoos, with all of Japanese mythology on their skin. Forever.

Meanwhile, they sell fried squid for three hundred yen to a little boy who came to the matsuri with his parents. They'll give the revenue to the oyabun and receive food, lodging, pocket money, and strict education in the ways of the world.

One of them, Shimura, is nineteen. He meets me in the morning, and we walk to the *sento,* the public bath. I see unfinished irezumi drawings on him. Sketches traced and half-colored in. When I admire the tattoos, he says to me, "You want to see how they do it? Come."

I go with him.

Doing Irezumi Tattoos

I go to visit Horimae—one of the few remaining irezumi tattoo master. Horimae leans over Shimura, who's lying with his back up. The master dips a bamboo needle in a jar of violet ink. He explains the rules of tattooing, the theory and practice.

"You dip the needle in the jar of ink. You put your left hand on the client's back, and you lean your right hand on your left." He aims the needle at the eye of the dragon on Shimura's back and inserts it beneath his skin. The dragon's eye is colored violet.

Shimura stiffens. He twists his face a little. Then he smiles.

"You dip the needle in a pigment—orange, for example—and you insert the needle under the skin again." He dips it into the edge of the dragon's eye. Shimura's skin turns yellow, and the dragon twists painfully on his back.

"You take a row of needles tied to each other and deep them in ink." He says something to Shimura. Shimura nods tensely. Horimae soothes him.

"You lay your left hand on the client's back again and lean the right hand on it, as it holds the needles. With a firm hand, you plunge the needles into the client's back. You do it with a quick series of jabs."

With a firm hand he jabs all of them together into Shimura's back. Shimura howls. Horimae wipes the perspiration from around the colorful wound that will be the dragon's head. He wipes the perspiration from his own brow. I look at Shimura, and he looks at me, smiling.

Later Shimura shows me his chest, where a symbol of the family in bright colors is beautifully tattooed. "It's stunning, isn't it? It's sexy. The girls die for it. Manly. But I wear long sleeves, always. That's the oyabun's order. No showing off. You've seen the bathhouses where there's a sign: no entry with irezumi! So I go with long sleeves. At the beach I cover myself with a towel, but when I go into the water I have to bare them, see? And then the crowd scatters. So I'm dating this girl, and she doesn't know at first. But somehow, a bit of my arm is exposed. And I see her dropping, woooooooo! Her breathing stops. And then in bed, she melts, every inch. Even now, when I have only half my back done.

"Irezumi is a dress you can't take off. You see? I'm not even a member yet, but I've put on this dress, and it's un-erasable! It's already deep in my skin, with the oybaun's name engraved in my chest. It's forever. There's no way back for me, and the oyabun knows it! He'll respect that. I'm here for the duration. Can't be a katagi anymore. I'm a Yakuza before I'm a Yakuza.

"And besides, irezumi is a useful reminder of the Yakuza values. Look, here: *Endurance* on my shoulder; *Restraint* on my belly; *Modesty* on the neck; *Fidelity* on my heart. So I'll remember. Others choose *Courage, The Path of Extremes, Devotion,* or *Anger* to be inscribed on their bodies. I'm so proud!" he says with a face twisted in pain.

Many times since that day, Yakuza friends proudly expose their tattoos for me, mostly in hot spring sites, where one goes naked into the pools. I then gape at these marvelous moving galleries displaying fish; tigers; legendary serpents and dragons; swords; spider webs; skeletons; monsters; witches; flowery calligraphies of mantras and prayers; icons of the goddess Kannon and of wrathful gods; vengeful demons; the bird of fire; kabuki figures; samurai committing hara-kiri; and other fiery mythological scenes. Some of the Yakuza are tattooed only around the shoulders, but some are fully covered, head to toe, including the penis, around and around. "Suits," they call it. "You should do it too, Sensei. What d'you say?"

*

Two years later, in a small pub in Tokyo, I interview Kometani Oyabun, a boss from the north. We talk about a variety of subjects, and we get to talking about tattoos. "I'm covered all over, Sensei. The artist is the grand master of irezumi, Horiyoshi the Third. It took years to complete. And, Sensei, I'm going to bequeath my skin to the

Medical Pathology Museum of Tokyo University. An original way to be commemorated, don't you think? When I die, expert doctors will remove the skin 'in one piece' [he says in English] and preserve it in oil. Then they'll seal it in airtight frames, and the work will be sold to a museum or a private collector. If you go to the Pathology Museum, you'll find more than one hundred works of art like that. Skins of dead oyabuns. Two or three of them were my best friends. On one of them, right in the eye of the Buddha, you can see the hole made by the bullet that killed the bastard!"

He bursts out in rowdy laughter, and right there, in the pub, he takes off his long-sleeved shirt and bares his densely decorated body with the profusion of red-blue-green colors. I am dumbfounded, and so are a dozen drunken customers, half of whom hastily stagger out of the pub. Kometani's big belly trembles violently.

Okawa Oyabun Speaks, Part Two

"After the robbery I spent seven years in prison. There I learned everything I needed to know about the ways of the Yakuza: the map of powers, the turfs, the figures, the methods, the negotiation techniques, the charisma—everything one needs to enter the Yakuza. Then I plowed my way into the top.

"My heart is in Korea. But my heart is also in Japan. To this day I'm a leading activist in the Japan-Korea Friendship Society. My mother is there, in a beautiful house I built for her in Seoul. I go see her often. Yes, my daughters speak a little Korean. The little one, Kimiko, isn't so good at languages. But the older one, Machiko, is a genius. She speaks English, French, a little Spanish, and Korean too. She speaks and reads Korean much better than I do!

"I'd like to take Machiko to the jolly places I control—Shinjuku, Kabuki-Cho—but she prefers books. A waste of time, no? Not that I'm against books and education. On the contrary. I want her to be educated, but there has to be a balance, right? With her, there isn't. She's all books, art, and philosophy.

"You see? I'm Korean, and I'm Japanese. Is Japan my home? Yes and no. My real home is the Yakuza. It's not a country, it's a home. Neither I nor thousands of other young man, Japanese or Korean, would have gained a life of honor and a livelihood, equality, and an opportunity for a good life without the Yakuza. Miura, the great founder oyabun of the Okawa-Kai family, adopted me when I got out of prison, then, at the end of the war. Miura didn't ask about my origins, about my past. Nothing. He taught me ways to make a living in miserable postwar Japan. He offered a home, warmth, honor, security, trust, friends. I wouldn't have gotten any of that outside. Miura Oyabun was my true father. His picture is with me, here, in my heart. His big picture decorates our office. You should come to our office."

At the Yakuza Office

I go to the family office. Following the address, I find an ordinary three-story office building not far from Kabuki-Cho, the busiest and most colorful sin city of Tokyo.

Outside the building are two red paper lanterns, with the family crest—two red maple leaves with a samurai sword between them—painted on them. I enter the building, climb the steps, and faintly knock at the door. There is a strong smell of cigarettes. On the door, in bold letters, is a sign: Okawa-Kai, and a drawing of an awesome Yakuza, his chest painted with irezumi in six colors, his face as if sculpted in stone, and the family crest, similar to the one outside the building.

I enter. Okawa Oyabun isn't here yet. A group of young men, all wearing suits and ties, sit at a table playing mahjong. Others are sprawled on a sofa watching TV. As I enter, they rise. Some even spring up to attention and bow deeply. Two of them are naked above the waist. One is tattooed, the other blank. A cup of Japanese tea is immediately served at the table. We all feel awkward.

On the wall across from me is a giant photograph of the legendary Miura Oyabun, the family founder. He wears a kimono. His arms are folded, eyes penetrating. Next to the picture, his name, Myura Oyabun, is tattooed in calligraphy in swirling characters. Beneath, a gigantic wooden sculpture of an eagle, wings spread, dominates half the wall. Its eyes frighten me. On another wall is a huge map of the east side of Kabuki-Cho, with red outlines around part of the quarter, the family turf. Next to the map is a big round Mickey Mouse clock. At the big office desk sits Sato, the family coordinator, wearing a suit and tie. He is speaking over the phone, grumbling, whispering, sometimes barking. He looks anxiously at the big clock across from him.

Several Yakuza are busy coming and going. They tell me they are on duty. They come every day, nine to six. Every week there's a different team.

Toward noon a boy comes with lunch, then a tofu-seller, and between them an elderly person, obviously a katagi, probably asking for help. He enters cautiously, bent over, stealthy. The conversation takes place in another room, not in my presence. After some time he comes out of the other room and hurries out. Then a policeman enters. Everyone is extremely polite to him. They serve him tea. He looks at me. They introduce me as a university professor.

"Is that so?" he says. "Nice to meet you." He asks a few trite questions.

They spend a few minutes gossiping and joking. The air is thick with courtesy. Then he takes out a little notebook, pretends to jot down something, and leaves.

At three o'clock Okawa Oyabun arrives. Everyone leaps to his feet and bows. "*Oooooooooooossss!*"

Okawa acknowledges my presence with a nod, goes for some time to the other room, and then reenters the room and addresses me with an air of a university lecturer. He speaks to the young Yakuza as well as to me. He speaks as if continuing an interrupted interview, answering my last imaginary question.

"Why is our office here? Why are we in the midst of the community like this? Because the Yakuza were here before most of the other residents. In the Edo period, just three houses away, was the home of the legendary Saeki Oyabun. His house was always open. People came and went, Yakuza and non-Yakuza. Saeki and the family maintained the neighborhood Shinto shrine. They donated the neighborhood's *mikoshi* portable shrine, which you can see to this day, carried around the neighborhood during the autumn festival. Yakuza take part in carrying the mikoshi, and the eyes of the girls in the neighborhood pop out when they see the irezumi tattoos. We're proud of our contribution to the matsuri. We create the atmosphere. We're the tradition. We're the peddlers, the fortune-tellers, the entertainers, and the craftsmen, the central actors at the matsuri. Many oyabuns in the past used to be labor contractors, employing many citizens, so there's an ancient bond between Yakuza and the neighborhood.

"People still come to us to resolve conflicts with the authorities, in the family, or with their neighbors. We solve problems quickly, and you can depend on us the way you can't depend on the courts. There every conflict about a fence can take years. The oyabuns were once prominent figures in the community. People respected them more then they respected the law.

"And we're open. You saw the signs outside. Our status in the Korean and Chinese communities of Japan is especially high, and also in the Buraku community, the descendants of the Edo period's untouchables.

"Sensei, the Koreans, the Chinese, and the Buraku feel no loyalty toward Japan or the Japanese authorities. They have always relied on representatives of their own laws, which is to say the oyabuns of the Yakuza families or affiliated organizations. The number of oyabuns of Korean or Buraku descent is very great. Me, for example. Here in the world of the Yakuza, everyone receives equal rights, the possibility of advancement, and a world of respect that they couldn't ever see in the Japanese world.

"We don't harm the people of the neighborhood. We come here in suits and ties. Nine to six. No loud music. No drugs. We try not to stand out. We cooperate with the police. Well, in certain matters. Our out-of-jail ceremonies are held at four in the morning so we don't disturb or block the roads. So, you see, we have respect, to a degree, for those who don't always respect us."

There's silence in the office. The young men listen to the oyabun's speech without uttering a syllable. They bow deeply.

Then, suddenly, the phone rings. The coordinator answers and says, "For you, Oyabun." The oyabun takes the receiver and enters the inner room with it. He motions to me to come in after him. I follow.

"Yes, Inspector Oba. I'm sorry to hear it. Certainly. I know the area. What do you say! For two days now! And I didn't know! I'm sorry for the inconvenience. Certainly, Inspector Oba, certainly! Don't worry. Sure. A pleasure to cooperate with you. Regard the matter as settled."

He hangs up. "It was Inspector Oba, who is in charge of the area. There are problems with a few *chimpira* hoodlums in the Shinjuku Nichome area. Maybe new people who came to the area. Maybe ours. I can't control all of them. Maybe Taiwanese. But I'll settle the matter, and the area will be quiet again by nighttime. We cooperate with the police to keep peace in the area. Don't think that keeping the peace and security in Japan's cities at night is only the work of the police. A lot of it is our work. It's our interest, after all. Yoshi, Taro, Chong, Hisao!"

Yoshi, Taro, Chong (a Korean), and Hisao are already outside before he finishes speaking, after a sharp bow and a guttural "Ooooooooooooooossss!" He utters a few words, and they leave.

We're alone again. Okawa looks at me and says, "Sensei, forget what I said a few minutes ago. It's not true. Nothing is true anymore. It's been a long time since we contributed to the shrine. In most neighborhoods they don't want to see us carrying the mikoshi anymore. We participate in festivals in very few traditional neighborhoods. In most places they drive us out of the neighborhood baths. Some of the conflicts we help resolve are conflicts of our own making, and for the rest we charge a lot of money. The residents don't like us. We're shit for them. We don't belong anywhere, and the police foul up our lives. We're fighting a rough war with the Taiwanese and Chinese gangs. They don't give a shit, and they'll shoot right away whenever there's a conflict between us. Our moral codes are deteriorating. I see the new generation, and it's a different world. Cruel, no values. And I'm sick with cancer. My liver is eaten up, and I won't be here in another year, and I don't know what will happen next. So forget everything I said before. Why did I say what I said? For the young men sitting there, so they'll have a little education. And I'm a Korean who's more Japanese than the Japanese. Isn't that funny? Yakuza life is not easy. It is always a biography of agony and suffering, believe me."

The Yakuza Life—A Short Biography

One day they'll leave their house, and they won't get back until the next day. They won't tell Dad or Mom where they're going. They'll get onto a motorcycle, pick up a red-haired girl all made up, and they'll rally, a herd of thirty motorcycles, next to the river.

You can hear them at night, dancing with their motorcycles, and the penetrating buzz pierces bedrooms along the river. Young boys, and young girls who hold onto them. Twenty, thirty, a hundred. They'll make their motorcycles leap among the hillocks and push the motors to their noisy limit, and you can hear the chorus howling and screeching and buzzing and screaming and mourning and weeping, and the screams of the crazy girls who rip the air to shreds. There are long knives there, and chains, and a great yowl at the world.

Then they'll go out onto the road and buzz in front of the police station, *vroom, vroom, vroooom,* and a dispirited desk sergeant will look at them and scribble something in the blotter. The air will be full of fierce humming, like cosmic bees cutting flesh.

Before morning they'll brawl, wound, weep, and holler and go back home, where their mothers will silently swallow the bumping of the door, sliding on its track.

From time to time they'll ride on the major highways of Japan, heads down, a look loathing the air. They'll petrify any decent driver on the road. They'll dance at his side, shout nasty words at him, circle his car, and continue onto the highways of hatred. Even policemen won't dare interfere. But sometimes a black car will pass their way and signal twice, blow on the horn twice, and twice more, and they'll signal back and wave their hands. It's a Yakuza car. Then they'll say in their hearts, "Some day we'll be Yakuza. We'll be real Yakuza."

One cold morning they'll furtively leave their homes without telling anyone. There's no one to tell, anyway. Dad's not at home. He hasn't been for a while. He left long ago and hasn't been in touch since. Like Dad they'll leave the house, without turning their heads back. They'll travel to the big city by motorcycle, or by train using money they've saved or stolen. They'll arrive at the big city, with or without an address, and they'll wend their ways through the streets, amazed by the city, fearful, no longing or hope in their hearts. Not one glance backward at the place they came from.

A boy will find another; a boy will join up with another. They'll use a knife, a fist. Sometimes the *Nirami* intimidating gaze that can kill. They'll choose a gang leader, and their actions won't betray the great fear in their hearts.

One day a tough guy will turn to them and tell them nice things about the Family, and they'll join. They'll have new brothers, fathers, big sisters. Scars will spring up on their faces like an ancient sacrificial script. At their oyabun's place they'll scour, polish, bring water and tea and various drinks, hold the child in unsure hands and gaze at the big brothers who come and go in the house. With head down they'll do the little chores with neither glory nor wealth, with only humility and submission and a great appetite for being.

Slowly they'll straighten their heads, wear red and black suits and shiny shoes, and no one will stand in their way when they pass.

Over small flames they'll heat little crystals that look like sugar and are called *shabu*, which gaijin call methamphetamine, and they'll inject it or grind the crystals into powder and snort it up their nostrils, and the white crystals will fill them with mighty potency. Their hair is short. Their eyes are black behind black glasses, and a tall girl with red hair clings to their ribs. Before a year is over they'll go to the tattoo master, and he'll etch something into their skin from which there is no returning: the oyabun's name, and immense flowers of ancient Japanese gods. They'll take bundles of banknotes out of hidden pockets and lay them here and there for little services. They'll have a second and third woman. They'll cover them all with money in return for the weeping, loneliness, fear, and vanity.

One day, with veins full of crystals, they'll beat someone unconscious or stab someone or shoot someone, and then they'll be summoned to the oyabun, and after that there are no more crystals because it's forbidden. One day someone will shoot them. One day they'll disgrace the family, and they'll have to pay for this. They'll prepare a knife and a piece of white cloth. They'll ask a friend to hold them, and they'll close their eyes, and with one blow they'll cut off the joint of their pinky. As penance. Blood will spurt onto the cloth, and they'll bring the offering to the oyabun, white–red, white-red, *Pardon, forgive, accept this, Father; please accept it. I won't stumble again.*

They'll enter this and that bar with a slightly swaggering gait, a sleeve rolled up to hint at the red and green flowers on their skin, and their heart will be filled with joy at the sight of katagi citizens shrinking in fear. Disgusting little worms. Maybe their father will be there, maybe their civics teacher, maybe the therapist or the social worker. Maybe they'll meet the whole chorus, all those straight people, educators, people who wanted the best for them, and maybe the heart of these honest people are humble now, and they'll ask for some pardon, some mercy for the little boy they crushed without mercy.

They'll walk about in the neighborhood holding the oyabun's wallet. They'll offer him a cigarette. They'll light it. Everybody will see them and know they're in the Family.

Other boys will come in their wake, with or without motorcycles, and their looks will ask for entry. They'll agree, and they'll be severe and hard and ruthless.

They will fight for honor and money. One day their oyabun will kill his rival with a pistol. They'll look at him with thanks and with yearning eyes. He'll look at them without batting an eyelid. They will bow, and will rise, without a blink will go and turn themselves over to the police and say, "I did it." They will spend years in a little cell in prison, bath three times a week. A bit of sky from the cell window. They will become the legend of the Path of Extremes that knows no compromises. Singers in red silk suits will sing of these men who know nothing but pain and honor and pride and chivalry, and war. They will be living legends in the little cell, year after year, loaded with loneliness and glory.

They'll grow stronger. They'll rise up and crash into the world without solace. Like the phoenix, they'll crash again and again. Night after night they'll wander in the world of fear they created. In their dreams they see little katagi people who will piss in their pants when confronting them, and they will have no mercy for them in their hearts. Men of blood, urine, and semen, their livers shattered from drinking. They will still seek love and will be consoled only in their raging masculinity.

They'll die with shattered livers, and maybe they'll bequeath their skin to laboratories.

Tetsuya, the Untouchable Crime Lord

We began the day early in the morning. Tetsuya was going to a memorial ceremony for Ikeda Oyabun, a Okawa-Kai man, and another victim in the escalating war between the Okawa-Kai and Yamada-Gumi families. The war is more intense on the northern island of Hokkaido, especially in the capital city of Sapporo, a virgin city for the Yakuza business. Although it has been agreed that Yamada-Gumi won't get into Tokyo, they violate that agreement almost daily. Last week a member of Yamada-Gumi tried to penetrate Ikeda's turf. One evening Ikeda shot and killed the Yamada-Gumi man. Then he shot himself, for the balance of deaths, and to keep the battle from expanding into a general warfare, so the fire wouldn't spread. It was an act of honor, highly revered by the Path of Extremes.

But the Okawa-Kai people fear things will get out of control. "Soon, Sensei," Tetsuya says while we drive to Ikeda's home, "Okawa Oyabun will die, and I will have to cope with the issue." Everyone in the family as well as in the Yakuza world knows Fujita Tetsuya will be the successor.

Tetsuya is regarded as one of the three "terrors" of northeastern Japan. But he's also a diplomat, a true disciple of Okawa in the art of assertive conciliation. He's the mediator, the intermediary, and the person who binds adversaries and fixes alliances with local families all over northeastern Japan, while expanding the boundaries of Okawa-Kai's control beyond Tokyo. His vision is no less than a Okawa-Kai empire. He knows the price, so he is already preparing the ground for confrontation with the two or three families, particularly the Yamada-Gumi. Tetsuya is a shrewd and smooth-tongued man. He is tall and thin, with a sharply chiseled face, and an ascetic demeanor. He's always dressed in an expensive suit and a conservative tie. One has a hard time picturing his infamously dreadful reputation.

I meet Tetsuya outside his house. After the memorial ceremony for Ikeda Oyabun, we plan to drive to the city of Fuji-Yoshida at the base of Mount Fuji. We will go to the Fire Festival, which marks the end of Mount Fuji climbing season. We enter the black Mercedes. Tetsuya wears a black suit and black tie, with a Okawa-Kai platinum badge on his lapel.

When we get at Ikeda's house, I see a very long convoy of black luxury cars along the street and the surrounding streets. Ikeda acted in a noble way by killing himself, and everyone has come to pay him respect before the funeral and cremation of his body. Neighborhood citizens sneak by furtively, never turning their gazes toward the ceaseless stream of big black suits, shortly trimmed heads, and black sunglasses. Rumors move fast, and they all know why these menacing men have gathered here. Better not look.

Tetsuya says, "Sensei, stay outside for now. This is a private family event, and I can't take you in. Wait in the car."

I sit in the car, looking at the string of black cars and the tough men gathering at Ikeda's place, and I think, *What if the Yamada-Gumi people come here to attack?* I shrink into the seat, and for the first time since I first encounter with the Yakuza, I'm afraid. I leave the black luxury car and sit in a nearby café until the ceremony is over.

*

An hour later Tetsuyy comes back, and we are on our way to the Fire Festival on Mount Fuji. Tetsuya's face is stern. He's worried.

He says, "One has to keep cool. They have to know it's impossible to penetrate our areas. It's a war for honor and money."

Soon he changes the subject and we chat about everything: international affairs, the Middle East conflict, religious festivals in Japanese culture, and the progress of my research. He talks on mourning and sorrow, and the restraint demanded of a Yakuza.

After a three-hour drive, we arrive in the town of Fuji-Yoshida, at the foot of Mount Fuji. Everything is ready for the fire festival, with the main setting seen all around the area—the straw columns, ready to be devoured by fire in the ceremony in two hours. Tetsuya's young kobuns are busy with the stalls, preparing them for the beginning of the matsuri.

We reach the parking lot. A kobun stands there, waiting, keeping a parking space for Oyabun Tetsuya. Tetsuya leaves the car and greets the kobun. The kobun bows deeply. Tetsuya removes a small suitcase from the car and takes out some clothes. Then and there, in the parking lot next to the car, he takes off his black mourning suit and stands in his underwear. The next moment, as if in a magic show, he is in striped brown trousers, a yellow shirt, and white shoes. Exit the ruffian-cum-diplomat in black suit and tie, enter the clown. He smiles at me. We walk among the booths with his kobun.

"Sensei, let's have a drink. Now I have to earn my living. Maybe I'll take in a million, a million and a half. Oh, what a beautiful day! *Hei*, Yoshi! Go get me a babe! What's up? Everything's ready? Pick up you head, Jiro! The customers will be here right away. Behave yourself, Yoshi, say hello to the sensei! Come, Sensei, let's sit in the izakaya and have some booze."

In the izakaya everybody shows Tetsuya a lot of respect. He doesn't have a bodyguard. He doesn't believe in bodyguards. We walk through and no one dares look at me. Not really, not openly. We order little plates of the house food and sake. We drink. Suddenly he becomes thoughtful and introspective. At his request we move to a private room. He drinks a lot. I look at him and see tears in those burning eyes that kill people and bring them to life. The great terror is weeping, his cheeks sunken. For some time he is impenetrable.

For some time he is silent, and then he speaks. "Sensei, I'm a *yotsu*," he says, spreading out four fingers. "Yotsu means four. Four means four legs. Four legs means an animal. Not a human being. An animal. Four legs means animal, a *Buraku*. I'm a Buraku. We Buraku are untouchables, the descendants of the Edo period untouchables. Inerasable untouchables, although everyone will deny it. Once they called us *Eta*, and now Buraku. The Buraku aren't human beings. They're animals. I was born to a Buraku family. My ancestors were Buraku. My grandfather was Buraku. My father was Buraku. So I'm Buraku. You can't clean it off.

"When I was a boy, I was skinny and gaunt. I would go out to play, my eyes always watching the surroundings, to avoid the mockery, to run away from the stones. I remember the bullying, the mockery. The kids calling me yotsu, spreading out four fingers. I could only play with my own kind, yotsu animals like myself.

"My parents put me up for adoption so I'd have a chance. I was moved from one foster family to another until I settled in with a loving family where I received a good education. My last foster father was the owner of a famous automobile company.

"You may laugh, Sensei, but I studied ballet when I was little. Maybe that's where I got my love for dancing. Ever seen me dance at a matsuri? My foster mother cultivated my sense of beauty. I love art and beautiful things. I must show you my calligraphy and my drawings, the scripts I wrote for movies. I'll show you my collection of rare Chinese porcelain. Ming. Quality. Only quality. I'm a man of quality.

"But I'm yotsu, not human, even if you can't see it on my face. We're a transparent race. But with ordinary Japanese, there's always somebody who'll find out, who'll investigate, who'll discover where you came from, from what village, what your family name was, somebody who heard about your mother. That she was yotsu. And they'll never let you forget that you're an animal.

"You can only be a butcher, or work in disposing of carrion. You'll tan leather. Sell flowers. it's within the death trade. You can only live far from Buraku, as far as possible. But I can't run away from the animal in me. I left the family that gave me a good education, art, calligraphy, dance, piano, and a lot of money. And a future, as they said. My foster father used to say he wanted to send me to the University of Tokyo. But I ran away. Because I'm impure, untouchable.

"I went back home to my lonely mother, much to her joy and sadness. It wasn't easy. Home wasn't home. Mama was loving but confused and weak. We went through a year of suffering together. After some time I joined a *bosozoku* motorcycle gang, but then things got complicated with the gang. After a year or so I left home for Tokyo. I disconnected myself from mama, and didn't see her for thirty years."

I ask Tetuya about the bosozoku motorcycle gangs. He looks at me softly. One day, he says, I will tell you.

*

Months later, we drive to Hokkaido, one of Tetuya's main business areas. He is driving now, and I'm dozing off. Suddenly there's a deafening buzz. A bosozoku motorcycle gang passes in front of us. Kawasaki 750. Honda 750. Yamaha 750. About thirty motorcycles. They scream. They're wearing leather jackets, decorated front and back with the slogan "The Executioners." Sunglasses. Helmets decorated with skulls. Behind the skulls, the faces of screaming girls. Japanese flags flutter. The motorcycles block the highway, driving slowly. One gang passes us, and another one can be seen in the distance.

Tetsuya is excited. He flickers his headlights and slows down. He honks twice. Again twice. Suddenly the gang in front of us slows down, and the motorcycles zigzag a dance. The skulls wave their arms happily.

Tetsuya stops, and the gang stops. Thirty motorcycles circle the car. A demonic ritual dance of engines and leather jackets. Again and again and again. What do they want, these skulls? I see embarrassed giggles.

Tetsuya puts his hand out the window and makes signs: thumb and index finger raised. They make the same signs back to him: thumb and index finger raised. The traffic stops completely. The leader stops next to Tetsuya, gets off the motorcycle, and bows deeply. He also makes a sign with his thumb and index finger. The other boys circle the car. They look at me curiously. They look at Miyuko and the baby in the backseat. I hear the word aniki again and again. Tetsuya shouts words of encouragement to them, and they shout back words of thanks. And they bow. Marvelously polite, these wild kids are. They ask and he answers, "Okawa-Kai." And they shout enthusiastically, passing the name from one to another. Then the leader makes a sign, and all the boys, and the girls, bow deeply. They raise their thumbs. Then they get back on their motorcycles and continue their shrieking ride.

Something's happened to Tetsuya. He takes out a cigarette, and his fingers are trembling. He's blushing. He looks at them, and a line of longing extends from his eyes to the exhaust pipes of the motorcycles until they disappear far off in the heart of the hills, as if a cord in his heart has broken.

"Those are the bosozoku, the speed tribes. They're our little brothers, Sensei. Part of us. We were like them. Some of them will come to us. One day they'll come and try to make an impression on one of us. They'll join. They're our youth. Our reserves. Future Yakuza. Those forgotten by the *kami* (Shinto deities) and society and their mother and father. Youth from the extremes, who have nothing to lose. My heart is with them, Sensei. We flash signals on the roads. We're the fucked-up side of Japan. We signal to each other.

"Sensei, I came from them. Remember I told you that I joined a bosozoku gang when I was a teenager? We were bosozoku under different names: Hell's Angels, The Traitors, The Black Emperor, The Red Scorpions, The Kamikaze, The Sharks, The Dragon God, The Mafia, The Wanderers, The Cobras, the Skulls, The Evil Vampires, The Black Princesses, Lovers of our Homeland, Banzai, The Blue Angels. We rode Honda CBX400s, Kawasaki FX400s. We wore the *toppuku* - the long, black bosozoku jackets. We put on what we called 'kamikaze clothes.' Leather. Sunglasses. Some of us wore purple, white, red. I was the leader of one of them, The Black Widows. On the back and on the helmet was a picture of a black widow. We wore black leather jackets. The neighbors were afraid. The local cops were afraid. We would fly by the police station at two in the morning. Let them try and catch us. We would gather on the broad riverbank. To fly there. To swallow the earth. To fuck the ground. It was a poor working class neighborhood. My motorcycle rally stood out there. Kawasaki FX400, 150,000 yen. How did I get the money? From here and there. But 150,000 isn't all. What about the mirror, that must be a Napoleon, and the blue flashing brake lights, the Pirelli tires, the Moriwaki horn, the paint, the pictures on the motorcycle, the colored chain guard, the saddle, the flags, the helmets, the outfits. That cost a lot!

"And the girls. Azzedine Alaia skirts. Goose-down jackets, orange, green, and purple hair, spiky, lots of silver sprinkles on the whole body, with a lot of vodka in the blood. Sometimes good girls, sometimes monsters. Frightening to death. Valentine Boogie. Rosemarie Ku-ku. Hiroko Desirée. Miyako Pussy. Sitting on the motorcycles like they were fucking them.

"At first, when it all began, we weren't really together. When we gathered in the park, with the girls, we'd see each other on the motorcycles. We'd look out at the little houses, the little apartments, the little gardens, the little families, the little people—they were all in prison, all of them hiding, all good, all bad, all dreaming impossible dreams. When we'd look out at the town, at the police station, the blood would rise in us. Explode into the motorcycle. A little edgy, a little frightened. Breathe in a little turpentine. Inhale shabu. Snort something.

"Then suddenly we would let out, *'Huun, huun, huuuun! Gwaaaan!'* and we'd go! Then, when the rally started going well, all of us—and I'm telling you all of us—would feel each others' presence. Our hearts would shout, *'Dun dun! Dun dun!'* It would really hurt. *'Ban ban!'* and then I'd shout, *'Ayaawww!'* and it's in the bones, the blood. We'd all turn into one giant monster, unconquerable. No fear.

"Then I'd feel it. Me and the motorcycle. I'm speeding. I'm the motor, I'm the flag, I'm the saddle, I'm the wheels, I'm the exhaust, I'm gas, I'm the road. And nothing blocks me. Nothing blocks me at all. Not the road, not the river, not the mountain, not the sky—nothing would stop me then.

"The most powerful mometns were when we wagged the tail. That is, running away from police pursuit. In zigzags, and then our heads became one. Really one. At that time, we became one flesh. It's huge. It's gigantic. It's divine. Maybe that's what the kamikaze felt back then. We were high. At a moment like that, it's really something. I'm not sure I've ever felt anything like that since then. Since I was sixteen, riding with the bikers boso tribes. And those guys we just met, they remind me of it. No one, no cop, no emperor, not the father I never knew, not the mother I loved, no one could stop me. Maybe death. And it wasn't even a sure thing that death would stop me. Who can feel that way in this fucked-up Japan? Tell me. Who? You know us so well. Who can feel that way? Who?

"To feel the people's eyes. Shaking with fear. Hating so much. The motors that roar. *Hun hun hun huuuun!* To see the people so much, so much wishing to be even for one moment in their lives, to be like us. To conquer the main street. To rouse all the weaklings out of their beds. To see the cops trembling.

"And think about the girl sitting behind me. If she was some softy, it was awful. She'd sit there quietly, trembling with fear, and not saying a thing. It would turn me off. Completely. But if she was a fox, if she shouted, 'You're greeeat! You're a giiiaaant! Go! Go! Go! Faster! Let's make fun of the cops! There they are behind us!' Like the craziest matsuri in Japan.

"And look at me now, Sensei. Look, I'm a boy again. I'm afraid of them now. I wouldn't dare get on a motorcycle with those crazy guys. But I have a lot of love for them. And respect. And longing. Just from the memory, I'm burning. Look, I'm trembling.

"But one time, Sensei, it was different. Once, when we finished a splendid boso in the city, three or four of us, around dawn, tired, wiped out, empty, we came back to our neighborhood. The sun was already up a little over the river. We got off the motorcycles and rested on the bank. A cigarette. Home. Sleep. To wake up tomorrow afternoon.

"A group of construction laborers approached on the way to work. Twenty men, approximately. They all lived in the neighborhood. Black work boots. Little lunchboxes. Tool belts around their waists. All kinds of wrenches in them, screwdrivers. Hammers. And now they stopped next to us. They stared. Nirami. Looks straight in the eyes. We knew they didn't come for a friendly conversation.

"One of them looked me in the eyes. I looked at him. He looked at me and said to me, 'What are you looking at, you piece of crap! Dog shit, what are you looking at? Get up and bow to an older man! Where are your manners, little chicken? Get up!'

"We look at each other cautiously. We also have tools, motorcycle tools. If I get up, he'll beat the shit out of me. If I don't get up, he'll beat the shit out of me. For all the noise we made there in the last few months.

"I get up, humble like, and the truth is, I'm scared. These guys aren't bank clerks. Their faces are lined from a lot of life. Their sons are sometimes with us. Their daughters are with us. Their kids don't go to the university. They're in our university. And I'm scared. Maybe his daughter was with me yesterday. Maybe on the motorcycle. Maybe on the tree. Under the tree. Maybe I brought her home ripped up beyond repair. Who knows?

"I get up and bow, sort of, and I sneak a look toward the motorcycle, figuring out how I can get to it fast. Then, the first blow, in the ribs. Then another and another. And I hear the others, their skin is exploding, a bone cracks, I hear the blood that nothing stops, I hear the beating of my heart like drums in the sky. The screams. I see with my eyes, red with blood, my friend Jiro all shrunk, torn up, and red.

"And the motorcycles, that hurts the most. Hurts the most. A pile of smoking metal junk. And the paint and the flags—ripped to shreds.

"I was in the hospital for two weeks. My mother sat there for hours. For two weeks she sat there. Didn't say one word. Her face had no expression. No mercy. No pain. No reproach. No question. No wish. Just laying wet cloths on the wounds.

"That's when I left for Tokyo. That's when I made up my mind to be my own boss and run my own life. No one was going to hurt me. Not the tough guys in my mama's neighborhood. No tough guy in the street. No one."

*

At the age of eighteen Tetsuya arrived in the Shinjuku Quarter of Tokyo, a Yakuza stronghold. There he did "all sorts of things," he says. Three youths joined him after a month. One joined him in drinking sake. Another helped him in a fight, without being asked. The third stood by him when someone blocked his way and gave him an intimidating, mean, nirami stare. In a day or two in that neighborhood you know you can't just let a guy stare at you and then walk on. So he attacked. A few youngsters joined the nirami starer. A fight broke, and Tetsuya's four-man gang won.

From that day on none of the other gangs in the neighborhood dared provoke Tetsuya's little gang. He rented a little room for himself in the heart of the quarter, above a sex shop. He didn't bother meeting Yakuza. Other youths turned to him, and he would interview them, test, calculate, and look into the soul of the aspirant. Let him wait for an answer. He didn't accept just anyone. They began calling him aniki, big brother. He didn't forbid it.

Half a year passed, and they were eight. Tetsuya's reputation was spreading fast in the neighborhood.

One day, when he was walking down one of the alleys, a young man in black trousers, sunglasses, and white shoes stopped him. Thin and stooped, he was imitating a Yakuza boss.

"Come with me," he said to Tetsuya.

"Who the fuck are you?" Tetsuya asked.

"Come. I'm telling you, and that's enough."

Tetsuya sensed seriousness. He didn't argue. They walked into a little bar. It was clear that Sunglasses was at home there.

"You—the time has come for you to grow up. You can't wander about like this much longer."

"I can."

"Try. But I suggest you think about it. Here's my business card. You see what family I belong to. The Okawa-Kai family. Okawa Oyabun. You've heard of him, right? My name is Azuki."

Tetsuya had heard of Okawa Oyabun. But he didn't take the card.

"Join us, and you'll be in the most honored place here. You and all your kid brothers." He was referring to his small gang.

"I'm okay the way I am."

"You're not okay."

"I'm okay, I said."

"You're not okay, I told you. Did you hear, fucker?"

Tetsuya tensed. His hand gripped his cup.

The young Yakuza placed a hard hand on his. "Don't try. If you want to talk to Okawa Oyabun, I can arrange it."

"I'm okay. I don't know who you are or who Okawa Oyabun is."

"Okay, you'll see." And he left.

Tetsuya put the card in his pocket.

From that day on, people kept their distance. In the pubs and bars, he didn't get the warm hospitality he was used to.

One day three youths came up to him and gave him stares. They weren't afraid anymore. One day one of his young guys came to him with his face black and blue and cigarette burns on the back of his hand. The people in the stalls on the edge of the neighborhood stopped paying when he came to collect money, and two big guys were standing next to them. Not a word was said. One day another gang member came and bared his back, to show dozens of burns.

Tetsuya realized it was time for a change. One evening he saw Azuki. He lowered his head.

Azuki said, "Come."

*

"That's how my Yakuza career began. I go and meet Okawa Oyabun for the first time. His gaze is soft, but he looks deep. For the first time I was frightened. He tells me, 'Stop messing around and come over to me. I'll make you a man of honor.' He doesn't ask anything about me or about my mother or about my grandfather or about my untouchable ancestors.

"Many years have passed. Since the day I met Okawa Oyabun, nobody has dared spread four fingers in front of me, like the children back then, forty years ago. Okawa Oyabun is the one who turned the world upside down for me. Shame to honor, failure to success, pain to pleasure. So I owe my life to Okawa Oyabun and to the Yakuza.

"You and I are brothers, Sensei. You're a nomad, Sensei, and a peddler, like me, trying to forget you're untouchable with some bits of honor. Yakuza and university—the same. Maybe you're very learned and respectable in the university, and you have a business card and people bow to you. But you're an outsider. I sell rootless bonsai pots and you sell useless knowledge. We are both vagabonds, Sensei."

Suddenly it's as if he's waking from a dream.

"I have cute Maltese dogs at home. They chirp like hoarse little mice, and they like to sit in my lap, but I also have other dogs that I raise in another place. Tosa Japanese bulldogs. They're huge carnivores. Size of donkeys. Nature's work of art. For me they're a combination of beauty and business. Sometimes I go to the kennel and look at them. I have an armchair opposite the kennel. I smoke a pipe and look at them for an hour, two hours. Sometimes I go into the kennel and talk to them. I pat them on the back and their hind legs. Masterpieces! And they're also for betting. Some day you'll come and see a Tosa dogfight. You won't believe how many of our honest Japanese love to bet on dogfights.

"Yakuza, Sensei, are the innards of the Japanese. If we didn't exist, they'd invent us. We're the spleen and the liver and the lungs and the guts. Not pleasant to look at, but you can't do without." Of the Ykuaza

*

"I didn't see my mom for thirty years. When I saw her again, a few years ago, she was sick. And I, one of the three terrors, wept out loud next to her bed. The funeral I held for her was the biggest and most

73

splendid funeral ever held in the city of Tokyo. I put her ashes in a golden urn. We're tough but we're soft, sensei. Better be tough."

*

One day, at his spacious home, we are drinking and chatting. Tetusya drinks more than usual. He is obviously in a shaky state. "You're too gentle, Sensei. I'm afraid you wouldn't qualify as a Yakuza. But I'll tell you something. Most of us don't qualify. Very few rise and don't fall. Many rise and fall, rise and fall, and fall. And fall. Some of us never rise. Most of us just fall. We hardly share our failures. We sometimes write sentimental letters. Some, like me, write poems and novels, film scripts, or secret journals, in which we tell our true story. Mostly in jail. Lots of free time there. You get there every two or three years, some times for a long stay. And you write. *Memoirs*, you call it? I'll give you a sample to read. Written by one of a young Yakuza I knew. One who could go big but fell badly. Handled to me by his only lover, Akiko, after he has vanished form the Yakuza scene. A fellow Yakuza found it on his body and sent it to her." He goes to little chest, opens one of the drawers, and takes out a scruffy masnuscript. "Handle with care. It's fragile," he says. I take the manuscript and begin reading.

The Rise and Fall of a *Chimpira* Hood -- Journal Excerpts

"Akiko snorts and smokes. She puts a flame under aluminum foil and all that. Her mother injects shabu (meth) under her nails, so you can't see the puncture marks. I like to grind it into powder and snort it straight up my nose. I travel from my village to Fukuoka to buy shabu. We sit in an old car, in an automobile graveyard, and snort. Dream. Akiko doesn't want anything, just to dream. I like to look at the beauty spot on her left ear.

My mother cries at night. She won't talk to me. But once she did talk to me. No, I said. I don't want to go to that school. Yes, I want to study and do something to become somebody. Yes, I want to be a Yakuza.

My dad? A sperm that got into my mother seventeen years ago. I bought flip-flops with high heels. I bought a purple silk shirt. I bought big black sunglasses. I had my hair done in a pa-ma. I watch the aniki in Fukuoka. I start walking like them. Swaggering, you know. It's not easy to walk so people will think I'm one of them. I start to talk with a rolled *rrrrr*. It's not easy. Akiko comes with me. She's my girl. People look at us.

I stopped a drunk in the street. I said, 'Give me money.' He gave. So easy.

*

"Mom committed suicide yesterday. Or the day before. Can't remember. Uncle Bunjiro took me to his house. The social worker, Oba-san, took me to eat *yakitori*. Asked fucking questions. What do I feel, questions like that. She suggested I should go here and go there. She's pretty, Oba-san. Too bad she's a social worker. But I haven't been with a girl yet. When she asked me if I wanted to go to a special school for boys 'that I could talk to,' the blood went to my head. I stabbed her hand with a wooden yakitori spit and ran away. I hope she burns.

*

"I stole money from Uncle Bunjiro. I didn't say good-bye to Akiko. I went to Tokyo. I'm living with a friend. In Shibuya you can get good shabu.

I like the smoke. I like the colored signs. I like the sound of the flip-flops in the alleys of Shibuya. I like to watch the couples going into 'love hotels.' I like to do nirami—the stare. I like it when a guy comes up to me and challenges me into a side alley. I hit him hard in the stomach and then in the face, and I leave him there. There's

75

a smell of blood and piss. There's a strong smell of sweat under my armpit. That's good.

*

"Today I went to a love hotel with Akiko. She came from Fukuoka, ran away from home. She's tall and has long legs, not crooked like most of the girls around Shibuya. We missed each other a lot. We went to the love hotel right away. I was very nervous because I didn't know exactly how you do it. Akiko instructed me. It wasn't all that interesting. One, two, I came, and that's it. I like the smell of bodily fluids. It's good. Akiko knows what she wants. Better than me. Lots of times I don't know.

*

"I look for fights. I always find them. One stare. One question, usually, 'Got a problem?' That always works. Especially with the rolled *rrrrs*. Then the chimpira either runs away or comes closer, and then that's the end of him—a face like chopped meat.

I changed my hairdo to a brush cut. Real short. It's nice to rub it with your hand. Nice when Akiko rubs it with her hand. I like the smell of bodily fluids.

The way they walk, the Yakuza aniki! How the katagi look at them! There he walks, the aniki, without a wallet, his back straight, and the other one behind him holds the wallet. There are bundles and bundles of banknotes in it. I saw. And that one, the young one, takes out the money, lights his cigarette, opens the door for him. I'm dying to be there. I will be.

*

"I saved a gaijin from a beating in Roppongi. His name's Jeff. A journalist, he says, but I don't believe him. After that he offered me grass. First to smoke. We did a little business. We sell to gaijin in Roppongi and to dumb Japanese, who don't ask questions about the price. Fuck 'em to hell. I love the smell of burning. We have lots of money.

I exchange my flip-flops for shoes. I'm growing up. My shoes are white. I have yellow pants and white pants. I go to the sado-maso show in Shinjuku. Ropes on the girls' tits and all that. People peek into the girls' holes. They clap hands. They sweat with excitement. One day I'll have a club like that.

They have mustaches, the oyabuns. No Japanese man has a mustache. It's beautiful. It's good. A mustache is macho.

Akiko bought a coat with spotted fake fur. Pretty sunglasses. She knows what she wants. One day I'll have a purple silk jacket.

Hachiro plucks his eyebrows. I say to him, what are you, a homo, or what? But he thinks it's really very manly.

I went to the *sento* (public bath) in Ikebukuru. I saw a Yakuza with irezumi all over his body. That's good. That's pretty. That's sexy. I told Akiko.

She said, 'You should do it too. I'll give you money.' If she gives me the money, I'll do irezumi. No one will ever erase that from me. Sometimes I think she's running me.

Akiko brought money. I don't know from where. She always brings me money. I go to the man who does tattoos. He asked if I have money. I showed him. He said, lie down! He made a little dragon on my back. I fainted. For a few months I had an infection. My back was like a lizard. Once I took off my shirt in a little club in Chiba. They gave me money to get out of there. That's good.

I like the red lanterns of the *sakariba* entertainment quarters. I like the smell of sake at night. I like to go to Sanjuro's place and eat yakitori. I like the sauce on the yakitori. The feeling of fat on my fingers. The skewers remind me of that place in Fukuoka, where I met the oba, the social worker. How is she now? I wonder. I would fuck her, except she's a fucking social worker. I like to see the oyabun's Mercedes-Benz in Ikebukuru. I like to see his kobun polish it when the oyabun is busy or something. I like to see his face reflected in the car. All twisted. How he combs his hair in front of the hood. That's nice.

*

"I go on selling grass and shabu. I stopped taking it myself. It messes up business. Your head gets blurry. Before you know it, you're in deep shit, and fucking chimpira take over the area.

A kid I knew in Fukuoka, Hiroji, got to Tokyo. He called me aniki! I gave him two slaps so he'd understand that you have to say aniki with a lot of respect. He made a deep bow. He said, 'Yes, aniki. I understand, aniki.' We go out and slug people. We collect a little money. But most of the money comes from Akiko. I don't know what it's from. Aniki, he called me!

Another kid, Osamu, also came from Fukuoka. He also called me aniki, more politely than Hiroji did. He has good manners, Osamu. But he wants to go out and hit people. A hothead. I've got to teach him manners—*giri, gaman* (endurance, restraint). Osamu's got no gaman. He also said something nasty about Akiko's fur scarf. I won't forget that.

The three of us went and kidnapped Jiro, the leader of the Daruma Boys. He was with us for a week, tied up, peeing in his pants. Getting hit. We got a million yen and let him go. Now they know about me. Another kid joined me, and another one, and another.

*

"Somebody from Okawa-Kai, calls himself Hiroaki, came up to me and said, 'Come to my office this evening.' I went. I called him aniki right away, the way you should. I knew it would come, that they'd invite me. I was with them in the office. I made a bow like you should. Yes, aniki; no, aniki. There were pictures of the oyabun

78

there! I saw Hiroaki take off his purple suit. I saw him in *fundoshi* (a loincloth). He doesn't give a shit. He took off his clothes and put on a black kimono. Like a samurai. A kimono is nice. I saw all the tattoos. A full body tattoo! Wow!

Then he said, 'Come to us with your whole gang. And don't argue. You understand, you piece of crap?'

*

"I do babysitting for aniki. I buy things at the grocery store. I wash dishes and serve tea. I polish the car. I get hit. I learn the bowing code and how to talk politely. I sleep in the room underneath the stairs. One day somebody will sleep in my house in the room under the stairs. That's good. Meanwhile I don't tell aniki about my business in Roppongi. I still don't know what he'll give me, so I tell Osamu and the others that it should stay between us.

*

"One day aniki says, 'Come!' and we drive to some place behind the Haneda Airport. Warehouses and stuff like that. I know they've found out. They light a candle in my ass, and I scream, 'Akikoooooo!' Then they whip me with a car antenna. On my back. On the infections from the new tattoos. 'Akikoooooo!'

'You come tomorrow,' they say, 'with all the details about your business. That's how you'll learn what giri is. Next time it'll be worse, worm!'

I tell them about my network, the sales stations in Shinjuku and Roppongi, and everything. Now I conscript young guys to sell. Aniki watches over me and helps me organize. We buy a four-gallon container for two thousand yen. On the streets we sell a little four-ounce bottle for two thousand yen. Big profit. That's good. Together we manage to sell more than a thousand bottles a day. I give most of the money to aniki. I get 10 percent.

Aniki tells me, 'Don't tell anyone, not one word, that we're selling this stuff. Okawa Oyabun doesn't allow us to sell shabu or drugs like that. Not a word! He'll kill us.'

*

"One day I get a place of my own. A little pink salon. I also have a little nomiya. Akiko manages things just right. We're rich. I have a kobun who walks with my wallet and bundles of money. I go around in a purple jacket, and I have a kimono. I have another girl, but Akiko doesn't know. Akiko is my woman. She's my money. Maybe I love her. We have our own place. We have respect. Life looks good. I'm gettng irezumi tattoos on my whole body. Akiko likes that.

I go to Hawaii with Akiko. At the airport in Honolulu they arrest me and send me back.

In Japan I tell the guys, 'They kicked me out of Hawaii! I'm on America's black list!' I'm so proud.

*

"I enlist a few young illegal Koreans. They know how to fight the way our guys have already forgotten. Now I also have responsibility.

Aniki puts me in a responsible position in the family. I'm in charge of the young men. "Do that for two years," he says. He gave me the job in order to check if I can take on important jobs. Fuck him! I'll educate the newcomers. I'll make them into proper soldiers. I'll teach them manners.

I bring in a lot of money for the family and myself. I send the young guys to persuade old katagi to leave their houses. I tell them to scare, not hurt. Most of the time it works. Sometimes the katagi get stubborn or bring in their sons. Then my kobuns settle in there and raise hell. They shout. They smash things here and there. They look at the people who walk into the houses. They scare them. Once somebody died. Maybe from fear. Maybe from a disease. I got a rebuke from aniki. I gave the young guys a rebuke, with a couple of blows. Idiots. A dead katagi is bad for business.

*

"The sakazuki ceremony. When I sipped the sake, my hand shook. A few drops spilled on my kimono. I disgraced the family and myself. I blushed. I wanted to excuse myself, but I saw they hadn't noticed. I passed the bowl to aniki, and he didn't even look at me. One day I'll force him to look at me. Now I'm officially aniki's kobun, an official member of aniki's "house" in the Okawa-Kai family.

I wore a black kimono. At the party I had a purple silk jacket. I wanted to bring Akiko but they said no. 'This is a man's ceremony.' Afterward I explained to her that it was a man's ceremony.

She said, 'Choose.' I slapped her. She slapped me hard.

That very day she left and never came back. I wanted to cry, but no tears came. I went and blasted my head with shabu. I was clear but sad. Sad but distant. Like there's a scar, and you don't really feel the skin. And I didn't have anyone to tell. I went to an izakaya in Ikebukuru, but there was no one who could listen.

I offered a bunch of money to find that bitch. I shouted, "Find me Akiko." I disgraced myself in the izakaya. The izakaya belongs to aniki's number five woman. What's the matter with me?

Aniki walked into the izakaya, and in front of everybody he said, "One more time we catch you like this with shabu, it's your pinky, and after that, out!"

I took a knife, tied up my pinky, took a towel, shouted, 'Akiko,' and cut off my finger. I threw it in his face, shouting, 'Take it!'

*

"I'm alone. That's not good.

Somebody arranged a reconciliation ceremony. Aniki forgave me because I'm a good businessman. I manage to sell a thousand little bottles a day in my network. Now I have to sell two thousand because the prices are going down in this fucked-up country. I don't know how to do anything else. I see the brothers doing all kinds of jobs, but I don't know how yet. I know how to scare katagi and how to sell shabu. Aniki forgave me also because he was afraid I would tell that we're selling drugs. Aniki really pisses me off.

When will I be an oyabun? I have fifteen kid brothers. Most of them are Koreans who are ready to die for me. I have everything I want. Three of them went to prison. Stupid street brawls. When they're young, they aren't ready yet. You need three or four years in the streets so you can keep yourself together in prison.

*

"One day I call one of my kobuns, Lee, a tiger who's not afraid of anything. I tell him, 'Come on, we're going to get big. We're going to finish aniki.'

Aniki goes to his number-five girlfriend once a week. But his bodyguards keep watch. Every day they're on watch. But on that day they're not there. When he comes out, he dies without a peep. Ten holes in his body. They accuse this gang and that one, even the Sumiyoshi-Kai family. But Okawa Oyabun decides not to start a war. He wants to investigate what happened. I'm afraid of him. The only person I'm afraid of is Okawa Oyabun. But he's sick. I hope he dies before he finds out. He has the head of a great man. He can find out. So that's the end of me. I'm afraid, but I go for it.

But he's going to die soon. It'll be a new world here.

*

"Aside from that, Aniki stank. He's been dead for a while. He didn't deserve to be an oyabun. Something flashed in his eyes like a sick dog. That's not good. They have to understand that today it's something else. I'll strangle the katagi even harder when I get to be an oyabun.

82

*

"They appoint me temporary oyabun of the house. A quick sakazuki ceremony, and just five or six people from the family. Without a party. Akiko! Where is she? I'll burn her when I find her. Now I'm the king of the eastern part of the sakariba of Akabane. In two days there are two dead Chinese and two of our Yakuza. One katagi. Too bad. Not good for business, a dead katagi. The Chinese did things to the Yakuza. Very cruel, these Chinese guys. I envy them. We can learn from them. Dragonhead is something fantastic! What a giant enemy! No giri consideration and all that junk. What an enemy! But an enemy we've got to destroy. I gave an order to kidnap the girl of one of the Chinese chimpira.

*

""I get a note. 'Free the Chinese girl or you'll get a woman's left ear. An ear with a mole, if you need a sign.' They found Akiko! I let the Chinese girl go.

*

"Everything got all mixed up. What's right and what's wrong. The Koreans are leaving me. In the izakaya they say I'm nuts. When I walk around, nobody looks at me. For a year now I've been taking shabu again. What kind of oyabun am I? It's not good. Not good for business. The streets aren't what they used to be. I lost everything. I'm living near the pond with a few rags. Akiko, where is she? I get a red postcard from the family. I don't understand what's written there.

I'm lying here under the trees next to Ueno Pond. The lotus flowers are so big. I wash in the public toilet. Fellow vagrants show me how to get cardboard boxes for sleeping. How to wash clothes in the pond. Where you get scraps of food. How to fold the cartons neatly and hide from the rain. How to get into Ueno Station when winter comes. Everything is very clear now, but how will I get money? One little bottle costs two thousand yen."

End of journal.

I finish reading the journal, amazed and wondering, whose journal is it really? "I see," I say to Tetsuya, "I see. I see," having nothing wiser to say.

"You see?" He says, and takes another drink. "So go on with you research, and see if you can find our true nature. Can you?"

Okawa Oyabun Speaks, Part Three

I own a company that transports gravel for construction. But you understand I don't make my living from that, don't you? It's for the income tax authorities. We are involved in a variety of activities. There's protection, for example. At the festivals, peddlers who aren't our members pay for their place. You know, the ones who sell jewelry, for example. Some foreigners, including Israelis. We do protection in sakariba, the entertainment districts, so that drunks won't act up and make trouble. So other Yakuza people won't bother them. No, we don't take protection money in regular residential areas, from katagi stores: a grocery, a fish store, a clothing store—like that. We don't touch them. We work only in the "water business" in the sakariba—restaurants, clubs, bars, pubs, izakaya, nomiya, pachinko.

Also blackmail. From big companies. Every big company has dark areas, and we are specialists in detecting them. Individuals have dark places too, you know: CEOs, politicians, especially people in high places. They're full of shit, these people. They're corrupt, heartless bastards. It is a society of impostors and posers. Believe me, what we do doesn't come up to their ankles. Not in the amount of money they slice off, not in wickedness, not in cynicism, not in self-righteousness, not in hypocrisy. We have a lot to learn from the "legal" companies in the matter of fraud, evil, crime. We have a lot to learn from the state of Japan. It's going to explode sometime, and then you'll see the power of darkness and its extent. So when we hear about problem in a certain firm, we get to the bottom of it, and then we go and visit them.

Fukuoka Ken'ichi—The Man of all Trades

One day I meet Fukuoka Ken'ichi in a small nomiya in Shinjuku. He's holding a big package wrapped in brown paper. He wants to consult with me about graphic design.

"Graphic design?"

"Yes. I'm a publisher."

"A publisher? Of what?"

"Of a newspaper."

"Since when have you been involved in journalism?"

"I'm involved with newspapers that expose corruption in major companies."

"Since when?"

"Oh, for a while. I move in and out of the business, according to the situation."

"Show me."

He pulls out a sheet from a newspaper.

Economic Affairs Weekly
Date, Place (Tokyo), Publisher (name, an indistinct address)

The main headline reads

Isozaki Holding Company Denies CEO's Involvement in Huge Bribery Incident

Isozaki Yasuo, CEO of Isozaki Holding Company, refused to be interviewed by our newspaper today regarding persistent rumors of a huge bribery incident. The company spokesman refused to answer our telephone calls. Employees of Isozaki Holding Company anonymously reported to our correspondent Hirosa about a huge bribery incident in which the company is involved. According to them, Isozaki, the CEO, paid ten million yen to a senior official of the Forestry Ministry for a concession.

The story goes on to supply interesting and embarrassing details regarding the public behavior of the Isozaki Company.

"What are you doing with this? Has it been published?"

"For the time being in a limited number of copies. I met Isozaki yesterday," Fukuoka says.

"Did you? And what did you tell him?"

"I showed him the newspaper."

"And then?"

"Then? What do you mean? Sensei, sometimes you really embarrass me. After all, you're a university professor, aren't you? Isozaki doesn't want the newspaper to be published, does he? Isozaki is a very corrupt man, but he isn't dumb. He won't want the newspaper to be published. You understand? By no means does he want the newspaper to be published. He'll buy up every copy! The whole edition is very expensive, if you know what I mean. And they'll pay for it. There are dark places here in Japan. I tell you, Sensei, our streets are safe—there's no robbery, no murder, no rape. But the soul is corrupt. Business is corrupt. Everybody's Yakuza. And if everybody's Yakuza, Sensei, then let them pay! A lot.

"And I want you to know that last week I donated, anonymously, five million yen to establish schools for disadvantaged youth, in my hometown, down in Kyushu. The money comes from men like Isozaki. I gave it anonymously, of course. If they knew where the money came from, they wouldn't want to take it. And now I'm going to meet Chairman Ito, from another corrupt company. I am very busy this week. See you."

*

"Chairman Ito, someone wants to see you, and he didn't make an appointment in advance. Here's his card."

"Show him in."

He enters. Suit, tie, and all the rest. Chairman Ito knows immediately by looking at the card. His hand slightly shakes.

"Hello. My name is Fukuoka. I own stocks in your company."

"Do you have a certificate?"

"Certainly. Here."

"True. A very small number of shares. However, it's true. You are a shareholder. Will you have some tea?"

"Coffee."

"Right away. Yes. What can I do for you?"

"I'd like to show you something."

He hands him the newspaper, and Ito reads out loud, "*Economic Affairs Weekly.*

Isozaki Holding Company Denies CEO's Involvement in Huge Bribery Incident. Isozaki Yasuo, CEO … Yes, we've heard about that matter. But we're not Isozaki, so what does it have to do with us? I'm a very busy man, and—"

"Certainly, certainly you're not Isozaki. I know how to read, and I know what company I own shares in. And you show great respect for shareholders, I know. And you're not Isozaki, and you've never given or taken a bribe in your life. But we are a number of stockholders, and we would like to be sure, you understand, to be sure that company is run properly and that there's no corruption *like* with Isozaki, and other things like that, that have been going on recently, and we just want to be sure. Of course there's no reason to disturb you now, because you're busy doing those important things that you chairmen are always taking care of. I just wanted to tell you that we're a group of shareholders with an interest in the company, and we want you to know that in a month, on June 15, you know— certainly you know, because you're the chairman of the company, after all—at the annual meeting of the shareholders, we thought, you know, of raising a number of questions, nothing special, just the way it's done properly at a meeting, only according to the bylaws, and not to be too much of a nuisance, and I have here a few examples of questions regarding the Yoshimura gravel company and the tender for building the new bridges in the Fukushima District, and also about Hokkaido, and about—"

"How much?"

*

One day I meet Fukuoka at a big hotel. He's wearing an elegant suit. His tie is a conservative color, I notice.

"Are you meeting the prime minister?" I ask.

"No, but somebody close."

He didn't volunteer any more information. After some idle chitchat and a cup of strong coffee, I see that he's expecting someone; he keeps looking at the entrance of the hotel.

Suddenly my eye catches one of his kobuns, whose name is Hida-chan, approaching with a little package in his hand. He makes a deep bow, mutters something, leaves the package on the table, and rushes out.

Fukuoka expertly opens the package and takes out a bundle of business cards. He hands me one. I read

SHOGUN
The Leading School for
Japanese Language Study
Tokyo (Address, Telephone Number)
Director: Fukuoka Ken'ichi

I look hard at Fukuoka and ask.

He says with great seriousness, "I'm opening a school."

"Yes, but what—"

"I'm opening a school. What's so strange about that?"

"Yes, but—"

"Sensei, do you doubt me?"

"No. It's because I don't doubt you that I'm asking. What is it?"

"A school for the study of the Japanese language. Can't you read? Look at the back."

I turn the card over. The same content, but in Chinese.

He begins to make sense. "Explain."

"There's some nice movement of Chinese people to Japan."

"Yes. I know. But it's mainly illegal workers, for construction and things like that."

"True, but recently the immigration officials have gotten stricter. It's hard to bring in Chinese workers. But if you want to study Japanese, for example, you get a student visa. So I opened a school. The Chinese ask for a permission to study Japanese, and they get a student visa for study of Japanese culture and language. Everything's fine."

Things are getting even clearer, but still I ask, "What about textbooks, teachers, tests, a building—do you have all that?"

"I have it all. You can come and register."

"Do people really study?"

"No, of course not. They register, they come to a meeting, and the next day I get construction work for them. And I get a commission. Sometimes it's a construction company that belongs to someone in the family, or in its many shadows."

"And who are you going to meet today?"

"Somebody important in the immigration ministry. Now, go away, Sensei. You don't want to be here now." He bursts into loud laughter.

I leave.

Half a year later the school closes. But by then there are many hundreds of Chinese in Japan, all of them students of the Japanese language. All of them live in dormitories rented by the Okawa-Kai family. All of them wear gray work clothes. All of them go out to work in the morning and come back at six p.m. They all wash in shared showers or in the public bath. They all cook Chinese food in woks in little apartments, at the entrance to which are piled up dozens of pairs of clogs, and they fill the neighborhood with Chinese food odors. All of them disperse in the evening to the clubs of Shinjuku Nichome, drink a lot of sake and beer, and then disappear in the back rooms of the clubs, where they lose their money in gambling parlors run by the Okawa-Kai family.

Okawa Oyabun Speaks, Part Four

I always tell my sons, the kobuns: you can violate the law, but you can't do bad things to people. Breaking the law and harming people isn't the same thing. You can be a criminal, but you should be a good person. Circumstances brought you to this world and to this place, but don't be a demon. Don't let evil enter and govern you. Be a criminal with a face, honor, and humanity. If you have to, go and blackmail corrupt, bad people. Do it without shame, without hesitation, without thinking twice. But if it's someone you should help, give him your last kimono. I educate my sons to be human beings even in this harsh world that we live in. It's good. It's right, and it's also important for the survival of our organization.

Yakuza Loneliness

"I want to grow up, Sensei," Fukuoka Ken'ichi says to me. "I'm forty-seven, and I want to grow up. I don't have any real friends. I don't really have a wife. I don't really have a daughter. My daughter hates me. My wife, she has nowhere else to go, so she stays with me. True, we Yakuza have giri. Giri means that I'm always there for my family brother, no questions asked. Always. If he's in trouble, I'm with him. I'll protect him. I'll hurt anyone who tries to hurt him. Kill if necessary. I'll take care of his children when he's in prison. I'll give him money when he gets out of jail. I'll take care of his family if he's killed. I'll give him shelter if he runs away. My brother will never be alone until he dies and even after he dies. He is with me, no question asked. And if I'm hurt, if I'm in jail, if I die, there will always be someone to take care of my family and me.

"But we're lonely people, Sensei. Lonely little children. Even Okawa Oyabun, *Oyaji* (Papa), as we call him, even he can't really be a father. I ran away from my little town in Kyushu when I was fourteen, but even then I hadn't seen my father for more than ten years. I have no idea who he is, where he is, if he's alive. Okawa Oyabun has been my father for many years. He gave me a livelihood, warmth, and love and care. He was severe with us, exacting, frightening, and punishing. But he educated us. And he's a father, but he's not.

"Most of us have a wife and mistress. Some of us have two more, or three. Some are faithful, some aren't. Some of us have just one wife. Me, for example. We have everything we need. We have money to give to our first wife, the second and the third. We have enough money to let our daughter study in the best school, in the best university, so that she has a secure future. We have everything.

"But we're little kids, you understand? Like back then, when we ran away from our little town in Kyushu, frightened, hating the world, and Dad and Mom. And we were lonely, and so terrified that we joined up with other scared children. We're still looking for our lost dad and mom, and a woman. We're looking for love.

"I never grew up, Sensei. I had an empire of clubs, lots of money, and status. People were afraid of me. I had women once. Everyone respected me. They were afraid of me. The name Fukuoka was pronounced with great fear. One day I had money. One day it was gone. One day I'm here. One day I'm in prison. I can't do the same thing for two weeks. Now I lost everything. I had a house but lost it. I hop, I move from place to place. People won't rent me an apartment. Now I have to move every year or two. They find out; they know. The police visit and frighten them.

"I'm afraid of my beeper. Every time it buzzes, I jump. It's on me twenty-four hours a day. It buzzes, and I answer immediately. I drop everything and go where I have to go. Something happened. There's an urgent consultation. There's action. A trouble, one of my kobuns did something. An emergency, a war broke.

"My time in prison was happy. It was to rest, study, think. I took courses–history, calligraphy, poem composing. And I wrote poems. A kind of diary. One poem for every single day in prison. Four years. Will you read my poems, Sensei? They're really nothing special, but I'd like you to read them. I have a notebook of poems. Will you read it? I'll send it to you, but only if you won't show anyone. For your eyes only. I'll send it.

"I'm alone, Sensei, and I'm a kid. What do you know about that, you straight people, katagi? What do you know?"

What do we know, really?

"Will you come and sleep at our house tonight, Sensei?"

Okawa Oyabun Speaks, Part Five

We also make money by importing foreign workers. That will be an important area in Japan. We bring them in legally and illegally. How do we bring them? Various methods. [He laughs loudly.] They come by themselves. Take construction, for example. Japanese people don't want to work in construction, so we bring them in from Korea, China, the Philippines, Bangladesh, Iran, even from Brazil—the grandchildren of Japanese immigrants.

We also bring in Philippine dancing women. We have a dancing school there, would you believe? We train them to perform in Japanese clubs. Some of them work as whores afterward. Today more and more of them are in prostitution. Japanese men like Filipinas; they're sexier than Japanese. But most of them are still working as dancers or hostesses. Are hostesses also whores? Depends on the club. There are decent clubs where it's a crime even to bare a knee, and there are others where they only flirt, but there are places where after the club they go for sex. For money, of course. We get a commission.

A variety, you see. Personal enterprise produces various ways of making money. But with us, people go up and down, they shoot up and fall down. Nothing is stable here.

The Poet

On my desk in my university office lies a big brown envelope. My name is written in fine calligraphy. I open it. There's a white envelope inside. I open it. Inside is a notebook with a piece of paper attached, and on it is written

> *To Yakobu Sensei, with deep feelings of brotherhood.*
> *From your brother, Fukuoka, "the Nobody"*

The notebook in the envelope bears the seal of the prison's authority. I open the notebook. On the inside front cover are dried flowers and a heading in colors:

> *Poems from Prison. Fukuoka Ken'ichi*

Next to a dried pansy a poem is drawn:

> "Endless Winter"
> *The flower's fragrance fades,*
> *But my love's fragrance*
> *Still lingers on*
> Elsewhere:
> *This is a way of no return*
> *Till my dying day*
> *I cannot erase*
> *The tattoos on my skin*

And other poems, a poem for every day of the four years in prison, are written in soft, flowing calligraphy, very feminine. And, like gems, words sparkle in it that were born in longing and in the freedom of imprisonment:

> *The prison library*
> *I pick a flower*
> *From the dictionary*

Okawa Oyabun Speaks, Part Six

We don't sell drugs in our family. In the Kansai Region (Kyoto-Osaka-Kobe) there are families that do sell drugs. Lots of shabu. Also in the Kanto area there are some families like that. With us in Okawa-Kai, there's none of it. We don't do drugs, and we don't sell them. It destroys you. Anyone who sells drugs isn't human anymore. And he's not useful to the family. His head is fucked up. If I hear that someone is doing drugs, he's kicked out immediately.

We also deal in real estate. Tokyo's going crazy with the property prices, and we're not the ones who caused it. But it'll explode. You see that the terrible processes caused by the legal society are severe, much more harmful, much, much more, than what we do. So we're also in property. Speculation. Investment. Brokering. Is it always done nicely? No! Sometimes we apply pressure. But in our family, we don't touch katagi. Yes, there are families that act with violence, but I can't get involved. Yakuza are in a process of gangsterization, no doubt about that. I'm worried. That's not my moral code. But even with respect to our survival, you have to look forward, many years forward. And globally. Gangsterization will destroy the Yakuza.

We're like political leaders. With us it's just like in your world. You need leaders with vision and a broad political perspective, and also a moral perspective. Yes, moral. Morality here is complicated and full of contradictions, exactly like in your world. So the violence we employ in real estate—that's not a good thing. It's not smart, and it'll bring about the total disqualification of the Yakuza. To throw people out of their houses, to force them, pay them a little and scare them—that's not good. That's not good! And it isn't effective, either. I still insist on our inner morality, but I see how it's rapidly disintegrating. With me, if somebody intimidates innocent people in the street, or in their houses, or just to show that they're Yakuza, he'll get a black postcard: he's banned. Some leave their pinky at my door. I don't like that. Cutting off pinkies is also an old-fashioned custom. A year ago I forbade that practice here in my family. We have to stop it. We have to look forward, be modern.

The older guys, they sometimes buy a false pinky so they won't be stand out in public. The best false pinkies are manufactured in London, but they're cheaper in Hong Kong. And it's closer.

The Pinky

A young man is walking along a narrow street. A young man comes toward him. They look at each other. Nirami. Their heads are lowered. Eyes penetrating. The heart explodes in the chest. The head says keep walking. The heart says no. The sake flows in the body and touches hidden places; it wants to break out. Action. Action. Simmering. The belly boils. The head says no. Don't do it. But the madness, that madness. What to do? The oyabun doesn't allow it. But that piece of shit looking at me that way. Every day he walks around here and provokes me. Look how he's staring at me. Those eyes. If I just walk away, I'm not a man. How can I look my friends in the eye? What can I tell them? But the oyabun doesn't allow it. Don't start personal fights, he said. The punishment will be severe, he said, but how can I go away now? And he's standing there, that prick, probably from the Yamada-Gumi, the shabu's coming out of those disgusting nostrils. The oyabun said don't get into unnecessary fights. So what if he said? Look, he's moving, he's moving, he'll pull a knife. Be smart and keep walking. No, how can I keep walking, and he's moving, and I'm afraid? I'm not afraid. I'll rip him to shreds. I'll rip him up, I'll rip him!

They're on each other. One man tears the other's skin, and the flesh is bared, and the blood stains the road, spreading over the asphalt. They squirm on the road. Is somebody whimpering? The blood mingles, and there's no way of knowing.

Suddenly there's a commotion. Young men from this gang, from that gang. They tear each other's skin and their mothers pray to Kannon to have mercy on that fire that burns and finds no repose. Oh, Kannon! Please!

Now there's a war in the offing. The next day two men attack the oyabun's office of the rival family. They shoot at the family crest. The day after two men come here and attack a group of young family men in an alley in Shinjuku. Soon a big battle is about to begin. And you can't tell where it will lead.

Then a telephone call between the two oyabuns. They understand. Yes, yes, today's young men. Sorry. No, I'm the one who should beg your pardon. No, no, I'm the one. After all, we're peaceful men. And how's your daughter? Yes, everything's okay with me. Yes, thanks, thanks. We'll see each other at Nomura's funeral.

The oyabun calls his kobun, telling him to tell his own kobun, to make it clear the young man who started the fight that he acted recklessly and improperly. And you know what to say.

That very day the young man comes to the family office. He makes a very deep bow to everyone present.

He asks for a big kitchen knife. He sits at the table. He spreads out a white cloth. He puts his left hand on the table. His hand is pretty and smooth and young, and he puts it on the table. He spreads his fingers. He ties a band of white cloth around his pinky. His hand trembles. He looks around him, ashamed. The men look at him. Their eyes are clear. You have to do what you have to do, the eyes say, and stop trembling. The faster you do it, the easier it is, stupid!

None of them is standing in front of him. They know.

The young man separates his pinky from the other fingers. He takes the big kitchen knife, the knife that has known so many pinkies. He puts the point of the knife to the left of the pinky, next to the first joint.

The young man shouts, "Oyabun! Forgive me for the embarrassment I caused! Forgive me!"

He shuts his eyes and shouts, "*Huuuuu!*" and lowers the knife in one fell swoop on the pinky joint.

The end of the finger flies off, and the blood spurts out. Like a pipe that's been opened. The figures dance before the young man. The men turn foggy, and everything is black. He tries to wrap what's left of the pinky. He faints. A red stain colors the white cloth, spreading.

Someone picks up the severed end. Wraps it in white cloth. Places it next to the young man. Someone spays him with water. Someone slaps him. Someone shakes him. "Get up, man!"

The young man will recover. He'll go to the oyabun's home. He'll go down on his knees and bow deeply before the door, even if no one sees him. He will place the fingertip there, wrapped in white cloth, and the knife, stained with the brown spots left on it. He'll go away proud and humiliated.

The oyabun will pick up the tip of the pinky. Someone will wash the stump. Someone will put the fingertip in a small bottle full of formaldehyde. The oyabun will place the bottle on a shelf, next to fifteen similar bottles.

The oyabun has nine natural fingers, whole and manicured, on his two hands.

He would like to revoke that outdated custom. We're modern men.

The Wife

"I soak the pinky stumps in formaldehyde in little medicine bottles and put them in the cabinet. Line after line, as you see up there. You have to wash the blood out of them and then soak them. Once every couple of months I find them at the door. But I stopped vomiting a long time ago." So says "Mama" Miyuko, Tetsuya's common-law wife and the mother of his son.

"It's what men do when they've strayed, they say. I don't know. A man without a pinky can't hold the hilt of a big samurai sword well, they say. Maybe, but for a long time now they haven't been fighting with swords, only in their stories. Well, it's not easy to hold the gun without the pinky either.

"Now I'm like a man. Years ago I was a dancer in a nightclub in the city of Sendai. I was a real woman then. I used to sing and dance. Sometimes I'd strip. Then I met Tetsuya and left that way of life to live with him. He would come and go, come and go. He would disappear without warning and come back a few days later. Tired, sometimes scarred. He'd ask how I was. Nowadays he's worried about the baby. Not a single word about what happened there, in those dark places where he goes. And even today he comes and goes, comes and goes. There's no end to his loneliness that you see on him when he comes back from those trips that I'm never allowed to ask about.

"The kobuns come to me when they're in trouble. When they're afraid of Tetsuya. I visit them when they're in prison. I bring them things, the newspapers they like. I give them smiles and warmth, as much as one can, you know. Most of them don't have a mother who'll come and visit. And if she does come, she won't smile. She'll just sit there quietly or cry. I smile at them. Even the big ones are little kids, believe me.

"Never ask a Yakuza's woman if she's happy. Can anyone answer? I very seldom meet the women of other family members. Mainly I meet the men. I know the men—the sons, the brothers, the uncles, Okawa Oyabun. Just men, men, men. Sometimes I'm a man myself. When he's in jail, I'm a strong man."

Okawa Oyabun Speaks, Part Seven

You have to see us as an entirely normal world. Normal. Just like yours. With Yakuza too, sometimes you need diplomacy. In the early

1980s I saw that our region, Tokyo, had become unbearable. There were turf wars. In the end the outside enemy began to threaten—Yamada-Gumi from the Kansai region, who haven't dared to come in here to this day. Something had to be done before we destroyed each other and before the police had an excuse to make our lives miserable.

I made some moves—one in connection with the police and one within our world of Yakuza. It took years of persuasion inside and outside. I wanted people to look far ahead. I had long meetings with the heads of the big Tokyo families, especially with Ninomiya Oyabun, the leader of the biggest family in the Tokyo region. There was an urgent need to make peace.

By long and dangerous diplomatic maneuvers, I managed to convince the big oyabuns to agree to map out the turfs and areas in the whole Kanto district. I also managed to set up a supervision and communication mechanism among the big oyabuns, to prevent unnecessary wars from breaking out because of a small fight between two individuals of two families.

Once a year, on February 20, we meet, the heads of the big families, in the New Otani Hotel. The police? Oh yes, sure. We inform them; you can't hold assemblies like that secretly. Every year we renew our understanding at a big, festive banquet. The peace treaty that I drafted five years ago is ceremonially ratified again every year. Since the peace treaty was signed five years ago, there have been no wars in the Tokyo region. Not a single one. And look what's happening in Kansai.

Aside from the annual gathering, there is a monthly meeting at a lower level, a mechanism for maintaining control and coordination among the big families of Tokyo and the region. Look at the pictures here. Here are the heads of the big families of Tokyo.

With the police, I created conditions for cooperation wherever possible. For example, safety of the streets. We help them very often with that. And it helps them save face. See, for example, our offices. Since our headquarters are in office buildings and sometimes in residential areas, I created a norm of behavior in our offices. This office is open from ten to six. My kobuns come dressed in suits and ties. There's no shouting, no wild behavior. No girls. Everything is managed perfectly. We don't disturb the neighborhood, and there's no reason to disturb us.

Or take, for example, the jail-release ceremonies. In the past, if some high-level member was released, we used to come to the jail with dozens of cars, block the traffic in the area, and act in a rowdy, arrogant way. That was enough of an excuse for the police to interfere. Now we hold the ceremonies early in the morning. We park the cars some distance from the rear gate of the prison and quietly hold the ceremony. In that way we were considerate toward the police and the community. If there's no need for it, we don't bother either of them. We have to manage our affairs discreetly, without unnecessary fuss. That's smarter. That's more decent. And it's also more profitable. We're visible. We're honorable. We're decent and trustful. That's why the police cooperate with us. Up to a limit, that is. Why don't you go and interview the police?"

At the Tokyo Police Headquarters

And so I did. I made an appointment at Tokyo Police Headquarters and went to interview a high officer, on the pretense of reporting them about my research. A minor official greeted me and asked what I wanted.

I told him, "I'm a visiting professor at the Tokyo University of Foreign Studies, and I've been conducting research on the Yakuza."

The man didn't appear to believe me. He asked, "You're collecting material from the press?"

"No. I'm connected with a family that adopted me."

"A Yakuza family?"

"Yes."

"Which family, if I may ask?"

"The Okawa-Kai family. Okawa Oyabun is the one who adopted me, three years ago," I announced, almost like a veteran Yakuza.

Silence. The man excused himself and left the room. Five minutes later he returned with an officer more senior than he, who repeated the questions, almost verbatim. I answered, as before, with the same answers. The man excused himself and left the room. Five minutes later he returned with someone senior to him, and again they left and returned until finally a senior officer entered and introduced himself as Mr. Oba, who is in charge of police supervision of the Yakuza in the Tokyo District. With a slightly crooked smile he announced that he knows Okawa Oyabun personally, and that Okawa is a very special person. I agreed with him.

He wondered how I reached Okawa, and I told him. He raised an eyebrow and said, "It is very difficult to reach Okawa Oyabun."

I said, "I know. It was very difficult."

He said, "You know you must be careful. Okawa-Kai and its sub-families are among the worst and most violent in Tokyo. You must be careful."

"I'm careful, and I don't feel endangered. I'm under the protection of Okawa Oyabun, and I feel no danger."

"Be careful, Sensei, they're bad men."

"Some of them are bad, and some are good," I said. "I've already spent three years with them, and I'm no more apprehensive than I am in the streets of Tel Aviv."

"I never heard about anyone who wanted to do research about the Yakuza. No one Japanese and no foreigner. The few Japanese who tried failed miserably. They don't let them in."

"I know about all the efforts. They failed because they're Japanese. I may have succeeded because I'm foreign. Maybe it's because I've formed a good and warm connection with Okawa Oyabun. As you said, a very special man."

"Did he make any requests of you regarding the results of the research?"

"No, on the contrary. He told me I have a free hand, and that he doesn't intend to intervene at all in the process of the research or its results. Until now I can only thank him for his openness and excellent cooperation."

"I've known that family for twenty years. Sometimes it seems to me we're doing similar things. You have to be a little bit criminal in order to know criminals. They also have to be a little like the police to know how to work with us. We work together a lot."

"I know. A month ago you called up Okawa Oyabun and talked with him about problems in the Ikebukuro Quarter. I was there."

The inspector looked embarrassed. He admitted that he called Okawa and spoke with him about a problem that Okawa helped him solve. "No doubt," he said, "the Yakuza are a secret police force in the streets, and they often succeed in places where the police doesn't succeed. The police and the Yakuza have many common interests. There are a lot of elements in the streets that both parties are interested in getting rid of: individual criminals, ad hoc coalitions of organizations that don't belong to the Yakuza, the Asian gangs—Taiwanese, Chinese, Thai, and violent youth gangs that assault entertainment and food establishments. The Yakuza is no less interested in the security of the streets in Japan than the police and the citizens. It's good for business. Robberies and theft, which are so rare in Japan, interfere with the Yakuza's good businesses. According to the code of most of the families, thieves and burglars are regarded as contemptible, and the punishment for petty theft is severe.

"Take my business card, and if you have a problem, or something else, you understand, don't hesitate to call. But be careful, Sensei. They're not what they seem sometimes. Not at all."

Thank you, Inspector Oba. You know I'll never call.

Tetsuya, My Brother

One day Tetsuya calls me and says, "Come to my house. It's been some time". He sounds formal. Do I feel tension? He picks me up in town, and we drive to his house in the suburbs. We enter the house, and Miyuko greets us. Along with her, two little Maltese terriers greet us with hoarse yips. Tetsuya sits in an armchair and puts them in his lap. Mama brings refreshments.

Next to the armchair is a low Japanese table, and on it lies a calligraphy set, carefully arranged—an ink stone, a small jar for water, brushes, Japanese paper spread out, and two sketches of Chinese characters in a sweeping style. Good calligraphy.

"That's my calligraphy," he says. "I've been studying and practicing for five months now. I also make ink paintings. But I'm still a beginner. Maybe somebody I'll get it. Who knows? How do you like it, Sensei?"

"They're excellent calligraphies," I say. "Could you do one for me?"

"Sure," he says, shyly. He spreads the paper on the tatami mat. Very carefully he places the weights. Then he prepares the ink, working in deep concentration, takes a deep breath, picks up the brush, and dips it cautiously.

He holds the brush over the paper, inhales deeply, and then, with one sweep, he slices the paper, and the character dragon bursts out, twisting, solid, splashed.

It's really beautiful.

"A brush with the sweep of a sword. And the ink is like blood," he says.

He carries two huge Chinese porcelain vases, blue and white. He hugs them. For a long time he talks about each vase. And drinks. On one of the vases is written, "May my five sons pass the imperial examinations." Next week, his daughter from a previous marriage will be taking the entrance exams to study Chinese medicine at the university. May she pass the examinations with success, he says. She'll be a doctor. She'll help people. She won't be bad like him. No, she won't be like him. She's a good girl. She ...

He wipes a hidden tear and drinks some more. He unrolls ancient scrolls for me. And he drinks. He shows me photographs from a matsuri, from past times, that are gone forever. And he drinks some more. He shows scripts he wrote for successful Yakuza movies. Miyuko serves us more and more tea. He drinks more and more whiskey.

I look at the son of untouchables who has risen to success, who does calligraphy, and who loves his mother. I look at the brush and at the Chinese vases, and I see there the matsuri spirit of Japan, and his days that are full of crimes and blackmail and fights. And now his eyes are moist.

We drink quietly. He closes his eyes. If it were possible, I would hug him.

I bow, suddenly. Deeply, to the floor.

"Tetsuya. I have nothing to show you. I'm very grateful. But I'll write a poem for you, with a brush. That will be my token of gratitude for everything."

He waves his arms dismissively.

I spread out paper, prepare the ink, take the brush, and dip it. My hand trembles. I write:

> *Between tear and tear*
> *I return to my hut*
> *And the summer hurries to perish*

Silence. And then he shouts, "Sake!" and sake immediately appears on our table.

"You and I, Sensei, are going to be brothers now. Five-five. No, no, you can't refuse. You and I will be brothers. Take the cup and repeat after me, 'I Yakobu Razu …' Take it, you're insulting me, take it! Take it! You won't have to commit any crimes, don't worry! Take the cup already! Repeat after me! 'I Yakobu Razu, with the drinking of this cup …'"

Thus we became brothers.

Chapter Four

On Yuki's Trail

Winter 1991

A telephone call shakes me up. It is Tetsuya.

"Sensei, maybe there's someone who can help find Yuki!"

Eight years have passed since he disappeared. I rush to meet Tetsuya. In a bar, he is drinking beer. His face is red.

"Hi. How are you? I may have some link to start a search for your Yuki. I'm not sure. But we will try. When the Yamada-Gumi began to penetrate the Sugamo district of Tokyo some years ago, hardly anybody noticed. Sugamo is a traditional neighborhood. There aren't big profits for Yakuza there. It's a boring neighborhood. Now they're suddenly there, the Yamada-Gumi. They get into the neighborhood clubs, bars, nomiya, izakaya. They talk politely to the owners. They threaten gently, almost unnoticed.

"One day, in the summer of 1983, a confrontation breaks out. Hey, you okay? Yes, I know you met Yuki that summer. When the small clashes begin, Hayashi Oyabun, the one you met in Sugamo, stops a filthy chimpira from the Yamada-Gumi and demands a full accounting about the types from Osaka who've been showing up in the Sugamo area recently. He demands full accounting for bothering the locals, and also for annoying the Yakuza, because it's his area, and who's the little prick that's getting in his way? The chimpira from the Yamada-Gumi draws a knife, and Hayashi almost goes.

But then the chimpira from Yamada-Gumi gets hit on the head with a heavy object—so I was told—and he falls down.

"The one who smashes his head with the heavy object is apparently that Yuki, your friend. Some blows are exchanged. Maybe your friend is even injured. He saves Hayashi's life, but he doesn't save the neighborhood. Within a month the area falls into the hands of a gang affiliated with Yamada-Gumi. We don't notice at the time because Sugamo is so boring, as I told you, and we have bigger problems in other places. Hayashi, Yuki, and some others scatter and disappear.

"I make some enquiries in the north to find out what's with Yuki' brother. Murata Yoshinori was a minor but very talented and promising oyabun in and around Hakodate City, southern Hokkaido. He was loosely allied with us. One day Yamada-Gumi men show up at Yoshinori's and tell him that his brother Yuki killed one of their men in Tokyo. They're willing to forgo revenge in return for parts of the Yoshinori turf. Murata doesn't believe them. His brother's a good boy, university graduate and all that. He shows them right away where they are and whom they're standing in front of. Before they finish one more sentence, they each have a deep scar on their faces. Very brave, that Yoshinori. There's blood. And maybe one or two Yamada-Gumi men are killed. Hokkaido is a rough area, I'm telling you. But Yoshinori also lost the area to a family affiliated with Yamada-Gumi.

"Since I heard about your search, I've been trying to find out what happened to the Murata brothers. Yoshinori, the big brother, disappeared. Maybe he changed his name. Maybe he changed his face. Maybe he ran away. Some people say he went abroad until things cool off in Hokkaido. I heard he was in the Philippines. I heard it was Brazil, I heard Hawaii. I don't know yet. I'll find out. And Yuki, we don't know. Somebody told me last week that maybe, somewhere, maybe somebody saw him in Hokkaido.

"We might find your Yuki. We might not. Eight years is a lot of time in our world. People disappear every month. Next month

I'm going to Hokkaido. Come with me. We'll try to find him there. Hokkaido is a tough place, I'm telling you. A tough place. But pretty. I like Hokkaido. But there's going to be a war there, in the future.

"In the meantime, come with me tomorrow. I'll introduce you to somebody who spent some years in Hokkaido. Maybe he knows something. We'll try."

The Homeless Yakuza

A winter day. It's cold.

I'm driving with Tetsuya in the rich neighborhood of Nishi Azabu of Tokyo. The fences are high. The gardens are well kept. Fashion stores sell scarves by Issey Miyake for a hundred thousand yen. Sedans. Here's Arisugawa Park, with its pools, and the arched bridges over little ponds. The Filipina nannies and the diplomats' babies in strollers. Patches of snow under the trees.

"Let's get out for a minute," Tetsuya says. I notice he looks around and into the car's mirrors before we get out. We walk through the park. There's a corner in the park, on the other side of the pretty pond, and in that corner sit three men in filthy clothes. They're sitting on the ground. Remnants of the night's frost spot the dirt.

One of them is wearing six layers of black jackets and crusts of filth. When he turns over from his right side to his left, you can see a red label on the lining, and also his skinny bare belly, and beneath it his shrunken member. The other one is wearing two suits. The upper one was once striped, and now it's also black. The third one—only his head is visible under a pile of black blankets. His arm sticks out, holding a bottle. He has no pinky on his left hand.

Between them are sake bottles, white rice in banana leaves, and a can of food. Their faces are various shades of black, like theatrical makeup for a Gorky play.

Tetsuya asks me to stand at a certain distance. He walks up to the three and quietly calls to the man under the black blankets.

"Brother!" A loud whisper. "Brother Ito!"

The three raise blank faces, their eyes slits. The man under the black blankets returns to the bottle.

Tetsuya approaches and gently raises him and takes him to the side. He sneaks a package under the man's rags and hurries to the car. The man returns to the two vagrants and sits down. We go back to the car.

"Ito was once a big oyabun in our family," Tetsuya explains. "He came to us when he was twenty-eight, not like the others who come when they're teenagers. Ito finished university and came to us after five years in the Foreign Office. For some reason he left. We never ask anyone about private affairs, or about the troubles that sent him to our world. I swore him in with the sakazuki ceremony.

"You know, company directors come to us, sales clerks and bank clerks, policemen come to us, and construction workers, and architects, and we never, ever ask questions. If Ito had a huge debt, or if he shamed his family, or fucked his sister, or stole money from the government, or got sick of Japanese life like me and my friends, we don't want to know. We give him a home.

"But in our family, you don't do drugs. Even if somebody sometimes sells it here and there, it's really forbidden to use it. 'Life or drugs? Stop doing drugs!' That's what we announce in our family magazine, right? If somebody smokes, you can't trust him. You can't tell whether he's here or there.

"And we didn't know Ito smoked. A lot. Ito was a very talented and ruthless man, and within two years he already had widespread businesses in the Machida region, and he didn't trust Japanese. His kobuns were from Korea and Taiwan. Foreign Office, no? Later he also built a little base for himself in Sapporo, Hokkaido. Small but profitable. Construction stuff, I think. We'd drink together, go out with girls. He was very successful. He had a big black car and a beautiful villa and bodyguards and beautiful women, number two, and number three, and number four—and he fed them and indulged them generously.

"But one day Ito had some fun with a girl in a love hotel, and he went out the next day cursing and screaming in the street, 'Fuck you all! Fuck fuck fuck you all!' He kicked cars and molested people. And when they went in to clean the room after his fucking, it stank of marijuana, and there was smashed furniture all over. It was a huge shame for the family.

"Two days later he came to Okawa Oyabun with his head shaved and left his left pinky, wrapped in cloth red with blood, outside the door. The Oyabun forgave him, after giving him a severe warning in front of everyone.

"But Ito didn't kick his habit. He was his own prisoner. One day he went back to the love hotel, and the next day they found him in drugged stupor, and next to him was a dead Korean girl. She'd ODed.

"So then they send him a black postcard. A black postcard is expulsion that can be revoked. If you're blackballed, you can't do business, and no one can meet with you, and no family is allowed to receive you. The postcard is sent to all the families in Japan. Then, after a year of banishment, they sent him a postcard accepting him back. We were glad he came back because we liked him. He was a good man.

"But he didn't stop. Then something happened, in Sapporo. And since then I have *on* (a debt of honor) to Ito. Since Sapporo. The situation in Hokkaido was very delicate, very tense for a long time. Okawa Oyabun told us to be careful. Not to start anything and not to cause any battle that wasn't planned from Tokyo. Not to be dragged in. The Yamada-Gumi keeps trying to draw us into battle before we're ready. Okawa is building a coalition of families in the north, and he's cautiously planning for the future and for the coming war. Meanwhile, by no means may we be dragged in. Whomever does anything like that will be punished.

"One day Ito and I are sitting in a pub in Sapporo, and two Yamada-Gumi men walk in. They sit at a nearby table and start nirami, staring at us. War eyes. I say to Ito, 'Let's get out! No fighting, not now. Okawa says not to start a fight under any circumstances now, unless there's no alternative. Don't get dragged in. You'll be punished!' I say to Ito, 'Let's go.'

"I don't know whether he's soaked with drugs or not, but he doesn't leave. He even sends nirami back to the two hoods. I drag him out, and they're following us. I drag him after me to our office in Sapporo. He shouts all kinds of stupid things to them. We go into the office. Five minutes later, they're there.

"Ito had never fought before. After all, he was from the Foreign Office. All his courage comes from cocaine. I try to stop the two Yamada-Gumi guys, and he's lying on the sofa, out of it. Out of nowhere two more come. And suddenly he gets up. That kid from the Foreign Office races to the sword rack and takes down the Oyabun's sword. And I shout to him, 'Forget it.' I throw him a pistol. Because if you don't know how to use a sword, it pulls you in every direction.

"Ito takes the pistol in his right hand and the sword in his left and screams, '*Yarrrrroooooooo!*' For a moment we all freeze with fear. I look at him and see that his eyes are tightly closed, and he sticks out the hand with the gun and shoots right into the stomach of one of them.

"And then, his eyes still closed, he waves the arm with the sword, and, like I thought, the sword pulls him all over the room, around and around. He shouts, '*Yarrrrooooooo!*' again.

Before I know what's happening, I see blood spurting and the Yamada-Gumi are dragging away their wounded. They disappear, and in the room I have a monster going crazy, a sword gripping a man and a gun shooting in every direction.

"'Ito!!' I shout to him from behind the sofa. 'Ito! Enough!'

"Suddenly it's quiet. Ito lies down. There's a sliver of glass stuck in his arm. He's shaking. His eyes are still closed tight, and there's a very strong smell of piss. I try to examine him, and I'm shaking too.

"It's not like in the Yakuza movies, Sensei. Ito was fighting with a lot of fear and cocaine inside him. His eyes were closed real tight.

But he saved me. And if you ask me whether other guys fight like in the Yakuza films, and how I fight, I won't answer you. But he saved me, and I owe him for it. I have *on* for him, and that's why I bring him food packages, against all family regulations. And the *on* that I have for Ito is as strong as what I have for the Oyabun. I have giri for the Oyabun and the family, but I also have giri for Ito. Giri versus giri. Unsettled conflict.

"He saved me, but he disobeyed orders. A little war broke out in Sapporo. In that war we also lost territories. We lost because we weren't ready. Okawa Oyabun was fuming with rage. You couldn't argue. 'Send him a red postcard,' he said softly.

Then they sent Ito a red postcard. A red postcard is final banishment. A red postcard, Sensei, kills you little by little. It's worse than death. A red postcard is absolute ostracism, and there's no way back. A man who receives a red postcard isn't allowed to run a business or keep an office or a rank or sons, and no one is allowed to be friends with him or drink with him or give him anything, and no family in Japan will accept him. Like a black postcard, but forever. No way back. And if with a black postcard we dare to call the guy up and visit him and tell him a little about what's going on, with a red postcard it's strictly forbidden. Whomever makes contact with a red postcard man is rebelling against his oyabun, and very harsh punishment is in store for him. Maybe getting a red postcard himself. Whomever gets a red postcard dies little by little, Sensei.

"But me, my giri to him is life. I owe him my life, even if I pay with my own life. That's gokudo, Sensei, the path of extremes. If they catch me giving him something one day, I'll join him in the park, and maybe I'll hear lectures from him about Japan's foreign affairs, and maybe I'll get food on the sly from one of my sons. And die little by little. But meanwhile, how can I see him hiding there in those black blankets? So I bring him packages."

That's what Tetsuya tells me in the car.

"And now it's impossible to talk to him. You saw. My stomach aches."

"Yes. I can see that. Do you think he knows something about Yuki?"

"Maybe. That's why I brought you here today. Maybe he knows. But not now, well, you saw for yourself."

*

We visit the park five times before Tetsuya decides it's possible. Then we bring Ito food again. We take him with us in the car. And he's black with filth, but there is no stench, maybe because of the winter. Tetsuya drives to a safe apartment. We help Ito up. He takes a dip in the hot bath. He is clearer now. His look is enquiring. He looks at me suspiciously. He bows deeply in gratitude for every cup of tea.

We ask about Yuki.

"Yuki? Murata Yuki? Yes, yes I remember. While doing business in Hokkaido. Somebody came to me, a messenger from the Ida family from Sapporo, a sister family of ours. He says to me, there's somebody who needs help. Help him. The man needs to change his face. His name is Yuki. Full name Murata Yukihira, whom I have to help, may have to change his name, place, documents, identity. Everything. And this man, whom I have to help, is important, or maybe some VIP's brother or son or lover. Otherwise they wouldn't ask me to change his face. And the sister families in Sapporo will be grateful for the help. Extremely grateful, they say.

"One day he comes, this Yuki. Wild. Frightened. Very thin. Looks around. One eye is like looking somewhere else. A scar on his cheek. With a knapsack. When he puts it on the table, books fall out of it. I'm an educated man, you know. I can recognize educated men. Books of poems by poets whose names I can't remember now. And I arrange a little apartment for him. I give him new documents. Everything. I switch his identity. A kind of cheap spy story. Three days later, he says to me, 'I also have a woman.' Wait a minute, they didn't tell me about that, I say. I call to find out, and they say, 'Yes, we forgot to mention it. There's a woman too. Be careful with her even more than with him. She's important. Very important. Change her too. And send her abroad. To Bangkok. To Kuala Lumpur. Jakarta. Manila. Send her away quick.'

"And there really was a woman. Not a woman. A girl. Thin as a twig. All orange. Orange hair, orange shirt, orange shoes. As if somebody poured orange paint on her. And she has a little bag. Orange. And the books that pour out of it are manga comics for teenyboppers. What are they doing together? All day they hug each other and make noises. They really eat each other up. They're running away. From who and why, I don't know. But they're running away. I change her identity too. Documents, names, clothes, everything.

"One day I hear a scrap of conversation between them. 'Your dad ...,' he says to her. Something about her dad. Then I hear the name: Sekida. Sekida Saburo! I know Sekida Oyabun. Her father is Sekida Oyabun!? They're running away from her father!? Are they crazy? He'll kill them! And why is it important for the men from the north to help them disappear?

"A few days later a story shows up in the papers about the kidnapping of Sekida's daughter. I check it out by telephone with the Ida guys in Sapporo. 'Are you crazy? Do you want a war? Did somebody decide to go to war about some stupid love affair? Are you out of your minds?' 'Help him,' they insist. 'And don't ask questions. If possible, abroad, too.' When I check up, I understand that Murata Oyabun is thought of as someone who, with his courage and intelligence, can stop Yamada-Gumi penetration into Sapporo, so they're trying to help out his brother as much as possible. But why the girl? No answer. You're out of your minds. If there was a kidnapping in order to threaten Sekida Oyabun, there'll be a war. And Okawa Oyabun won't allow that. You remember what happened to me afterward.

"So now I understand. Maybe there's a stupid love story here. But what came out of it, unintentionally, is a story about pressure on Sekida Oyabun, so that he won't side with the Yamada-Gumi. Apparently. Maybe. Too complicated for me.

"I have connections with the Foreign Office, and I find out if its possible to do something to help them. Then I decided: First, a total change of faces. Then, a cooling-off period in Hokkaido. Then, out. Jakarta, or Manila, maybe. But he has to get settled first. He's a kid. He reads poetry books. He has to be trained. He's just a kid!

"After that I sent him to Hokkaido, to Hakodate. To one of our guys who runs gambling joints. I think I got him work in our Athene club, in Hakodate. As a guard, I set up for him, something like that. In the meantime they will train him. Guns and stuff. I make sure that somebody would make arrangements for him in Manila after that; at that time we started business in Manila. So he'll have rice to eat abroad. Whether he got there or not, I don't know. What happened to him, I don't know. Because after that, I got into my own troubles. Check in Manila. A strange guy, that Yuki. And now, Tetsuya Aniki, get me out of here. You don't want to get a red postcard. You're going to be a great oyabun, and you don't have to get fouled up with me. Get me out of here.

"Oh, yes, Tetsuya. I remember now. The name I arranged for Yuki is Suzuki Taro. Suzuki Taro. As gray as possible. So they won't think a lot. The name I gave her? Nakamoto Natsuko, I think. What was her real name? I can't remember. I also painted her in new colors. I don't know what she did with that. Now, get me out of here."

Tetsuya returns him to the park. He doesn't give him a change of clothes so no one will figure out that somebody's taking care of him. Just gives him food, and a little money. He sits in the car and cries.

I ask about Tatuya about Sekida and the kidnapping. Tetsuya is pensive. He remembers something that shook the Yakuza world a few years ago. He doesn't remember the details. Sekida Oyabun died two years ago, he thinks, and his family was swallowed up in other families.

Tracing Yuki's Past

The kidnapping of Sekida's daughter? I think. 'That's what he said, 'The kidnapping of Sekida's daughter.' I go to search in newspapers archives.

Two hours spent in the Asahi Newspaper archives produced the following item:

October, 1983:

Where has Sekida Mayumi Disappeared?
Kidnapping in the Yakuza World?

Investigative reporter Hiraoka reports from informed Yakuza sources that Sekida Mayumi, the daughter of Sekida Akira Oyabun, the boss of the Sekida-Gumi gang, from the Sugamo District of Tokyo, disappeared without a trace several days ago. Sekida-Gumi is a small veteran gang in the area, going back to Edo days. It has become known to us that Mayumi, the beloved daughter of Sekida Oyabun, was recently placed under close and constant guard by her father because of tension in the district.

The great tension in the Sugamo District began when elements foreign to the area, apparently from the Yamada-Gumi gang from Kansai, penetrated the quarter as part of repeated efforts of the biggest crime gang in Japan to enter the Tokyo region and thus violate the turf agreement that exists between Yamada-Gumi and the Yakuza gangs of Tokyo ... There have been a number of violent incidents in the Sugamo District, one of the quietest and most traditional neighborhoods of "Old" Tokyo. In these incidents, Yamada-Gumi men were beaten mercilessly by Okawa-Kai men.

There are rumors, as yet unsubstantiated, that Mayumi was kidnapped by Okawa-Kai men, maybe in order to warn Sekida not to side with the Yamada-Gumi in their attempts to penetrate Tokyo. Nevertheless, according to senior sources in the Yakuza, there is a mystery here because the Yakuza do not usually kidnap family daughters for revenge or as a way of exerting pressure. If the Okawa-Kai family really did use this method, it means a declaration of war, in the style of the American Mafia, first within the families of Tokyo and also between the Okawa-Kai family and the Yamada-Gumi. If the kidnapping was committed by a Yakuza family, this is a dramatic turning point, symptomatic of what many people both in the Yakuza and out of it have been fearing recently: that the Yakuza is undergoing "gangsterization." The violence will increase, the public will rebel, and the legislature will be called upon to act more firmly.

I read in amazement and recall the order of events at that time, in 1983. Mayumi is the girl in orange! Yuki and the girl disappeared at the same time. I remember going to place Hirano's in Golden-Gai to look for Yuki. He wasn't there. She wasn't there. Yuki? Is he the kidnapper? Or was that just lovers escaping? What's the meaning of this?

The next day I go to the library and poke around in the newspapers of late 1983 and early 1984. There are tabloids that specialize in Yakuza affairs. Stories about warsfare, honor, sex, and the internal politics of the Yakuza, interviews with big oyabuns, adventure stories, gossip, and many pictures of oyabuns in kimonos or in expensive suits. Blood, sweat, and semen, all in huge bold titles, drip from the pages on my curious hands.

Very little about Sekida and Mayumi. The tabloids feast with banner headlines:

Where Has Mayumi Disappeared to?
Sekida Oyabun Does Not Conceal His Concern and His Tears!
Sekida Oyabun Swears He Will Find the
Kidnapper and Take Revenge!
No Ransom Demands!

Okawa-Kai Headquarters in Tokyo denies any connection with the kidnapping. This is not the way of the Okawa-Kai, says the family spokesman in a press realease today. We do not kidnap girls. We will not be dragged into any provocation. Kidnapping is not the Yakuza Way. Sekida Oyabun should check very well which of his kobuns lusted after his Little Daughter, adds the spokesman.

Disappeared, as if she'd never existed. No doubt it's the girl in orange. She's the girl whose name Ito changed to Nakamoto Natsuko. How can I find Nakamoto Natsuko, who has probably changed her name, her face, her dresses, and her soul a thousand times since she disappeared? They both ran away, Yuki and Mayumi.

Leads in the Far North

After the meeting with Ito, the homeless Yakuza, it seems that all traces lead to Hokkaido, Yuki's native region. So I go north with Tetsuya, Miyuko, and little Kotaro. He travels there regularly, for the northern festivals, a branch of his business. We reach Hakodate, the southernmost city on the island of Hokkaido. On the way Tetsuya stopped in a number of places. He would disappear for a few hours and return. Sometimes he seemed perturbed. Sometimes content. Mostly he would return drunk. Always glad to see the baby. We stayed in various *minshuku* B&B's, and it always seemed that they'd known him for a long time, and they gave him great respect. In the city of Hakodate, he's involved in the matsuri that's taking place there. Maybe we'll hear something about Yuki. We drive to a small minshuku, and the proprietors greet me with a big smile. "Welcome, Sensei, welcome. Tetsuya-san told us about you."

A table laden with about thirty small plates awaits us, and each one is a miracle of taste, fragrance, and color. The proprietors are an elderly couple. Tetsuya goes to take care of some business and will return later. We sit at the table. Green tea. Fans. It's very humid.

"We like Tetsuya-san," they tell me. "We know where he comes from and who his friends are. But he's a man with a huge heart. Maybe he's a criminal. Maybe he does bad things in other places. We're simple people, and we don't know. But he's been staying with us every year for fifteen years now, on the dates of the great matsuri. He likes the matsuri. He supports our matsuri with a lot of money. You should see him bearing the mikoshi on his shoulder with the others. Tetsuya is a matsuri man. He knows every matsuri in northern Japan. For twenty years he's been following the same routes throughout the country, on the path of the matsuri. He's good to his kobuns. He's good to us. Sometimes he comes with the child. He's good to his son".

Tetsuya returns, his face red. He's a little drunk. He sits down and says nothing for a while. He keeps his silence even longer. Then he says, "Come, let's see what's going on at the matsuri. And tomorrow, when everything's taken care of at the matsuri, we'll go look for Yuki. I mean, Suzuki Taro."

At the Athene Gambling Joint

Evening. We drive to the sakariba of Hakodate, the city that sends tongues of light into the sea at night. There, in the alleys where Tetsuya walks as though in his own home, we stop in front of the red door of a club. A neon sign says Athene. It's the club Ito mentioned. Will there by anything about Yuki here, eight years later? Who'll remember? Who's stable in the Path of Extremes for more than six months? Who'll even give a hint? Who'll give any information? Maybe Tetsuya's company will encourage people to talk.

We go in. Athene looks like an ordinary club. Men in suits slump next to girls who encourage them to drink, chat, and do some bar-side cuddling. The mamasan is working hard behind the bar, pouring, serving, wiping, surveying the place with a strict eye. She sends subtle signs to the girls: mind the skirt, the drink, the talk, the leg, the shoe, the man who needs attention. You look around and see nothing special. But it's just the innocent face of a big gambling club, I note to myself. My heart pounds, and I look around.

"Not here," Tetsuya says, "there."

"There" is an ordinary gray door at the back of the club. In front of the door is a table draped in red cloth, like the other tables. Next to it sit two people, a man and a girl, a hostess. She fondles him with the dry, hoarse sexiness of club hostesses. He smokes and looks out into the club, a look you can't mistake. He sees Tetsuya, springs to his feet, and bows deeply. "*Ooooossss!*" he whisper-shouts, and rushes to open the door.

Behind it is an office, and in back of the office is another door. A young man is standing in front of that one with his legs spread and his arms crossed over his stomach. When he sees me, he takes a very little step forward. When he sees Tetsuya, he calms down, bows deeply, and withdraws. He opens the door and barks something inside. We enter a heavy cloud of smoke and dim light. I cough. Everybody looks at us. For some time I can't see anything.

Gradually I notice the details. In the cloud floats colorful drawings, red and blue, yellow, purple, white. Dragons, snakes, kabuki figures, tigers, deeply engraved in the skin, so they can't be erased. They sit around the low table. Tattooed bodies. Naked to the waist. Others, with a *haramaki* loincloth bound around their waist. Like mythical diapers. Some of them wear trousers. They all smoke cigarettes. They're playing with *hanafuda* colorful cards. Every card has a picture of a flower or the moon or rain according to the season. The pictures stand out in red and yellow alongside brightly colored men.

The dance of colors in a smoky cloud dazzles me. Between the cards are stacks of money. Giant piles of bills, some tall as a beer bottle. And there are smaller stacks. There are also men with no money in front of them, and their faces are gloomy. Some of the half-naked tattooed men have peaceful eyes, and others have taken off their suits and loosened their ties. Their eyes yearn toward the table. A beam of light shines on the faces of the men sitting around the table and moving in and out of the light.

When I get used to the darkness, I see that I'm in a big room, where two other groups are playing. Coughs and grumbles and short barks—there's almost no talking. Everybody's facing someone who's completely in darkness. When the heads move into the light, you can see split lips, scarred faces, rotten teeth, gold watches, and a lot of dragons on the arms. Sweat. And smoke. And the sour smell of tension and greed.

Suddenly everything stops dead. A blow on the table, and two men leap toward each other. Somebody barks, and the two freeze. Somebody raises a hand. They thaw and return to their places.

Tetsuya has disappeared. Where is he? I seek him but dare not move. It's frightening here. Where has he gone?

Somebody says, "I'm going to pee." He gets up and passes very close by me. Odors of tobacco. Sake. Perfume? When he passes, he brushes against me and sends a defiant smile. He murmurs, "I'll be back," to the cloudy interior.

I tremble. Where's Tetsuya?

And Tetsuya is over there, far off. He says out loud, almost shouting, "Sensei! Come over here!" Why is he shouting? Why "sensei" out loud? I hurry into the smoky darkness. He hurries to the end of the room and is swallowed up in a door. How many inner rooms does this place have?

Inside, someone is sitting in a faded armchair. A small lamp on a small table, above it a small fixture, and on it a small sheet of aluminum foil. Something is burning, raising swirls of white smoke. Leaning close, the man holds a piece of paper, rolled into a kind of hollow cigar. The paper is a ten thousand yen bill. The man inhales smoke through the rolled paper. He holds his breath, exhales. He looks content.

"Clear, very clear now. It's clear to me now.

"You, who you are, clear, clear, you're the one Tetsuya told me about. You're the gaijin. Sorry, okay? Sorry. But you're gaijin, no? You're looking for Yuki. Or Suzuki Taro. That's what Tetsuya said. Or Murata Yukihira. Many names, many faces, this guy. I know him. Of course I know him. I also know that he came here as Suzuki Taro. But a long time ago. A good man. Not exactly one of us, but a good man. A man of giri. He had a good brother, the oyabun of a brave little family. But I don't know where he is now. Disappeared one day. Maybe he went to a far, faraway land."

"Where did you meet Yuki?"

"Here, a few years ago. I don't remember how many, gaijin-san. Yes, I've been here for ten years. Haven't moved. Every night in this room. What else can I do? I can't do big business, gaijin-san. Happy that papa gives me this. Kind of Papa Yamanaka. He's best. He gives me. Always. It spreads all over your body, and you feel clear, clear. The clearest. You're clear. Your glasses. Your clothes. Everything is clear. Ookh, so good."

"Yuki?"

"Yes. Yuki. Excuse me." Silence.

"Yuki."

"Ah, yes, Yuki was here. Did I tell you? Here. Years ago. I don't remember when. I knew him. Somebody from the family said help him. Said he was running from the cops and also from the Yamada-Gumi. Needed shelter, change of face and identity, work. So I arranged all this. No questions. He started as a guard outside a gambling den. You need some alarm, no? You know, the police, and all sorts of other pests. That's how you start in the Yakuza. His face was so scary, that even a Yakuza would run away. Ha-ha-ha. Good. So good. I don't even know if he was a Yakuza before that.

"This Yuki, he could have made a career with his brother, Murata Yoshinori Oyabun. A real man, a samurai. But the kid brother didn't want to. Didn't want to, they said. What did I say? I can see through your clothes. Yes, fine, fine. Everything is pleasant and clear and transparent, trans … parent. Yuki? Oh, yes. Yes, after some time he began to work inside the club. To supervise, so people don't cheat, stuff like that. And whether anybody was armed. He was supposed to keep an eye out. After a month the jerk said he'd never fired a weapon. So I took him out of the city for training. It was very funny. That Yuki. He held the gun and trembled. Shouted something to encourage himself. Shot with his eyes closed. We broke some windows in old houses, and a few carcasses of old cars. Never hit a thing. Always shaking. I took him out for more training, and more. Never came to anything. He was fit to be an 'intelli-Yakuza'—like the lawyers and stuff like that. Business. I think he was in finance. University. Business. You know. Not guns. Except those guys, the educated ones don't know giri. They forgot what sweat is. They forget what it is to pee when you're in a fight. What fear is. What it's like to pull your friend out of the grave, deep, deep from there, and give him life. With your air, you give him life. And to say thanks. Air. Is there air here? Clear, clear, everything's sharp, biting sharp, gaijin-san.

"Yuki? Ah, yes, Yuki. He worked here for a few months. Not made to be a Yakuza, the guy, even if he did have an impressive scar on his right cheek. The guy was at least in one fight, so they say. We went out to drink together sometimes. Nice guy. His eyes were always sad. One eye is never there. So scary he was, I tell you. He never wanted to snort shabu. But he drank. Sometimes when he was really drunk he'd talk about some girl. Girls—screw them all. He loved poems. Even wrote poems, I think. But he disappeared. Maybe he went to the girl. Maybe abroad. But he had a head for business. Somebody in the family heard about him on business stuff and offered him a job. But he vanished. That's how they are, young guys. They come and go, and you don't know where. Rumor was that maybe he ran away out of the country. But I don't ask. With us, you don't ask. You go, you come. You make friends. You separate. Always leaving, we are. Always longing. Always alone. Alone, gaijin-san. What are you? What's your connection with Yuki? Something he did for you? Something you did for him? What are you, brothers or something? You did sakazuki with him, or something? You also don't look like a Yakuza or anything like that, gaijin-san. Maybe you're brothers, huh?"

"Yes," I tell him. "We're brothers."

"So look in Sapporo. Maybe in the Kimura Family. Something I heard. Maybe he was an advisor, or something like that. That's something maybe I remember. He was something in economics, the guy, no? Not sure …"

The Ex-Cop

"Sensei, it's the beer," the man says to me. We're on the beach, in the city of Hakodate, Hokkaido. "You see this round belly? It's beer. Lots of beer. I love Asahi Dry. Most refreshing. Goes to your head the most."

The speaker, Hisao, is sitting on a lounger, his feet paddling in the water, wearing only shorts. Above them, a huge belly that attracts the attention of the other people on the beach. Every evening during the matsuri, he sells slush with syrup. Purple slush, yellow slush, red slush, pink slush, green slush—whatever the children ask for. He also drives a truck that carries goods to the matsuri. He's about forty-five but a novice in the family. He treats the others, most of them much younger than he, with great respect and awe. He relates to Tetsuya with the extreme honor due to an oyabun. He addresses the senior members as aniki. He even addresses me with a great honor after he sees the demonstrative friendship between Tetsuya and me. A middle-aged Yakuza novice.

A few minutes later, after three beers, he says, "Sensei, once I was this!" He swings his fist to the middle of his forehead. A fist in the middle of the forehead means police. The insignia on the front of a policeman's hat.

It's hot at the beach, and he offers me a beer. He pours for himself too. His sixth glass since we've been sitting here.

He lowers his voice, peers to the side a little, and says, "I was there, on the other side. I quit two years ago, and I was unemployed for a year and a half. It was impossible to get work. I was a middle-ranking officer. What am I doing here, you're probably wondering. The truth is I didn't quit. I was kicked out with great shame. I even thought of suicide. My kids didn't want to see me. I had a beat. I was in charge of the small police station of a nice little community, and it killed me. Boring. Little quarrels among neighbors, the dog that messes, the loudness of the music. I would go into the bars of the little sakariba of the neighborhood and envy the people who were drinking and had no inhibitions. I would see a Yakuza. There weren't many of them. Until one of them came to live in the neighborhood with his family. The people of the neighborhood didn't like it and started pressure to get him out of there. I visited his place a few times, politely. Got to know the wife, the kids. He wasn't a successful Yakuza. Did one thing once and then another. Clubs. Blackmail here and there. Some gambling. I found out about him. Not impressive. He gave me respect, told me one thing and another.

"One day I get a report me about exceptional noise coming from his house. I raced over by bicycle. Somebody was running out of the place. There was shooting. The neighbors were peeking out of the windows. Nobody came out. It was quiet. I went in. The man was wounded. He was on the telephone, talking rapidly and quietly, almost collapsing. And there was blood. The wife was crying. He didn't let her come near him. The little girl was silent. I ran to him, but he wouldn't let me near him. Somebody had shot him. I wanted to throw up. Never seen anything like that. Blood, like in the movies. But not like in the movies. I wanted to throw up. The Yakuza gradually caved in. It stank there. I called my superior. He called his superior. My superior officer got back to me two minutes later with details. A turf war between two families, and the man belonged to the family that was gradually losing its territory. I should leave everything and get out of there. I ran away and called an ambulance. But when it came, they didn't find the Yakuza at home. Just a weeping woman who didn't know anything.

"In the next few days we hear about a number of events in the nearby neighborhoods, especially in the entertainment areas. A little war is expanding in the area, and I don't know what to do. One day I'm invited to a meeting. My superior is there, and another police officer, even more senior, and another guy who looks like a Yakuza. There's a lot of respect between the officer and the man. The man talks briefly, softly. In a few words he describes the situation, the map of turf divisions between the families, and he promises he'll take care of this disturbance and apologizes for the unpleasantness that was caused to us and to the residents. The officer and the Yakuza give us a briefing. I can't believe what I'm seeing, the relaxed ambience between police and the gangster. They talk about the Taiwanese danger, about the Chinese thugs who slaughter like butchers. I want to puke. I miss the boredom I had until a few days ago. I don't understand very well. I want to go.

"Two days later they summon me to help in the sakariba of a nearby area. We survey the sakariba, among the bars, the nomiya, the alleys. Then I hear a faint noise. I go into an alley, and there's a little light coming from a distant bar, and there, in front of me, five guys are literally crushing someone. They whisper sharp things in a foreign language, Chinese maybe. I run away and puke. I know that's not for me. Maybe it's that way abroad. Maybe in America, or in Hong Kong. Here we're not used to that kind of thing. It's not for me.

"In the following days I have to meet with the Yakuza a few times. My stomach is flipping, and I don't understand how I chose to be a cop. Now I don't know. And I don't like them. Those coarse, hard, ruthless hoods. And we become like them. Otherwise we wouldn't be policemen. But these guys—I can't stand them.

"Later I was promoted and made an officer and moved to the district. And I saw things. Sensei, I saw things.

"Then I start drinking. At first a little. Then a lot. Really a lot. And in the following months I meet with more Yakuza, and I see the Yakuza in me. No big difference. One day I don't understand why I'm doing what I'm doing. I don't understand my colleagues. Who's fighting against whom. I get fed up. One day I get up in the morning, and I don't know who's on which side.

"One day I'm out. And one day, a year later, I'm here. Professional contacts, you know. And when I call up Fujita Tetsuya Oyabun, he doesn't ask questions. He says, 'Come.' And I come. And I go to work, and I feel good and pleasant.

"But some time ago, when I was driving the family car and I crashed into a truck. I was totally drunk. Fujita Tetsuya Oyabun called me and warned me. If I keep drinking like that, he'll throw me out. 'Drinking,' he said, 'is your personal business.' Well, I try, but not with big success. On the other hand, because I used to be a cop, I have a promising future here in the Yakuza. But I have to prove myself. There's a demand for people like me here. Now I sell slush and drive a truck, but I can get big here. I became family advisor on police matters. There's a big future here. And money, too. A lot of money. I can't stop drinking. But I must.

"If they throw me out, I'll have nowhere to go."

Tetsuya approaches. He's carrying little Kotaro in his arms. A year and a half old. A big smile. Tetsuya is wearing a long-sleeved jersey to cover his tattoos. He comes up to Hisao, the ex-cop, and gently lays Kotaro on his enormous belly. "Take care of him for a few minutes," he says and walks off. Hisao puts a fat, hesitant hand on the little one and steadies the glass of beer in the sand with his other hand.

We sit on the sand for another little while, and he goes on shooting the breeze until something dawns on me.

"Hey!" I say. "You said you served in Hokkaido for some time. Did you ever hear about Murata Yoshinori Oyabun?"

"Murata who?"

"Murata Yoshinori. An oyabun who was active here in Hakodate."

"I recall something. Let me think. Yes, somebody who could have been big in the Yakuza and fell. Why he fell I don't remember. Murata Yoshinori fell. Disappeared. We looked for him, in connection with the gang wars, stuff like that. They said he, with a few of his fighters, was stopping the penetration of the Yamada-Gumi into Hokkaido. He disappeared after that and never came back. He went abroad, I think. Ask me later, when I'm sober, okay?"

"You're never sober. It's important. Try to remember."

"Why is he important to you, that Murata?"

"Not him. His brother. His name is Yuki. Or Suzuki. Suzuki Taro. He changed his name."

"You're kidding, Sensei. Do you know how many Suzukis there are in Japan? What, he changed his name? Why? What do you have to do with his brother? Is he a Yakuza? Is it his real brother, or his Yakuza brother?"

"His real brother. I got friendly with him. Yuki had a food stand in Tokyo, and one day he disappeared. I'm looking for him, any way possible."

"Do you have any hint about what happened to him?"

"Very little. That he was working in a gambling club in Hakodate. That both the police and the Yamada-Gumi were after him a few years ago."

"Yes, yes. I remember something … ask me when I'm not drunk? Okay. Okay. I can't go to the police now, but I have one or two old friends in the police who might help. Maybe they know something. I'll check and let you know."

The Business Genius

A few days later he calls. "I got it."

"What?"

"Maybe there's somebody who knows about your man."

127

How many times have I heard that sentence by now?

We meet in a gloomy and very dark nomiya called Okhotsk on the outskirts of Hakodate. Hisao, the ex-cop, is sitting there with someone. Smooth, ironed. Hello. Nice to meet you. Business card. Name is Katayama, a financial consultant, of course. He's missing a pinky on his left hand and another on his right.

"Hello. I knew your man. We don't usually disclose details of our brothers, you know. But I am told you are a friend of Fujita Tetsuya's. That's a great honor, you know. I wonder, but I don't ask. You Israeli Yakuza or something? Never mind. Yes, I knew Yuki very well. He is the brother of Murata Yoshinori. His was an amazing story in out circles. When I first met him, he didn't know much about our world, although his brother was an oyabun. He didn't know our laws, didn't know what giri is, but he had giri like no one else. Giri from birth, the kind you can't learn anywhere. Sometime in 1983 Yuki hit a chimpira from the Yamada-Gumi in Sugamo in Tokyo to save his oyabun, Hayashi. Maybe the chimpira died, maybe not. We don't know. But the Yamada-Gumi said the chimpira died, and they wanted revenge, or they were looking for an excuse to make trouble and get into Tokyo. Yuki had to run away, change his name, his face, shave his head, and get to the distant north to hide. They looked for him for three years but didn't find him. But they didn't forget.

"Then they found out he ran away to the north. But Yuki was different now: new name, new face. His mother wouldn't recognize him. He worked as guard in a gambling club, salesman in stands, debt collector, truck driver, translator—English and Spanish—with representatives of interested groups from the Philippines, from Hawaii, Hong Kong. That sort, you know. Meanwhile his brother falls in Hokkaido and loses his family and everything and runs out of the country. Maybe to Hawaii. Maybe the Philippines. Or Brazil. They're starting Yakuza business there too. And him, the one you call Yuki, works here and there. By then they were calling him Watanabe, his new name. Who knows how many times he changed names by then. So Yuki was now Watanabe.

"One day, Kimura Oyabun, an important boss in Sapporo, sits with him and a few new guys, hears Yuki-Watanabe's story, and learns that he's Yoshinori Oyabun's brother. He asks how he can help Yuki. He's in a fine mood that day, Kimura Oyabun. But then Yuki-Watanabe asks Kimura Oyabun: 'How can I, Watanabe, help *you*?' Do you know what it means? That miserable mouse, who was at most a truck driver, asks the great Kimura Oyabun if he can help *him*.

"That day Kimura Oyabun is in a good mood, and he isn't insulted. He could have cut him up, that Yuki, you know. And his bodyguards are happy to so just that, but he's in a good mood. And he says to Yuki, 'Business isn't good. We do collection, protection, *sokaya*—stocks, that kind of thing. Blackmail, a little drugs. The cops are getting in our way in the matsuri business. There are matsuri that you can't get into anymore because of the cops. And it's hard to make a living. We smell a recession.' Then he asks Yuki-Watanabe, 'What do you have to say? How do you think you can help me? They say you studied economics. Well, let's hear.'

"So Yuki-Watanabe says to him, 'The business is too small. You've got to grow, Oyabun! For three years now I've been studying Yakuza business thoroughly. And I'm learning about the shit that's going to happen in the Japanese economy. There's an opportunity now. There's no more business in the traditional lines of work. The big money is in controlling companies. Control of firms, control of politics. Just there. Once the Yakuza used to be strong in politics, but since the Lockheed affair, we've fallen down. We hid. We apologized. But now, I can be useful, if you permit me. Let's talk about banks. Let me tell you a few of the thoughts I have about Yakuza business and about banks.'

"That's what Yuki-Watanabe says to the great Kimura Oyabun. 'Come, let's talk about banks.' What daring. Or stupidity. But that's how he talks, and he talks with the oyabun, and soon he rises up high, polishing his ideas more and more and the money flowed. A genius."

*

"He started small. Local politics. Bribes here and there. Extortions. But he was an ambitious man. He wanted to go into big business. Preferable legal business.

"We've changed, Sensei. Until a few years ago we used to be in the gray world of business. But the police have been pressing us more violently. So let them pay. We have to live, no? On the one hand, we went over into more aggressive ways of making money—drugs, more violent extortion. On the other hand, we're moving closer to the gentle forms of violence that are socially acceptable—banks, businesses, control of banks, crooked tenders, implicit and explicit pressure. Nice and conventional violence. We've become like everybody else. We have to live, no? One of my kobuns sits on the board of directors of a company that's in trouble. Since he joined, the creditors stopped coming. ... We've stopped being 'the men who walk in the sun' so that decent people can walk in the shade. Decent people? Fehh!

"And your Yuki? He got bigger and bigger, from one idea to the next. Until this extraordinary takeover plan. The historic business deal that was closed in Nanohana's teahouse. Nanohana was the most famous geisha in the area. I was there on that Autumn evening."

At Nanohana's Teahouse

The paper doors slide open, and the geishas, kneeling on the other side, bow deeply. Signs of autumn, dainty maple leaves on the hems of their white kimonos. They glide into the room, secretive and charming. On red wooden trays sit little wooden bowls, and there are bowls on the low table, already served, as if they had glided there by themselves.

The yolk of a quail's egg rests in clear lavender soup. Like the full moon of September.

The owner of this elegant teahouse is a sixty-six-year-old geisha whose name is Nanohana, or Nano-chan to her many admirers.

130

In this beautiful place she has entertained honored guests from a variety of worlds, bright and dark alike. She jokes with one of the notables, whose face is red from the seven little cups of sake he has sipped so far. Red Face is the Head of the Business Department of Bank D. He lectures to the small audience about his theories of the true origin of the Japanese people. Nanohana knows how to show respect to the lecturer and his theories, and also to grind them up with fatal innocence. Now she's a little girl, now she's a coquette, ironic, erotic, wise woman.

Nano-chan kneels at Red Face's side, converses with him and with others while watching with piercing delicacy the three other geishas, and signals a variety of instructions with an invisible wink; the doors slide to the right and left, bottles of sake arrive, disappear, the tables are cleared, and new dishes appear as though from outer space, as though from the lovely paper doors. A red moon is painted on the doors.

Three men in expensive suits are sitting at one side of the table. They are wearing colorful ties. They move as if the world is in their hands, to play with as they please. One of them is Red Face. Next to him is his assistant, invisibly efficient. The third man doesn't utter a syllable all night long, has short hair, and doesn't hide his left hand, which is missing a pinky. He's *their* Yakuza.

On the other side of the table sit three men in no less expensive suits and ties. Almost the twins of the ones across from them. Two of them have very short hair. All three are Yakuza: one is Kimura, the prominent oyabun from Sapporo. The other is Katayama, representative of Okawa-Kai, and the third man is Watanabe, alias Yuki. They all introduce themselves, with impressive business cards: all three are senior executives in A-Corp, a respectable investment company whose center is now the city of Sapporo, Hokkaido.

Watanabe-Yuki introduces himself as the assistant financial advisor of A-Corp. A blue suit. A yellow tie with red spots. His hands are delicate. A scar, well disguised by makeup, on his right cheek. His eyes stare. One as though dreaming, and the other sharp, making people tremble. He looks younger than the other two.

The invitation letters sent to the participants were drawn in an artistic hand that emphasized the red leaves already falling from the maple tree and the chill of autumn, and the full moon. The Nanohana teahouse is situated deep in an anonymous alley on the edges of a street along which flows a canal of pure water. There's no name or sign on the simple wooden door. It is a place for the initiates. The canal is decorated with weeping cherry trees, their branches bending down, touching the water. The leaves are red, their hearts torn, and their brothers already float in the canal. Red lanterns are reflected between the floating leaves, as is the sound of the *shamisen* lute and the mournful voice of a young geisha, slightly trembling, slightly unripe, slightly hoarse, young, but redolent with sadness that is enough to soften the hearts of the hard men who have gathered here.

The first course is brought. And then another, and another. They stream with the sweet music that flows in from the shamisen.

Nano-chan, the adept conductor, leads the conversation. The autumn, the new pottery in her collections, yes, the prime minister's resignation, again, who knows, maybe the next prime minister … because it's not possible … the price of a square meter in the Ginza … I too have a restaurant there … they say that … I don't believe it, it can't be … see who's sitting now in the House of Representatives, unbelievable … entertainers, actors … yes, certainly everyone has a place … the Takashimaya Department Store, yes, just yesterday one of my customers told me that … somebody, you know I can't tell you … yes, Nano-chan is a locked safe [they laugh] … I know the man …

And then Nano-chan sends a hidden code, and the young geisha girls bow deeply, and with invincible charm slip out of the room. So does the shamisen player.

Do speak, honored guests, and trust confidentiality, says Nano-chan to the guests.

Kimura Oyabun speaks first. "Gentlemen. Not to repay a debt is an extremely regrettable act. This country is in big trouble, very big trouble. A Japanese who doesn't pay his debts is a shame to this country. Such deplorable behavior splashes mud on Japan in the eyes of the world. Our firm was established in the eighteenth century, and it has had since then an excellent reputation. Our economic situation is surprisingly solid, taking into account these hard times in Japan's economy. We moved to Hokkaido about two years ago and we have invested extensively in this economically virgin region. In spite of the tremendous difficulties we are ready to consider the request you transmitted to us by your men the other day. Watanabe-san serves as our assistant financial advisor. Times are hard, very hard, but we shall be happy to assist. Of course we have to consult our board of directors, but—" He leaves his words hanging.

"Certainly, certainly," says Red Face, the head of the business department, who knows all he needs to know about Kimura Oyabun. "Your honorable family is well known to us. After all, your fathers' fathers dwelled in Kagura-Zaka, and they had no equal in trade in paper, tobacco, and copper, and there has been a long cooperation between our families. There's a place for your firm in this region, no doubt ... we're looking forward to your activities here. ... I knew the late Kinoshita Oyabun. That's the reason why it would be an honor for us—"

"For us as well, for us as well," Kimura says. "And the bad debts. Bad debts are the mother of all evil. Not to pay back that way, so up front ... what terrible morality. That can topple Japan ... reliability was always the backbone of Japan. ... According to the data we have, your bank suffers from bad debts on the order of twenty billion yen, or am I wrong ..." A paper magically appears in his hand.

Red Face laughs nervously. He sips a cup of sake and coughs. "No, not that much, not that much ... but it's certainly very disconcerting. We have a list of the bad borrowers. Very respectable, very respectable, and we have no doubt they'll pay the money back. They're all well-established companies that we've been dealing with for ... with a little support, I am sure we will—"

"Absolutely not reliable, Mr. Head of Business Department! Those companies are wiped out! And they'll never return the money! You know that, don't you?"

Silence in the room. On the other side of the paper door, the geisha's song is faintly heard. Red Face blushes. He puts his sake down very slowly, and Nano-chan, in a soft voice says, "You haven't tasted our next course yet ..."

The doors slide, and trays smoothly move onto the table, decorated with diamond-shaped plates, made of rough clay glazed in a marvelously well-ordered random pattern. In each plate, carefully designed, are slices of dried persimmon and pickled radish in lemon juice. The food softens what could have been the bitter end of the evening.

All eat in silence.

Red Face says, "It will be hard, but I—"

"You know, you know very well those loans of yours are lost, unless, well, there might be an idea ... you know ..."

"It's very generous of you. ... What idea do you have in mind ...?"

"To buy your bad debts."

"That's very generous of you, but—"

"It's not generous; it's worthwhile. We can buy your debts for substantial amount. That will support your group for a considerable time ..."

Coughs, clearing of throats, Kimura drinks more and more. His hand slips sometimes, and his speech is slurred. But his eyes pierce, and it's evident that Red Face would prefer to talk about other things.

"Without consulting with my superiors, I can't decide about such gigantic sums."

"That you'll lose altogether if you don't agree!"

"Give me a few days ..."

"Maybe I'll also give you a membership in a golf club that we're opening now east of Sapporo. Maybe not. We'll ask for three billion more to compensate for losses in the stock exchange in the past two

years on Ishii Oyabun's investments, and maybe we'll buy more
debts from you on the range of a few more billion yen ..."

"What other debts?"

"Here, on this paper!"

Watanabe, in a blue suit with a yellow tie, who hasn't said a word
until now, removes papers from an elegant briefcase.

Red Face looks at the papers. The chopsticks shake in his hand.
He swallows the slice of persimmon without enjoying it and turns
to Nano-chan for rescue. A bottle of beer appears at the table, and
she whispers something in his ear.

Then he says, hesitant as to whether he should address Kimura
or this Watanabe, "But these aren't bad loans! They're loans to well-
established companies. They're solid loans that are being paid back
regularly. We're talking about Nikko Holding Company, Fukui
International Investments, the Shimura Group!"

Then, suddenly, Watanabe speaks. Quickly, briefly, in a delicate
voice, as in prayer, one eye penetrating the manager, the other eye
looking into space at the ink drawing on the wall. "Soon they'll
follow in the footsteps of the other companies! Think about it,
Mister Business Department! Think! You're capable of it, aren't you?"

"I've had the honor of doing business with Kinoshita Oyabun,
and I wish to emphasize that—"

"Kinoshita Oyabun lived at a time when a bank's word was
sacred!"

The doors slide open, an intermezzo for soothing the atmosphere.

Chestnuts in vinegar arrive at the table. Silence. Watanabe, who
hasn't drunk until now, sips from the cup of sake and adds in his
soft prayer voice, "And we repeat, compensation for Ishii Oyabun's
losses on investments in the stock exchange. All because of your
incompetent management!"

"That isn't the style—"

"This isn't a school of manners!"

"You're embarrassing our Nano-chan ..."

"It's out of respect for Nano-chan I'm not saying other things that come to my mind!"

"This is a new world …"

"It certainly is! We expect to hear your proposals within a week. You know that we're not a gang of tattooed gamblers anymore, the way you think. It's a new world, as you say. A week! And if not, we'll consider …"

Silence. The Head of Business Department takes a deep breath. After putting a chestnut in vinegar in his mouth, he says, "In fact, ahem … I have here a preliminary proposal from our board of directors …"

Silence.

"Fine! And what's the proposal?"

A muffled discussion. Nano-chan, at the edge of the table, smiles, scolds, proposes, guides, chants a hymn to autumn and the falling leaves and the full moon and the sounds of insects, and pays full respect to this one and also to that one.

Mr. Advisor from the Finance Ministry, and Mr. Chief Advisor in the Department of Justice, and even the Chairman of the Board of a sister company—all of them are regular clients in this teahouse—and there's no doubt that with good spirit and goodwill we will find a way…

The air suddenly echoes with laughter, with jokes, with guttural comments. The karaoke system starts, and the bank officer sings about two lovers parting at the entrance to the subway station in Ginza. An enthusiastic applause from the Yakuza, who also sings with a fine voice about Hokkaido, the snow country, so very beautiful, and its beautiful foxes, and all the faces are red, the ties loosened, and the jackets laid at the side, and the girls are here again, and the shamisen player sings a song of the gloom of autumn, and what does she know about bad debts to the amount of so many billion yen, and also good debts, and stock options, and compensation for losses of investments, and so many additional percentages of control and complete silence at the upcoming stockholders' meeting? What does she know about all these things when the cloud obscures the moon, and the ivy reddens on the walls, and the plaintive voice of the stag, echoing among the mountains, seeking his mate, who went down into the valleys and is not to be found. In a week they'll meet here again.

Everyone leaves. Yuki-Watanabe, the assistant financial advisor, in his blue suit and yellow tie, stays and makes a deep bow to the girls and to Nano-chan. He gives the girls a look that confuses them. He leaves a small package, wrapped in silk, on the tatami floor. With brief words he apologizes for the embarrassment. Nano-chan bows, her head down to the floor. She takes the package, rises, and bows again. The door slides soundlessly in its track.

A Week Later. Same Place

Watanabe, in a soft voice, says to the Head of the Business Department, "A little matter we didn't talk about last week. The Agricultural Bank of Hokkaido, one of your group's subsidiaries, is to be included in any arrangement. In this framework there will be changes in the management of the bank. The bank isn't managed well, and there's a need to change the personnel, especially the board of directors ..."

"True, there were some problems in recent years, but—"

"Aside from that, we propose a new member in the board of directors of your bank, someone who will help lead the bank to a new place."

"Who is that?"

"Me. And you'll be free of the debtors."

Yuki's Getaway

"I was there, at Nano-chan's," Katayama tells me, while we're sitting in the Okhotsk nomiya, on the outskirts of Hakodate. Hisao, the rogue policeman, listens, and his eyes are glazed.

"There was a new style at Nano-chan's," Katayama says. "Modern. Daring. We asked Yuki-Watanabe why he insisted on changes in the management of the Agricultural Bank of Hokkaido, but he won't specify. He joined the board of directors of the D Bank, and within a week he saw to the dismissal of several of the chief managers, with rapidity and a style that was rare in Japan. He especially insisted on getting rid of the chairman of the board of directors of the Agricultural Bank, a certain Mr. Hanaoka. We asked why, but he never answered. At most he would mumble something about inefficient management. It seems like there was something almost personal in the way he insisted on removing Hanaoka. I found out about the man, Hanaoka. He had been the CEO of the Agricultural Bank in Hokkaido, a bank that was a subsidiary of the D Bank. There were stories about corruption, embezzlement, and lawsuits by farmers who claimed that they were impoverished because of Hanaoka's corruption. The trial lasted for years and ended inconclusively. What was that guy to Yuki-Watanabe? To this day I don't know. I let the matter go, and because of Yuki's maverick actions, we all lost interest in Hanaoka's fate.

"Watanabe, your Yuki, turned out to be a financial genius. He led us to wealth and satisfaction and strength, and to the new generation. In a short time we had everything we wanted. Money, women, fine cars, villas all over the city, endless trips to everywhere in the world—until we were put on the blacklist in America and Australia. Everybody predicted a big future for your Yuki-Watanabe.

"But one day everything changed. On that unforgettable day Yuki asked for a meeting with Kimura Oyabun. He came dressed in a kimono. We all sensed that something wasn't right. Why in a kimono? He began a short speech and thanked Kimura Oyabun for the years he was favorite member in Kimura's family and for the help and opportunities he was granted, and that he owes his life to Kimura Oyabun and all the friends, that he'll never forget, and so on and so on, but now he has to go. He's going, parting, going on his way. All he did was to get enough money because he had a personal matter that he had to resolve.

"Kimura was stunned. Here was a young man who he saw as his possible successor. This was someone he loved almost like a son. He had been about to appoint him to a high position in the family, despite the objections of the senior brothers. And now, this rag was telling him he was going. Departing the enterprise he'd built up. Who would manage things with the banks? Where would they find a business talent like that? And how can you just leave a family? Is he crazy? Doesn't he know you can't just leave a family? Where is he going? But Yuki wouldn't tell.

"Then he understood. Kimura Oyabun is a very smart man, and he sees the woman there, with Watanabe-Suzuki-Yuki, or whoever the talented and well-liked young man before him might be. He sensed the woman who would bring him down beyond repair. He was very angry.

"Kimura Oyabun was silent for a long time, looking at Yuki with narrow, narrow eyes, and finally he said to him, 'Watanabe! Do you remember the words of the oath? "Even if your wife and son go hungry, throw your life away on behalf of the family, on behalf of your oyabun." Do you remember those words that you swore at your sakazuki ceremony? You dare to go away from here without my permission?' He hit the floor, and the house shook.

"Yuki knelt and spread his arms on the tatami floor. He lowered his head to the delicate straw weave and begged, 'Kimura Oyabun! I will never forget what you did for me. I owe you my life. But nothing, not even my life, can change my determination to go and do what I have to do. Please, forgive me! Aside from that, Kimura Oyabun, I never had a sakazuki ceremony. I'm not your kobun.'

"And before anyone could blink an eye, he drew a large knife from his kimono, and before a questioning hand could be extended, before looks could be exchanged, the blood spattered on the oyabun's face and his clothing, and the tip of the pinky lay before him, exiled from the finger.

"Kimura Oyabun's face turned red. One of the kobuns leaped forward and tried to wipe the blood from the oyabun's face. The oyabun slapped him. He wiped the blood himself. Then the suit. But the oyabun had no choice but to accept the fingertip. Then he'd see what he'd do.

"That night it was impossible to find Yuki at home.

"Kimura Oyabun was seething with rage, and he ordered his men to send out a black postcard of ostracism all over the country, and two men are to search for, find, and bring Yuki to him, at any price. But alive and well.

"Two months later he sends a red postcard all over the country. Yuki is banished for good, no way back. But he has vanished, nowhere to be found.

"Now he's hounded by both the Yamada-Gumi and by the Okawa-Kai, through Kimura Oyabun, and also by the police—first priority—for his part in extorting money from the banks. But he evaporated. I'd pay a lot of money to know what happened to this Yuki, your friend, brother, or whatever he is to you.

"One last thing, Sensei. While he was here in Hokkaido, I was in charge of monthly meetings between Yuki-Watanabe and his aged mother in neutral, secret places in Sapporo. But two days after Yuki-Watanabe disappeared, his mother disappeared too. Can I guess that she's living in São Paolo? Maybe with his brother? Who knows. We stopped asking a long time ago. But I'll ask. But you should know, Sensei, that whatever I find, if I find anything, has to be approved first by Okawa Oyabun. We're talking about a man who got a red postcard."

The Oyabun's Daughter. 1992

One day an American journalist calls me, the editor of an English language magazine in Japan. He asks me for an interview. He's heard about my research and about my connections with the Yakuza, and he wants to interview me for his magazine. We meet in a small café.

This is the first interview I give about my Yakuza connection, and I feel a bit nervous.

I don't tell him about the storms, the disappointments, the fears, or the despair, and I don't tell him about the excitement, the friendship, the loneliness, or the stories that take place, out there or in my heart. I don't tell him about the man I miss and wonder about where he is, after he rose so high and disappeared so thoroughly. But I do tell him about my meetings with very special people, who are always on the edge of a precipice from which either flight or a fall awaits them.

I tell him about the strange and extraordinary man, Okawa Oyabun, the king of crime, a man of morality, a great leader, and that his days are numbered.

And I tell him, incidentally, as it were, about his daughter Machiko, about how she lives in a house where tough and menacing men come and go, uncles of courtesy and war. About her involvement in the tea ceremony, her love for Japanese ink drawings, and for the art of the European Renaissance, about her singsong way of speaking Korean, French, and Spanish. About her being his daughter.

The journalist looks excited. "Maybe I can interview her?" he asks.

I say, "No." Then I say, "Perhaps." And then I say, "I have to ask her, and of course get her parents' permission. But if you interview her, there's one condition. Never, I repeat, never ask her about her father."

He says, "We've got a deal."

I say, "I'll ask her father, then her, and then her mother. If they all agree, I'll call."

I come and go in the home of Okawa Oyabun. I talk with Okawa. He's very ill. He's weak but strong. I tell him about the interview, and about the request, and about the condition.

He says, "I have no objection."

And I talk with Machiko, who has no objection either, nor does her mother object. I call up the journalist and say they agreed, and I repeat the condition: "Never, not once, not even with a hint are you to ask her about her father and his business!"

And he says, "I promise."

A month later, her father is hospitalized. I visit him in the hospital often. It was then that we arrange the interview with the journalist in Kyoto. She returns that evening. I call, and her mother answers.

"How is she?" I ask.

"Not well. She came back in tears." There's a short pause. "He asked her about her father. He also said something like, 'How can you live when you know that your father is a top criminal?' I don't know what to say. It isn't good for Machiko. It isn't good, Sensei."

An enormous anger rises in me. I immediately call the man in Kyoto and tell him, to my own surprise, in a menacing way, "You'd better, I repeat, you'd better call now. Not later. Now. And apologize. Say that you promised me not to ask her questions about her father. Now! You'd better do it. And you don't publish a word of the interview with her. Or the interview with me!"

I don't know what I'm saying or what I mean by "You'd better not." I simply threatened the man, didn't I? The feel of Yakuza.

The man is clearly frightened. The smell of fear is on the telephone line. He calls and apologizes to the mother and to Machiko. And I have no more dealings with him.

The next day I go visit Okawa Oyabun in the hospital. Tetsuya is standing in the entrance hall on the ground floor. His legs are spread, arms folded on his chest. With no preliminaries he says, "You can't, Sensei. We trusted you. And you betrayed us. My kobuns were your friends. We bathed together. We traveled together. We laughed together. We opened our hearts to you, the way we never open them to each other."

"He promised … I didn't know …"

"You've been in Japan for a long time. You're almost Japanese. You teach at a university. You ought to know. It doesn't matter to me whether you knew or not. I trusted you. I exposed my belly to you. I wanted to come visit you in Israel. You served as a mediator between the journalist and Machiko. So you're responsible. No excuses. I don't want to have any connection with you. We never touch the private family, never. Don't come to visit Okawa Oyabun. And forget about your research. Also, forget about me helping you in any way to find Yuki."

"Does he know?"

"No. He's sick. Now please go."

I go away. All at once the world has turned dark. I wander hour after hour in the city streets and can't go back home. Thinking. The four years of fragile fabric that I embroidered. The friends I made. The trust that I built between us, with mindfulness, with subtlety, with careful, careful heedfulness. Or so I imagined. Some of Tetsuya's kobuns used to call me aniki, my big brother. Now what am I to them? In an instant of stupidity I lost dear friends, and the research is null. And Okawa Oyabun there in the hospital. I, a man of no giri, betrayed them. And Machiko. What can I say to her?

I try to call the family office, and there's no courtesy on the telephone. There's no 'How are you?' and no 'Come and visit.' No 'Sensei.' I remain silent and I call no more. Once I call Tetsuya's house, and Miyuko answers and tells me gently not to call again, and says no more.

The silence continues for a month, another month, and then another. I call the hospital to enquire about Okawa Oyabun's condition. I know that he's not well. Did they tell him?

In my place, a Yakuza man would take a knife and a big towel, someone would hold him, and he'd cut off the end of his left pinky and bring it, wrapped in white cloth, soaked with blood, to his oyabun and place it on his doorstep.

I'm afraid now. Have I not witnessed the dark power of vengeance in their world?

One day I'm sitting next to the telephone and staring at it, and dare not call the one person I owe the tip of my pinky to, Machiko. And then I call. Okawa's wife answers. Relief in her voice? Concern?

"How are you, Sensei? I was a little worried about you. Yes, Machiko is here. Machiko!"

We arrange to meet in a small, stylish café. She's glad to see me.

"Sensei, I apologize for the embarrassment I caused you. I feel terrible. And I'm worried. Among my Yakuza uncles, you know, there are some hotheads. I'm sorry."

"No. I'm the one who has to ask forgiveness. I'm the one who's sorry for the embarrassment I caused you."

"No, Sensei, I've forgotten all about it. I'm spoiled. I'm sorry. I got too upset there, during the interview. Do you think this is the first time someone asks me about Dad?

"You know, I'm twenty-one, and I feel as if I'm sixty. I can't talk about it. I'm the daughter of Okawa Oyabun. He's so angry with me because I'm immersed in books and don't enjoy what he can offer me. He's sick now, and I love him, and I'm worried about him. He's going to die. I don't know what will happen to me and to Mother and to Kimiko, my sister, and the family. I know how important peace in the family is to him. How proud he is of his sons. How proud he is of what he does. Always, always when they come to the house, we're upstairs in our room or we go out for a walk, and we don't know and don't hear, and we're not part of that world. But we are, aren't we? We never talk about the family but Sensei, we know everything. I don't know what Kimiko knows. But I think she knows a lot. We never talk about Yakuza. She loves ikebana, and she loves singing *enka* pop songs. You know, the sentimentality. Departures and solitude and sadness, platforms and departing trains. She knows what that is. Each time they come to visit, the smell of solitude is in the house. And Dad, he tries to give those kids a house. Warmth. Family. Education. Yes, education. I don't know anything, but I know a lot. I hear. Everything. They used to take me for walks. They were my babysitters. They would take me to kindergarten. To school. And drop me off at some distance so that no one will identify the types. They would drive me to summer camp, polish my shoes, clean my room when I was a kid. I've always been with them.

"Did you ever think about what I used to say when they asked me about my father's profession in school? 'A businessman.' 'What company does he work for? What's his job there?' Did you think about what I used to tell my girlfriends? What stories I made up? I'm the ultimate storyteller. My girlfriends never came to my house. Our house looks good, bourgeois, respectable. No one could suspect anything. But one can never know. When will there be an emergency? When will the young men come, with those suits and that short hair and the missing pinky, and a scar on their cheek? And the gruff speech, even though they try very hard to be polite. And the show of marvelous tattoos when my father is away. And when will a convoy of ten big black cars come over and big, hard men will emerge from them? So what can I say to my girlfriends? That my dad is a film director, and they're shooting a Yakuza picture at our house?

"But, Sensei, I love them. I don't know what they do. I read newspapers. I hear the radio. I read books about the Yakuza. Sometimes they talk about Okawa-Kai. But none of them really knows the heart of those men. To journalists they're gangsters, clowns, movie characters, and sexy stories. Not people. I love them. They're evil, and they're good. They're lonely. They've been thrown out of their families. Out of their jobs. They wanted to do what their hearts told them to do, and someone wouldn't let them. The family. The father. Society. School. They were suffocated, I know. Sometimes they would tell me. There are Koreans there. They call themselves Miyake and Kuroda and Fujita and Ito, but they're really Chong and Kim and Lin and Park. I know. They're homeless in Japan. They have nowhere to go. And Dad. I know my father gave them a home. He didn't ask who or what or why or where. He just said, 'Come, be with us.' I see them swell up with pride and become good men by his side. And they have good eyes, and they would be willing to die for their brother, for their oyabun. For me. Without batting an eyelid. To the end. Without fear. And they can live. Live. Sometimes I feel like an old woman.

"That journalist asked me how it is to live with the knowledge that my father is a master criminal. What does he know? How his eyes sparkled when we met, as if he were watching a porn movie.

"I know that Tetsuya is very angry at you. I can't do anything. They've sort of blackballed you. A black postcard. And I'm worried. I tried to talk with him, but now it's impossible. Mom tried too. After all, you're a gaijin, and you don't know exactly how people behave here. I don't know what is going to happen to your research. And I know you have another issue, the search for your lost friend, Yuki. You see? I know everything. The daughter of an Oyabun, am I not? Let time cure the wounds, and I will see what can be done.

"Aside from that, Dad asks about you. He asked you to come. Yes, yes, they'll let you visit. Please go to the hospital. He doesn't have a long time to live."

Reconciliation

I go to the hospital. The Yakuza on the ground floor ignores me. Nobody detains me, and I go up to the fifth floor. A private room for Okawa Oyabun. There are no bodyguards anywhere. It's dark here. Okawa is pale. His cheeks are sunken, and his eyes, his tiger-eyes, smile at me.

"Hey, Sensei! Where have you been? Did you go out on your fieldwork again?"

He doesn't know anything. I'm deeply grateful to Tetsuya.

The conversation flows.

And then I tell him everything. About the journalist, the ban. And the meeting with his daughter. He looks at me with sunken cheeks, the breath of a man about to die, but his eyes are lively as always. "Sensei! You were very stupid. But who isn't? So they sent a black postcard, eh?"

And he laughs out loud, coughs, and says, "What will you learn from that? That's what's important, what you'll learn. Think hard. Without doing something like that, none of the sons can be a true son. Foolishness. Failure. Weakness. A fall. Very good for polishing. And now we'll move on. From my place here I don't have a lot of time for that kind of foolishness, as you see. Maybe in another day, another month, I won't be here. I'll talk to Tetsuya. Everything will be okay. We've sent postcards of redress for more serious things than that. We'll send you a redress postcard. Aside from that, Sensei, I'm going to die soon. Be careful not to get a red postcard, okay?"

The coughing laughter makes me shudder.

*

Three more months of silence.

Then one day, Miyuko, Tetsuya's consort, calls my room at the university.

"Sensei, Tetsuya is waiting for you in the Hinotori izakaya in Shinjuku. Come!"

The breath is knocked out of me for a moment. I immediately cancel everything and take a taxi to the Hinotori izakaya.

I enter. Tetsuya and Machiko are there, sitting on the tatami. Tetsuya's face is red. He's been drinking a lot. He leans on one hand and holds a glass of *shochu* liquor in the other. He waves the cup, and with a smile that has no end, he almost shouts, "So, Sensei, when are we going to Israel? Is February good for you?"

Dire Straits

For a long time after the reconciliation, things aren't what they had been. There is a need to rebuild what has been spoiled after the incidence.

The Yakuza are concerned about bigger issues, and I am soon forgotten. On March 1, 1992, the Japanese House of Representatives passes the "anti-gang law." At first I didn't understand its immediate import. During the months after the law passed, I notice many changes in the world of Yakuza.

People avoid me. Tetsuya doesn't authorize meetings easily, repeatedly apologizing, saying it has nothing to do with the Machiko incident. The friends I've made no longer go easily with me to the nomiya of Shinjuku. It's hard to meet Tetsuya. He's polite but nervous. Rumors circulate.

One day we drive together to visit Okawa in the hospital, and Tetsuya, tired, worried, nervous, and apologetic tells me, "Sensei. Our world is changing. You know that the House of Representatives passed the anti-gang law. From now on they're not making arrests on suspicion of committing crimes. Now the police can designate any group as a criminal organization if more than 10 percent of its members have been convicted. Several big families were marked right away. Ours too. Since then life has been hard. There are police raids on the private homes of oyabuns and on offices; pressure on hotels and other places not to host our meetings and ceremonies. Pressure on Buddhist temples not to hold funerals or burials for members. The police are encouraging citizens' groups to complain and act against Yakuza. They arrest our members, almost daily, even those who haven't committed crimes, and there's no protection of law for us.

"From now on our men are arrested for belonging to the Yakuza, not on suspicion of committing a crime. The police itself are acting in the gray areas of the constitution. Much like the American RICO Act against Mafia activities, where the leaders of the organization are held responsible for the actions of their men. Now almost half the members of the Yakuza are liable to be arrested, even if they haven't done anything criminal. We immediately started a counteroffensive. Our lawyers have sued the police and the government for violation of human rights, for unconstitutional action. Sometimes we've won cases. But we gave an order to the members to duck, to go underground, to remove the public signs, to change the business cards, to limit the appetite that some of us have for newspaper interviews.

"Members are leaving us. Along with Buddhist and Christian civil organizations the police is establishing counseling centers for Yakuza who want to leave. Brothers are buying false pinkies.

"Our income sources are dwindling because of the weak economy. The turf wars in the streets are getting more violent. You've certainly heard that citizens have been hit in the wars. That never happened before.

"Chinese crime organizations from Taiwan and Hong Kong, with rules of their own, have appeared again and again on the streets of Japan. Our traditional laws of honor don't apply with them. The battles for the streets are tougher. Okawa Oyabun has appointed me as his successor, as you know. When he dies, I'm going to take over a family that's in worse shape, after years of being a leading family in the Path of Extremes. I don't know what's going to happen.

"But, Sensei, we've gone through hard times in the past. We'll overcome! Let's go upstairs and visit Papa Okawa now."

A month later he is arrested.

Arrest

Tetsuya is arrested and subsequently sentenced to three years in prison. He will probably get out after two years. There was a fight. Tetsuya was there. Someone, a katagi on his way home, was in the line of fire between Tetsuya's gun and the Yamada-Gumi man, and the katagi was wounded. The Yamada-Gumi man was also wounded. The police decided to intervene. Too many common citizens have been wounded recently. Public opinion was unforgiving. Action was demanded.

Tetsuya turned himself in and didn't wait for any of his kobuns to do the *migawari*—that is to turn himself in in the stead of his oyabun. The man, who is about to inherit the Okawa-Kai after Okawa's death, is now placed in detention, awaiting trial.

From there he writes to me.

Jacob Raz

Letters from Prison—1

Sensei,

On [date] I was involved in an incident that was defined as attempted murder, and I turned myself in to the police. Now I'm in detention, awaiting trial. As you surely understand, Sensei, they'll sentence me to prison. In this case I acted as was proper for a Yakuza, and I have no regrets. You will understand that I can't continue to help you with your research, and I'm sorry about that. Please forgive me. It can't be helped. It is pity, especially now, when we've gotten to know and understand each other so well. Too bad. I'm really sorry. I have a life here that you can't imagine. I'm not good at writing, so excuse me for my clumsy style.

As for your temporary banishment, I hope you understand. You did something very bad. Not very wise, if I may say so. It was impossible to ignore. But, Sensei, you understand, don't you? You're a brother. Otherwise we wouldn't have banished you. And if you felt a small death, that's not terrible, right?

Sensei, Okawa Oyabun is about to die. Go visit him. He likes you. Go visit him often. He'll be happy. And send him my love.

So, good-bye, brother,

Fujita Tetsuya
[date]

*

I send a letter to the detention house, but it is returned. I enquire. Only family members are permitted to send a letter. _What's a family?_ I wonder.

At Okawa's Deathbed

I visit Okawa Oyabun in the hospital every evening. He's alone after seven p.m. No bodyguards to be seen. He's very ill.

One day I find him grayer than usual. And he talks. "Sit, Sensei. Thank you for coming. How are you? How's your research? Are you going to publish an important book about us? I never told you what to write in it, and I never kept track of your research, but now, when I'm going to depart, I'm curious. But I don't have enough strength to hear. I'm sure it will be a good book.

"I want to tell you something. Sit, sit and listen. I'm going to die now. I'm not afraid. People don't talk about it around me, but I know. Another day, two days, a week, and I won't be here. Sensei, I'm proud of my life. Out there are thousands of men, maybe tens of thousands of men, whom I helped to live a better life. A life of honor. I'm not ashamed. I talk with my daughter, and I know she won't follow my path. But she knows that in my way I was a good man. No government and no big economic firm can look me in the face and say, 'You're a criminal. You're violent. You blackmail people. You violate the law.' None of them can. Especially not the Japanese government or the big corporations. Because they're the real violent criminals. Much bigger than I am. And none is a bigger criminal than governments. Your governments in the Middle East, for example, they're the worst Yakuza. So I'm going to die without any twinges of conscience.

"Sensei, you've been good with us. When you came to me in the Washington Hotel you were looking for human beings, not clowns or demons. You've been good with me and with my daughter. That's good. You were a welcome guest in our home. You helped Machiko in ways that you don't understand. And I, I never told you what to write. How to write. Whom to see. Whom to interview. Whom not to. I never stowed away the darkness from you. I don't know what will happen to Japan. What will happen to my homeland, Korea, split and torn as it is? What will happen to the Yakuza? How I'll be born next time. Maybe as a Christian priest? That'll be fun. But I don't care that much. If I'm given the choice, I'll choose the same path. I had a full life that I lived in every nook and cranny, in every extreme, in every fold. I have no regret. How many people can say that? Write that down. I've lived without regret. Write that I lived in the world to its extremes. That's something I'm asking you to write.

"You know what's happening now with the new law. I gave an order to restrain activities for a while. I ordered some members to go underground. It's harder to make a living. The turf war is tougher and more violent. I'm afraid a general war will break out. It will be for survival at any price. It's a new world, Sensei. And that's where Yuki, your man, comes in. The man you're looking for."

For a while, I stop breathing.

"We've asked about Yuki, your man. Katayama, the men you met with in Hokkaido, Tetsuya, and others, helped in searching for the man in Japan and all over Southeast Asia. Just recently I learned that your man is probably in the Philippines. He's well camouflaged. He changed identities with such speed that not even we can follow them. I wonder if he can. Recently he apparently made big business deals with people from the Chinese Dragonhead organization. The Dragonhead used to work with us until three years ago. Then they became competitors, which means they became our enemies, both at home, in Japan, and also in Thailand, Hawaii, and the Philippines. Never mind the details. We've suffered tremendous damage. We have to reevaluate all of our activities in Southeast Asia. There have also been wars. People have been killed on both sides. Maybe Yuki doesn't know about all that. Maybe he has some big plan in his extraordinary mind.

"Sensei, the new law will change the face of the Yakuza. It will be a world of new men, violent men, who don't care about anything. Who go underground. A new world. Thuggish. Cruel. With no values. I'm worried. It won't be the way it's been up to now. We need new deals, new alignments. Or refresh old ones. The daring new deal demands brave leaders, with a vision. Modern leaders. There will be a need for a new kind of leader. Maybe your man is such a man. They say he's very sharp, that he thinks big.

"I gave an order not to harm him. Meanwhile, I hope the Yamada-Gumi won't get to him. I know they're pursuing him. The Japanese police too. But I gave an order not to hurt him. There were three cases in the past, just three, of a pardon after a red postcard. I'm willing to grant him a pardon. But there's a condition. You have to find him. I think if you locate him he will talk to you. I remember your story about your short friendship. Our people will help you get close to him. And you'll give him a message, in writing, with the conditions for a pardon. There are some things he must do in order to return to the family."

"Okawa-san, I haven't seen Yuki for many years. How will I find him? I doubt if I can recognize him. And if I do find him, why will he accept anything from me? Why are you asking me to do something you can't do? Who says he'll recognize me, who says he'll see me? They say his mother wouldn't recognize him. Maybe he won't remember our pledge. Maybe our pledge was no more than a romantic game for him nine years ago."

"Sensei, excuse my impatience. I'm living my last minutes now. If he's worth anything, that man of yours, he'll honor the vow between you two. In our world, you're brothers, and that's something you can't get divorced from. Maybe because of that, maybe because you're a gaijin, he'll accept it from you. I don't know. Our people will help you get to him or close to him. Don't worry. We'll keep watch over you. And you'll give him the letter. Everything's written in it. And he'll do what's it tells him to do.

"If not, he's got to face his own fate. Is that clear to you?"

It's as clear as the fading light in this man's body. I bow. For a moment he's my leader. My oyabun. And I miss him already. He's fallen asleep now.

Suddenly he opens his eyes and says in a weak voice, "Sorry. You see. The great Okawa Oyabun. Dead already ..." He sighs. "But think it through, Sensei. We're all social outcasts. That's what they say about us, right? And that's what we ourselves say about ourselves. We're outcast from family, community, the law. We're misfits who can't adapt."

He closes his eyes again. He pants. His cheeks are like a slack bellows, sucked against his teeth and inflating again, as if he were blowing a whistle. He opens his eyes and smiles.

"But, look, please, Sensei. You've been with us for years. We ran away from the civil society and took refuge in the Yakuza society. But the laws of this new society are stricter, more severe and uncompromising, than the laws of the society that we ran away from. In our world the hierarchy is more precise, it's better kept. In our world, the punishments are extremely severe, and deadly. And they're by far more effective than the penal system of the decent society. And very few dare to violate our moral code. 'Misfits'? Not a single 'well-adjusted' katagi would last a single day in our world. So can you think about what should have been done for those youngsters, before they came here? Think it through."

His eyes are like black candles in the darkness of the room. You can see the breath withdrawing and disappearing within him. Weakness. Flickering. The cheeks are deeply sunken into the face, which led thousands on the path of no regrets. Here's a friend about to depart. I take his hand. He opens his eyes. I press his hand gently.

He smiles and says, "Go now. Thank you."

A week later Okawa Oyabun dies.

Photos from The Funeral

I choose not to attend the funeral. A tall foreigner will stand out in a funeral of such national scale. Representatives from all the big families will attend. Questions will be asked. The family will be embarrassed.

A week later I visit Okawa's house. His wife and daughters show me pictures from the funeral.

Here's a photo of the close family members: his wife, the daughters, Fukuoka, the senior Yakuza brothers, all in black kimonos. Hundreds of men fill the temple courtyard, all in black suits, black ties, with the family crest on their ties. A small white plastic garland is attached to the lower pocket of the suit, and a ribbon swirls down from it with the name of the deceased, Okawa Hiroaki Oyabun.

Here is picture of the end of the cremation. The Buddhist priest waves the dead man's Adam's apple, holding it with big chopsticks, before the awestruck crowd. Their Great Oyabun has turned to ashes.

Thousands of garlands. White, red, yellow, all plastic. More and more men with shorn hair, holding white prayer beads, bowing deeply to the widow and the daughters.

The temple courtyard, painted with the black crowd.

The Buddhist priest, in a white kimono, bald. He and the Yakuza, how similar they look.

The family elders, one by one, before the microphone. Their eyes testify to their words.

A man with tears in his eyes. Another man with tears in his eyes.

A curtain of incense. Every man bearing his incense stick, holding it with delicacy so rare to those fingers. You can almost smell the scent.

A line of people waiting. Like soldiers. Like children. Who will love them?

Lines of dark sunglasses.

Long panels above the wreaths. With names of the families sending condolences.

Even the oyabun of the Yamada-Gumi is there, staring straight into the camera, his eyes boldly declare his undisputed presence. It is a gaze of respect for an honored rival, who is now in an urn of ashes.

Above the altar, a photograph of Okawa, soft and pleasant, as he seemed to the innocent eye during his lifetime. A photograph of his wife, expressionless.

Bodyguards, five for each oyabun, looking all around for an invisible assassin.

Okawa is dead, and Tetsuya is in prison. I feel orphaned.

Letters from Prison—2

Tetsuya's second letter was smuggled out to me by Okawa Oyabun's widow.

> *Yakobu Sensei,*
>> *Okawa Oyabun is dead. A great man is dead. I weep for him every day. I don't know when another leader of that magnitude will arise. It is certainly not I. I'm afraid.*
>> *It's still cold here, and there isn't enough heat. But I'm a Yakuza, and I'm not allowed to complain. You're a gaijin, so I permit myself to complain to you. In a little while the cherries will blossom, and here we won't go to the cherry-blossom viewing. The prison courtyard is bare of trees. But I'll watch it on television.*
>> *I'm using the opportunity of a visit by my Big Sister* (Okawa Oyabun's widow). *Today is the memorial day for Oyaji (Papa) Okawa. We will pray for him here. We will think about him and remember him. Right after Oyaji's death clashes broke between our family and Yamada-Gumi. People died on both sides. The situation is explosive. The chain of clashes threatened to develop into a real war. We tried to hold a reconciliation ceremony, but failed. If Oyaji had been alive, I think the matter would have been resolved with no killings.*
>> *Sensei, I can write things to you that I don't dare to say to other people in the family. I'm Okawa Oyabun's successor, according to his will and explicit instruction. It's an enormous responsibility. But I'm afraid. You can understand that, right? I'm really frightened. I, the*

Yakuza Terror of the North, of whom everyone is afraid,
I'm very frightened. Don't tell anyone, please.
    About the man you're looking for, Sensei. Go and
meet Jimmy, the blond brother, and he'll tell you what to
do with your friend.

Good-bye from your friend, Fujita Tetsuya
[date]

The Blond Yakuza

Jimmy receives me in his office after getting an order from Tetsuya
to do so. Blond hair, straight nose, otherwise a Japanese face. Short.
His feet on the table. He skips the courtesies. Two young Koreans
serve him. A look from Jimmy, a raised finger, a tilt of the head,
sometimes a bark in broken English, and they rush into action. A
giant picture of the writer Mishima hangs on the wall behind Jimmy.

Since I saw him at the Washington Hotel, five years ago, I've been
wondering what he's doing here, yellow hair among the Japanese.

He smiles. I introduce myself again. "Sit down." He gets up and
serves me tea. He says he's been interested in my research. I ask him
about his origins. He looks at me, smiling.

He speaks Japanese, and occasionally turns to English. "My real
name is Giancarlo James Bertolini, which is where 'Jimmy' comes
from. My mother was Japanese, from Okinawa. My father was an
American from Chicago, of Sicilian origin. Funny, no? My dad was
an American soldier in Okinawa. That's where he met my mom,
who played shamisen in one of the bars of the city of Naha. They
got married, had me, and got divorced when I was eight. My dad
went to America and never came back. No contact. I don't know
where he is now. Once I went to Chicago to look for him. I met a
friend of my dad's, and I got a lot of information from him. He told
me my father's parents were immigrants from Sicily. Decent people.
My grandfather owned a garage in Chicago. But my uncle, my dad's

brother, joined the Cosa Nostra, the Mafia, as you call it. Yes, yes, we're proud Mafiosi in the family.. But after that visit to Chicago I decided I didn't want to see my father or have any connection with him.

"I, Sensei, am a mongrel. Mixed. *Ainoko*. In Japan ainoko is constant ostracism. Worse than gaijin. My mom left Okinawa with me. We moved to Tokyo when I was ten. Then she started working in the clubs and bars of Shinjuku. She was a great player and a great singer. She saved penny after penny so I could go study at the university. She died two years ago.

"In high school I was a hood, but everybody recognized my talents, and I managed to get by. I passed the university entrance examination easily. I went to Asia University, known for its nationalist character. I studied history. I didn't study much there, but I was very active in politics. At the university I organized a group of 'New Lovers of the Homeland.' Extreme right. Long live the emperor, and all that. We were a small group with a big presence. The leftists were afraid of us.

"Why the extreme right? Because the left is a bluff. Their love of mankind went as far as the place where they saw me, a blond Japanese, and it didn't fit in with their ideas about human brotherhood.

"After I finished university, with an undistinguished record, we continued our activism. We grew. Now we were fifty members. Enthusiastic young people. We got together to study the doctrine of *minzoku* (the ethnic-nationalist doctrine of the 1930s), and the teachings and speeches of Mishima Yukio Sensei. We bought a big black car with big loudspeakers. We shouted in front of the Soviet embassy. We embittered the life of the Communist Teacher's Union. We beat up leftist students. We bullied members of the ultra-leftist Chukako-Ha. We did some bad things here and there. The ones we hated most were the members of the Sekigun-Ha, the Japanese Red Army. Have you ever heard of the Japanese Red Army? Sure you have. Once they sprayed bullets at people in your Tel Aviv airport over there. Okamoto. Yes, yes. Okamoto. They hate Japan; they're enemies of the emperor. Once we used to look for them to smash them with iron rods. They're rat shit. There was an order to find them and break them. That wasn't business. That was ideology. Then they disappeared from Japan. Lebanon. North Korea. Libya. The Philippines. Once we went especially to the Philippines to find them. To attack. Even to kill.

"Not all the members were actually real patriots. Some joined for other reasons. The extreme right, Sensei, is a place of refuge. If the society vomits you out, you go either to the Yakuza or to the extreme right. What happened to me is a combination of the two. The people of Okinawa hate the emperor, and, I, half-foreign, an Okinawan, fought for the emperor. Can you explain that? How can I, the ultimate outsider, fight for Japan? Explain that to me. You're a professor, aren't you? I fight for Japan, because that way I am in the heart of Japan. Nobody can say that I am an outsider. I am a patriot, ain't I? No fuckin' Japanese can throw me out because I am more of a true patriot than most soft-headed, benevolent Japanese. But then I shit on Japan. Fucking racist society. You can write that. Did you write it?

"During my childhood my mother already changed my name to Hamano Takehiro. That's my official name. The Italian-American past has been erased. But I won't dye my hair. Why? Because now I live in a family that doesn't care where I come from or what color my hair is. The Yakuza family.

"I have a little army in the spirit of Mishima Sensei. We publish a newspaper, hold conferences. We still annoy the Russians, so that they'll return the Northern Islands to Japan. We still beat up Communists. We have a secret base in the mountains, and we train there. When the police harass us, that's where we hide. We are under the surveillance of the guys from the Unit for the War on Terror, not to the Unit for the War on Yakuza. But we don't give a shit.

"When we were a group of partisans after the university, we didn't last long. We needed backing. The members dispersed. The zeal melted away. The men were weak. They didn't know how to fight. In general, Sensei, today's young Japanese don't know how to fight. They don't know how to hit. Cowards. Squeamish chicks.

"It went on that way until we met Okawa Oyabun. He may be Korean, but he preserves the spirit of Japan more than the weaklings in suits who run around here. Those of us who were left joined Okawa's family. I'm Sicilian, I'm American. I'm Japanese. What am I? I studied history, and I know that if I'm Sicilian, I'm Arab, or maybe also Swedish, and French. What not? So what am I?

"What am I? I'm Yakuza. This is the place where they don't ask questions. I'll never forget how Okawa accepted me. Simple. 'Come,' he said, and that's all.

"We put out a paper, I told you. Also a magazine. About Japanese patriotism. Here, look. We also organize demonstrations and meetings and we invite various people to discuss Japanese nationalism. How do I make a living? From here and there. They hire me sometimes. But mainly I recruit people for the newspaper and the magazine. Subscriptions. After all, it's patriotic journalism, isn't it? I go to a big company and ask for a subscription or a donation. Then I send the newspaper. How much does a subscription cost? A lot. We have our expenses, don't we? It's a subscription and it's also a contribution. The amount depends, according to the company's economic condition. We ask for a million yen, ten million yen, fifty million yen. It depends. What if someone doesn't want to subscribe or contribute? I convince him that it's worth his while. Usually they pay up.

"So, Sensei, that's how I combine ideology and business. Do I have other sources of livelihood? I do. This and that. My kobuns see to various sources of income. We have a research department, and we look into various things about companies, and then it's easy for us to obtain contributions. It's called extortion. Once a month the police come. They enquire. They drink tea with us. Sometimes they bother us. Sometimes people lodge complaints with them.

"I recruit my new kobuns from Korea, not Japan. Most of my kobuns are Koreans. The young Japanese, I told you, don't know how to fight. They have it too good. Are you recording this? Excellent. Write it down, Sensei. I'm proud to be a Yakuza. It's a warm family like you can't find in Japan. Without them I'd be nothing. I'd be an outsider. Now I'm an insider. Blond or not blond. I never dye my hair. Go try to be blond, mixed, out therein a firm, in a school, in government service. I'm a Yakuza, and things are good for me. I chose it. And things are good for me.

"I'm not Japanese, not American, not Sicilian. I'm a Yakuza.

"Now, about your business. You're looking for somebody, Sensei. I don't know exactly where he is, but maybe I know approximately. We also have dealings in the backyards of Manila. We have business there. I'll send you to our man in Manila, Imai Kazuo, and he'll help you proceed, if the man you're looking for really is in Manila. He knows everything you need to know about Yakuza or ex-Yakuza in Manila. Here's the address. Also, take this envelope. There are three letters here. One is an introduction letter written by the late Okawa Oyabun. The letter introduces you and should be the best visa to anywhere in the Yakuza world. The other one is letter of introduction from me. You will hand these two to Imai. The third letter is Okawa Oyabun's letter, addressed to your Yuki, or whatever his name is. You are to hand it to him personally.

"Sensei, one last thing. You're emotionally involved. That's dangerous. Be careful. That man may have forgotten you long ago. Good luck."

Manila

I'm sitting in the Au Bon Vivant Restaurant on Guerrero Street in Manila. My partner is Imai Kazuo, the man mentioned by Jimmy-Takehiro. He has just returned from a gambling party at the Philippine Cockers Club, where they bet on fighting cocks with sharp blades fastened on their spurs. He is in a good mood. Bundles of money peek out of the inside pocket of his violet silk suit, covering an orange tie with a winking Mickey Mouse. Manicured fingernails.

Two rings. Beneath the sleeves, the ends of tattooed decorations. We drink from silvery-framed glasses.

I hand him the letters of introduction, one from Jimmy, one from Okawa Oyabun. He grumbles with admiration. "Well, you can't argue with a letter of introduction from the Great Okawa Oyabun," he says. "Whatever you want, you'll get. Akh! Akh! Okawa Oyabun! A real giant! None like him now. There won't be anymore. Maybe he is the last; who knows? Nothing's going to be the same after his death. And you, gaijin-san, you are very privileged, I'd say."

I don't tell him yet about the other letter burning in my own inner pocket, the one addressed from Okawa to Yuki, if I find him.

Imai takes out his business card.

EL CAMINO
Manila Central Academy
of Performing Arts
Director: Kazuo Imai

Young Filipinas learn how to sing and dance at the El Camino Academy, he explains. "All kinds of girls study with us," Imai tells me. "Girls who were whores and got tired of it, girls who are sick of their mamas or just ordinary girls whose parents have pushed them to study, so they can go to Japan or Bangkok, Singapore, Kuala-Lumpur, Hong Kong, or Jakarta, and make good money in the nightclubs and send it back home to their parents in the Philippines. Some of the students are dreaming of a big entertainment career in Southeast Asia or in Japan. There are quite a few dance academies here: Las Vegas, Hollywood, Los Monjes. Very creative names, aren't they?"

But the both parents and girls know that the way lead to prostitution. Graduate students will be "exported" to Japan by the Yakuza. It all begins with gentle persuasion. After all, the girl may be an experienced whore already, so what's wrong about that. Now she's going to add a bit of art, and there's good money in it. She can help her parents. Just for a little while, and then she can sing and dance. Maybe she can dance a serve the clients after work. If she refuses, they'll lock the girl up in a little apartment. They'll keep her passport in a safe. She won't be able to leave the apartment. Maybe she'll run away one day, but if she's caught, they'll beat her up. Appeals to the Philippine embassy won't help in most instances. Sometimes she's lucky to get to the press, or to some Buddhist and Catholic organization, and she'll be saved.

Imai Kazuo runs a dance academy. He is a new kind of Yakuza, unknown to the old generation. He is modern. Global. He is fluent in English and Spanish. He can converse in passable Chinese and Tagalog. He doesn't like to be told about the old values of the Yakuza.

"Stories," he says, "just stories. We're the shit of society. So what. Society itself is shit. The Yakuza 'path of chivalry' is passé—or it never existed.

"What the newspapers like to hear is about Yakuza who love the motherland, who hate Communists, who help the weak and harm the powerful, who walk on the sunny side of the street so that the katagi can walk in the shade. Bullshit. But me, I like to strangle the little man. Like this [he demonstrates]. I'm sick of the little Japanese katagi. He's a slave. He's a hypocrite. He hates me, and he wants to strangle me. I won't help him. Let him help himself. If I can I will exploit him, frighten him, cheat him, blackmail him, beat the shit out of him, I'll do it with great pleasure.

"We're men of the world. It's a world of interests, not loyalties and all that crap. Whoever helps me is a friend. We trade guns, whores, drugs. Everything. We trade even with the Communists, believe me. Even terrorist groups, Red Army and all these shit ideologists. If it helps to make money, I will hug the devil.

"So you're looking for somebody called Yuki, or some other different names. That's what it says in the letter. Well, it won't be easy. Even Okawa Oyabun didn't know exactly where he was, that Yuki man. I understand he fled here from Japan. You know how many Yakuza are living in Manila? Hundreds. Manila is big business. Maybe I've met him; who knows? In business. Drugs. Entertainment girls. But we're elusive, you know. And I don't even know his name now. Probably Ferdinand Marcos. Maybe he bought a passport in Hong Kong. If he wanted to hide from the Yakuza or from somebody else, he could have had some plastic surgery, so that even his mom wouldn't recognize him. If he has other identifying marks, you know … something on his ass. On the inside of his arm. I know, I know you didn't sleep with him, but maybe you went to the baths together, hot springs. Something inside. Something in the heart, that you can't operate on."

"His eyes," I say. "One looks straight, and the other looks to the side. Like a toad. He has a scar on his right cheek, and in his heart, a kind of melancholy you can't erase. And there may be a crazy woman with him. Maybe she wears orange."

He listens and thinks. He suddenly says, "Well, very romantic of you, gaijin. But wait a minute. You, gaijin-san, what's your business with him? Why are you looking for that guy? I'm not sure I can just give you information like that, even if you have a letter from Okawa Oyabun. I can't burn myself, you understand? I have businesses here and a lot of connections, and a lot of trust people put in me. It's not the way things were once. Even the power of Okawa Oyabun isn't what it once was. He's already dead, and we're in a new world. Fujita Tetsuya is in prison, and I don't know what's going to happen to the family when he gets out. They don't have authority here. Certainly not in the Philippines. It's like the Wild West here. So what's your business with him?"

"Giri," I tell him. And I tell him the whole story. Almost, minus the red postcard.

He's silent. Looks at me. Suddenly he asks, "Are you brothers?"

I say, "Something like that. Yes, yes, we're brothers."

He stares. His face floats up in the smoke, and his eyes, black points, stare at the ceiling. Then he looks at me thoughtfully.

"I'll help you, gaijin-san. Even though I don't understand a thing. I'll help you. Maybe because I still have a lot of respect for the memory of Okawa Oyabun. And maybe because of the giri. It's bigger than me."

*

Imai takes me to meetings in bars, nightclubs, private homes, public parks, villages. It is Easter—*Pascua*—in Manila, and the Filipinos go mad with the sufferings of Christ. The streets become the Via Dolorosa. They carry huge crosses, wear crowns of thorns on their brows, and compete with each other: Who will truly be crucified? Real nails will penetrate their hands and nail them to the wood, and the blood will flow from the hands, truly black, truly thick, and they will be one with Christ, and will bear the *los pecados del mundo*, and they will cry, *"Eli Eli Lama Sabachthani?"* ("My God, my God, why hast thou forsaken me?") And I can smell Yuki's scent in the city.

Another meeting and yet another. He might have been seen here and there. There are some fingerprints. He and the woman at his side, who may be the real operator behind the scenes. Well, we don't really know, but, yes, the woman ... maybe he is Hirose, maybe he is Sato, maybe Watanabe, maybe Nakasone, maybe Hayashi, maybe Villa or Corason. Maybe he's a trafficker in women. Maybe he smuggles arms. Maybe he sells drugs. I see pictures. I visit the police—a professorial business card and a few thousand pesos folded up in my passport—and I ask. He's not in Manila, they tell me, or the plastic surgeon worked a miracle. Articles about the activities of the Yakuza in Manila appear every day in the newspapers, although the police deny faintly that the Yakuza are active here. Wars break out between the Yakuza and Filipinos or Chinese gangs—especially with the Dragonheads. I hear of violent clashes. Men killed on both sides. But people often die in Manila, where there are guns and whores and drugs, and lots of dead bodies and no one asks questions.

Every night I return to the hotel, and I wonder why I am searching for that man.

One day Imai calls and says, "Come, we're going to meet somebody."

We go to a bar. He leads me to a dark corner, and I can't see anything. I hand over my business card. The darkness doesn't give me a card in exchange. There are big black sunglasses that reflect the little lightbulbs over the bar. I'm used to black sunglasses. But here the glasses are very big. I don't know whether he's looking at me or through me or in an entirely different direction. He looks like someone disguised as a threatening Yakuza. He is menacing indeed. Darkness within darkness. Why did I get into all this?

"Imai told me about you and about the guy you're looking for," says a voice that seems to be distorted and camouflaged. "People know you're looking for him. And I tell you, go away. I'm telling you because you were like a son to Okawa Oyabun. Go away, gaijin. No, no, I won't tell you anything. I'm just telling you to go away. It's not healthy for you to be here. Even if you think you're brothers and all that shit. I'm told you're a professor. So I hope you understand."

"I understand. Thanks. Just give him my business card, please. And this letter, too."

Both card and letter are grabbed and swallowed up the dark jacket. I know now that Darkness will deliver the letter to Yuki. Okawa will forgive me for not handing it personally.

Darkness doesn't say a thing. He just spreads its legs wide. He exhales smoke into the bar. I'm glad to leave the place. Imai also takes a deep breath when we get out into the street.

The next day I fly back to Tokyo. It's spring there, and people are going crazy over the cherry blossoms.

Letters from Prison—3

The letter was smuggled out by Miyuko.

Yakobu Sensei,

I hear news on the radio about the advancing front of cherry blossoms. It's warmer, and life in prison is a little easier. If you make it through the cold, life isn't so hard. I get up at seven in the morning, wash in the central furo *(bath) twice a week. I exercise every day for half an hour. They allow me three visitors per day. I buy in the canteen various things like milk, candies, fruit, canned food, magazines, and such. I lack nothing. Well, just "women, sake, and freedom." I can read books at leisure and listen to the radio. I feel very tranquil. But I have no freedom, and they're very strict about rules and regulations. I have a three-tatami room. Some prisoners live in bigger rooms in larger groups.*

I can see you again, Sensei, in a few years. I don't know how many they'll give me. Three, five years. Good behavior, and maybe I'll get out in two years, including the months of detention. Not so bad. So I'll tell you then everything about life in prison. I'll visit you in Israel, and we'll meet there, or wherever you say. I'll take my son, Kotaro, with me. I'll show him the world. He'll decide on his way when he's grown. I'll try to use the time in prison to study, at least one thing, so that I'll know the days here weren't wasted. I'll do whatever's possible to help your research. You know, I can send instructions from here. No one will challenge my orders.

I hope you're progressing in your research, and also in your personal search for that man. I hope you're not endangering yourself, even though you have the protection of Okawa Oyabun. Be careful.

I have plenty of time here in prison to plan for the family when I get out of here, and get the position of oyabun of the Okawa-Kai. I'm still concerned, but less. Good-bye. I miss you.

Your brother, Tetsuya
[date]

*

I buy a big box of candy, big enough to feed a whole group in a prison cell. I buy a number of books of the kind Tetsuya likes.

With no prior warning I arrive at the Tokyo prison. At the gate I address the guard, hand him my business card (Professor, etc.), and tell him I wish to visit Fujita Tetsuya. The guard is polite but strict. He goes inside, returns with a negative answer. Only family members are allowed. My pleas and arguments don't get me very far. I ask, at least, give the box and the books to Fujita Tetsuya, with a little letter from me. He should take just one candy and give the rest to the others, because he's got diabetes, and the books are for him. Could you tell him that I wish he would write more, that I'm very moved by his letters? Thanks. He will deliver the candies.

The Manila Times

Every day, in Tokyo, I read the *Manila Times*. Maybe I'll find something.

Nothing. Until I despair. I go to Manila and came back. I ask people to keep track of crime news. Anything. No results.

But on the morning of May 14, 1993, I see another headline about the increase of Yakuza activity in Manila. I've gotten tired of these articles, so I read, weary:

Activity of Japanese Yakuza on Rise in Manila

Last night the Manila police raided a luxury villa on Roxas Boulevard after neighbors complained of gunshots and screams coming from inside. According to police sources, the villa belongs to Furukawa Saburo, a wealthy Japanese businessman, and has recently been the focus of suspicious activity. According to these sources, the Manila police have reason to believe Furukawa is an ex-Yakuza (Japanese criminal organizations), who has been acting as a lone wolf. Lately the activity of the Yakuza has been on the rise in Manila, so much so that it has become a main target of the Manila police. Yakuza activity concentrates on prostitution, drugs, and arms smuggling. Unofficial rumors say that Furukawa is connected with various crime groups: Chinese groups in Burma, Corsican gangs in Laos, Triad groups in Hong-Kong, and criminal elements here in the Philippines. In Manila he is thought to be in close contact with Mercedes Salonga, who heads the city's largest prostitution syndicate. It is also known that Furukawa has been in contact with a number of the Chinese "Dragonhead" bosses, a connection that is a matter of deep concern to the Japanese Yakuza in Manila.

The police found the villa empty. The screams, it turned out, were of a pet monkey who was frightened by shots that apparently had come from inside the villa earlier. The interior of the villa was in a complete chaos. Furniture had been slashed and the contents of drawers strewn on the floor. It seems a search had been hastily made, and intruders fled when they heard the police approach.

Two photographs from inside the villa accompanied the story: one shows a large, splendid room opening onto a garden and pool. It's a mess. The second is a photograph of the terrified monkey, sitting on a dresser, with an expression of dread on its face. Behind the monkey I notice a picture frame leaning against the wall, and in it, in large letters, a print of a poem in English. Most of the words are clearly legible. I bring it close to my eyes:

> "I will break God's seamless skull,
> And I will break His kiss-less mouth,
> O I'll break out of His faultless shell
> And fall me upon Eve's gold mouth."
>
> —Jose Garcia Villa

It's him! Furukawa is Yuki! That poem by Jose Garcia Villa! It's him!

I don't need more proof. It's him!

I call the newspaper in Manila. I explain I'm a professor at … etc. Doing research, etc. May I please speak to the editor in chief?

I wait. And then he is on the line. And again, explaining who I am, what I'm investigating, etc. "You have a special reporter in Tokyo—of course. Yes, yes, I read it in the story. To investigate about the Yakuza, yes, yes, I know, … I'd like to meet him. I can help. I have a lot to offer. Yes, I have a special interest in Furukawa. Thank you, thank you. Here's my phone number. Thanks. You don't have to promise anything. I'm very grateful to you. Yes, yes, I know you can't promise anything. I'm used to that."

*

I meet Bienvenido Arroyo, tailored and polished, in the Cafe La Mille in Shinjuku, and almost without delay I offer to make an exchange: rich information about the Yakuza, except for truly secret material in return for every possible detail about Furukawa. All information will remain absolutely confident.

Arroyo asks for two days to consult with his superiors. We'll meet here again.

*

We meet two days later. Arroyo is very friendly. He's heard about me from "reliable sources." He has a lot of respect for the courage and depth, etc. The editor of his paper would be happy to exchange information. He just isn't sure how much serious information he has about Furukawa. "The world of the Yakuza, you know, is elusive, and people are here today and somewhere else tomorrow. Manila, São Paolo, Bangkok."

"Yes, yes, I know. I know. So what do you know about Furukawa?"

Arroyo speaks hesitantly. "We have all kinds of information gathered from various sources. Men from the Yamada-Gumi were about to kill Furukawa. They identified him as the one who, so they say, killed a senior family member in Tokyo. At the time he had a different name, apparently."

"Yuki. Murata Yukihira."

"Maybe. It seems that he's also wanted by another group ..."

"Okawa-Kai."

"Maybe. Aside from revenge, there's a story of betrayal. The Yakuza blame him establishing connections with the Chinese Dragonhead, the archenemy of the Yakuza in Japan and in the Philippines. But as for his identity, the information is contradictory."

"Meaning?"

"The sources say the man apparently changed identities many times in the past years. He became a lone wolf, and he doesn't actually belong to any family in Japan. The Japanese don't like that. But he manages to conceal his criminal connections beneath the disguise of an extremely successful businessman. Plastic surgery and identity change. And the man has disappeared within himself. His areas of activity are varied: finance, import-export, and maybe arms. And behind all that is a powerful woman. She also had plastic surgery and changed identities. She also wouldn't be able to identify herself, apparently. Strong. Sharp. Crazy, they say. Maybe because of years of cocaine. Someone who saw her says she's gaunt, and nothing remains of the beauty she may once have had. They also talk about loud arguments between them, recently.

"The confidential sources say that he travels very little. In the past three years he's gone to Laos once. Twice to Japan. Twice to Hong Kong. Three times to São Paolo, Brazil. Three Brazilian bodyguards of Japanese origin work for him. But that doesn't seem like a good enough reason to go there.

"Aside from that, he loves poetry, apparently, and he has a big collection of the poetry of Jose Garcia Villa. It seems strange and flattering, or highly embarrassing, that the man loves our beloved poet Jose Garcia Villa so much. Especially when we're talking about such a major criminal. Can you explain it?"

"No. Can you explain anything, at all?"

We agree that it's impossible.

At other meetings I tell him things about the Yakuza. And even though there's no divulging of secrets, and even though Arroyo could have found out what I told him from other sources, it leaves a bitter taste in my mouth to tell the stories about my intimate friends.

And the summer comes.

Letters from Prison—4
The letter is smuggled by Miyuko.

> *Yakobu-san,*
>   *Thank you very much for the candies. I was moved to*
> *a group cell, and I gave the candies to the other prisoners.*

I told them about you with great pride. Some of them know you. You have thanks from all of them.

Today the Sanja matsuri in Asakusa is starting, and I won't take part. On May 7 I was transferred to a cell with six men instead of the painful little cell where I was before. I've been in prison before, but this is the first time I've been in a group cell. They're all Yakuza. All from other families, but there's one young guy from our family. I spend my days happily. In the other cell I felt very isolated. I couldn't talk with anyone. Here I can talk, and that's a relief.

Every day friends from the family come to visit me, and also Miyuko and Kotaro, and that makes me happy. Kotaro has grown a lot, and he already talks a little. "Hi, Daddy," he says. Would you believe it? He's so cute. Every time he visits me, I leave a little of my heart in the visitors room. Maybe he understands with his child's mind that this time we'll be separated for a long time, because when move from detention to prison, they don't let little children visit. One day he said, "I'm not going. I won't say good-bye to Daddy," and I cried. Maybe I'll see him in another year or two.

Life in prison isn't hard. I have no worries. I just have to reconcile myself to the years of imprisonment, but they, Miyuko and Kotaro, live out there, and it's very hard for them. Although the brothers and sisters from the family take care of them, it's hard. On the other hand I can live here quietly, knowing they're not alone. I intend to read a lot and learn a lot and make use of the time.

Prison, Sensei, is giving me a rest. Recharging the batteries. Here there's room for thoughts, writing, reading, quiet conversations, philosophical discussions, listening to music, studying. A few of us are learning crafts. Others

*study history, writing poetry, calligraphy. But it's a waste
of time. We'll forget everything when we get out.*

*We learn a big lesson in prison. A lesson in patience,
restraint, devotion, and the power of silence. I long for
my woman, the child, friends. But I don't tell that to the
others. We all miss something or somebody. Here we hear
songs. Most of us like the enka songs of Naniwa Bushi.
You see? We're very sentimental. Very conservative. Soft.
Lonely. Little boys. Here we'll check who we're afraid of.
Here we ask what's with the Yakuza. Every day. Is it good
for me? Is it bad for me? Here I decide time after time to
stay because it's my world. I also understand that I don't
have the strength or time or persistence to raise children. I
love them very much and want them to have only what's
good. But I don't have the time or strength to raise them.*

*Yakuza in prison get privileges. Our status is high
here. We aren't like little thieves, rapists, murderers,
robbers. Or little confidence men. Such people disgust
me. A Yakuza would die before he steals. The guards also
respect us more than the little criminals.*

*The matter of your man Yuki still isn't clear. But
it turns out maybe he did something big for our family.
What my sources tell me is that the man is in danger.
They don't know where he is. But the Yamada-Gumi
are looking for him. They even tried to kill him. We were
looking for him, too. You know why. But just now this
man managed to make a connection with Dragonhead
men, to make an alliance with them. That took a lot
of courage, I imagine. With all the danger that he's in.
They tell me that he managed to write a draft of a treaty
between Okawa-Kai and the Dragonhead, and he's
about to present it to us for approval. Okawa Oyabun
initiated that before his death, but how the instructions
reached him, I don't know. Maybe you know? The goal of*

the alliance, from our point of view, is help in removing the Yamada-Gumi from Tokyo and northern Japan, and especially from areas of influence in Southeast Asia. All of that is in return for partnership in interests in various areas of Tokyo, Manila, Bangkok, and in Hawaii, help in getting arms, and other things. If he really managed to forge the alliance, he did something that will boost the status of Okawa-Kai in Southeast Asia significantly. It will be a historic event.

He has an international mind, your man. He reads the international map. He understands the difficulties of our economy. He sees the need for international connections. He understands that we need to expand out of Japan. And he knows how to camouflage all of that so as not to bring shame on the family. If it's all true, we're going to invite him into the family with great honor, to revoke the red postcard—a rare event. We will hold a reconciliation ceremony, to give him an important job in the new economy of the Yakuza.

When I get out of here, and I'm the head of the family, if I'm the head of the family, I'll go into the subject very deeply and give him everything he deserves.

Sensei, do you have any part in this?

Sometimes, Sensei, I'm tired of all this and I want to be a lone wolf.

From now on I'll call you Yakobu, okay?

Yours,
Your brother,
Tetsuya
[date]

The Life of Yuki

Two months later a fat envelope lands on my desk at the university. The stamp is from Hong Kong. The postmark is blurred. There's no name on the envelope.

I know it's from him.

I tear open the envelope. The pages are in order, but the handwriting is cluttered. The paper trembles in my hand, and the deciphering takes hours. I read once, and I read again.

Sensei,

I know you've been looking for me for years. Maybe I owe you my life. Maybe I owe you my death. But you're my brother. So I owe you my story.

You see? I'm in a hurry. I have no time. And the main points will be enough.

I don't look the way I did when you knew me. My eyes don't bulge, and people don't call me a toad anymore. But the eye that drifts to the side could only be changed a little. Maybe it would have been possible with a different surgeon. The scar is artfully covered. I had my eyelid sewn so I don't have that telltale blink. That's how far! I don't know if you'd recognize me. I don't recognize myself.

I was born in a small village near Hakodate, on the Island of Hokkaido. I'm *ainoko*—mixed. My mother is Japanese, and my father was one of the Ainu people. Maybe he himself was mixed. I don't know. He didn't stay with us long. He drowned in a fishing boat on the Okhotsk Sea. I have pictures of him: tall, hairy, protruding eyes. A long beard. A man from legends. I'm "a fisherman's son with no home." Do you remember Yukihira's poem? Mom loved ancient Japanese poetry, and she chose my given name—after the poet Ariwara No Yukihira, who wrote that poem. And my love of poetry—my mother's inspiration? My name?

Usually mixed breed people are handsome. Not us, the Murata brothers.

It was hard after Dad died. My big brother, Yoshinori (we called him Yoshi) supported us. Construction work. Tourism. Work in

176

nature reserves. Truck driver. Then he joined up with bad guys. He would disappear, return, bring money. Disappear again. He was always good to me. Like in the books, a criminal with a good heart. His looks were always frightening. And whatever my thoughts about his new company, it was impossible to argue with the money that was flowing in. He refused to say who his friends were. He never would bring them home. Yoshi would take us on trips, mainly in Hokkaido. Twice we traveled to faraway Tokyo.

From time to time I liked to go to Hakodate, to the Trappist monastery. There was the charm of distant lands there, of distant religions. Of crucified gods. The gaijin god always fascinated me. Nails in his hands and blood flowing on his chest, his head bent. I liked the red bricks, the boulevard leading to the monastery, the sight of the monastery in winter, the trees like white mushrooms. I liked the sad-faced Madonna in the frame of red leaves in the autumn. There was a charm of a land in heaven.

I liked the monks' stories. The stories about the Mother of God, about Jesus, about the crucifixion, about the sufferings he took upon himself to redeem the world, about "Why hast thou forsaken me?" I was especially fascinated by the story about Barabbas the robber, who was pardoned from crucifixion. I liked the meaning of his name, "The Son of the Father."

I read books from all over the world. Yoshi was happy about that. He was glad to see me reading in English and Spanish. "Sometime that will be useful," he said.

One day, when I was sixteen, he said to me, "Come." I went with him to a little storage shed outside the city. Twenty men were there. Their hair was short. Some had shaven heads. And some of them had pa-ma, Afro hairdos. Most wore sunglasses. Some wore kimonos.

My brother told me, "Sit at the side and don't say a word." Somebody poured sake into a little cup with great formality. They said things in incomprehensible Japanese. My brother stood in the middle. Somebody in a kimono exchanged cups with him. They drank. They swore an oath, like in the Yakuza movies. Everybody's hands trembled.

Afterward, on the way home, he said, "Those are my brothers now. No less than you. Good men. They'll also help me bring food home. I wanted you to see. Maybe one day you too ... who knows? But you'll be at the university, apparently. That's good." I heard and trembled. My knees shook.

He took good care of us. Later he went to live in the city of Sapporo. Two years later I went to the University of Sapporo to study literature. Then Mom came, and we lived together. He paid for everything. Sometimes I would visit his office. I gradually understood he was getting bigger there, in that world of tattooed men. People respected him.

One day he said to me, "I have a house in the Yakuza." That meant he had become a small oyabun.

"I see," I said, "You don't kill people, I hope."

"We don't kill people," he said. "Look at me. Am I capable of killing people?"

"Anybody can," I said.

He slapped me.

I didn't have sex with a woman until I was twenty-three. Books were everything to me. At twenty-three I met Sayumi. She was the daughter of Hanaoka, the CEO of the Agricultural Bank in the Hokkaido region. He was a short, guilty-looking man. I didn't like him.

On my first night with Sayumi I wanted to end my virginity. I thought it was natural. That it was what everybody did. She laughed. And she refused. It was half a year before she yielded. One day she pulled me into the forest, and that's where we were joined. I thanked her. I felt like someone who has attained awakening. And she was my Master. I kissed her like a woman. I hadn't known that the joining of body to body could be so spiritual. There was no shame. *Teach me*, I told her, *and I'll be a shield unto you. Teach me.*

We wrote *tanka* traditional poems to each other. She was working as a saleswoman in a clothing store. Always smiling. Always observing. She designed children's clothes. She would bring my mother dolls made of pieces of cloth she'd gathered. Once a week she would go to a *zazen* meditation session with an old, smiling Zen teacher, who worked as an accountant.

Yoshi's visits became scarce. I ran the household. Investments. Savings. He praised me for my economic talent. One day he said, "Go and study business."

I said, "Are you crazy? I'd better study astrophysics." But the seed was sown.

I decided to study for a master's degree. I first graduated in literature. I did my master's thesis on Octavio Paz. I discovered the Spanish-speaking world, and the marvelous modern Filipino poetry in Spanish, English, and Tagalog. I got to the Philippine poet Jose Garcia Villa and fell in love with him. Didn't know why then.

In my second year of studies I also registered for a master's degree in economics. I graduated with honors. They wanted me to continue on an academic career at the university. I didn't want to. Why should I?

Sayumi and I began to live together. We started a little business manufacturing rag dolls. It was wonderful. It was amusing. We made fantastic figures from faded pieces of cloth. We started to sell in Hokkaido and then in Tokyo. We made a lot of money. Yoshi didn't like the idea.

"You were meant for great things," he said. "Rag dolls aren't a business for you." But I liked the dolls.

I knew Sayumi and I would never part. Ours was the kind of love they write about in the most romantic books. I didn't understand then what Jose Garcia Villa was talking about in his gloomy poems. Why did he write about the end of love? What did he know? He was disturbed, I thought. Sayumi and I used to laugh like mad. We read poems. One room in our house was crammed with colorful rags. There was joy like a fountain.

One day Sayumi announced there was a baby in her womb. I dived into the rags screaming with joy.

I never told her about Yoshi. Maybe she guessed.

One day Yoshi visited Mom's house. He was in a rage, nasty and ugly. More frightening than ever. He shut himself up in my room and spoke on the phone for a long time. Now and then voices could be heard from there. Barks in Yakuza slang. I trembled. The man in that room wasn't my brother. It was a demon. I wanted to peek— maybe somebody had gone in there and kidnapped my brother. It was hard to understand what he was saying. But I understood an address, and an hour of date. I heard an order.

I went to the place at the appointed hour. It was a storage shed. Three black cars were parked outside. Trembling with fear, I walked quietly to one of the sidewalls. I looked in. It was dark. My knees shook. I peeked.

A short man stood there with his back to me. A few other men were there, facing me. My brother stood in the center. His face was more frightening than ever. He spoke softly, and I didn't understand what he was saying. The short man with his back to me suddenly fell to his knees. Somebody shouted to him, "Get up!" He was shaking. He said something I couldn't understand.

Then I noticed a puddle spreading at his feet.

They let him go. They gave him his briefcase. He turned toward the door, his pants wet. Then I saw his face. It was Hanaoka, Sayumi's father.

I collapsed next to the storage shed. My brother found me there, and he hit me in the face. Once. But the blow is still there, next to my eye.

"He's an evil man!" he shouted. "Do you hear? A very evil man! You know how many families that man has shattered without batting an eye? I'm going to do justice! Do you hear? I'm returning the money to the people that evil man stole from! And I'd better not see you this way again, ever! Next time I won't just hit you once! Now get the hell out of here!"

I couldn't go back home. I went to the Trappist monastery and stayed overnight there. I went to the abbot and told him what happened.

He said, "Go to her, my son. Go and ask her forgiveness. And do something to atone for your brother's deeds. And say a prayer."

"But I'm not Christian," I said.

"No matter. Say a prayer." And he made the sign of the cross in front of my eyes. My knees were still shaking.

The next day I went home. Sayumi was lying on the futon. She didn't ask. She didn't say anything. I told her. She kept silence. Afterward she went to the sink and vomited. I followed her and vomited too.

The next morning I found her standing in the doorway of the rag room, her legs spread, a red puddle between them.

She went away that day and never returned. I haven't seen her since.

I went to Tokyo. I tried various jobs. Sales agent for a small company that marketed vitamins. Salesman in a bookstore. But I kept quitting. I kept wandering to a new place. And I was always reading poetry. But one day I was flat broke, and somebody came to me and offered me a stand in Sugamo. In Hayashi Oyabun's turf. I knew Yoshi was there, in the background, watching. Sending emissaries. Arranging my life. By then he was already a respected oyabun in Hokkaido.

I liked going to Golden Gai, to Hirano-san in Murasaki. Remember? That's where I discovered Mayumi, the girl in orange. Remember you asked me about her? That was where she started talking with me. That was where she told me one day that I was hers. That her father, Sekida Oyabun, was a great and terrible boss in the Tokyo Yakuza. That nobody must know about us. That one day we'd run away from there. That one day wealth and death would come to us. That one day we'd run away, and we'd never stop.

She knew everything, that crazy girl. She knew who I was. What I was thinking. Who I was running away from. As if she was attached to my brain. She told me she was an incarnation of Sayumi. She was crazy, and she was the only sane refuge I had. A hiding place of sanity, from Sayumi, from Sayumi's father, from grief, from shame, from the end of love, from the puddles of urine and blood, from the God who had left me, from the holes in my hands that bleed like that Son of God, so sad, hanging from the cross in the Trappist monastery in Hakodate. Sometimes the shame was in the image of Sayumi. Like the sad Mother of God hidden in a niche, on a snowy day, in that monastery.

Mayumi and I became secret lovers. Café lovers. Park lovers. We made love in the time cracks through which she managed to slip away from her bodyguards. For some time we just talked. No sex. But then the sweetness of madness stuck to me, and I surfed down the waterfall. There was no park in Tokyo, large or small, that did not serve as our love bed. Sneaking away from her bodyguards became an art. Danger was a thrill. We were on a high, almost praying to be caught by a bodyguard. Then Big Shibata, the goon, began to turn a blind eye. Probably in conspiration with Mayumi. I think he was afraid of her more than of her old man. And me, after some time the demons returned, and I found no comfort in this madness.

That was the time, soaked with shame, confused, crazy, that I met you. Fearful, tortured, taking solace in small doses of tormented poets from distant lands.

One day, toward dawn, when I was going home, I saw Hayashi in the street, talking with a chimpira hood of the Yamada-Gumi. Everything happened with lightning speed. The flash of a knife. The threat against Hayashi. My hand found a stone. The hand hit. Then it was covered with blood. The sunglasses shattered. The groans. The fight. The slash of knife. The taste of blood dripping from my cheek into my mouth. The trembling in my knees that hasn't stopped to this day. The flight. Hayashi's gratitude. Run away from here, fast! I was told. Today!

I went to the Murasaki. I passed a note to Mayumi via Hirano-san. A meeting place and a time.

We ran away.

I wanted to say good-bye to you, but I couldn't.

Since then, wanderings. You know. You investigated, didn't you? On my tracks were Mayumi's father, Sekida Oyabun, and Yamada-Gumi men. A minor oyabun of the Okawa-Kai named Ito spirited me up to the north, gave me new identity papers. A new passport. The first plastic surgery. A minimal operation. Various jobs. The Athene gambling club. Various services for the oyabuns in the North. Everything, I know, was made possible through Yoshi's intervention. I fled from place to place. I only saw Yoshi once. He had troubles of his own.

One day I was told Yoshi's "house" had collapsed too. He had disappeared. He'd fled, they said. Maybe to a foreign country. It was as if my father had died again. In time he wrote a letter handed personally to me. He had gone to live in São Paolo, Brazil. I saw my mother occasionally, in hiding places.

During the many hours of waiting at the entrances of gambling clubs, I could think, observe, plan. And then, one day, I knew how to weld evil with evil: the evil of the world of business, for some reason called decent, and the world of the Yakuza. But I still didn't dare. I consulted with Mayumi. She thought for a few days, until one day she told me exactly what I had to do. And I did it. And the memory of those two puddles and my trembling knees was still with me.

Then, as advised by Mayumi, I asked for the conversation with Kimura Oyabun. I set out my ideas. He listened. I remember his generosity on that day. His attention. He sensed an opportunity. So I was given the opportunity to bring the Yakuza into today's economy. At that time my name was Watanabe. With every new name, I was a new man.

Then the meetings at Nano-chan's, the geisha. Our dizzying success. Within a short time I was on the board of directors of D Bank. Even before the meeting at Nano-chan's I knew D Bank was the parent company of the Agricultural Bank. Then I heard about the appalling actions committed by Sayumi's father, the corrupt Hanaoka, when he was the bank CEO, and about the dozens of farmers ruined because of his villainy. I remembered what my brother had told me about the man. I set out on a campaign of punishment against this and other bad guys. Within a few days, Hanaoka was unemployed. I took revenge, but there was no relief in my heart. The avenging evil became my shadow, my teacher, my goad, my friend, my brother, my oyabun.

Our house, the house of Kimura Oyabun, got rich. And I became the constant shadow, under a name that wasn't my own, with a face that wasn't my own, with a luxury car that wasn't mine, with money that wasn't mine, with courage that wasn't mine. Every day I swore not to be evil. And every single day I did more evil. Every day I swore I was doing evil in order to do good. I had my own plan, one that not even Mayumi knew about. And I was bad. Worse and worse.

And all of this, Sensei, was to atone for the night that I saw Sayumi's father pissing in his pants and shaking with fear of my big brother. I did what I did to prevent such evil. To punish evil. With a great sweep, I hoped, I would do something beyond imaginable dimensions, something that would wipe out the house that had brought me up. I wanted to bring goodness to the world. There was enormous good within me. There was enormous evil in me. There was a madness of gods and demons in me. I was about to bring good on the scale of a mythical disaster.

One day a messenger brought me news from my brother from São Paolo. I should immediately send him our mother, that times had changed, that there was no safety here for her or for me. He didn't even dare write a letter.

That very week I sent my mother to São Paolo. She traveled with a tattered little suitcase that she chose. In the airport she said to me, "Yukihira, you were destined to write poetry. Not for what you're doing now. You've already killed me. Why deliver my dead body to another country?"

I bowed deeply to her. And left.

But then one day all was meaningless. The money. The power, the evil. Then I went to Kimura Oyabun. Quick. Decisive. Crazy. Loving. Purging the world from its sins. I told him I was leaving. I wasn't afraid of his anger. I left the tip of my pinky with him. Sensei, what's the tip of a pinky compared to the constant pain of the nail holes in my hands? To the unceasing trembling of my knees? To the God who forsakes? To the baby who became a puddle of blood between Sayumi's legs?

I left my pinky tip with Kimura Oyabun and added him to the list of my pursuers. In two hours I left Japan with Sayumi. My money has been deposited in foreign banks. On the plane to Manila we rolled with laughter, thinking about the long line of pursuers: Sekida Oyabun, Mayumi's father, Kimura Oyabun, the Yamada-Gumi, the police, and maybe my brother, who apparently decided to intervene and halt the shame. They were all on our heels. We rolled with laughter. The stewardess asked us to calm down because we were disturbing the passengers. First class, no?

In Manila I did great things under the name of Furukawa, after another deep plastic surgery. It was impossible to identify me. Who could stop me? I joined up with Corsicans in Laos, with Chinese in Hong Kong, with rebels in the Philippines, with women traffickers and drug manufacturers. Who could stop me? I smuggled arms from here to there. Whores from there to here. I even had a dancing school. I called it *Las Vegas*. That's where we trained the girls who were then sent to Japan, as entertainers, prostitutes. I was an empire. And it was all behind the scenes. No one could track me down in any investment or operation, criminal or legal. No one could identify me. It was only in *Las Vegas* that I risked exposure. I would visit the place from time to time. I like dancing.

I planned to gather enough power in order to go back to Japan in a little while, in a few months perhaps, and stir up the gigantic economic revolution in the Yakuza, a revolution that nobody could resist. With international forces on my side. To bring down my good

God. And Mayumi was at my side, a man among men. We had a villa on Roxas Avenue. Two cars. Servants. And a pet monkey—Octavio, after Octavio Paz.

And I read a lot of poetry to remind me of the battlefields of the world.

And one day Okawa Oyabun's letter reached me by a messenger. I knew then that the Okawa-Kai people found me. The messenger said, a gaijin from Japan handled it. Directly from Okawa Oyabun. "For you, personally," he said. I asked who the gaijin was, and he gave a description. I knew it was you.

I opened the letter with excitement:

> *Murata Yukihira,*
> *I will die soon. When this letter reaches you, I won't be here. I'm sending you the letter by the hand of Yakobu Sensei.*
> *I'm writing you for two reasons. One is the intervention of Yakobu Sensei. The other is an opportunity we have for a historic change in the world of Gokudo—the Path of Extremes.*
> *You're under pursuit, and you know that sooner or later they'll find you. We'll find you. Actually we have a very good idea of your whereabouts. Kimura Oyabun will find you sooner or later and will settle accounts with you for leaving him, or Sekida Oyabun will find you and will settle accounts with you for kidnapping his daughter, or the Yamada-Gumi will find you and will settle accounts with you for the one they claim you killed ten years ago. Or the police will find you. I don't know whom you're playing off against whom over there in the Philippines, but as tough as you may have become, perhaps, in the past ten years, you're not made of material that can survive pressure like that. I've asked about you. You're made of material like my daughter, Machiko. Books and*

art. When they find you in the Philippines, it won't be according to the rules we practice in Japan. You're not even a member of any family. You're abandoned to your own fate.

You owe a debt of gratitude to Yakobu Sensei, who wanted to find you so much. Why? I don't know. If he's not too late, he'll save your life. It would be better if this letter reached you before your pursuers.

You also owe a debt of gratitude to your brother, who did great things for the Okawa-Kai family in Hokkaido. Without him, we wouldn't be the biggest family there. I hope he's doing well, wherever in the world he is.

For your brother's sake and for Sensei's sake, I'm offering you life. Return to the family and an honorable life.

I have another reason. You're one of the few who understand the meaning of the future of the modern Yakuza. You understand the meaning of the new anti-gang law very well. From now on, it's not arms that will bring power. Not the fist. Not intimidating the owners of little clubs, and not even the owners of companies of one kind or another. Only control. Control of the economy in a new way. Control of politics in a new way. According to their rules. Exactly. You understand that, and I understand that you understand it. I believe I understand how well you understand it. And also your ability to do it.

I'm worried about the future of the Path of Extremes. I know that only modernization will save it. And the process of international connections. No less. You can do it. We need a man like you with us.

But you have to pay for what you did. By action. I know that you've made contacts with Dragonhead men. Today they're our enemy, in Japan and in Southeast Asia.

They're strong. We have to admit that. We can't stay in the little Japanese hothouse anymore. If you want to come back—bring the Dragonhead to us. Make a treaty with them. Offer them spheres of influence in Japan and abroad. The Okawa-Kai family and the Dragonhead can control Southeast Asia. I authorize you to negotiate with them. Fujita Tetsuya, my successor, who's in prison now, will examine the agreement and authorize it when the time comes.

[Here were written the details of the offer that Okawa wanted to make to the Dragonhead.]

One last thing. Keep Sensei out of the picture. He doesn't know about the contents of this letter. He doesn't know how close he was to you and to danger. Keep him at a distance.

Make immediate contact with our people, right after the treaty with the Dragonhead. And come to Japan. You're not safe in the Philippines, no matter how rich and strong you may be.

When you return, we'll hold a reconciliation sakazuki ceremony. You'll receive a senior position in the family. Don't wait.

Okawa Hiroaki

Those are the main things he wrote there.

You brought me back. I've thought about you during all these years, about our strange brotherhood, about the inexplicable bond, about our short friendship, about what we didn't manage to say. The farewell that didn't take place. How close we were. How far we were. Growing apart. How unworthy I felt. How I vowed not to see you again. Ever. Because of the shame.

But you've returned. I couldn't even remember what you looked like. You were something vague that might not have existed.

I decided to act. I went to the Dragonhead people. I waited until Charlie Long, their boss, came to Manila for a business visit. I'd had various business deals with him for two years. But a surprise was in store for me there. After I explained to him what I proposed to do, meaning to renew the treaty with the Okawa-Kai, he thought I wanted to sell him out. He threw me inside a little room in his Manila house, where I sat for two days, tied to a chair with ropes that bit into my flesh, with a knife at my throat, and a candle ready to burn me. No food. No toilet. He wasn't willing to listen. I couldn't speak. I was scared. I sat there for two days, no food, no sleep, pissing on the chair.

As usual, it was Mayumi who saved me. On the second day they let me make one phone call to her. Under supervision. On the third day she went straight to Charlie Long's house, walked past one bodyguard, slapped another one in the face when he stood in her way, and shouted, "Charlie Long! Long! Come here! I'm going to talk to you!"

Even the bodyguards were in a panic and didn't know what to do. Crazy. Maybe the look in her eyes panicked them. I don't know. Long came out to her, and after five minutes he was sitting with her and negotiating. And I was in the next room.

Ten minutes later they brought me in. I still stank of piss and blood. I didn't know then how she convinced them to listen to me. They let me shower.

I returned to the room, and she commanded, "Explain to them!"

And I explained. For three hours I explained my plans and ideas. All the rest was processing the details—economic, political, the ways of preserving interests, mutual guarantees.

Charlie Long looked at Mayumi with enormous hatred and admiration. It seems he was convinced there was something to discuss.

Now it was possible to hold meetings between the leaders on neutral territory, on the island of Phuket, for example. And the rumors sped, as part of the tactic, and they spread. Even the *Asahi Geino* magazine published rumors about the historical treaty between the Japanese Okawa-Kai and the Chinese Dragonhead organizations.

I asked Mayumi how she convinced Charlie Long to talk to me. She said, "The details don't matter. But you should know that all the bosses you're dealing with—Chinese, Corsicans, Filipinos, and Thai—for every one of them, there's somebody who can get to him, or his son, or his father, or his mother. For example, somebody is constantly lying in wait for Pietro Demirelli's mother in his little village in Corsica. It's too far to from Vientiane or from the poppy fields of the Golden Triangle to Corsica.... He'd be better off giving in, or talking, at least. Charlie Long isn't exempt from that. He became fully aware of that after one telephone call to his mother in a well-guarded villa in Jakarta. 'Yes,' his mother said, 'a peddler dressed in a green sarong did knock on the gate this morning; what about him?'

"Exactly the description I gave Long. He burst with rage. He told me how I'd pay for it when the time came. But he sat down to do business. As you saw, a historic alliance came out of that house. The alliance will help both him and you, and his mother in Jakarta. And me. And those commandos like the one in Jakarta, they're cheap. All of soldiers who want to atone for something dirty they did. One in Taipei, one in a little village in Corsica, one in Bangkok, one in Vientiane, and one, especially well trained, in Jakarta. That's just first aid. In the end you don't get anything with violence. But it's first aid, you know. Don't forget, I grew up in a house of professionals. Where did I get the money? Shares in Dad's wealth."

That's what she told me, that crazy woman.

The treaty between Okawa-Kai and the Dragonhead was signed. I made contact with the Okawa-Kai people in Japan. After some time they announced a reconciliation ceremony would take place in Japan in two months. But there's no happiness in me.

And then, one day, they, whoever they are, invaded my villa in Manila. Had someone betrayed me? I don't know. I managed to escape. They wrote about that incident in the newspaper. Octavio was left behind. I saw his frightened picture in the newspaper. I loved him so much. I asked my servants to take care of him. I had to hide again.

One day I got tired of it all. The gargantuan and the small, the vision and the failure, life and death—everything was mixed into one doughy mess, without any sense. It didn't matter anymore if I was high or low, dead or alive, with or without money, with or without Mayumi.

I'm in Hong Kong now. I know I can't stay here for long. Mayumi disappeared on the day of my escape. She never contacted me. I don't even know if she's alive or dead. I'll never forget the look Charlie Long gave her, the respect and the venom. She'll also be pursued all her life. But she likes that, that crazy woman. She'll survive. One day Charlie Long may forget the insult. Maybe they'll join forces. Maybe he'll fear for his mother in Jakarta. Maybe he'll do his sums. Who knows?

Have my pursuers abandoned the trail? After all, I've been forgiven, and there's going to be a big reconciliation ceremony, with great praises, big rewards, big advancement, and great honor, and a lot of money—and I won't be there. Who's running after me now? I don't even know. I don't care.

Sensei, I don't know if I'll go back to the Path of Extremes. I don't know whether I'll return to any world. I'm going to atone for what I've done. I don't want the money I made. If I manage to get to it before Mayumi, I'll give it all away. I've failed in this lifetime. Do you understand? I failed.

And now a new betrayal is in the offing.

I don't have the strength to pay my debt to you. I'll never be able to repay the debt.

I can't say, "I'll be seeing you."
Forgive me,
Yuki.
PS

> "Tight, swarming, like a million parasitic worms,
> In our brains, a nation of Demons carouses,
> And when we breathe, Death descends into our lungs,
> An invisible river, with muffled cries of pain."

Baudelaire, *The Flowers of Evil*, "To the Reader"

A Trace in Tokyo

My trembling hands put the sheets of paper back in the envelope.

Nothing remained for me to do. Just to observe and wait. To ask. To sense that he is on his way here. Miserable, extinguished, failed, tormented. Like those lines from Villa's poetry. Already in Japan? On the way?

I wander about Kabuki-Cho, in Golden Gai. I ask, sniff around. In the family no one knows anything about him. Friends from the Yakuza introduce me to the world of Filipina dancers and prostitutes. Maybe they know something. Maybe one of them studied at *Las Vegas*. Maybe they met him in Manila. Maybe they could identify him if they saw him. Maybe they saw or heard. If they see him, they'll tell me.

In Golden Gai I go again to Hirano's place, the Murasaki, to ask about Yuki. Hirano just hints with his eyes, sadly. No. Nothing new. Yuki hasn't come back.

*

Thus it is for weeks, until that night.

In a place called The King's Palace, in Kabuki-Cho, after midnight, I take refuge from the cold.

The staircase, covered with a wine-colored carpet, leads to the second floor. The people sitting on the ground floor are multiplied a hundred times when you look at them through dusty glass stalactites hanging from the chandelier. Johann, from Munich, sits on a red velvet sofa with little Noriko, and they exchange words, very close. One of his hands grasps her shoulder while his other hand rests on the white piano, at the other end of which sits a pianist in black velvet. She plays, and with her looks she encourages a singer wearing a blue and pink garment, with shiny metal icicles on his arm. Three couples sway on the dance floor. Two Yakuza in silk suits drink, their rings glittering. I sit on a sofa, reading, occasionally looking up for someone I know will not come.

It's three a.m. now. Two old men at a table. Their heads lean on the table, all carved and covered with peeling gold. They're sleeping. Between them stand empty soup bowls.

Two girls who look Filipina climb up to the second floor. One sits next to a man whose head is nodding, and tries to seduce him. The other goes into the lavatory with a towel and a few other things that she pulls out of her little bag, and in a short time she comes out, scrubbed and combed, and she takes her friend's place next to the man whose head is wobbling, and she too tries to entice him.

A chubby girl, also a Filipina, is sitting at the nearby table. She smiles a doll's smile at me. She looks around and says, "Hi. Who are you? I Linda." Without delay she tells me, in fluent but faulty English, that "for fuck," which she offers to the lonely men of the city, she gets ten thousand yen and a place to sleep at night, because she has nowhere else to sleep except at the hotel with any man who'll pay her, because her father treated her very, very bad in the little village in the Philippines, and because of him she left the village and went to Manila.

"Very, very, very bad he treat me, yes? Jesus forgive him and forgive me. You understand, yes? One day Japanese men they come to village, give money to Dad, take me to Manila, teach me dance. I glad to leave Dad. I learn to dance and will be work as dancer.

Japanese man with the glasses, they say this. Will be work in Tokyo. Lots money. Meanwhile, he die, my dad. May Jesus forgive him for everything he do to me. And in Manila I learn in dancing school. Yes, yes, I'm graduate of dancing school. *Las Vegas.* That was name of school. Yes, *Las Vegas.* That's in America, yes? You know Las Vegas?

"Hey, what you so excited about, gaijin-san? Hey, gaijin-san, what's matter with you? You okay? You need doctor? Okay, okay. You go Manila? Really? Wow! How proud for me. I miss Manila. No, not really. Fuck Manila. When we studying in *Las Vegas,* Japanese men come and look. Glasses. Always black glasses. Some of them not nice, some nice. Then they give me plane ticket to Tokyo. I come Tokyo, and I dance in nightclub, and it is very nice, lots of tips. I buy clothes in Harajuku, and we go to church on Sunday. But one day, no work in dancing, now there's striptease. I send money to Mom. Lots. And I write her once how I working in theater, one time reception clerk in respectable hotel. One time I appear in movie. Maybe she believe this shit.

"And one day they tell me striptease not enough, I also have to do work like now. Like that, exactly like now. And situation in Japan not like before. Less money. Prices they go down. Prices of apartments and prices of whores together. Down. And the Yakuza also come and take, even from fucking ten thousand yen. Impossible not give. There are beatings. I don't know where they take my passport. And they also protect me, yes. Because there are some really bad Yakuza. Very, very bad. They come and take. Some good. Some very bad. But you get used. In Manila, in *Las Vegas,* one bad guy always come, and he talk very scary. But one day somebody else come, like boss. Oyabun, you know. And that one very nice. Very, very nice Japanese man. First I afraid of him. Scary eyes. Yes, scary eyes."

"Like a frog?"

"Yes, yes, maybe like frog. A little bit. You know him? Hey, why you excited? Maybe like dragon, a little, his face. But after I see that he is very nice, and if we have problems with Yakuza in Manila, he fix everything. He not want anything back. Not money. Not fuck. Nothing. Good man. But I saw that Yakuza there give him honor. Even Chinese. Sometimes he come with woman, thin like noodle, and all fucked up in head. She not nice, you know? Hey, gaijin-san you know tha lady? Really not nice, she is, and she also yell and sometimes hit us. But he protect us. I think she do shabu, you know? And she not nice at all. Not nice, people they scared of them, you know? You want snort?"

"What was his name?"

"I not know. How I know? But he was kind of oyabun. Anyway, I see him here two days before. What's the matter with you, hey? You okay? What's the matter with you? I call doctor? Sure I'm sure! I see him, what, I look like liar? Maybe he come to visit his Mom or for business or something, and he go back to Manila, and he take me back, too. I have not anything in Manila. One time he visit us in hotel in Manila, I see he was very sad. I smell lonely people, no problem. Sad and lonely—that's my business, no? He very sad there in Manila, with crazy woman. But when he come to me in the little hotel in Manila, before I go to Tokyo, I make him a little happy. I see he is thankful. He also give lot of money. I see him here, sure. I even say hello to him: 'Remember me from Manila, Mr. Oyabun?' But he look to me like a fish and go away. He don't look good, if you ask me. He also look different from Manila. Bad clothes. Like homeless. Maybe not him? In Manila he have suit and everything, like big oyabun. But here, really nothing. How I know what's the matter with him? Too bad. Maybe his head go soft because girlfriend. I think maybe he help me here like he help me there. Too bad. No, no. I don't see him again. Was here in second alley from here.

"And when no one want take me to hotel, I come here, 'cause open here until morning, and I buy soup and put my head on table like them two down there, that I don't know, but they come here three nights already, and they old. Who know where they from and where they go from here? They really alone, them two, eh?"

A chandelier, and a piano, and whores, and two homeless men, and two silk suits, and steps that rise in an elegant spiral, and a carved wooden banister, and sofas in what was once velvet, and three people who don't want a home. Art-deco.

"Linda. Here's a telephone number. If you see that Japanese guy again, call me right away, okay? Please! And please take this money. No, no. no fuck. Take it."

"Sure, gaijin-san. Sure. If I see him I call you, sure. He and you friends? Ok ok."

"Good night, Linda. Actually, good morning. And don't foget to call, please."

He's here.

The Jail-Release Ceremony. November 1993

Fukuoka calls one day and says, "Come to the office, tomorrow evening. They'll come and get you. Where? Don't ask. Come. Eight o'clock."

I'm used to not asking questions in this world. When they summon me this way, something important is happening. I'm curious.

I go to the office at eight o'clock the next evening. Fukuoka is waiting for me. I haven't seen him for months. He says, "Come! You're sleeping at my house tonight. Tomorrow morning we're going to greet someone. Early in the morning. Come, so we'll have time to sleep."

I ask questions. He doesn't answer.

He wakes me at three o'clock the next morning.

We're going to a prison, an hour's drive, he says. Who's getting out? Fukuoka is very excited. Tetsuya?

Now the prison building is seen in the distance. We approach and see black cars gathered, like a swarm of giant ants, at the rear gate. From time to time, in the darkness, they signal to each other. Then Fukuoka tells me that Tetsuya is getting out. A new chapter in the history of Okawa-Kai is about to begin today.

It's four in the morning and still dark. Opposite the rear gate of the prison is a street lamp, illuminating the surroundings with a dim light. A policeman emerges from the gate, looks into the darkness, and retreats.

More than sixty black cars have gathered this night in the lot opposite the back gate. In black convoys they've come from the ends of the land to the meeting place at the appointed time, which is four-thirty, dawn. Everyone who honors the man being released is present here, everyone whose place and security and honor are precious to him. This impressive turnout is a sign to Tetsuya and the Okawa-Kai of the respect the visitors hold for the man and his family. The new oyabun of the Okawa-Kai family is getting out.

And there's more. Everybody who's here today is placing himself and his family on Tetsuya's side in the war against the Yamada-Gumi family. The visitors are declaring, we're with you, Fujita Tetsuya, soon-to-be oyabun. This is a challenge to the largest family in Japan.

About three hundred present.

The cars are arranged on either side of the gate. Thirty or so on each side. Nose to nose. In the middle, a broad passageway. The Okawa-Kai members place their cars opposite the gate, at an angle. Fukuoka tells me to go sit in Ishida's car, Okawa's temporary successor. I go there, and Ishida signals to me to stay where I am and gets out. He doesn't like me, this temporary oyabun. I can see that even in the darkness of dawn. From within the car I see the whole ceremony, framed by the window.

The dark men silently emerge from the cars and stand in triangular columns in front of the cars. Each column is a sub-family. They bow deeply to each other. Everything is done in absolute silence.

The door opens, and Tetsuya appears at the frame. The lamp above the door shines on his thin silhouette. He looks around, blinking. He turns to the black community awaiting him. He makes a long, deep bow. Everyone bows back. Now he turns toward Ishida Oyabun and bows deeply to him. Ishida's reign over the family has lasted two years, a temporary authority according to a decision of the council of director-brothers, all done with respect to the explicit instructions of Okawa Oyabun. Who knows how long he will respect Okawa's wish? Will he choose a war with Tetsuya?

Suddenly Tetsuya falls to his knees and presses his head to the earth. Then he rises to his feet and approaches Ishida and cries: "Pardon me, my brother Ishida! Pardon me, Okawa Oyabun, who is no longer with us! Pardon me for the embarrassment and shame I brought upon you! I have thrown mud on our crest! Pardon me! I have no words to excuse myself!"

He turns to the other visitors and says, "My brothers! My honored friends! Friends on the Path of Extremes! I, Fujita Tetsuya, who was born in Kumamoto, which is in Kyushu, I who am a kobun, the son of Okawa Oyabun of the Okawa-Kai noble house! I humbly request: pardon, pardon! Please forgive me for the embarrassment and shame, and please let me apologize for your trouble—how can I repay you? I will never be able to repay you! Please forgive me, humble and prostrate, a contemptible doormat at your feet!"

Patches of red appear in the sky. Tetsuya passes along the corridor between the black cars. He stands there, bows deeply, and enters Ishsa's car, and sits by my side. "Ah, Yakobu. You're here. We haven't seen each other for two years. Thank you for coming, brother!"

His lips tremble. He says nothing until we reach Tokyo.

The New Oyabun

In two weeks the sakazuki ceremony is held to enthrone Tetsuya as the Great Oyabun of the Okawa-Kai.

Sakurai, the master of ceremonies, hands the saje cup to Tetsuya, and says, "When you drink from this bowl, you, Fujita Tetsuya, the senior kobun of the late Okawa Oyabun, thereby accept the position of oyabun of the Okawa-Kai family! Please, drink!"

"I, Sakurai Hideo, in the name of Ishida Taro, the elder of the family, hereby do the bidding of Okawa Oyabun and appoint you oyabun of the Okawa-Kai family!"

And the new oyabun says, at the end of his first speech, "The man who was the living spirit behind the renewal of the alliance between Okawa-Kai and the Dragonhead family is not here with us. Furukawa Saburo, also known to us by his real name of Murata Yukihira, or Yuki, did the impossible, and by his efforts the alliance with the Dragonhead was formed. I am sorry that he is unable to be here with us today. I wish to announce on this occasion his appointment as a member of the senior council of the family. As such he receives the full honor, and also the full protection of the family. Let it be known hereby that Murata Yukihira receives our personal protection, after every earlier decision in his regard has been rescinded and is null and void."

And the rest is history.

At Sanya, the Town of the Cursed

One day Tetsuya calls me and says, "Maybe there's something."

I straighten up. "What?"

"Come with me tomorrow. To Sanya."

Minami-Senju is a wiped-out subway station, around which is a cursed slum known as Sanya. Sanya accomodates people who have erased their faces and their past. They spend their days gambling, the smell of vomit and sake being their bedding. It's a place of forgotten people, anonymous to themselves. The inner bowels of Japan.

One is very careful when visiting Sanya. Like walking through a place of worship. Regular people don't just get off at the Minami-Senju station for no reason. The smell of vomit rises up the iron steps that descend into the station. You don't ask the faceless people here where they came from. They don't remember anyway.

At an afternoon hour, Tetsuya and I arrive at the edge of Sanya in his black car. We park near the Minami-Senju station and proceed on foot into the heart of the quarter. Three bodyguards surround us, as befits a big oyabun and his guest.

We're walking in the alleys of Sanya.

People don't sell houses in Sanya because no one would buy. The air here is clear of car pollution because there are no cars. No cameras, no fashion shops, no ads for cosmetics or fancy restaurants. No tea ceremonies here. The Sanya drunks lie on piles of garbage among heaps of empty bottles and the remains of leftover fish.

The only stores here sell black work shoes, brown work smocks, clear sake, and plastic containers with prepared soup—nothing else. Catholic priests and Buddhist monks, with blank faces and merciful hearts, labor over meals in soup kitchens.

We enter tattered, dark bars. Hostels where black shoes are arrayed at the entrance.

Tetsuya has a lead. But he won't tell me what it is.

I imagine Yuki here, faded among the faded. And I shrink.

Suddenly he stops and asks, "Is he still important to you, this Yuki?"

"Yes. I don't know why, Tetsuya. But yes. We're brothers. You must understand. Don't you? If he's he's in trouble, I have to help him, right? And he did something enormous for the family, didn't he?"

"Sure. You learned your Yakuza lesson, didn't you? I'm proud of you. But I want to make something clear. If it's Yuki, we have a delicate account to settle with him. He could be at the top. But he can also be in the sewer. It depends on him. If he runs away again now, even the spirit of Okawa can't save him. If I declare that he's an honored member, and that he's under my protection, and he ignores it and runs away—if—then he's throwing mud in my face, and I can't pass over it." Silence. "I hope he has very good reasons for being in this place, in this condition. If it's him at all. You understand?"

Silence.

"If he made me lose face, I'm sorry to say this to you, brother, but your giri won't help him this time."

Silence.

"I'm sorry."

Silence.

"But let's see. Maybe it isn't him. Maybe he has reasons. Maybe he really needs help."

I have nothing to say. We go on.

In the middle of one street people are standing around a round table. With gloomy enthusiasm, they bet themselves to death. The Yakuza are attentive to the lonely people of Sanya, so they'll bet on the dice. The Kimura family owns this place. It specializes in the miseries of the faceless. In the mornings they provide work in construction, in agriculture. But when afternoon comes, they organize gambling. In the streets. Out in the open. And the wretched, in dirty work clothes, black work shoes, the vapor of sake in their mouths, gather around the gambling booths. Dice. Cards. They throw the bills. Today's pay, which is all they have.

Morimoto, a Kimura family soldier, leaves his luxury car next to the station and enters on foot with a team of kobuns. Fragrant with expensive aftershave, with his brand-new black sunglasses, he deftly commands the gaming. He stuffs the bills into an inner pocket of his suit. At the end of the day he leaves. Next to his luxury car he hands the money to his aniki, his Yakuza big brother.

The next morning, at five, Kawashima, another Kimura man, will arrive here and arrange work for a few hundred men, at various construction sites in the heart of Tokyo. In the afternoon, Morimoto and the others will come and set up the gambling booths, and so day after day. Kawashima the morning man, Morimoto the afternoon guy.

When you pass the gamblers, don't tarry, don't stand there, and don't really look into the men's eyes or you'll get into big trouble.

Tetsuya addresses one of the young Yakuza and takes him aside. He asks him something. From the young man's body language, I conclude he doesn't know. Tetsuya looks helpless for a moment. He looks at me, hesitates, and then motions to me to come with him. We go on. We enter a dark bar. Tetsuya introduces me to the mama-san and tells me, "Wait for me here. You're in good hands. But don't even think about going out of here into the street. You're in good hands."

After a few minutes he introduces me to Kawashima and leaves. Kawashima is a man of thirty, but his soul is old. He sits in the bar, under its thin light, and drinks a white drink, 60 percent alcohol, distilled from potatoes or rice or barley.

Kawashima starts chatting with me as if we'd known each other forever. He tells me about his daughter, Yoko, who's now in the sixth grade in a small village in the south. She's an excellent student. How does he know? That's how she was five years ago, when he left his home.

"I'm sure she still is," says the proud father, from a distance.

"Have you been in contact with her?"

"No. I'm ashamed. I don't want to shame her."

"Why did you leave?"

"I had a business designing greeting cards. It was going well. Then it went badly. Big debts. And I couldn't stand the shame. Now I can't stand the shame of the shame. I'm the employment agent for miserable men like myself who take refuge here. I take a commission and give a percentage to the Yakuza. So I know a lot of the new men who come into this black hole. I'm also an agent for the Buddhist and the Catholic organizations that work here. Soup kitchens and that kind of thing. Sanya is the last step before these creatures go to sleep in the passageways of the Shinjuku station or next to the lotus pools in Ueno. So I make a respectable life possible for them here. So what are you looking for here? Yuki? I don't know any Yuki. The name isn't important. Anyway, it won't help. Maybe Furukawa, you say? You kidding? The people here don't have names. And if they have, they've changed them a thousand times. Do you really think that my name is Kawashima? Yuki. To look for a Yuki here, or a Furukawa. You make me laugh."

I tell him a few possible details about Yuki—true or imaginary or invented. I tell him about the scar and the protruding eyes. About the eye that drifts to the side. About the bottomless sorrow and the poetry books that the man might have in his knapsack. A little about the dates of his possible arrival here. If it's him.

Maybe he's seen him. He doesn't remember. He hiccups. Kawashima tells me he'll check. We should come tomorrow.

Yuki?

The next day we find Kawashima in the dark bar.

"Did you find him?"

"I don't know. Come."

We go out and come to a small hostel. Clean. A sign in nice calligraphy outside. Work shoes arranged in front of it. The odor of sake. We take off our shoes. We go inside. Laundry hangs in the corridor. Through the laundry, we enter a room.

Kawashima, Tetsuya, Tetsuya's bodyguards, and I, fill the room with our breath. On the futon lies a man. His face is black. My neck stiffens. My mouth is dry.

"Is that him?" Tetsuya asks.

"Is it him?" Kawashima asks.

I look at the man and don't recognize him. Does he recognize himself. Who is this man? The man is looking at me, maybe, and if he is looking at me, he doesn't recognize me. I try to look into his eyes, but his eyes aren't here. They're puffed up. I look for a twitching eye. But the eyes are almost closed. He could be Yuki. He could be anyone.

"Why did you think it was him?" I ask Tetsuya.

"It started with information from a Filipina whore who identified him," he says. "We followed him for a few days. He disappeared and reappeared. Probably a mistaken identity. Don't forget, we're looking for him now no less than you are. They sent me identifying marks, they said to ask Kawashima. Maybe he's in Sanya. That's why we came here. What do you say?"

"I don't know. I'm not sure. But please help him."

Tetsuya is silent, and then, "You know, don't you? If it's him …"

"I know."

He turns to the black man lying there. "You know too, right?"

203

The man is silent. We are silent.

"I'll help him," Tetsuya says, and he goes out. His two bodyguards go with him.

I stare at the faceless man. I leave the room. I am sick. I want to go back to the room but I can't.

*

A week later, in one of the family safe houses, I am with Fukuoka, who has been appointed to be with me during the interrogation of the man.

The man is clean now. Emaciated. But his gaze is direct, two tiny points through the slits of his swollen eyes. I observe him. I realize I don't remember how Yuki looked. And even if he hadn't undergone plastic surgery, God knows how many times in the excellent clinics of Manila and Hong Kong, I wouldn't be able to identify him. However, maybe by his eyes, I hoped. Eyes like that are impossible to forget. But that, too, can be operated on and corrected, I'm told. I look for a twitch in the left eye. There isn't any. My eye goes to the hands. Does he have a left pinky or not? Yes, he has. It could be false. I see that Fukuoka is also looking there.

Fukuoka interrogates him. "What's your name?"

"Hirosaki. What do you want from me? Who are you? I don't know you, and I want to go," he grumbles hoarsely.

"Where are you from?"

"From a village next to Morioka."

"Not from Hokkaido?"

"I've never been there. What do you want from me? Let me go."

I look in those swollen eyes that are looking at me. I look for a spark. Of what? He's not afraid, this man. Boundless indifference. No fear.

"Does the name Murata Yukihira mean anything to you?"

"No."

"The name Furukawa?"

"No. Who are you?"

"We're from the Okawa-Kai family. Does that mean anything to you?"

"No. Can I go? I didn't do you any harm."

I observe. This man, whether or not he's Yuki, has been many persons. Layer upon layer of men, so it's impossible to find out who he is. His hands don't match the eyes. The ears don't match the chest. The feet are foreign to the lips. And none of these match his heart.

"My name is Yakobu. I was Yuki's friend. I'm looking for him to help him. If it's you, please tell me."

"I don't know him, and I don't know about him! Let me go! Let me go, please."

"How did you get to Sanya?"

"Aren't you ashamed to ask a question like that?"

I am ashamed. We all are silent.

Suddenly Fukuoka says, "Go. You can go."

The man is stunned. He looks at me. He looks at Fukuoka. He sits up. Looks at me. Did I see something familiar there? A twitch? I'm not sure of anything.

"I can go?"

"Yes. We'll drive you wherever you want to go."

"Drive me to the Ueno station."

"Fine. Where will you go?"

"I'll go to die in my native village. What do you care?"

Fukuoka barks an order outside. A young kobun presents himself. He hears instructions and starts leading the man outside.

"Wait a minute," I call out.

They stop. The man stands still, his back to me, a silhouette in the doorway. He doesn't turn around.

"Does the name Sayumi mean anything to you?"

There's no movement in the silhouette in the doorway.

"No," he mutters and leaves.

Fukuoka looks at me and says, "It's him."

"Are you sure? Then why—"

"Because he would never have admitted it. Not even torture would have broken him. He has nothing to lose, that man. That man isn't afraid of anything. The end of the pursuit. Keep this between us."

"How do you know? And why didn't you—"

"Sensei. The way a horse breeder knows his horse. The way a farmer knows his cow. The way a mother knows her son. The way an archer shoots with his eyes closed and hits the target. We know. Someone who has changed himself a thousand times, until he doesn't know anymore. We're the experts. Haven't you learned anything?

"He who rose and fell a thousand times, until he cares no more.

"He who has known complete wealth and lost it perfectly.

"He who has seen everything and can't be surprised.

"He who has been at all the extremes and can't be challenged with extremes.

"He who has done things he'd rather forget.

"He who's not afraid of anything.

"He who's changed a thousand masks, so that he doesn't know his original face.

"He who is an outcast and hunted, so each minute is a gift of just one minute.

"He who has been all that knows his fellow, believe me. Even in the dark.

"Besides, I've been in prison, remember? I even wrote poetry there, remember? That man, the whole world is his prison. I'm surprised at you, Sensei. We're faithful unto death, but we also disappear in a wink. Haven't you learned that? Aside from that, he was so ashamed before you that he didn't recognize you. And he was so ashamed before himself that he didn't recognize himself. Let's go. Leave him. Leave him, Sensei. I'll tell Tetsuya Oyabun it wasn't him. Maybe it really wasn't. What do we know? Don't look for him anymore. He chose to go into the darkness. Let's go. Come on!"

The man I was looking for remained a silhouette in the doorway. Like a stained-glass window of longing.

With Tetsuya, in a Bar

What did I learn from Tetsuya today, in a small bar in the land of Japan? Okawa Oyabun is dead. The world has changed. The world of the Yakuza has changed. And we're sitting in a bar. What did I learn from Tetsuya? That the whiskey we're sharing has the correct degree of dryness because of the smoke from the casks, and if you sniff delicately, you can also smell the distant fragrance of the sea, and there is nothing like this kind of whiskey to raise your spirits. Thus he explains in detail, so he won't cry. So I won't cry.

After the whiskey he orders espresso in a tiny cup. No sugar. He drinks and doesn't grimace. The mama asks with her eyes whether to call the hostess, and he waves a hand. Not now.

Tetsuya, the dreadful Yakuza leader, grimaces. His eyes tear.

He weeps and asks why I'm going back to my country and leaving him alone.

Afterword

The End of the Day—
Siloam Church

My research is over. My search is over. The Yakuza world has changed dramatically. Families go underground. More and more members are leaving. Many of them try to fit into the katagi world in one way or another. They practice changing their gait, their clothing, their speech. Many of them buy false pinkies, made to perfection.

Only the splendid tattoos that cover their whole body cannot be erased.

At Siloam Church, Mission Barabbas, in Funabashi Town, not far from Tokyo, I meet Reverend Suzuki.

Suzuki Hiroyuki, formerly an active Yakuza member, today Pastor Suzuki, founded Mission Barabbas in Funabashi on July 30, 1995. Over the years other ex-Yakuza joined him, some of them men who had been deep in the Yakuza darkness, some who had been imprisoned for many years. Active Yakuza members also join the mission.

The church is called Siloam. It is unassuming building at the end of a small street. The interior is modest. On the back wall of the church is a golden cross, and on either side of it are stained glass windows with pictures from the life of Jesus.

On one of the walls the following scripture is drawn in artistic calligraphy:

> And as Jesus passed by, he saw a man which was blind from his birth. And his disciples asked him, saying, Master, who did sin, this man or his parents, that he was born blind? Jesus answered, Neither hath this man sinned, nor his parents: but that the works of God should be made manifest in him. I must work the works of Him that sent me, while it is day: the night cometh, when no man can work. As long as I am in the world, I am the light of the world. When he had thus spoken, he spat on the ground and made clay of the spittle, and he anointed the eyes of the blind man with the clay, and said unto him, Go, wash in the pool of Siloam. He went his way therefore, and washed, and came seeing. (John 9)

Suzuki is still the head of the mission, and he made it a place of social commitment. Suzuki and his men go out into the streets to find young people who are on their way to becoming Yakuza, and they bring them to the bosom of Christianity. They work with the homeless. They work with Yakuza who wish to leave the world of crime, and they help to rehabilitate them and find them jobs.

Sometimes some curious journalist or a researcher from some university comes, and he'll ask him questions about Mission Barabbas. And then he explains. "Barabbas means 'son of the father' in Aramaic. He was a killer, a thief and a rebel. Pardoned from the cross, he repented, perhaps, and established a church of his own. He too is the son of the Father, is he not?

"We're called tattooed Christians. Our wives are called the wives of Barabbas. Our oyabun is Jesus. What else do you have to know, my brother?"

Today the Mission Barabbas numbers more than two hundred members, some of whom are still active Yakuza.

Could Yuki be here? I won't ask. No one will answer anyway.

Suzuki is covered with tattoos from head to foot. Sometimes he gives his Sunday sermons with his upper body bare, and the cross swings before the wild irezumi images. Both his right and his left pinkies are missing, and he doesn't conceal it.

About the Author

Jacob Raz is professor of Buddhism, Zen Buddhism, and Japanese culture at the Department of East Asian Studies, Tel Aviv University, Tel Aviv. He is the author of numerous books and articles on Buddhism, Japanese aesthetics, and Japanese anthropology, in Hebrew, English, Russian, and Japanese. He translated into Hebrew many masterpieces of Japanese literature and poetry. He also authored fiction and poetry books.

On November 24, 2006, he was awarded by the Japanese government the decoration "The Order of the Rising Sun, Gold Rays with Neck Ribbon" (*Kunsho*) for his contribution to Japanese studies and for his "outstanding contribution to the friendship and mutual understanding between Japan and Israel."

Jacob Raz is a social activist, leading several NGO's working in the fields of peace and social action, and the world of people with special needs. He is also active in the cultivation and dissemination of Buddhism as everyday practice in various professional, institutional, political, and personal spheres in the modern Western world.